Broken Souls (Primani Book Four)

LAURIE OLERICH

DEDICATION

For all broken souls who yearn for healing and the healers
who make them whole again.

ACKNOWLEDGEMENTS

I am beyond excited to release *Broken Souls*! It's a special book for me because it stars my beloved healer Declan. He's the lovable Primani who's captured the hearts of so many readers. In addition to my family and friends, there are some extraordinary people who deserve a special shout out for making this sexy, dark love story possible! A million thanks to:

Jo Spring for her excellent editing work and advice. I can't thank her enough for her words of wisdom and support. She kept me on track and in good spirits! Thanks, Jo!

Ann, David, Deborah, and Tracy, my beta readers, for their honest feedback and suggestions. Ann and Deb, I'm humbled by your genuine love for Declan and the rest of the Primani. I'm blessed to have you rooting for me!

My wonderful friend Angela Bauer for the stunning cover! Her designs are breathtaking every single time. This cover is nothing short of amazing. I'm so lucky to have you in my life!

HeatherLynn Portraits for the beautiful model photo. Heather works magic with her camera! I can't wait to finish more books so we can work together again!

Eric Penalver for being such a dead ringer for Declan! His career as a cover model is just beginning, but I see a bright, busy future in store for him! You're awesome, Eric!

Brenna Zinn and Elaine Barris for your mentorship, friendship, and laughter. You two have encouraged me more than you'll ever know. I can't wait to see where the future takes us!

LAURIE OLERICH

Only a taste for now, but soon she would be his until death do they part. Hers, not his. -- Azrael

Prologue:

Brooklyn, New York, 1987:

"FORGIVE ME, FATHER, FOR I HAVE SINNED."

Confession.

It was good for the soul. Cleansing and purifying, confession would lead to absolution and forgiveness. Or so she'd been taught. If only it were that simple.

"It's been two months since my last confession."

To 24-year-old Annalisa, those hushed words damned her as much as her sins. If only she'd come to confession earlier, she wouldn't be in this situation. A month ago, she'd been ashamed. She avoided confession out of horror of her own behavior. She knew what she was doing was wrong, yet she was in too deep to stop herself. Now, the simple words were like a neon sign, flashing her guilt for everyone to see. She slumped lower in the confessional. Peering through the screen, she watched the cleaning lady for evidence that she could hear them. The little old lady from Queens dribbled more lemon oil onto a pew and half-heartedly rubbed it in. Was it her imagination, or did she seem to cock her head in the direction of the confessional?

Pausing to dab at her eyes, she continued, "I'm afraid I can't be forgiven. It's too late." There were some sins that were too consequential, too heinous, for forgiveness. Surely even God himself would turn away with disgust.

"There is always forgiveness, my child, if one is truly repentant. Why don't you tell me what you've done?" The priest's tone was encouraging, as usual. Patient, caring, his manner was comforting when hearing her confessions. This time though, he was about to get an earful.

She'd been taught that sins would be forgiven if the sinner was genuinely remorseful. She tried to live her life by the teachings of the church, and honestly felt bad when she strayed. Her parents and the nuns had ensured she felt guilty whenever she did something wrong.

Truly repentant? That was going to be a problem this time.

"I had sex outside of marriage, Father."

Way outside of marriage.

She swallowed hard and rushed on before she could lose her courage. "I had sex with an angel, and I'm pregnant."

Dead silence.

Finally, he asked, "Does he know?"

Shaking her head though he couldn't see her, the dam gave way and she sobbed, "I killed him!"

Chapter 1: Running From Angels

THE POUNDING OF HER HEART brought her gasping awake in the colorless light of early morning. Blinking in confusion, Rori Austin struggled to get her bearings. Where was she? *When* was she? With her vision still wonky from yet another dream, she scanned the room and sagged in relief. She was home. Thank God.

As the normal lightheadedness eased up, she panicked and dove for the notepad lying on the milk crate that acted as a dresser. I have to write it down. Write it down. Write it down. The mantra flowed in her mind like a curse. Write it down. Scribbling like a crazy person, she wrote everything she could remember. After ten minutes, she ran out of juice and stared at the pad in horror.

Two words--over and over again. *Only* two words? How was that possible? The vision was so real! It was long and winding... it kept her up half the night. *Surely* there was more than that. She closed her eyes, straining to recapture the vision, but it was gone. The barest hint of heat, fire maybe, teased at the edges of her memory. Jesus, help her. She was losing her mind. Shaking her head in frustration, she climbed off the lumpy futon and headed for the shower. Slouching under the weak stream, she sniggered at her own stupid optimism. Rori Austin, why on earth are you praying for help when you know Jesus turned a blind eye to you a long time ago? And for some crazy ass reason you still pray. Ridiculous! Ladies and gentlemen, God has left the building. With that cheery thought, she shoved her face into the water for a last rinse. She was talking to herself in the third person again. Not only was she an idiot, she was a crazy person. How much worse can this get?

"What the hell?"

Declan Manning rolled over and shot out of bed in the wink of an eye. Instantly alert, he scanned the room for threats but relaxed when he saw who had dragged him out of a sound sleep. He relaxed for the nanosecond it took to get a good look at her face. Oh, shit.

Splaying his hands in a gesture of peace, he flashed a weak smile. "Now Dani--"

She marched into the room and shoved her finger into his chest. "Don't you 'Dani' me! What the hell is the matter with you?" Her eyes cut to the rumpled sheets, gleaming with an unholy light.

Closing his eyes against the sight, he pried her finger out of his chest and tried again, "Don't you knock?"

Clearly furious, Dani stalked him backwards until he came up against the bedroom wall with a thunk. She yanked his face down to her level for some eye-to-eye contact.

"You have a naked woman in your bed." Her voice dropped to a hiss. Reaching out one delicate hand, she dragged her nails lightly across his belly, eyes hardening to granite as he sucked in his stomach. She pressed her nails just above his, uh, personal assets, pinning him in place.

Dani Taylor was more than pissed. How could he do this to her? She thought they had an understanding. She had been so careful to keep him interested while she figured out what she wanted to do. It wasn't her fault it was taking a while to make up her mind. She had other things to consider besides her hormones and his hot body. Finding him in bed with someone was NOT in the plan.

"And you're naked too. How could you?" The question was more or less rhetorical since she knew perfectly well how he could do it. Still, she wasn't letting him off the hook. Not by a long shot. She glared while he searched for the right answer. Her on again, off again Plan B looked at her now with so many emotions flickering over his face that she felt a grin trying to sneak out. Growling softly, she kept up the pressure, smirking when he hitched in his breath. He had beautiful carved abs covered with soft, tanned skin. It would be a shame to damage them too much. Once upon a time, she'd run her hands over them with more than pain in mind.

He finally sighed, long and hard, a hint of a smile curving his lips. A familiar woodsy fragrance floated around them, lifting the tension, filling her with calm. Suddenly she wasn't sure why she was mad. She inhaled, blinked, and took a really good look at the man standing in front of her. Tall, lean, tightly muscled, he was rock hard and golden-skinned. There was a fine dusting of pale gold hair scattered over his chest, tapering to a more burnished happy trail dissecting those sculpted abs and drawing her eyes downward to his quite lovely...

"Go ahead. Look at me, darlin'. Maybe you'll appreciate what you're missing." He wrapped strong fingers around her wrist, flattening her hand against his beating heart. With his other hand, he tilted her chin back and fixed her with a hard stare. "I haven't done anything wrong tonight. But even if I had, I don't answer to you." He pushed her gently back and grunted, "Your choice, remember?"

He crossed his arms and tried not to think about his junk hanging out in the cold room. It was really hard being hard on her (no pun intended) when he was buck ass naked. Goose bumps popped up on his arms, and his boys retreated to warmer climes. Ah, hell. Would she just yell at him and get out of here before he was totally humiliated? It was all he could do not to reach for a blanket. Instead, he stared her down and waited for her to throw out another insult or two before stomping out of the room, as usual.

A sleepy moan from the bed saved Dani from another undignified retreat. Her eyes practically fell out of her head when she glanced over.

"Abby?"

Three nights later, Dec leaned against the kitchen counter inside the Primani headquarters. The farmhouse was nestled inside a huge wooded lot outside of Plattsburgh, New York. His ops cell had used it for years. It felt a little more like home than anyplace else they'd been in several centuries. Of course, nothing could ever replace his real home, but that was long since gone.

The only woman he'd ever been able to count on was throwing together dinner while two of her three toddlers were out from under her feet. Mica Leahy was his best friend. The sun and moon rose and set behind her beautiful denim eyes--really, they did. He loved her from the first second he laid eyes on her about, oh, eight years ago. She had been young and naive and in a whole lot of trouble. Lucky for her, he had a soft spot for damsels in distress. She was as far from 'damsel' as he could imagine now. He'd watched her take apart a demon using nothing but the power of her mind. Yeah, that was pretty freakin' creepy, but hey, they all had their special abilities. It made them what they were. Telekinesis just happened to be one of her stronger talents. Her husband, Killian, was his Primani leader, and the older brother he never had. They were tight.

BROKEN SOULS

But no matter how much he loved Killian, he still loved Mica more. She was way nicer than her uptight husband. Even so, he'd been trying for weeks to find a way to bring up his problems with Dani, but wasn't sure how Mica would react. Dani's latest temper tantrum was pretty much the last straw. He was through being dicked around and wanted Mica's advice before he made his choice.

She squeezed his shoulder and dropped a kiss on his cheek on the way to the oven. "Okay, I'm going to be straight with you, Dec. I don't want to hurt your feelings, but you need to hear the truth." She paused to see if he was paying attention before continuing, "You know I love Dani; she's a good friend to me, and she's an awesome nanny for the kids. But damn it, Dec, she's sucked the life out of you. You've been moody for months. You're not yourself anymore, and I've been a little worried about you. I'm glad you asked for my input; I was about to give it to you whether you asked or not!" She shot him a quick grin and pulled out the tray of blueberry muffins that were baking.

"Look, the love of your life is supposed to feed your soul, not strangle it. She's supposed to build you up, have your back, nourish your dreams. That's just not Dani. She's left you hanging every step of the way. I can't explain her attitude. She isn't much of a sharer. You deserve better, though. Move on. You'll find a woman who's worthy of all that you are."

"Are you serious right now? I can't believe you'd say that! I thought you'd take her side."

She caught him in a sisterly hug and murmured, "Oh, sweetie, you'll always be my favorite. You're good and kind," she met his amused eyes with a grin, "and just completely adorable. You and I have been through too much for me to side with her over you." She pulled the tiny golden locket out of her shirt and waved it with a smile. "Blood is truly thicker than friendship."

Kissing the top of her head, he ignored her mangled quote and remarked, "Yeah, I *have* saved your life a few times. Thanks, sweetheart. It's not what I wanted to hear, but I'll think about it."

They were interrupted by the anguished howls of two of the triplets. Guess they were done napping. Mica beat him to the living room, where the boys had been snoozing on a fat sleeping bag. Michael Declan, his namesake and the youngest, was crying and rubbing his ear, but Rafe had gone rogue and was scaling the bookcase trying to get to God only knew what. He was clearly terrified, hence the howls, but he kept climbing, taking action in the face of fear! He would be a killer warrior someday. Good thing too; he had a big job to do.

Mica tossed him a hassled look and begged, "Dec, baby, please go grab Rafe before he falls!" She gestured with her elbow; her other hand was full with Michael who was squalling in protest as his mother slipped the spoon of purple medicine into his crying mouth. Dec's heart tightened when he spotted the first tear running down the little cheek. The youngest two were fighting off a cold, while Killian Jr. was healthy as a horse. That kid never got sick. Ever. It was eerie.

"Here, let me have this one. You go after Rafe." He plucked the unhappy toddler from Mica's grasp and lifted him over his head until he stopped crying. Squalls turned to whimpers and then giggles. There we go. Better. He kissed the top of Michael's sweaty head and said, "Come on, little dude, no crying today. You're all right. Where's your daddy?" Michael sniffed and pointed to the back door.

On cue, Killian materialized in the doorway. Letting his molecules settle for a nanosecond, he shook his fingers out and zeroed in on Mica. "Everything okay? I swear I heard the screaming in transit." He pulled Rafe from his mother's arms, studying his pale face before setting him down again. "Fever's gone?"

Mica gave him a distracted kiss and agreed. "And the cough is just about gone too. They're okay, just crabby. It's hard for them to be stuck inside all day. This weather sucks."

A sudden shower of rain struck the kitchen window. Fall in New York... chilly, rainy, dark. It reminded Dec a whole lot of England some days. He shuddered at the thought. He totally didn't miss England. His memories were not so good. When he peered into the darkest places of his mind, he could still see Sean's face covered by the stone angel. With skin bleached white and eyes bloody red, he'd suffered a fate worse than death... all for the greater good. He'd sacrificed himself to save millions from what would've been the worst smallpox outbreak mankind had ever seen. It'd been three years since they'd cleared Sean's name and gotten him freed. Even so, the nightmare images were still too close to his heart. *Sean* might be fine now, but he wasn't. They'd nearly lost Sean completely. He never wanted to go to England again.

Mica was right. He was brooding. Shaking his head clear of those maudlin images, he passed Michael to Killian who held him close for a second before setting him down and ordering, "Go play with your brother, Michael." Turning to Mica, he asked, "Little Killian's not back yet?"

Over the past year, Killian Jr. had shown signs of significant psychic powers. The archangels were intrigued and not just a little smug. To have such a strong asset on their side was a huge boon for them. Even though the triplets were only three years old, they were all showing signs of their strengths. All of the boys had powers from Killian, Sean, and Declan. Killian Jr. had inherited his father's most dominant power: the ability to control natural forces. He'd been doing it since before he was born, but they hadn't put the pieces together until he called forth lightning on his first birthday. Raphael had insisted they begin training about one minute later.

Mica smiled up at her husband and said, "He's not due back for another day. Raphael wanted to keep him for another week, but I told him you'd lose your mind." Tugging him by his belt loop, she slipped her cold hands under his shirt. With a wink at Dec, she suggested, "I think you need a nap. Dec volunteered to babysit for a few hours."

He rolled his eyes and shook his head. *You gotta be kidding me... Did everyone have sex on the brain? Must be something in the air. Full moon?*

An hour later, he slouched on the porch swing, scowling into the dripping trees. He wasn't trying to listen, really. But his hearing *was* supernatural. It wasn't his fault he could hear everything inside the house. He couldn't exactly crank up his iPod since he was babysitting. It was a nightmare trying to drown out *some* noises while also keeping his ears open for crying kids. The damn happy couple was quiet now, probably snuggling in some supernatural afterglow, but he was left with a teeth gritting, throbbing ache that was making him mental. He looked down at his lap and scowled some more. *Go back to sleep! Shit. At this rate, he'd need some alone time before dinner!* He flashed a grin that no one saw. Yeah, he was pathetic, but it was funny as hell.

Out of the three Primani in his ops cell, he was the one with the strongest ability to influence the minds of anyone around him. It was a powerful weapon in their arsenal. They all had that ability to some degree, true. But he was actually charming. Ladies liked that. Women responded to him in ways that boggled Sean and Killian's minds. Even Dimitri shook his head, and that was saying something.

With a mental wave of his hand, he could distort memories, charm the pants off of someone (literally or figuratively), or loosen up a stubborn suspect they needed to question. Theoretically, he could use these psychic abilities to get *more* women to sleep with him. Not to mention, he was also easy on the eyes. Modest, too. He *could* get laid every day if he wanted. But he didn't, for more than one reason.

Unable to sit still, he paced the length of the covered porch and studied the trees some more. It was still raining, but more softly now. Mother Nature must be running out of juice. The wind shifted, and he caught the faint peal of Mica's throaty laughter.

Ah, hell.

He couldn't stand living here any longer. It'd been three years since they all moved in together and things had been great at first. The triplets were a riot, and Mica and Killian were two of his favorite people. He'd gladly die for either one of them, but they, well, they had way too much sex. And damn it, he wasn't getting any. If he was being honest with himself, he'd admit he was jealous of what they had. They were crazy for each other, and everyone could see it. Mica looked at Killian with such intensity it hurt to watch. He wanted a woman to undress him with her eyes, to drag him off to bed... to just give a shit about him... yeah, he wanted that too. But that dream was so distant it might as well be nonexistent. And... he'd be fronting himself if he didn't admit he was just plain horny.

It had been *years*.

Stupid tool that he was, he'd been saving himself for Dani. He cared about her and didn't want her to think he wasn't picky. He liked sex, but he wasn't a man-whore like Rivin or Dimitri. Those two got more ass than they deserved. He missed the playfulness of it all, the warmth, the fun, and hell, the explosion of a spectacular orgasm. Damn. He needed to get laid. He adjusted his jeans with an irritated shove. Apparently there was some urgency. It was time to get his own space before the party in his pants turned into a full riot. Chewing on the tip of his index finger, he planned his escape. Could he really walk away?

"Uncle Dec! Why are you sad?" Rafe's piping voice snagged his attention away from the blond-haired angel that was invading his thoughts. Her stormy grey eyes glittered with anger and accusation. She was always angry these days, even before the Abby incident. Why she was mad was a mystery he couldn't figure out. Truth? He was sick to death of trying. He was just done.

Could he walk away from her? No. He couldn't.

He was about to sprint.

Sighing with regret, again, he turned to the toddler and forced a smile. "I'm not sad, Rafe, just feeling a little off today. That's all." Standing and sweeping the boy onto his shoulders in one move, he loped down the steps and headed for the boys' playhouse at the bottom of the porch. It was a stroke of genius, if he did say so himself. He and Sean had surprised their godsons with it a few months ago, and it turned out to be the perfect gift. Like a treehouse on the ground, it was fully enclosed with a couple of cool windows and an escape hatch in the back. They'd insulated it so it would be warm, and Mica'd lined it with soft carpet and some heavy curtains for winter. With three cozy chairs and a bunch of their favorite toys, it was a perfect place to hang out. Even if you were only three...

"Come on, buddy. Let's see what Michael's done with your racetrack." As he ducked inside, he glanced at the forest. A trickle of warning slid over his shoulder blades and he froze. Setting Rafe down, he shooed him inside, closing the door with a click.

There it was again. A feeling of eyes watching him... Straightening to his full height, he let his Primani senses take control and felt the hum of his *saol* revving him up. The energy readied him for battle, giving him strength and power that no human could ever hope to have. His eyes burned with a low blue flame as he used telepathy to search the woods. Come on, come on... show yourself... Where are you hiding? A chill swept over him like a shadow blocking the sun. He swiveled to the right, scanning the woods again. Nothing. No humans, no demons, not even a bear. The creepy feeling was still there though, and he tensed for a fight. What the hell is out there?

Switching his gaze towards the road, he studied the dense line of pine trees that loomed like sentinels across the front of the property. The dim afternoon light barely penetrated the canopy of branches, leaving the ground murky with shadows. A gust of wind bent the trees sideways, sending shadows flying in all directions. One shadow remained still... separate from the tall pines and larger than any tree trunk. Red eyes glittered within the darkness, the acrid stench of burnt earth drifted on the breeze. Gotcha.

Without a sound, he let his molecules scatter and dematerialized. Rematerializing directly behind the shadow, he pulled his silver Primani blade and skewered the darkness in front of him.

What the hell?

It was gone. His blade hit nothing but air. Impossible! Looking left and right, he was shocked to find himself alone. The air still reeked of evil though... something wasn't right... a shrill scream brought his head up and the blade out. The boys!

Acting on sheer instinct, he launched himself into the playhouse. If it wasn't so serious, he might've laughed at the sight that greeted him when he rematerialized inside. Most of the small space was filled with the bulky frame of a demon who'd been trying to grab the boys. He held Michael with one hand, leaning as far away as possible. The little boy was kicking and swinging his tiny fists at the demon's stomach while Rafe clung to his back screaming like a rabid howler monkey. Rafe had jammed his fingers into the demon's eye sockets and was practically ripping them out of his head. Black demon blood spattered the new carpet. It was hard to tell who was yelling the loudest... the demon or the boys.

The demon cursed, "You little bastards! Let go of me before I skin you alive and eat you!" Twisting this way and that, he finally flung Michael off. Dec caught him easily and set him down by the door. "Michael, run to your father. Now."

Michael shook his head. "No! He's got Rafe!"

He shoved him out the door. "Don't argue. Just go!"

He turned to the demon who was desperately trying to shimmer, his form wavering in and out of the plane. The human facade shifted back and forth to his real scaly self. Rafe was still screaming at the top of his lungs, the sound deafening in the tiny cabin. Clearly he took after his mother. All right, as amusing as this was... it was time to wrap it up. He was getting a headache.

"Rafe! Buddy, stop! For God's sake, stop." His sharp tone broke through the noise and Rafe immediately stopped yelling. His bright blue eyes snapped open and he broke into tears of relief.

"Good work, little dude. I'll take it from here." To the demon, he said, "So, demon, you seem to be stuck here." He circled closer, blade at the ready. "Looks like your intel sucks."

"I'm going to rip your scales off one at a time. Then I'm going to carve out chunks of your flesh and send each piece back to Hell in a special package for your boss to open." Mica's eyes burned with a white-hot flame as her anger threatened to turn her into a torch. You just didn't touch a woman's kids and expect to keep your naughty bits.

Since he wasn't needed for anything, Dec leaned against the railing and watched her work. As she circled the demon, her tone sent a shiver of fear through *him*, and he had a twinge of pity for the stupid demon. Said demon was tied to a chair, blood still covering his face, eyes blinded by a berserk three year old, and furiously trying to shimmer out. Sadly for him, this place had a new security system. No way was this demon getting out of the chair. Killian made it shimmer proof. Sometimes magic was a good thing.

The sound of heavy boots on the stairs distracted him. He glanced up at Killian as he ducked his head to enter the basement. "Well?"

"Dani's on her way. Do you want to meet her and fill her in?"

He shrugged. "Not particularly, no."

Killian shot a meaningful look in Mica's direction and said, "You two have to get past this. It's not helpful." To Mica, he said, "Babe, I've got this. Would you go upstairs and wait for Dani?"

The sound of her teeth grinding together was loud and clear as she stomped over to them. Glaring up, she snapped, "Dani doesn't need help. I'm going to carve this asshole into dog food, and then I'm going to finish dinner. We still need to eat."

He choked on a laugh and turned his back before she caught him. This was exactly the reason he loved Mica so much. Ruthless *and* practical.

Later that night, they sat around the dining room table bullshitting about this and that. He waited for the right time to bring up his plans. Fidgeting in his chair, he drummed his fingers against the side of his thigh and tried to find the words. Leaving wouldn't be easy. He'd miss them. He rested his gaze on the two little boys giggling together at the end of the table, and he sighed again. How could he do it? How could he leave them? He was their godfather. They needed him. As he sank deeper into thought, Domino's warm nose prodded his hand demanding his attention. The pretty little Dalmatian seemed to look right inside his mind.

You're leaving again?

Gently fondling her silky ears, he cringed. Was he so obvious? She rubbed her head on his leg and snorted a blob of dog snot all over his knee. Nice.

Duh!

Best get it over with. Straightening a bit, he blurted, "I'm moving out. Tomorrow."

Mica choked on her wine. "What? Why?"

He hated the shock on her face. But surely she suspected? She was psychic, after all. "I... I need some space. It's not you guys!" He tried to avoid looking at Dani, but his eyes slid that way on their own. She clamped her lips together and glared daggers.

"This isn't my fault!" she hissed.

Purposely ignoring her, he spoke to Mica and Killian instead. "It's not a big deal, Mica. I've been on my own for a long time. I'm used to more solitude than I've had here. I just need some space to do my own thing for a while." He gestured with his hands and added with half a smile, "Don't try to tell me you haven't suspected anything."

Sighing into her wine glass, she took a sip and set it down before saying, "It's okay, Dec. I can feel your unhappiness." Her eyes cut to Dani, and she hastily turned back to Dec. "You have a right to your own life, your own happiness. We don't expect you to live here until the apocalypse begins. God only knows how many years that will be!"

Feeling the first spark of excitement he'd had in weeks, he shot up and went around the table to hug her. He should've known she'd understand. She knew him better than anyone else; anyone in this lifetime, anyhow. "Thanks for understanding, darlin'. I didn't want to let you down. I swear I'll be here whenever you need me. I'm still on the team for ops, and I'm still the best godfather the triplets have. I'll be here for them too."

She squeezed him back with a cheeky wink. "Don't be a dork, dork. We totally get it. You want your space. You got it. You can come back any time you want."

"Can I help you pack, Dec?" Dani asked.

He gave her a level stare and said, "You've done enough already."

Chapter 2: Daydreams and Night Things

"SHIT, SHIT, SHIT! I AM SO LATE!" Rori balanced on one foot desperately shoving her toes into the strappy sandal that was about to lose her job for her. Stupid shoes weren't cooperating this morning, and she was way out of time. After jamming two toes through the side straps, ripping her pinky toenail and falling on her ass, she finally threw it into the wall. "Frickin' shoe!"

Five minutes, and a lot more cursing later, she slammed the apartment door and flew down the three flights of stairs to the lobby. Damn, damn, damn! She was so late. Again! Her boss would fire her if she was late one more time, and then where would she be? She barely had enough money to pay for the dump she lived in, and forget about eating. There was precious spare change for silly little things like food. These days she was living on noodles and the rare piece of fruit she snagged from the corner store. She was pretty sure Raul knew she was stealing his fruit, but he never said anything. He always turned his back when she came into the store. She was thankful for the small kindness. Those things were rare in her world.

Glancing at her watch, she picked up her pace. She never had enough time. In her universe, it ran in fast-forward. It didn't matter how much time she gave herself to get ready, she was always late. And of course, she was out of bus money so she was walking - no, make that running - the ten blocks to the flower shop where she worked. The owner, Angela Donatucci, was a total bi-otch about time. She was opening, so technically Angela wouldn't know if she was on time or not...but she had a pissy habit of showing up out of the blue. "Spot checks", she called it. She'd been busted three times in the last month. One more time, and she was jobless. And jobless meant *homeless* soooo... Crap! Dodging around a kid on a scooter, she hung a fast right and cut through the alley behind the Downward Dog Chinese slop shop. A couple of delivery trucks were pulled up to the back door. No problem. She'd just squeeze through. With her mind on the time, she didn't see the backup lights until it was too late.

A starburst exploded and then... nothing but darkness. Excited voices babbled nearby, but they drifted on the wind. Sirens warbled in the distance, the sound fuzzy and faint.

"Hey! Are you all right?" a man's voice snapped next to her ear.

Yes, yes, I'm fine! She tried to speak, but her mouth wasn't working. No sounds came out. This was so not good. Why couldn't they hear her?

"Holy shit, Ramirez, you killed her!"

What? No way! I can't be dead! She struggled to move, to show them she wasn't dead, to sit up, something, anything, but she was frozen inside her uncooperative body. A wave of dizziness rolled in slow motion through her brain, spreading from head to toe. She was too weak to twitch. She strained to lift her hand, but vicious pain stabbed into her belly. Why wasn't anyone doing anything? Didn't she moan? She could've sworn she'd moaned out loud. If ever there was a time to moan, this was definitely it. No one responded, so maybe she hadn't. Darkness pressed in, her inner vision tunneling to a single spear of bright light. Seriously? Damn... *I* am *dying*. Well, this sucks.

I should've seen this coming.

"Hang in there, darlin'. You're going to be all right." In contrast to the muted sounds around her, the soft words rang clear as a bell inside her head.

Someone loosened the hoodie's zipper before lifting the tiny gold cross she wore around her neck. An amused chuckle floated in her head, and the voice came again. "Nice metal. Okay, hang on to your heartbeat; I'm gonna rock your world."

Dec studied the woman's pale face and prepared to work a little miracle 'cuz that's what he did. Piece of cake. No way was he letting her die. He was in the right place at the right time and he could fix this. Looks like it was her lucky day! He laid his cheek against her breast to listen for the music of her heartbeat. When it faded to quiet, he got to work. Okay, sweetheart, time for a little preventative kissing. This is the fun part... Carefully parting her lips, he gave her mouth-to-mouth while the ambulance screamed from blocks away. A small crowd had formed, chattering loudly, but he didn't care. They had no idea he was using his powers to heal her. In between breaths, he ran his hands over her body, searching for injuries. Poor woman had some internal bleeding. He could hear the blood pooling in her abdomen, sloshing against the side of the visceral peritoneum. Where is it? Ah ha, here we go. Celiac artery. Not good. It was damaged enough that blood was flowing at a good clip. She'd never make it to the hospital without bleeding out. Soooo, time for that miracle. He tucked his hand inside her hoodie. With palm flat overtop of the torn artery, he got to work. After a few seconds, the ragged edges were neatly knit back together. Now back to her lovely mouth... she seemed to be breathing, but it wouldn't hurt to be extra positive.

Rori's back arched off the ground. Her arms opened to welcome what her brain didn't yet understand. Glorious fire warmed her from the inside out. Brilliant light flooded her mind, blocking all memories, all thought, until there was nothing but tranquility. Floating weightlessly, all substance drifting away... she was nothing and everything at last. There was no time, no place; nothing but the light pulling her higher.

Peaceful, so peaceful...

Settling like a feather to the earth once again, she gradually came back to herself. The blinding light dimmed to a soft luminescence behind her eyes. She must be dead after all and this was Heaven. The excruciating pain in her abdomen vanished. Her inner vision was still taking a siesta, but she was acutely aware of the strong fingers that held her jaw, the lips that pressed against her own... slightly rough. Male. The loops and whorls of his fingerprints branded the soft skin of her face. Capable hands... A fresh green scent washed over her, sending her mind to a fantasy of forests and waterfalls. As her heartbeat steadied to normal, she could almost see him in her mind's eye. The images came in fragments... ghostly and unclear. Windblown blond hair... cobalt blue eyes... a lean face was taking shape when the voice came again.

"Gotta bolt, beautiful. Have a nice life."

The half-formed face scattered like dandelion fluff just before she sank into a dream-free sleep.

Leaning against the stone wall of the penthouse garden, he closed his eyes and thought about the woman he'd rescued. She was a tiny little thing, half starved, too thin. No wonder she'd been hurt so badly; she didn't have any extra muscle on her bones. Aside from that, she was intriguing, pretty but not perfect. Fresh blood trickling down the side of her face couldn't hide the fine texture of her skin or the height of her cheekbones. She had a small pearly scar above her left eye. Shaped like a bird's wing, it lay parallel to the winged arch of her eyebrow. Her eyes had been closed, curly lashes sweeping her cheek. He'd wanted to see the color, but couldn't exactly pry them open while he was giving her mouth-to-mouth. That would've been uncool.

He rubbed a finger over his lower lip and had a clear flash of her mouth as his lips brushed against hers. The image surprised him, and he held his breath waiting for more. He felt the silky texture of her tongue when she held him closer and fell into their kiss. Encouraged, he threaded his fingers through her hair, tilting her head back for better access.

Jolting awake, he snorted at his own daydreaming. This was getting out of hand. Three years was definitely the max he could deprive himself without going insane. At the rate he was going, he would be ambisextrous in another month. It was bad enough that he had waaaay too much alone time with his immoral compass, Mr. Crowley. As far as penis nicknames went, it was his favorite. Named after one of his favorite Ozzy Osbourne songs, Crowley was not to be trusted. He had absolutely no sense. For example, right now, Crowley was all but yelling to tap that ass. He was even pointing in her direction, like a helpful little compass...little being figurative, not literal.

Smacking himself in the forehead, he shoved *those* thoughts to the back of his mind. He wasn't going to think of her that way. Rori wasn't an ass to be tapped--At least not by his tapper. She was just a woman he helped--one of, oh, probably 200,000 or so since he'd become Primani more than 1,500 years ago. Saving her was just part of their job description: Hunt and kill demons and save pretty women. Well, technically, they didn't have to be 'pretty' or even 'women', for that matter. Saving humans was something they did occasionally. 'Course, sometimes they *hunted* the humans and killed them too. Depended on the mission.

In Rori's case, she was lucky he'd been on his way to grab a bagel. Right place, right time. Good for both of them. She got to keep living, and his funky mood was gone. Win-win. Forcefully dismissing her from his mind, he let the night sounds of the city wash over him. The hum of traffic blended with the deep vibrations of bass in the apartment building across from this one. In the distance, a baby cried, and he smiled inside.

Crying meant living. Go ahead, little dude. Cry. Live. Make your parents mental. It's your job. Grow up to be someone you believe in. Be someone you like.

Up here, on the 18th floor, he was completely alone. Alone to think, alone to breathe a few deep breaths. He'd wanted this, hadn't he? Yeah, sure he did. He'd wanted to get away, get some space. Mostly he wanted to get away from Dani. He scrubbed a hand over his eyes to brush away her image, but she stayed put. Shoving away from the wall, he stalked across the patio, zeroing his gaze on the park so far below him. Dark now, there wasn't much to see.

Three years! He'd given her three years to come around! He felt like such a dumbass now. He'd thought he had everything all figured out. She had to be into him, didn't she? The signs were all there. They'd hung out together. She'd been sweet to him, right? She'd shared a kiss or two and a few other things that kept him waiting for more. He was pathetic. He hoarded those kisses like morphine, dragging the memories out when loneliness got to be too much. She laughed at his jokes... and most of them were pretty lame, too! She wouldn't do that if she didn't really like him, would she? In his mind, the biggest sign was jealousy. Dani had a fit every time he even friggin' looked at Abby. He slammed a hand into the railing and closed his eyes.

Abby.

With her rebel pink hair and grass green eyes, she was a pretty little thing. She wore a funky diamond nose stud that made him stare at her face. Pretty sure that was the point. She didn't need to bother with that, though. Fit, adorable, and energetic, it was impossible to ignore her. God knew he tried hard enough for more years than he could count. She just wouldn't give up on him. She'd be a friggin' stalker if she wasn't so damn likable.

He'd hurt Abby's feelings so many times his karma was on life support. She deserved better than him. He was dangerous. His *life* was dangerous. Abby didn't know all that. She'd wormed her way into his heart without him even knowing it. He'd tried to keep her at a distance for what felt like forever. She was Mica's baby sister, for crying out loud! He couldn't hook up with her. *Wouldn't* hook up with her. Even though he'd drawn that line, he still spent more time with her than he should.

How could he say no to a woman like her? He honestly didn't want to. He liked her. She was so in love with life, with living each and every day. She was fun to be around. He felt damn good around her. He loved her wide-eyed approach to new things, her passion for the people around her. She cared about people, truly cared. It was a rare thing these days. In the past few months, he found himself looking forward to seeing her when she wasn't around…the second he realized this, alarm bells, whistles, and sirens went off inside his head.

Time to walk away.

Her humanity would weaken him, would change him. It'd taken him centuries to finally be the Primani he was today. The future was murkier than ever and he, none of them, could afford to be vulnerable. Besides, she was human. That alone was a deal breaker. He wanted a forever kind of love.

He'd thought that love would come from Dani. After all, she was beyond death; an angel in the truest sense of the word. She could stand by him for his eternity. But Dani... well, she was just jerking him around all this time. Damn it to Hell anyway. Mica was right. He wanted to kick himself for being so blind. Flopping down onto a chaise, he remembered Dani's last words. Was it really only three days ago? Yeah, guess so. Time flies when you've been kicked in the teeth by a pain-in-the-ass, blond working angel.

Before he left for Manhattan, she'd followed him to his car and watched silently as he loaded it with a couple of suitcases and a backpack. The new Dodge Challenger was a gift to himself for not murdering her. The iridescent blue paint sparkled in the morning light. Feeling a wee bit heavy hearted, he'd closed the trunk and turned to find her waiting.

"What do you want, Dani? Come to make sure I leave?"

"It's not like that, Declan. You should know better." She was using a snotty tone that he was just about sick to death of. She pulled it out when she knew she was wrong, but didn't want to admit it. He'd heard it more times than he could count. With any luck at all, he'd never hear it again.

Her fine hair fluttered in the breeze, and he pulled his eyes away from it. "Really? What's it like then? 'Cuz I sure as hell don't know what to think anymore."

She sighed and tossed her hair like he was being a difficult child. He really hated when she did that. It made him feel childish, unreasonable. Who did she think she was? "Tick-tock. I'm waiting. No words now? Not another insult to send me on my way? That's a surprise."

Her eyes flashed, and she snapped, "You have no idea what I'm thinking, so give it a rest."

He flinched at her tone and studied her face one last time. He'd really thought he might love her, but she was right. He didn't know her at all. That's exactly how she wanted it, too. Sharing next to nothing about herself, she had kept him at arm's length all this time. He'd been stupid. Shrugging with nonchalance he didn't really feel, he buried the pain behind sarcasm. "And that's our problem, isn't it? You never talk to me. So I don't know you at all, do I? And now, I'm not sure I want to."

She grimaced at his words, grabbing at his arm to stop him. "Wait--"

Jerking his arm away, he cut her off. "No, Dani. I get it. You don't want me. You don't need to beat me over the head with it. I'm finally seeing things clearly. Shit, girl, I just wish I'd seen the truth years ago. I've wasted too much time waiting on you. I'm through." He gave her a hard look and got into the car.

Even here in Manhattan, she followed him. It was beyond annoying. She didn't want him, but he couldn't get her out of his head. He was a moron. Go away, Dani! Mentally scrubbing her face from his mind, he stomped back into the kitchen. A quick recon through the pantry turned up a nice fresh bottle of Jim Beam. Just what the doctor ordered. He'd just downed a double when there was a subtle shift in air pressure. Company. Please don't be Alex. He wasn't in the mood for their boss.

"Yo, Dec!"

He perked up. Now *Sean* he could stand in the mood he was in. Sean was his other Primani 'brother'. More like him than Killian was, Sean was practically his twin. Except he had a sense of humor and Sean, well, he just didn't. Ha. His timing was perfect! If anyone understood misplaced love, it was Sean. After all, Mica had ended up with Killian... after starting out with Sean. He'd get a ton of sympathy from Sean. "In here drowning Dani in bourbon. Come on in."

Sean strolled into the kitchen and frowned at the bottle. He shook his head and straddled a stool. "Don't drink alone, man. It's lame."

The morning brought a brand new day full of sun, and sunlight, and more sunlight. All of it was trying to kill him. Swearing very quietly, Dec shoved his head under a pillow and wished for the energy to close the blinds. Just the idea of getting up sent a shaft of pain through his skull. Not gonna happen. A few hours later, he dragged himself out of bed and stumbled into the shower. While the scalding waterfall sluiced over his back, he let his *saol* purge the toxins from his body. With arms folded against the glass, he rested his cheek on his crossed forearms and sighed. Breathing slowly and deeply, he let nature do its thing. At his command, the *saol* released a gentle pulse of healing energy that raced through his cells, burning off the garbage that was making him feel like crap. The rhythmic vibrations were soothing, so he took the world's longest shower.

Hot water on demand was a blessing that no one who wasn't immortal would ever appreciate. Two hundred years ago, he was lucky if he got a bath in a tub. Most of the time, the Primani settled for a scrub in a creek or a swim in a freezing lake, unless of course, they were working ops in Paris or another cultured city. The wealthy had bathtubs, sometimes. He smiled at a flash of memory. Mmm, Paris. He'd had a few girlfriends there. The last one died in 1777. Beautiful, pampered... blond and sweet, Justina. The youngest unmarried daughter of a fat, old count, she was left to her own devices more often than not. They'd met at a winter ball, of all things, and the chemistry was potent. At 23, s*he* was potent. Tall, willowy, with lush breasts, she was stunning. She also had all of her teeth, which was a rare thing back then.

It had started out as a simple fling. She wouldn't take no for an answer, and he didn't really want to say no.

Despite the work he was doing, he was able to squeeze in time to see her. Day visits turned to night visits faster than he could say '*ménage a trois*.' Apparently, her bedroom was soundproofed, because they never got caught by her parents. He still wondered if they ever found her toy box.

Justina.

He'd never met any woman who had such a passion for sex, before or since. On their third 'date,' they were at a party when she suggested a visit to the stables. She had to see the horses. After oohing and ahhing over the horses for about, oh, ten minutes, she unlaced his breeches and gave Mr. Crowley the royal treatment. Twice.

On their fifth 'date,' she smuggled him into her bedroom via the servants' stairs and a secret passage in the wall. They'd laughed and kissed and drank wine until after midnight. As the clock struck 12:00, she gave him a sly grin and dragged a carved wooden chest out from a hidden cabinet in the wall. Grinning hugely, she popped it open and told him to take his pick. Judging by her cries of pleasure and the claw marks on his back, he'd chosen well.

The chemistry burned too hot to last though. He knew that now. Then? He was addicted to Justina and the joys of her box. More than once, Sean warned him that nothing good could come from seeing her. They couldn't get married, and the count would demand it if she got pregnant. He accused Sean of being jealous. Sean shrugged it off with a knowing look and let the matter drop. But it turned out he was right.

The girl might have seemed innocent on the outside, but she did things that rocked him to the core. Worse, she let him do things that should have terrified her. But she begged, demanded more, and he gave it. God help them both, he gave her whatever she asked for. On more than one dawn, he'd crawled home feeling as though she took his soul along with his seed. The last night they were together, she drugged him. In his stupid lust-crazed head, he thought that was a good plan. On one level, it was the best sex he'd ever, ever had. Hallucinations blew his mind while she blew his... Every cell in his body burned, no *exploded*, with even the lightest touch of her tongue. And God only knew she touched him with way more than her tongue.

They'd emptied her entire box.

The overwhelming physical sensations were downright evil, and he still twitched at the memory of that night. Sometimes evil could feel heavenly...

He'd woken up to find both Sean and Killian shaking their heads at the foot of the huge four-posted bed. As he'd yawned awake, he realized the bed curtains were ripped down, the pillows scattered across the room. He, himself, was lying spread-eagled across the bed, shaved clean.

He tried to sit up and hissed at a sudden prick of pain on his stomach. Killian nearly died laughing. All he could do was point. He followed Killian's finger and nearly stroked out. Oh, my God!

The brilliant hummingbird's beak was poised to suck nectar from his cock.

At least it would if it ever got erect enough to reach his stomach again...right now, it was curled into a fetal position searching for the warm nest of curlies that were long gone. At this point, Killian had collapsed against the side of the bed. Sean was torn between humor and sympathy. Having been busted in inappropriate beds a few times himself, he understood the draw of forbidden sex way more than Killian. The fact that he'd been caught with his dick in a sling just a few months earlier didn't stop him from laughing out loud. As Dec struggled to sit up, he realized he was tied to the bed. Even now, he could just imagine the look of shock on his face.

Sean had finally given in to the urge that was strangling him. "I tried to warn you."

He shifted so the shower spray hit his stomach and let the memory surface. Ah, good times. He had millions of memories inside his head. Most he shuffled to the back and never brought up to the light. You'd go mental if you tried to keep up with that many. All of them did that; it was how they kept sane after all these years. Justina though... Well, she had been some kind of woman. It had taken him a month of focused healing to get that tattoo to vanish. He had to admit, it was amazing work. The artist had been talented. The tiny bird wore a studded collar around its delicate throat. He didn't know what that meant back then. Now? He was a little shocked. He didn't realize she wanted him to own her. He was up for kinky fun and games, but it never crossed his mind to take it to another level. Not that level, anyhow.

Probably just as well they never saw each other again. After Killian stopped laughing, he'd announced they were done in Paris. Time to move to America... wherever the hell that was...

A face full of cold water snapped him back to the present. Time to get his ass in gear. The past is the past. Justina's long dead, and he had more important things to do in this century. First thing on the agenda was following up on that pretty little accident victim. After all, he had saved her life. He should at least make sure she was still alive.

Rori. Her name was Rori. Pretty name. It meant 'brilliance' in his home country of Ireland. 'Brilliance' was a lot to live up to. Still, maybe it fit her. He'd have to judge that for himself. He ran the word around his head and finally said it out loud, "Rori Austin."

The instant the words ran off his tongue, an odd chill rolled across his skin. With a slight shiver, he opened his sight. A fleeting glimpse...an impression of something hovered out of his vision. Was it a shadow? A light? It was gone too fast to see. A sense of sorrow and pain lingered. Was she in trouble? There was something about her that tugged at him a little. He was always a sucker for a sad face, but this was... different somehow. He couldn't quite put his finger on it, but he was going to keep an eye on her. If nothing else, she was a diversion.

Rori closed her eyes and let the dream pull her under again. It was maddeningly close to the surface, the images skipping through her vision like an old black and white film. Again and again, she saw what she didn't want to see, what she would never remember. The dream's images were blurry, indistinct... the barest hint of reality. Flames licked at the edges, darkness lingered in the center. Framed against a gleaming arched window, the wings spread wide... the wings, the wings...

With a sharp cry, she jerked upright, heart in her throat, hand on her chest. Squeezing her eyes closed, she clung to the last rays of golden light that had appeared so suddenly in her vision.

The light was gone. Again.

Damn it!

Shoving her tangled hair away from her eyes, she squinted into the darkness of her room. Every day for three days, she'd had this same dream. It was making her crazy. Before her accident, she'd dreamed of the wings and the fire. But now there was a new element--the golden light. It invaded the darkness and chased the wings away. It radiated safety, escape, protection. Symbolic? Maybe. What did it mean? Shit. What did any of this mean? Most people dreamed random, disjoined images that were dredged up from their subconscious, their brains tidying up the loose ends of the day's work. She liked to think of it as the brain dumping the cookies and temp files it created after a long day of functioning. Kind of like a wicked powerful computer. *Most* people wouldn't find any significance in what they saw floating around inside their skulls at 2:00 in the morning. Huffing with frustration, she looked at the notepad and read her scribbled words.

What she wouldn't give to be like *most* people.

Chapter 3: The Devil You Don't

APPLES? ORANGES? BOTH? A girl needed fruit, right? It was healthy. Prevented scurvy and shit like that. Dec shrugged and tossed both into the basket. It was the least he could do, really. All things considered, he owed it to her. Right? Sure he did. Then why did he feel like he was doing something wrong? Guilt nibbled at his good intentions even as he dropped some cereal in with the fruit. He followed it with milk, bread, and some chicken breasts, crossing his fingers she wasn't vegan.

Trying hard to respect her privacy, he'd been sneaking up to her door and leaving boxes of food for the past two weeks. She needed a break. He could give her one. It was simple. He'd saved her from death, so he wanted to keep her healthy. He did *not* want to hook up with her, no matter how cute she was. It was not on his radar. Still…he felt a little dirty sneaking around like this. She'd probably think he was stalking her if she caught him. Good thing he could teleport!

Spring's Grocery was a typical NYC grocery store. Arizona Spring opened her little family business here in

1952. It fit the needs of the neighborhood and thrived even when money was tight. After all, who didn't need to eat? Most people who lived in the city shopped at these cramped little markets. It was one of the things he liked about living in a crowded city. He loved the energy of millions of souls converging in one place! He loved to walk down the street and watch the kaleidoscope of colors swarming around him. The hum of the people was music to his ears.

Mrs. Spring had recently put in a fresh grub bar with a broad selection of takeout items. Since restaurant food was insanely expensive, a ton of people started coming here to grab lunch. The narrow aisles couldn't exactly accommodate the crowd, but everyone was usually patient about it. It was odd how a shared love of eating brought people together. In this case, they were all *very* together as they inched their way to the cash register at the front of the store. Always polite, he raised the small basket over his head to make room for a Marilyn Manson groupie edging past him. The asshole didn't return the favor and thoroughly invaded his personal space with a full frontal slide-by.

"Dude!" Latching onto the asshole's arm, he pushed him backwards into the Cheetos rack. Bags went flying before all hell broke loose.

The man swung around and sucker punched him in the gut twice before jamming a needle between his ribs.

"Sonofabitch!" This guy had a death wish. He swung around to clock him, but his arm didn't respond. Rooted in place, he swayed but couldn't lift them. They'd turned to lead. He felt it then. His lungs not expanding, breathing slowed. He saw sparkling spots. Not good. Someone screamed. The sound warbled in his head, fading to a low ringing. He shook his head like a dog, or at least he tried to. The ringing continued.

The walls shifted 45 degrees. Spirals of color exploded from the stacks of fruit like a Skittles commercial.

"Enjoy the ride, Primani," Marilyn Manson grunted in his ear. As he swayed, Manson steadied him, a freaky rictus splitting his face. The man's gory make up melted over his chin followed by a stream of bright red blood. The plopping blood echoed like a church bell in the tiny room.

Lurching into customers and knocking over display racks, he used the last of his strength to get outside. He made it to the sidewalk before his world tunneled to a black dot.

A bucket of freezing water dumped over his head jump started his heart. The shock of it nearly gave him a stroke. Gasping at the cold, he snorted water and blood from his nose. Laughter brought his head snapping to the right even as his *saol* lit him up for combat. Awesome. He had company: two demons and a couple of rats lurking along the wall. An empty plastic bucket lay on the floor between them.

One of the demons gave him a jaunty wave. "Welcome back. We thought you'd be out all week. Francisco got a little carried away with the party drugs. Sorry about that."

Sonofabitch. This wasn't good. He yanked at metal cuffs, coming up short. He tested the cuffs at his ankles. No give there either. No problem. He'd just teleport.

"Don't even think about it. You, my wingless friend, are sitting on a very special chair. I wouldn't suggest shifting your weight even an inch. Things might get exciting if you do." He eased slightly closer and commented, "Nice laser eyes. Might want to tone them down before your eyeballs melt. You're not going anywhere."

Growling deep in his throat, he shut the smarmy voice out to focus on the chair. His hands and ankles were cuffed to it. It was wooden, nothing special…a little rickety… ah. There it was. A disk of metal rested just under his left butt cheek. A pressure plate. Now that he was paying attention, he smelled the telltale odor of almonds. Almonds and blood. He inhaled sharply which led to the discovery that one of his eyes was swollen nearly shut, and his nose hurt like a bitch. A vicious stab of pain in his side had him fighting another nap. His vision went spotty as he tried to stay conscious. Which one of these pricks kicked him? At least a couple of ribs were snapped, crushed by the feel of the pain. On a scale of one to ten, he was feeling about 120. Sonofabitches! When he got out of this chair, someone was going to die.

Locking eyes with the demon, he asked, "Do you want to explain why I've got a brick of C4 strapped to my ass? Seriously?" He wiggled his wrist as far as it would go, nearly slipping free of the cuff. With his voice just above a hiss, he swore, "When I get out of this chair, gutting you will be the very first thing I do."

The knife moved so fast he didn't have time to register it before it skewered his wrist to the chair. Pain swamped him like a tidal wave. Flashes of light burst behind his eyes as the nerves sent their screaming SOS's to his brain. He bit his tongue, tasting blood and bile.

The demon crouched before him, jerking his chin up, eyes burning like two coals. "Watch your fucking mouth, Primani. I've got orders to keep you alive. But no one said I couldn't damage you a bit while we wait for the boss."

With that cryptic piece of news, the demon yanked another blade from its sheath and thrust it under his left ear. "Keep talking and this goes. I don't think you can grow a new one."

The sudden blast of energy sent the demon sailing into the wall with a satisfying crash. Before he could hit him again, the other demon jammed a needle into his neck.

"Maybe we haven't taken the right precautions? Hold him."

Waking up the next time was even less of a party. He was still strapped to the friggin' chair, the athame pinning his wrist in place, broken ribs screaming with every breath, but now the scent of fresh blood curled his stomach. Glancing down, he nearly howled at the sight. The bastard had carved an angel trap into the top of his good hand. The sigil would bind his powers and mask his location, making it impossible for him to reach Sean. It neutralized the comms. Shit. There'd be no calling for help. He'd already sent a telepathic distress signal, of sorts, the second he came to earlier... whenever that was. The room was dark now. Even with the narrow windows blocking most of the outside, he could tell night had fallen, but he had no idea what day it was. How many days had he been missing? Sean would be looking for him--they'd had plans to go hunting the night he was grabbed. Surely he was tracking him? But if he was, why wasn't he already here? Sean was the best tracker he knew. His skills were legendary, really, and add them to their tight personal bond... well, he should be able to sense him without any trouble. Unless... glancing around, he looked for more sigils. It was technically possible to hide him from the other Primani with the right knowledge. Was it too much to hope that these yahoos were idiots?

"Don't bother looking. You're not getting out of here." The chatty demon was back.

Damn. Figures.

Alone this time, though..."Says you."

He sniggered, his full mouth curling into a genuine smile, teeth gleaming. Waving a hand in his prisoner's general direction, he said, "You're white as a ghost. How's your hand? Hurt much?" Pausing just out of reach, he sniffed at the air and added, "Sweating too. Huh. You still haven't healed yourself? I'm surprised. What's the matter with your mojo?"

LAURIE OLERICH

I haven't had TIME to heal myself, you dick. He thought about saying that out loud and opted to bite his tongue. He had some pressing issues that were about to become major problems and losing his ear wouldn't help things.

He was strapped to a bomb.

His hand burned like a mother.

His telekinetic powers were bound.

Oh, and one more thing, he had to piss like a racehorse.

This was not going to end well.

"So, is the plan to bore me to death, or is there a reason you're going to all this trouble? I don't recognize you, demon. Want to share your name?"

Most demons were assholes with ginormous egos. When spending time topside in the human plane, they preferred to wear what they thought were macho human facades. They thought it made them look badass. Usually they looked stupid... Primani didn't take too many of these yahoos seriously. Normally the demons didn't get the drop on them. Typical conflicts were like business transactions. Primani hunted them, and they fought with knives or energy to the death. Usually the demons were smoked, literally, with minimal Primani losses over the millennia. They were just that good. Having been superior soldiers as humans, they were a thousand times more powerful after an archangel made them Primani.

Demons were tricky; they had powers, they had weapons, they had Satan on their side. But in the grand scheme of things, they tried to avoid extermination *a la* Primani. In other words, they ran away a lot. Grabbing him and tying him to a friggin' chair in the middle of a cliché abandoned warehouse was a bizarre tactic that he couldn't get his fairly brilliant mind around. What was the game?

The chatty demon with the shitty attitude chose to dress in a suit--with a *tie* and black and white *wingtips*.

Aaaand the nauseating mess was all topped off with a hankie in the breast pocket. *Clearly* he'd watched too many old gangster movies. In an oddly fussy gesture, he tucked the small square of fabric back into its home and steepled his fingers. He kept his dark eyes hooded while he lost himself in thought. Just for a second though, they revealed his true nature. Yellow reptilian eyes winked into the deep set sockets before changing back to the deep green human versions.

Finally he answered, "You can call me Nick."

As the last melancholy notes melted into the night, Killian released a slow even breath. Twelve bells. Twelve. Midnight. Nearly time. Moonless and thick with summer heat, Rome slumbered like a great sprawling beast. It was preternaturally silent as though every creature knew there was great evil present. The subtle vibrations of it slithered over his neck, making him clench teeth that were already jammed together. He jogged in a crouch to the corner of the religious articles warehouse. The hundred-year-old building was wedged between an abandoned house built in the Middle Ages and a crumbling church built during Pope Benedict XIV--circa 1750 something or other. He'd been in Rome often enough to recognize the style but wasn't going to study the historical plaque over the door. A guard walked right into him as he rounded the corner. He didn't have time to shout before the fire was snuffed from his eyes. He yanked the blade out of the bony chest and wiped it on the dead human's pants. That's what you get for working with demons. With a hand signal to Sean, he raised his weapon and kept moving.

Sean nodded and vanished.

Come on, Dec... Where are you, little brother? They'd had a bitch of a time tracking him so far. He was supposed to be in Manhattan! How the fuck did he end up in Rome? And so fast? There was no way he took a plane. There wasn't enough time to get here from New York. Lucky for him, Raphael was thoroughly pissed off and sent out his own sources to sniff him out. They'd narrowed it down to this street. Raphael was as chill as they came--the inventor of original Zen. He had only seen his maker this furious on a handful of occasions; Dec's disappearance was another. Guess he had a soft spot for the guy. They lost him once. He'd be damned if they'd lose him to another demon. He'd go to Hell himself and set the place on fire. Hell hath no fury like a pissed off archangel. Just ask Lucifer... It was good to have Raphael on their side.

He took a sec to bring Dec's face to mind and set his jaw again. His family needed Declan--They'd all been stronger from having known his light. Everyone he touched, he saved in his own way. It was his gentle gift. Probably he'd never admit to loving the goofball, but he'd sacrifice a large chunk of the planet just to get him back. Besides, Mica would murder him if he didn't. With this cheery thought in mind, he stopped to get his bearings. The place seemed deserted. He'd killed one human guard already and heard the muffled sound of Sean taking out another. They'd cleared the perimeter without any other contacts.

A crunch of gravel warned him he had spoken too soon. Wheeling around, he swung his knife hand just as the click of a hammer sounded beside his ear.

Nick was the most heinous of all demons. A true poster child of evil, his cruelty knew no end. Dec's eyes dropped to the floor. Shuddering at the sight, he ground his molars together and debated the usefulness of prayer.

After an hour of torturing him with it, the bastard left the hose pouring water into a drain at his feet. Nick had decided to carve him up like a chicken, but opted to shove the hose in his mouth instead. After perfecting his version of waterboarding, he'd shimmered out. The next visit would be with his boss; so said the trustworthy demon. Who knew when the asshat would show up? His new buddy Nick the Dick had issued dire warnings twice, and so far, the boss demon had been a no show. He got the impression the plan was unravelling. Nick had been pissed off when he got here earlier. He'd ranted, raved, and took off without cutting off any body parts. Seemed kind of distracted. He even tortured him in a half-ass way. Honestly, he should be a little insulted at the lack of attention. After all, he'd been tied to this friggin' chair for the angels only knew how long, and his patience was getting pretty short. Someone either needed to rescue his ass or kill him. Things were getting bad.

Trying desperately to ignore the effect the water had on his bladder, he focused on healing what he could. His *saol* had warmed him and repaired the ribs just like it was supposed to, but it couldn't erase the sigil carved in his hand, which was still seeping a steady stream of blood, or push out the damn athame in his other wrist. Fuck. It hurt. He wasn't a wuss about pain, but every breath brought excruciating agony throughout his arm. Demon weapons were a bitch that way--all of them were toxic. To add insult to injury, he could look down and see it sticking there. The blood made him... uncomfortable. The obsidian toothpick turned him into a horror movie prop. Seriously, it was obscene. Now there were three of them... Crap! He was going to pass out again... oh, no, no, no! Now wasn't the time for that. They'd be back any minute.

To keep the dizziness from pulling him under, he bit his lip and took inventory of his arm. Staring hard and focusing on every inch, the lightheadedness waned by the time he made it to the wrist. Golden skin, fine blond hair sprinkling his forearm and wrist... nails short, not manicured, and long, lean fingers. Just your standard, attractive hand. The maroon trail of congealed blood added a dramatic splash to the bland colors... As if protesting the scrutiny, his middle finger twitched, sending an arrow of fire shooting up the rest of his arm. Unable to stifle the groan, he let it go and closed his eyes. No one was here to hear him anyhow.

"Where are you, Sean?" he muttered under his breath. "Any time now would be great."

On cue, Sean rematerialized in the shadows near the back of the room. Staying out of sight, he scanned the rest of the building for heat signatures. Finding none bigger than a rat, he zoned in on his hunting buddy. Even without his supernatural senses, he wouldn't have missed him. The smell of torture hit him like a shockwave; the rage he'd been resisting flickered to life. He would skin these bastards alive if Dec was dead.

"Dec!" He flashed over to his side and started to snap the handcuffs off when Dec's eyes flew open.

"Don't touch me! God, don't touch me!" His eyes bugged with real fear.

Sean froze in mid-yank. WTF? Dec wasn't afraid of anything. "Dude, we need to go. You need help."

Now that he'd released the cuff, Dec relaxed with a whoosh of breath and a ghost of a smile. "No shit, genius. I also need to piss like a racehorse, but you can't help with that... unless you want…" He let the words hang and gave a nod to his crotch.

Sean crossed his arms and said, "Not gonna happen."

Dec shrugged. "Worth a shot. Look under the chair. Tell me what you see there."

He crouched and whistled. Shit. He flipped onto his back, sliding under the chair to check out the explosives. Okay, a lot of plastique and a nest of wires that led to the assorted components. No problem. He'd just disarm the fucker, and they'd be on their way.

Pulling himself upright again, he rolled his eyeballs over Dec to check for injuries. All moving parts were still attached. Good sign. The sickening odor of blood seemed to be coming from the angel trap carved into his hand. Bad sign.

They needed to get moving. Dec didn't look good at all. He held himself stiffly, barely exhaling. His gaze landed on the athame, the obscene sight dragging a snarl from his throat.

"Yeah, it fucking hurts. I'd love you forever if you'd pull that thing out."

"I got it. Hold your breath." With that command, he yanked the blade out in one quick movement.

Dec made a strangled sound as his eyes rolled back in his head. Sean stared in horror as the wounded hand jumped in spasms. Blood pooled thick and hot across the arm of the chair. The smell of it added more fuel to his rage. Someone was going to pay for this. Dec's face blanched white, and he swayed forward.

Sean grabbed Dec's jaw, squeezing to leave fingerprints. "Don't you pass out on me! Suck it up!"

Dec bit down on his lip hard to steady himself. After a couple of deep breaths, he nodded. "I'll live. Just get it done."

He dug in a pocket of his pants and pulled out a Leatherman. Finding the wire cutter, he crawled back under the chair to get to work.

He considered himself a pretty experienced demolitions man. He and Dec had set tons of explosives over the years. He had a delicate touch, sensitive fingers, and a quick eye for details. He'd be the first to admit that Dec was better, though. He had an understanding of architecture and physics that was uncanny sometimes. He could eyeball a structure for five minutes and know exactly where to place the charges to create max destruction with minimum collateral. They worked in perfect synch with each other. In, out, done. Not today though. He closed his eyes and groaned inwardly. This wasn't good.

"What are you doing under there? Just cut the red wire." Dec's tone was more exasperated than scared now. "Hurry up, man!"

He didn't respond.

"What's the matter? Why aren't you doing anything?"

With a long, pained sigh, he answered, "All the wires are red."

Loooonnngg pause.

"Dude. Who *does* that?"

"Demons with a sense of humor." Killian dropped from the scaffolding, landing like a cat; a big, predatory cat. He elbowed Sean out of the way and poked his head under the chair.

"I got this. Move over."

Sean couldn't resist muttering, "My hero," but he moved out of the way. Killian wasn't just a *Primani*. He had other powers handed down from his ancestors long before the Druids thought to build their first rock altar. He was scary good.

While Killian squeezed his broad shoulders under the chair, Dec began to sweat, his face white with strain. Sean tore off a strip of his t-shirt and gently wrapped it around his bleeding wrist. "Hang in there. It'll be over soon."

In a tight voice, Dec replied, "You've got no idea," and squeezed his eyes shut.

After that, there didn't seem to be anything else to say, so they kept their mouths closed while Killian concentrated and worked his magic.

Five long minutes later, Killian gave a grunt of satisfaction and heaved himself out from under the chair. "Okay, that does it. Let's go before we have company."

His mouth dropped open. "That's it? What'd you do?"

Killian shrugged like it was no big deal. "You use your eyes. I use my mind. Easy." He dropped his gaze to the angel trap and pulled out *Sgaine Dutre*. The thin blade was Killian's most powerful weapon, forged from silver and tempered by his blood, its clear blue stone sparked to life at the touch of its master's fingers. "Give me your hand, little brother."

Blanching even more impossibly white, Dec sucked in a gallon of air and ground out, "Get it over with."

The stone blazed as Killian destroyed the angel trap with a couple of quick flicks of his wrist. With a subtle shake of his head, Killian wiped the blade on his pants and said, "It's done. You should be able to use your powers to get out of here. We need to bolt. You're too weakened to fight, and they're coming back."

Dec wanted to leave. Really, he did, but his legs didn't want to cooperate. He trusted Killian, but he'd sat so long his muscles were frozen. He started to sweat again. The sounds of boots hitting the sidewalk and the faint click of ammo belts had been steadily growing closer. Killian was right. They were about to have company, and he wasn't in any condition to fight. The toxin had to be purged first.

Sean helped him out by hauling him to his feet and gripping his shoulders so he wouldn't fall on his face. "Come on. Let's go!"

He swayed and found his balance again. There was something he needed to do before he teleported anywhere. He gritted his teeth and fumbled with his zipper. "You might want to stand back."

The reentry into the penthouse was less than smooth. His powers weren't working at full strength, so he'd miscalculated the landing site by 50 feet. Normally, he'd land inside the foyer without any issues. This time though, he'd landed at the edge of the rooftop garden. As soon as his molecules reformed to solid mass, he swore, "Oh, shit!" and promptly took a header off the 18th floor. With arms and legs sprawling in a freefall, he heard Sean shout above him. As the faded red roof of a parked car zoomed towards him, he closed his eyes and sent an SOS to his maker.

"Declan!" A firm hand gripped his bicep in a persistent squeeze. The voice was familiar.

Raphael.

His ears rang as he gradually regained consciousness and everything came flooding back. He kept his eyes shut against the pain he knew was waiting for him. He didn't feel dead… at the moment. But he'd been dead before, and it hadn't hurt then either, so…

Raphael shook his shoulder. "You will be the death of me yet. Wake up and let's get you healed."

He slit his lids to find several faces hovering above him. Oh, awesome, an audience. Sean's smart ass mouth curled into a grin which just got wider in response to Dec's glare. Killian simply rubbed at his jaw and chuckled. Raphael frowned with real concern and more than a little exasperation. Pushing himself into a more manly position, Dec took a quick inventory. Nothing broken… his hands hurt like a bitch though, and he saw spots from the sudden bolt of pain through his wrist.

Raphael folded his arms and asked, "What were you thinking? You're lucky I caught you."

"Yeah, what were you thinking?" Sean contributed, his smile threatening to hit his ears in another minute.

Killian's battle with dignity disintegrated into bursts of laughter. After a minute, he wiped his eyes and managed to wheeze, "You should've seen the look on your face when you went over. God, it was priceless."

"Oh, yeah, sure. Hilarious. You guys are such assholes." He didn't find this funny. Not even a little bit. He was exhausted, in a ridiculous amount of pain, his bladder was probably broken, and he stank. "Get lost so I can chill." The room tilted, and he snagged a fistful of couch, groaning as the broken bones in his hand ground together. He swallowed bile when his stomach roiled. Don't puke. Don't puke. There would be no living that down. Ever.

Obviously taking pity on him, Raphael ordered softly, "Close your eyes, warrior. You need my help." With that, he placed his palm over Dec's heart, his touch light, fingers hot.

The effect was immediate and welcome. All of the archangels had the power to heal others, but he was the angel of health. Healing came with a mere thought. Raphael's energy swarmed into his chest, unfurling across every muscle fiber, every capillary, every cell, burning away the demon's toxins until he was clean again. A burst of heat whipped through him for a few seconds before cooling to his normal temperature.

Raphael spoke quietly inside his mind. His words and the timbre of his voice were as soothing as his touch. *I am cleansing you. Healing you. You are my warrior, my Primani. I have made you, and so I will keep you well.* Un vita, *Declan.*

With a slight twinge of pressure, the bones and tendons in his wrist quickly knitted together, the shocking pain gone. Next, his hand tingled and burned as the hated angel trap was erased, leaving him with fresh, new skin. The process only lasted a few seconds. When he was done, Raphael sat back with a smile, his blue eyes glowing gently with the evidence of his immense power.

"Good as new. Now, tell me what happened."

The blessings of his maker humbled him. Lowering his chin to his chest, he collected his thoughts before speaking.

"Thank you, Raphael. I am grateful for your care." He nodded his head with respect before slapping on his bard hat. After relating the bizarre tale of the Marilyn Manson impersonator, the oddly powerful psychedelic drugs, the cocky new demon on the block, Nick, and the C4 strapped to his ass, he sat back and waited for the inevitable barrage of questions from the captivated listeners.

Raphael was the first to speak, his tone pensive. "It seems unusual for a demon to take such actions without a reason. Did he not question you?"

He shook his head, hair brushing his cheeks, and slugged a glass of water before answering. "It's weird, right? I woke up tied to the friggin' chair expecting some idiot to torture me." He smiled ruefully and commented, "Torture me they did, but not for information. I think he just wanted to screw with me." He shuddered at the memory of the water hose. Torture by full bladder? That was crazy--even for demons.

Killian had been pacing during the last half of the story. His face had that intense, focused expression that he wore whenever he was putting his supercomputer brain to work. Now he stopped and squatted next to the couch where Dec was sitting. "He didn't ask you anything specific?"

His mind had been clouded with drugs and pain, but nothing came to mind. "Not really. But he was waiting for someone else to show. He kept saying the boss was coming for me, and that he wasn't allowed to kill me. Wouldn't give me anything else to go on. I don't know who the boss was. Nick got pissed when he didn't show up though. He'd shimmered off to find the guy when you two dropped in."

Killian studied his nails for a few seconds before pacing again. "I don't like it. It smacks of turf war. Who's this Nick? I've never heard of him. Grabbing a Primani would give any demon some street cred. With some of the big players out of the way now, it seems we may have some up and comers jockeying for position."

Sean spoke up. "I've still got some underground contacts. I could do some hunting and see what rumors are floating."

Sean had spent a lot of time undercover as a fallen angel. He'd lived with demons, trained them to fight, and quietly killed them off when no one was paying attention.

He'd barely made it out of Hell alive once his cover was blown. That was a few years ago, but his demon contacts still answered when he called. They might be evil, but they were savvy enough to keep their options open. Regime changes were fatal. Sometimes they secretly bargained with Primani for help with exterminating particularly brutal leaders. On the flip side, Primani used them as snitches when they needed to. Personally, he wasn't thrilled with using demons for info. Duh. They were *demons*. They lied.

The sun was long gone when Raphael finally stood and stretched his arms over his head. "I think we've exhausted the topic of Nick. Sean, go hunting. Killian, get to work on your contacts in Europe. Maybe Gabriel's team will know more about the demons in Rome. Call Alexandyr. And Declan," he paused and flashed a genuine smile, "stay off the roof."

Everybody's a comedian. "That's it? No instructions for me?"

Raphael clapped him on the back, laughing, "You know what to do. You're my best detective. Go investigate new demons in the area. Oh, and check up on that young woman. I sense she'll need a protector very soon. Consider her your new charge." He locked his eyes with Dec's. "The clock is ticking with that one, though I am unsure what is coming. Watch her, but don't cling."

A storm was coming. Thunder grumbled in the distance and lightning flickered through the heavy clouds that swallowed the tops of skyscrapers. In Brooklyn, Mother Nature's display bounced across the bedroom window like a funky strobe light. The summer heat was smothering everyone and the hot rain wasn't going to make it better. Tempers were frayed to the breaking point. Rori's was teetering on the edge. It had been a shitty week.

She sighed like a deflated balloon and started to pull the curtain closed. The thin fabric wasn't much, but it was the only barrier between her and the perv next door. She was sick and fucking tired of catching him peeping into her bedroom at night. If she was going to put on a strip show, she'd at least go get paid for it! Friggin' creep!

It was going to be miserable tonight. She stuck her face out of the window and wished for clean, fresh, mountain air. Once upon a time, she'd lived in the country with a mountain view. It was cool, clean, and quiet. She missed it every summer since moving to the city. That tiny slice of rural life was one of her better childhood memories. Karen and James Castle had made her feel welcome and safe. Warm and loving, they had been gentle with her at a time when her world was upside down. She'd had two years with them before a car accident killed them both. That was ten years ago. She'd never lived in the country again. Someday, though…

She rolled her eyes when a few fat drops of rain plopped on her hands. Damn it! Now she'd have to close the frickin' window! Was it possible to suffocate inside an apartment? She'd sell her soul for an air conditioner right now. A light moved in the shadows on the street down below. Faint, pale yellow, it bobbed like someone carrying a flashlight. She rubbed her eyes and squinted. A clap of thunder shook the building, making her squeak in surprise. When she got her heart out of her mouth, the light was gone.

All lights were gone. Her alarm clock flashed at 12:00. Great. No power. *Again*. She swiped at a bead of sweat running into her eye. She hated this dump.

As the summer storm raged outside, she tossed and turned, hot and miserable. The light show kept her awake, even after the hookers had gone home. Shoving her tangled mane of hair into a ponytail clip, she groaned at the time on her cellphone. I've got to get some sleep! Tomorrow would be a nightmare without sleep. Frustrated to the point of cussing out Mother Nature, her apartment super, and

Brooklyn in general, she flung herself onto her back and slammed her eyes closed again. Must sleep! Eventually, exhaustion won out.

He watched her from the window, eyes hidden in shadow, dark, forbidding. With arms crossed over his chest, careful not to touch anything, careful not to leave a trace of his presence, he breathed in her scent. Lush, rich, she smelled of the earth... of green plants and flowers. Inhaling slowly, he let the fragrance settle into his memory, his very bones. Oh yes, she was perfect. She was exactly right. Years of waiting nearly over... he'd found her. He'd proceed carefully. No mistakes this time.

As insubstantial as a sigh, he slipped into her dreams just as she sank into the deepest of sleep. Her mind responded to the images, the scents, and sounds while she lay limp with paralysis. His woman moaned and flung out a delicate hand, clutching at the tangled sheet. Fully under the dream's pull, she was oblivious to the waking world. And she would stay that way until he decided otherwise. It was time to play.

Hear me, Rori.

Obediently, she opened her eyes to darkness and flickering light. The soft glow soothed her, made her languid and pliant on the bed. Silky sheets caressed her naked skin, slithering around her thighs and over her belly. She was flushed from the heat, damp with sweat.

Close your eyes, Rori.

His voice was compelling... sexy, commanding. Her eyes fluttered closed. Her heart began to race even as she lay limp as a doll.

That's good. You listen well.

With that compliment, he caressed her jaw, stroking her cheek, teasing her mouth. Her lips parted for his finger, and he smiled in the darkness. Too easy. Positioning her hands above her head, he admired the roundness of her breasts as they thrust forward against the sheet. He glanced at the silk still sliding between her parted legs. With a thought, the silk lay motionless again. He could smell her desire. The spicy fragrance only added to her appeal. Tempting, oh, so tempting she was. Her breasts were small, pert, and creamy smooth. The sight made him want to play a different game tonight. He reached out to stroke her and stopped. He couldn't be sidetracked now. There were some things more important than *his* lust.

Like *hers*.

"Please..."

Ask me nicely.

She nearly flew off the bed when his hot mouth latched onto her breast, sucking her in, stroking her with his tongue. As his mouth worked her nipple in and out, his hand slid to her belly. There was nothing for her but the heat of his body and the fire erupting inside her own. He switched to her other nipple and bit the tip until she arched against him, pulling at her hands. Connected as they were, he felt her fall as the sensations overwhelmed her. So deeply entranced, she couldn't hear the thunder crashing overhead as he leaned into her face.

"Please, please..."

Please what? Ask me, Rori. Ask for what you want.

"I want you to..."

The shattering of the glass window brought her stumbling out of bed, tripping over a scratchy yellow sheet and falling to her knees. Grabbing at the milk crate for support, she landed in a heap. The storm! Expecting to see a watery mess, she was stunned to find no rain had come in at all. The floor was covered in broken glass though. Great, just great. She picked her way to the window and stopped dead. It wasn't even storming now. What the hell happened to the window? She glared at the ragged space, daring it to answer her. It didn't. The hair on the back of her neck stood up, and she froze.

Chapter 4: The Forecast Calls for Raine

TO KNOCK OR NOT TO KNOCK... that was the question. On one hand, Dec wanted to see her. On the other hand, it was not a good idea. He really, really didn't need to get involved with a woman right now. Human or otherwise! He'd dragged his sorry butt to the penthouse to have some alone time. He had to take some action if he wanted to stay sane. Dani needed to be exorcised--heartless witch--and he needed to make some plans. Things were changing. He knew he had to find his balance again. A woman was a completely bad idea. Period.

He knew that, sure. But still... he was lonely. He wanted to play, to *live*. What was the point of life if you didn't live it? He'd been pondering such deep thoughts for a year now. He had a job to do, true, but he wanted to enjoy this planet too. All work and no play made him a very unhappy Primani. The man inside of him wasn't too thrilled either. When was the last time he'd gone to a concert? Years? It'd been too long since he'd let himself go. Maybe he should call Rivin and hit New Zealand again. The waves were killer.

Did Rori surf? Had she ever seen the ocean? She'd probably love the water.

A woman was a completely bad idea... Yeah, yeah, he knew that.

But, on the other hand…

Raphael *did* tell him to keep an eye on her. He should absolutely listen to his maker, right? He was charged with keeping her safe. Surely it wouldn't hurt to do that in person? As the logical part of his brain argued its points, the rest of him stood across the street, ghosting in the shadows of a dumpster. No one could see him in ghost mode, but he hung back anyway. Force of habit. He didn't sense any demons, but he hadn't lived this long by being careless. Who's this?

A man lurched across the sidewalk to his right. He looked so out of place that Dec's mouth dropped open as he tried to figure out where he'd come from. Buzzed grey hair stuck out from the side of his head like a hedgehog. A faded green field jacket swallowed the man's scrawny frame while a filthy backpack slid off of one shoulder. It was too hot for a field jacket; the creepy dude had to be roasting. Muttering on his way past Dec's spot, he hesitated and stared directly into Dec's invisible blue eyes.

Pointing a trembling finger, he whispered, "Come to save us all? Hurry up before it's too late!"

What the hell? Can he see me? No way. He must be stoned, hallucinating or something. Dec slipped further into nothing, prepared to bolt if the man made another move.

"Oh, I see you all right. Wadda ya think you are? Invisible?" He rubbed at his stubbly chin and spit on the sidewalk. "You sure did take yer time, didn't you?"

The sun blinded her as she came around the corner of the Chase Bank building. Digging for her sunglasses, she stepped around one of the many people selling crap on the corners. This man wore dreads and a black Bob Marley concert shirt. Baggy shorts and flip flops completed his look.

"Hey, Rori! You're not going say hi?"

She slowed and waded back upstream with a smile. Raine. Out of all the street vendors, performers, pick pockets, and homeless people she knew, he was one of her faves. Just as broke as she was, he managed to scrounge a living by selling knock off Rolexes, umbrellas, sunglasses, and whatever else he had. The cheerful red glasses perched on her nose were a gift from him last week. He was kind that way.

"Holy shit, Raine! I didn't recognize you with your new hair! What the hell did you do?" She gestured at the dreads and grinned.

The last time she'd talked to him, his hair was a floaty blond cloud brushing his shoulders and hiding most of his face. He'd worn it that way for as long as she'd known him. It was wavy and shiny. Honestly, she'd always wanted to drag her hands through it but never had the courage to ask. Now he'd cut his hair to the collar and sported thin, twisted locks. Softer looking than the ones she usually saw, they almost seemed loose, springy... fascinating. Huh... Who knew?

Flashing a rare, boyish grin, he shrugged. "You know how it is. I just got sick of it in my eyes. Needed a change." He bobbed his head so the dreads bounced. "What do you think?"

Laughing at the twinkle in his clear green eyes, she had to admit he looked good. Make that hot. She'd never had a clear view of his face before. Dreads weren't usually her thing, but they gave him an exotic air, something wild, pagan... something other than the good-natured street person she'd known these past few months. The tiny silver hoop earring sent a shiver down her spine. Yum! Letting her eyes drift over his high cheekbones and straight nose, she got lost for a minute. Why hadn't she noticed how fine he was before today?

His laughter drifted off, the leaf green of his eyes turning mossy with male intuition. He licked his lips, and she watched the tip of his tongue against his full lower lip, wondering for just a split second how it might feel stroking her mouth.

"Are you checking me out?" He moved closer, voice dropping to an amused purr. Taking her hand, he stroked her palm with the pad of his thumb. He broke into a smug grin when she jerked her hand away.

Omigod! What was she thinking? This was no time to be getting hot and bothered by anyone--let alone one of the only friends she had in the city! Desperate to leave with some dignity, she forced an expression of disdain and sniffed, "I was thinking about something. Not you."

Lame. So lame!

Raine continued to grin and nodded with mock seriousness. "Sure. Of course. Not me. Got it. Well, I have to get back to work, or I won't eat tonight. Have fun at the library!"

Before she could escape, he caught her hand, kissing it softly, letting the heat of his mouth linger against her knuckles. "Think about me later, okay?"

Was it possible to die from embarrassment? With face on fire, she bolted down the sidewalk, weaving in and out of business suits and cellphones. She had no smooth whatsoever! She'd never be able to talk to Raine again. Ever. That was the only solution. God, he probably thought she was such a moron. Mentally smacking herself in the forehead, she skipped up the steps to the impressive doors of the most fabulous place on earth--the New York Public Library.

Closing her eyes just inside the doors, she inhaled with sheer joy. The smell of it! Furniture polish, leather, paper... Mmmm. When she died, she wanted to be buried right here. Or if that wasn't doable, maybe she'd just haunt it. If she had a home away from home, this would be it. Since her crappy apartment sucked ass and wouldn't be considered a home by any stretch of the imagination, she'd just call this place 'home'. It was Heaven! She moved to the side of the foyer and thought about her mission. Where to start today?

"There's my sweet girl!" The scratchy greeting came from a frail old gentleman named Arthur Annison. Standing barely a hair taller than the water fountain on which he leaned, he was both ancient and absolutely adorable. Despite the warm summer weather, he was dressed in the only clothes he seemed to own: grey wool pants and crisp white shirt. Today he had a soft blue sweatshirt on top. Frayed at the cuffs and stretched out, it had seen better days.

He'd been coming here on Thursdays for more years than she could remember. The sweet old guy was the reason she made a point of spending Thursday afternoons here. He'd taken her under his wing when she was broken and lost. No questions asked. He just listened to the words she couldn't say out loud. He'd simply sat with her, a steady presence when she'd needed one. That day, ten years ago, was the best day of her life. She wouldn't be alive if it weren't for him.

Leaning down to place a peck on his papery forehead, she smiled into his murky brown eyes, wondering if he could still see her clearly. His eyes were cloudier than ever. "Handsome flirt! Are you stalking me again?"

The tired old joke sent him into wheezes of laughter. "Only you, my sweet girl, only you."

"Oh, really? You say that to all the pretty ladies, don't you?"

Supporting him by the elbow, she guided him down the polished corridor to their favorite reading spot. After helping him get comfortable with his favorite selection of newspapers, she caught him up on the excitement of her week--he always thought she lived on the edge. Sure she did. She worked at the flower shop and trudged up three flights of steps to a shitty flat. Yep, her life was hot damn exciting! It didn't matter though. He never got tired of hearing her silly stories of lovesick customers and crazy street people.

Chuckling at her description of the dread-covered Raine, Arthur broke into a coughing fit that left him breathless. She patted him on the back, frowning at the phlegmy sounds coming from her old friend.

"Are you all right, Arthur? You don't sound so good." Oh, please don't be sick!

He wiped his nose with a shaky hand and coughed again. "I'm fine, worrywart. Don't you fret about me. Old men cough up a lung now and again. It's what we do." Smiling broadly to show off bright white dentures, he patted her arm, shooing her concerns away. "Leave me be for a bit. I have reading to do and you need to get to the computers before they're all taken up. I'll be right here when you're done. Then I'm going to get you a taxi home." His tone was light, but something in his eyes hurt her heart. He looked away as he promised to wait.

Acting on impulse, she reached out and hugged him. As usual, he smelled of Brut aftershave, but hadn't actually shaved in days. His prickly cheek chafed her jaw as she declared, "I love you, you old cotton top. You know that, right?"

"Yeah, yeah, I know it. All the ladies do. You can't help yourself. Now get moving!"

She headed to the computer lab with more than a little reluctance. But she didn't have much choice. This was her only day off and she had to take advantage of it. No rest for the wicked and all that jazz. Three hours later, she leaned back, rubbing tired eyes. The sun had slanted deeply west, sending a misleading darkness over the building. It wasn't totally dark outside yet, but she needed to get moving. She had a long walk home and didn't want to be caught outside her building in the blackness.

As she turned into the main reading room, she couldn't help but smile at the sight of Arthur napping at the table. With one arm cushioning his cheek, he dozed on top of his papers. His bent up gold reading glasses lay off to the side near the open fingers of his sprawled hand. Poor old guy, she'd left him waiting longer than usual today. He usually conked out around 5:00. It was past 6:00 already. Her heart swelled as she noticed the serene smile curving his dry lips. He'd had a good day. She was thankful for that. He deserved good days.

He looked so comfortable, she hated to wake him, but he'd need to get home too. Through some unspoken agreement, they followed the same comfortable routine every week. After she was done in the lab, she hailed him a taxi and saw him off before she headed home. It was a small act of kindness that she was compelled to do. As far as she knew, he had no one else to do for him, but had enough money to remain self-sufficient in his old age. Every week he tried to get her a taxi, to do something nice for her. Every week she turned him down--gently but firmly. She didn't want him to spend his money on her. She was young. She could walk home. It wouldn't kill her.

"Arthur." She shook his shoulder gently and froze. No! "Oh, no, Arthur!"

Dropping to her knees beside him, she took his wrist to check his pulse, but she knew it was too late. He was gone. Just like that. Oh, Arthur. No. You can't leave me yet. I'm not ready to live without you! With shaking fingers, she gently smoothed a wayward strand of hair from his eyes. Damn.

So now what? She swallowed a howl of grief as the ambulance pulled away from the steps. No lights, no sirens, no fanfare at all… just a slow merge into traffic carrying her friend away forever. She clenched her fists to keep from breaking down and bawling all over the sidewalk. What was she supposed to do now? She'd had Arthur's company for as long as she'd lived here. He'd befriended her, cared about her. He helped her put the pain and anger into perspective. Her chest hurt. Her heart hurt. She just wanted to curl up and cry. He wouldn't want her to weep for him; she knew that. He'd say it was his time to go… he'd say he was glad to go in his sleep… he'd say she had to be strong and live for him now. But how could she? He was all she had here. And now he was gone.

"I'll miss you, you old flirt," she whispered, voice breaking into a sob. Sinking to a step, she buried her face in her hands and quietly lost it.

Standing against one of the massive columns behind the steps, Dec watched Rori, feeling her heartache like a kick in the gut. Who was that old man? Not her father… he'd done a background check already. Her birth certificate didn't have anyone listed as her father. He looked way too old to be her father anyhow. Grandfather? No. He didn't think she had any living male relatives. What had he missed?

He'd been dropping in and out of her life since Raphael told him to watch her. Nothing exciting had popped up on his radar, so he hadn't gone to 24-hour surveillance. If things went south in Rori's world, he'd have to drag the rest of the team in. Sean and Killian were both busy on other projects, but they'd be freed up to help him with surveillance.

This morning he was intrigued when he noticed her heading towards the library so he traveled ahead to park his butt at a good vantage point inside. He'd wondered about the old man, but Rori had glowed like a candle when she'd seen him in the entrance way. Obviously he was important to her. What had he missed though? He'd left for a couple of hours to grab some grub and when he came back, the ambulance was pulling away. Always a sucker for tears, he stepped forward, intending to go comfort his charge. Probably she'd look at him like he was crazy. He'd worry about explanations later.

His hero intentions screeched to a halt as some dude in dreads got to her first. He eased himself down to the step and gently draped an arm around her shaking shoulders. She jumped as soon as he touched her, but the man said something against her ear and tucked her into his chest. Dec's own chest tightened with some emotion he didn't want to name when Rori wrapped her arms around his waist and sobbed. Dread Head rubbed her back in that way that guys did when a woman was crying in their arms. He ground his teeth together. That was *his* job! Catching himself growling out loud, he slammed the lid on his emotions. What the hell was the matter with him? Rori was clearly devastated, and he was feeling punchy because some other guy was helping her out. He should be thanking him. He should be feeling relieved that he didn't have to get too close to her.

Along those lines… yeah, he should bolt. There was no good reason to keep hanging around here. He was hiding behind a column for crying out loud. He looked like an idiot. Obviously, this guy knew Rori and would probably make sure she got home safely. See? Definitely no reason to stay.

But it *was* dark. They'd probably be walking back to her place. It was pretty far from here. Did he mention it was dark? Surely it would be okay, necessary even, for him to make sure they got home in one piece? Really, you just didn't know what could happen to a couple walking in her part of town.

Thankful for his arms around her, Rori curled against the warmth of Raine's chest. She needed comfort right now, and he was offering. Oh, Arthur, I'm going to miss you more than you could know. She pictured his teasing smile and laughing brown eyes. That's all she would have now... memories of the sweet old man who'd brightened her life. The thought triggered another bout of sobbing that had Raine pulling her closer, murmuring against the top of her head. Despite her sadness, she eventually ran out of steam. As the tears slowed to a trickle, she became more and more aware of Raine... the heat of his body, the scent of his skin, the vibration of his heartbeat. Funny how something so natural just a few minutes ago, now seemed awkward. She dabbed at her running nose and stinging eyes with the sleeve of his shirt, hoping he wouldn't notice the smudges of mascara and snot she left behind.

Putting some space between their chests, she cleared her throat and said, "Thanks, Raine. I... I don't know what to say."

He kissed her tenderly on the forehead before resting his against hers. "It's okay. This is what friends do." He thumbed a fresh tear from the corner of her eye, whispering, "I've got you. Just breathe."

Out of tears, but still not ready to face the world, she clung until the slicing pain of grief was gone. His arms promised protection; they promised sanctuary. As he rubbed random circles over her back, she realized she could breathe again. She could handle this curveball. His quiet strength reminded her that she had her own. She just needed to draw from it. The hectic world around them disappeared for too short a sliver of time. The blaring of a car alarm startled her out of the numb daze she'd fallen into. Coming back to full awareness, she realized her face was pressed intimately against the curve of Raine's neck. Snuggled up on the steps of the library? Crazy. And even more crazy? She liked the way it felt. When she woke up today, she had no idea she'd lose her dearest friend. Had she somehow gained another?

How on earth did this happen?

"I should probably get going. It's late, and I have to get up for work tomorrow."

He tugged her to her feet, steadying her by the elbows. "Do you want me to get you a cab?"

That would be awesome if she had money to pay for one, which she didn't. "No thanks. I'll walk."

"Okay, sounds good. I can use the exercise."

Too good to be true. "Seriously? You're walking me home?"

Raine hefted a duffel full of merchandise and replied, "Yes, ma'am. Let's go. I'm starving. Let's grab pizza on the way." He jingled a pocketful of change. "My treat."

The thin sliver of moon marched over the horizon and vanished for another night. Even his favorite lunar view didn't lift his funky mood. Dec bounced on the balls of his feet, hugging the disgusting rat-filled shadows--again. Finally! The light in her bedroom window winked out after what seemed like hours. He scowled up at the broken fire escape, jaw set, fingers tapping his thigh. He should go up there. Something smelled off about this entire day. He couldn't pinpoint the exact moment things had gone from normal to weird. It could've been a number of things: The death of the old guy; Dread Head riding to the rescue in orange flip-flops, or maybe it was his gut clenching with jealousy.

That whole jealousy garbage should've sent him screaming after some mouthy demons so he could slice and dice his negative feelings away. He knew better than to show personal interest in his charges. But instead of going demon hunting with Sean, he was steaming in the friggin' stench of the city, staring up at her broken window. He'd followed them back here, kept a respectful distance, waited until homeboy said goodnight and made sure he left. No kiss goodnight.

He didn't want to dwell on how relieved he was... nope, he wasn't even thinking about it. He was behaving himself. He was most definitely not getting personally involved with Rori. She was his charge; he was her protector. End of story. He was a good Primani. A smile snuck out, and he let it go. Hell, he *was* a good Primani. He'd destroyed as many demons and killers as any other of his brothers. He was one of the best demolitions guys they had, too. He was awesome at his job. But when it came to his off time... well, he just liked humans more than he should. They were fun.

He flipped a glance at his cell and yawned. Time to go. Giving the street one last eyeball for trouble, he got ready to travel. Screw walking home. It was too hot.

A shrill cry froze him in mid-transition.

"Dec! You've got to slow down, man. I can't understand you," Sean exclaimed. "Look, I'm pulling into the penthouse. Just meet me here."

He ground his molars together, shifting his weight with impatience. "Dude, I am *not* moving from this spot. Park and travel. You know where I am." With that, he shoved the phone back into his pocket and resumed his Killian-like pose--arms crossed in front, scowl in place, and mouth clamped in an unforgiving line. Staring a hole through the walls wasn't giving him any satisfaction. He wanted to get back inside her place.

"You look intense. What's got you in a knot?" With eyes burning on low flame, Sean blinked a couple of time to clear the residual energy. Looking human again, he mimicked Dec's Killian pose.

One dimple popped out, but he refused to laugh, though he did dial back the intensity a hair. "It's not funny. I barely got there in time. It could've been bad."

"Spill it. What happened?"

"Long story. Short version is I wanted to check up on her. She had a bad day, so I was hanging out, keeping an eye on things."

He stopped and cocked his head, listening. People were moving about, waking up for work. The sun was creeping into the city. They'd have company soon. Turning back to glare at the apartment some more, he seethed, "By the time I got to her room, he had her on her back, but she was sound asleep! He took one look at me and shimmered out. Bastard!"

Sean looked up at the apartment and murmured, "Well, that's not a good sign. Who is she? What would a demon want with her?"

He studied the apartment before answering. What *did* the demon want with her? That's the question of the day. Not the usual vic. She wasn't rich, had no influence in politics or business, and had no access to holy artifacts. He'd done a thorough background check on her. If she had occult ties somewhere in her family tree, it was a carefully buried secret. As far as he could tell, she was the complete opposite of the usual possession victims. She was dirt poor without family money. She didn't have any Indiana Jones-esque artifacts... no grimoires... no psychic powers... no powers at all. Hold up. He'd sensed something when she was dying. There was a connection between them, a spark of awareness. Did she have some kind of psychic abilities? Did she know?

"I know that look. She's got powers, doesn't she?" Sean barked a laugh that startled a handful of pigeons milling around the sidewalk. As the birds exploded into flight, they both ducked out of the line of fire.

As the feathers settled, Sean scrubbed a hand over his head and shuddered as he flicked a stray feather into the air. He muttered, "Rats with wings," before facing Dec and teasing, "Any special physical powers I need to know about?"

"Don't even think about it!" Sean thought he was hilarious. Idiot.

"Don't get your panties in a bunch. I'm not poaching."

"You suck. It's not like that. I'm just worried about this demon. It's weird he can get to her in her sleep."

Sean lost his smirk and eyeballed the broken window. "I might as well stick around to give you a hand. Aisling's gone again, and the demons have been freaky quiet since Dec-napping you. I've got feelers out for intel, but it's going to take some time."

Aisling was Sean's baby mama and sometime friend. Usually she was a pain in their asses, but once in a while she was cool. A former Primani, she was formally released by her maker Gabriel, and allowed to live on earth since she'd had a baby with Sean. Full-blooded Primani babies were ridiculously rare since there were very few female Primani made by the archangels. Once upon a time, Aisling had been a unique weapon in their arsenal. Today? Not so much.

"Wait! Here she comes. Let's follow her." Dec was across the street as soon as the words left his mouth.

The hot summer air slapped her in the face as soon as she opened the lobby door. Gagging on the smell, she sucked in some oxygen and coughed it back out. The rain had washed away some of the garbage stench, but it was still rank. God, she hated this neighborhood. Filled with bottom feeders and predators, she wondered for the millionth time what she'd done in a past life to end up here. Slamming the door behind her, she took off jogging to work. She was going to be late again. After getting creamed by that truck, she had a more relaxed attitude about the whole timeliness bullshit. Oh, she'd rush to get there on time, but she wasn't going to have a panic attack over it.

Before she could clear her own block, someone whistled at her. Damn it! Not again! What would it take to get rid of this guy? Hector Ramirez was a cocky young gangbanger who actually thought she'd sleep with him if he treated her like dirt. As if. There was nothing about him that rang her bell. He was short and overly muscled for his height. He wore his hair shaved nearly bald. A chin curtain hid the weak jaw that made him look younger than his age, but didn't help the fact that he seemed to be missing his neck. All of this was topped off with beady mud-colored eyes. Even if he was good-looking, his attitude was a no-go.

He whistled again, and then shouted her name. Refusing to look in his direction, she kept moving. She totally didn't have time for this, or for him. He'd been a... *problem* recently. Fixated on her in a creepy "Criminal Minds" sort of way, he watched her apartment window with an arrogant gleam in his eyes that spelled trouble for her. The more she said no, the worse things were getting. Last week, he'd cornered her in the lobby, shoving his hand up her shirt while offering his protection from the gang. Not really an offer, not really protection. Honestly, he was scaring the crap out of her. One of these days she was going to buy a stun gun if she could scrape up enough cash. It was a plan at least.

He caught up with her and jerked her around. Losing her balance, she stumbled against his chest to the delight of two gang brothers hanging out on the corner. He gripped her by one wrist, holding it up like a trophy. His nasally voice usually grated on her nerves, but today there was an underlying threat of violence in it that gave her chills. "Where do you think you're going? I called you, my bitch. Don't you know to come when you're called?"

One of his friends added, "Woof. Woof!"

Squirming against his grip, she stomped hard on his instep. "Let go of me!"

Five dollar plastic sandals were completely useless as weapons. He just laughed harder and tried to cop a feel of her ass. She'd give up her first born for a Taser right about now.

"I said let go of me!" She slapped him with her free hand, the sound echoing in the stunned silence that followed.

His eyes went flat as a snake's, and he raised his fist. "You bitch!"

Before she could react, Hector flew backwards into the side of a parked car. The shattering window glass scattered like shotgun pellets. Two men stalked to the car so fast they were just a blur. Unable to believe her eyes, she blinked several times. The men were still there, and they weren't standing still. Whoa! Where did they come from? Between their looks, their clothes, and their total disrespect for the gangbanger, they were clearly not from around here. And the way they moved? Aggressive, powerful, controlled... Their muscles rippled with every movement. *Dangerous* men. She shivered as those words crossed her mind. A sane woman would probably run in the other direction, but her brain was too busy oohing and ahhing to give any commands to her feet.

Gawking with no restraint whatsoever? Priceless. A woman just didn't dismiss eye candy this sweet without taking a good, long look. It would be rude not to memorize every inch of them for future reference. Not only were they hot, they were clearly trained in martial arts. She wasn't usually into violence, but damn! She couldn't turn away as they took on Hector and his friends. There was so much testosterone flying through the air, her lady parts were screaming, "oh, yeah!" at no one in particular.

Since no one was paying attention to her now, she'd just do a little ogling before running in the other direction. The more brutal of the two men practically screamed 'Navy SEAL', from his black t-shirt all the way down to his camouflage pants and black combat boots. He had short, spiky black hair, a lean face, brilliant blue eyes, and a hard mouth. That mouth was growling something ugly at Hector while a blond-haired guy bent his arm behind his back. There was something familiar about the blonde. She knew him from somewhere... tall and gorgeously made, he seemed younger, more approachable. He damn sure wasn't smiling now, but he had the kind of mouth that curled naturally upwards at its corners. Considering she was usually surrounded by dark-skinned gangbangers and dusty old men, this guy was like an Australian beer commercial come to life. Surely she'd remember a man this fine? Where had she seen him before? He had the same high cheekbones as the SEAL guy. Hmm... She wondered if they were related. Brothers maybe? Yes... they could be. They moved together like they were used to fighting side-by-side. Each one seemed to know what the other was going to do. Fascinating. She was so lost in dissecting them, she missed his approach. In two steps the Aussie was standing in front of her, asking her questions that her mouth just couldn't seem to answer.

"I asked if you're okay. You look like you're in shock."

Despite the curt tone, the sound of his voice sent her hormones pulsing. He had an accent on top of that sexy body? That was just wrong. She absolutely couldn't help it; she glanced down until he cleared his throat to get her attention.

"Hello? Can you hear me?"

Flushing beet red, she stammered, "Oh, Jesus. I'm sorry! I wasn't listening to you. I was... was... uh..."

"Sorry, not Jesus. The name's Declan. Everyone calls me Dec." His curt tone changed to teasing amusement that sent a swirl of warmth into her belly.

If he was there to rescue her, she was completely on board with that plan. Declan smiled and her heart melted on the spot. Consider me rescued! Normally she'd snap out some kind of sarcastic comment, but she was stuck in staring mode. He had the most impressive dimples she'd ever seen. Ever. His eyes were so clear a blue she wanted to dive into them. His smiled widened, and those eyes crinkled... Shit! She was staring again.

Closing her mouth with a gentle touch of his finger, he spoke very slowly, "Uh, darlin', are you all right? You seem a little shocky to me. Maybe you should sit down. Did he hurt you?" He gave her arm a little shake. "Are you hurt?"

Oh, my God, she was going to die on the spot. She'd lost her mind right then and there. He must think she's a complete moron. She wasn't usually this awkward! This was all Hector's fault--his attack short-circuited her brain. What was she thinking? With a single step forward and a wave of heat, Declan swamped her personal space. He stood with a perplexed expression. He seemed to be waiting for her to do something. He wiped his hands on the back of his jeans and winked. Thunking herself in the forehead, she squeezed her eyes shut. He's looking for an answer. I'm an idiot.

Snapping out of her embarrassing trance, she cried, "I have to go!"

"Was it something I said?" he mused under his breath as she bolted like a deer. Wow. That was the first time in a long time that he'd stunned a pretty woman with a smile. And she didn't even have a head injury.

He was torn between wanting to chase her down and wanting to beat the hell out of her attacker. Deciding she'd freak out if he started running after her, he flexed his fingers and opted for violence. Spinning around with every intention of clocking the tool one last time, he stopped abruptly and fumed. The *tool* was out cold. Damn it! Now who could he hit? Where was Dread Head? His blood was pounding with adrenaline that he really needed to release. Worse, his *saol* was still amped up higher than it should be. It coursed through him like a current of electricity, making muscles stronger, vision sharper, hearing stronger. Mica called it soldier-mode; he called it cool. But bad things happened if they let their energy run too hot.

"Dude! You couldn't wait for me?"

Sean knelt over the prone man. He glanced up at Dec's accusation. Lips pressed tight to keep his power under control, Sean waved a hand over the general direction of the guy's torso and suggested, "Want to kick him while he's down?"

One of the asshole's friends objected, "No!" He moved in to take a swing at Sean.

Sean pivoted out of range then kicked him in the side, breaking a couple of ribs. The guy grunted, going down hard. On his knees now, he couldn't move fast enough to escape one last roundhouse to the side of his melon.

The other banger pulled a knife and jumped at Sean's back. Dec dove into the helpful, but stupid, friend's side, slamming him into the ground. The two rolled across the sidewalk into the street. After getting one solid punch to his side, he grunted and slammed his fist into the guy's tattooed face with a tad more force than necessary. Lights out.

Rolling smoothly to his feet, he hollered at Sean to get a move on. They had more important things to do.

The bells clattered as the door swung closed. Her customer, Alex Taylor, turned to wave as he walked out. Forcing a bright smile, she lifted her own hand before sagging against the counter. Geez. Mr. Taylor was nice enough, but she wasn't really in the mood to hear all about his beautiful wife's birthday plans. He'd scored tickets to an off-Broadway show, and then they'd be off to a surprise party at some fancy restaurant. If that wasn't enough, one dozen crimson roses and a chocolate teddy bear would probably earn him a blow job after the party. He'd babbled on and on about his secret plans, minus the blow job part, while she wrapped up his order. She absolutely couldn't move fast enough.

Oh, they were so happy! She was the best thing to ever happen to him... Rori wanted to puke. Yeah, yeah, I'm sure the sun and moon rise and set on her... whatever. Please go away so I can think! She thought those words, but would never say them aloud. He had a right to be happy, she got that, but right now she really needed to be alone. The routine of opening the store and handling orders helped settle her nerves. She'd finally stopped twitching over the ugly scene with Hector and those other men. In the grand scheme of things, they were minor distractions. She had bigger worries. She had to think. The dreams were getting worse, more vivid, more frequent. She thought she could handle that, but now she was losing time again. Arthur was gone... there was no one to ask now. What was happening to her?

Hello, Rori. I've been waiting for you.

Blinding pain forced her to her knees. Light seared the inside of her eyes as she clutched her temples, desperate to crush the pain before it killed her. No, no, not again! Whimpering like a wounded animal, she curled into a ball. Trying to fight it just made it worse. Breathe, just breathe. There was a vague sense of darkness, another blinding flash, and then nothing. As abruptly as it came, the searing agony was gone.

Dec rounded the corner and stopped in front of a two-window storefront. There was a green and white metal awning hanging over the sidewalk and half a dozen lifelike photos of flower arrangements covering the windows. A bright yellow sign announced the place as "Angela's Flowers and Gifts."

"Here's the shop. Come on. Let's go."

Sean parked his butt against the side of the building and pointed to the door with his chin. "You go on. I'll wait here. God knows you can use a little… distraction. I'd just be in the way. You know how it is. The minute she sees me, it'll be all over for you!"

"Yeah, right. I've got no worries. Besides, this is business. I'm not looking to hook up with her. She's human for crying out loud."

"Yeah, sure. A very pretty little human with big problems. Just your style. Go on. I'll wait. Yell if you need any help." He grinned and pointed to the door again.

Everybody's a comedian… He yanked on the door handle much harder than was necessary to get the thing open. The metal bells clanked loudly against the glass. With an apology on the tip of his tongue, he realized he was alone. Where was Rori? Drawing his Sig, he circled around to the storage closet, easing the door aside with the toe of his boot. Nothing. Same thing with the bathroom. The skin on the back of his neck prickled. Where did she go? Tightening his grip on the gun, he headed back to the front. A faint shuffling noise snatched his attention straight to the checkout counter.

"Rori?" Jamming the weapon back into its holster, he vaulted the counter. "Sean!"

She lay curled into a fetal position, fingers digging into the side of her head. Both eyes were open, staring at nothing, terrified.

"Oh, God. Don't be dead!" He slipped straight into healing mode, checking for signs of life, muttering prayers under his breath.

Her pulse was fast and thready. Good. Not dead. But not normal either… the pallor of her skin scared him. Chalk white, blue around the lips and under her eyes… We need to get her to a hospital.

"Stop! Look up!" Sean ordered. Pointing to the ceiling, he kept his hand on Dec's arm.

"What the hell?"

Chapter 5: Dazed and Confused

"HEY, YOU'RE AWAKE." Moving slowly so he wouldn't scare her, Dec leaned into her field of vision from a chair next to the bed.

His little mystery woman had been out for hours. Just now easing awake, she was disoriented and groggy. Intending to comfort her, he wrapped his fingers around her cold hand. Flinching like he'd shocked her, she jerked her hand away with a gasp.

"Sorry, sweetheart."

Oops. He needed to dial it back some. Their *saol* did that to people if they didn't rein it in before contact. She scooted against the headboard, eyes wide with fear and confusion. As they darted around the room, he got a good look at them. Cognac? No. Bourbon. Definitely bourbon. Her eyes were the shade of top shelf Kentucky bourbon. Tilted up at the corners, heavily lashed, with thick black rings around her pupils, they were stunning. Cheetah eyes. Beautiful and hypnotic. Exotic. He couldn't look away. For the first time ever, he was speechless.

His eyes drifted over the rest of her face, taking in the pallor and dark circles. She frowned, shielding herself with the sheet as if it would protect her. Nothing could protect her from him. He could do anything he wanted. But he wouldn't. He didn't have it in him. Her vulnerability called to the warrior in him. He sensed her emotions as easily as he read her expression. She was scared, confused, and desperately trying to remember how she'd gotten here. He should say something... anything. He had a pretty speech all planned out until she opened her eyes and destroyed his ability to think.

She watched the man's eyes linger on her face and tried to force her own expression to stay blank. Who was he? *Where* was she? When? Her mind raced in a mad scramble for information. This was not good. She wasn't where she was supposed to be. How did she get here? This hadn't happened before. She always woke up where she fell asleep. Glancing around the room, she searched for a clock or a calendar... anything with a date on it. Nothing jumped out and waved at her. The bedroom was simply furnished. The dresser and bed were made from dark wood with intricate carvings. The sheets were purple. There was a small framed picture of a couple sitting on the nightstand. She studied it more closely for a clue, a date stamp, something in the background maybe. The pair were obviously in love. Their faces glowed with happiness. Not helpful, that.

Where the hell was she?

The man cleared his throat. "Rori. Look at me, darlin'. We need to talk."

Snapping her head towards his voice, she found him studying her from six inches away. She jerked back, smacking her head against the headboard hard enough to see stars.

"Ow! What are you trying to do, kill me?" She rubbed at the back of her head, and he burst into laughter.

His lopsided smile was natural and bright. "You've been asleep for 24 hours. If I wanted to kill you, I've had plenty of time. Though truthfully, I've been sitting here waiting for you to wake up just to see the color of your eyes." He reached out and traced a circle around her right eye, calloused fingertip just skimming the tender skin. "And you do not disappoint, do you?"

Her skin tingled, her blood bubbled, tickling her from the inside out. Gasping at the sudden burst of pleasure, she smiled into his eyes. She'd never been this alive. His expression was somber as he touched her, tracing the curve of her jaw and moving to her left eye. After tracing its shape, he rested his fingertip beside the delicate skin near the corner.

"Beautiful," he murmured.

She should move. She should slap his hand away. She should...

"So your Sleeping Beauty woke up? Did she say anything?" Sean sliced into his steak and waited for Dec to answer.

The two of them had been cooling their heels all afternoon until Sean declared he needed some cow. Sometimes room service was a beautiful thing. He pushed his empty plate across the marble bar and tossed a napkin basketball into the sink. He'd killed his steak, fries, and a beer in record time. Saving damsels gave him an appetite.

"Yes and no. She woke up totally freaking out and didn't even recognize me. I caught some of her thoughts but nothing that made sense. She seemed confused about the date. No idea what that was about. I put her back to sleep."

Sean sat his fork down and leaned back. His mouth turned up at one corner. "Exactly why would you do that? You know the protocol. You're supposed to get her up, get her talking, and get her out of here. You can't keep knocking her out. You'll scramble her brains."

He chuckled. "Stop nagging, grandma. Unlike you, I can always heal her brains if I break them. She just seemed so upset... I thought more rest would help. Why don't you go check out her place--see if you can find that demon. I'll stay here and keep her company until she wakes up."

Giving him the hairy eyeball, Sean stood and stretched. "Uh-huh, sure. 'Cuz demons always leave traces behind when they appear in someone's dreams. But sure, why not? This could be the first time." He picked up his cellphone and added more seriously, "Be careful, okay? You don't know this woman, and there's a demon involved. She could be bait."

That thought had already occurred to him, so he just shrugged and said, "I know what I'm doing. It's all good."

The second Sean left, he bolted back to the spare bedroom. As he approached the door, a low keening sound stopped him in his tracks. The mournful cry made his skin crawl. Rori! He ripped open the door to find her right where he left her except the sheets and pillow were scattered across the floor. Suddenly she clutched at her head, the same keening cry coming from deep inside her chest. Tears rolled down her cheeks.

The tears did it.

"Ah, hell, woman."

Folding her in his arms, he rocked her, crooning words of comfort. Her pain was like a knife to his chest. What nightmares haunted this woman? What did she see when she closed her eyes?

"Shh. It's okay." He smoothed the hair away from her eyes until she settled. Carefully stroking, soothing her, he kissed her temple, resting his lips against her damp skin. She mumbled in her sleep, and he held her closer. The words terrified him. She was in some serious trouble. Trouble she couldn't handle alone.

When her tears slowed and her breathing steadied, he ran his hands over her back. Didn't she eat? Didn't she have food? She was so slight she was nothing against his strength. Lifting her up and down once, he realized her bottom fit perfectly against his lap. He wasn't the biggest guy on the planet, but he overwhelmed her, covering her like a blanket. He flashed a grin at his helpful imagination. Probably that wasn't the best analogy. It made him think of beds... and beds were made for more than nightmares. But that was a thought for another day, another female.

She was calm now, her breath coming in deep, even measures; her heart beating normally. He tipped her back to look down at her face. Her eyelids were closed and still. The nightmare was probably gone. Her lips parted just a bit. One last tear trickled into her hair.

"No more tears, sweetheart." He caught the drop with a stroke of his bottom lip. That tiny drop of liquid unleashed a flood of sensations inside of him. His mouth watered. A hot flash lit him up just as his vision went white. He was paralyzed to resist the images ricocheting through his mind. Bracing himself against a killer wave of dizziness, he held on for the ride.

Flickering flashes of color... reds... oranges... yellows bombarded his inner vision, drawing his eye, blinding him. Shifting walls in every nuance of black and grey... obsidian, charcoal, cold silver... gleaming, shimmering, knifed through the schizophrenic colors. The walls rose up like mountains through lava. Flickering and shifting, blinding light and sucking blackness, drew him deeper, pushed him to the edge. Just as he thought he was lost, the images coalesced to reveal leaping flames and shadows.

Shadows and flames... very slowly the focus of the vision zoomed in to reveal a woman standing in the center of a cavernous space. Its inky blackness was broken only by the glow of orange and red flames. Insubstantial as a wraith, she drifted towards a massive, arched window in the front of the room. As she moved, the fire dogged her steps, licking at the walls, undulating and swirling into the shadows, but never touching her. It nudged her forward.

Within the darker recesses, something moved. It slipped in and out of the shadows, faster than his eyes could track until suddenly the entire vision vanished into an empty void... then as abruptly as it disappeared, it burst back into view.

They were in front of the window... just out of focus... black as night... sleek, powerful, inviting. Eerily beautiful, seductive. The woman was mesmerized. She tilted her face to rub it against their softness. They unfolded into a graceful arc across the window. She reached to touch them and...

"Rori! Wake up!" He tried to shake her awake. When she didn't respond fast enough for his jangled nerves, he shot her with a hard jolt of his *soal*. Unused to the force of the current, she yelped in surprise and sat straight up. Sorry about that.

Her eyes went huge when she saw where she was sitting. Scrambling to get up, she slid straight towards the carpet even as he grabbed her arm. Instinctively latching on, she tumbled backwards with him in tow.

He landed sprawled atop her, his hands just catching the weight of his body. Laughing out loud, Dec grinned into her shocked face.

"Get off me!"

Totally enjoying the humor of the situation, he scolded, "That's not very romantic. You can do better than that, right?"

Apparently not. She panicked, pushing at him, her pupils unfocused with sudden terror. "I have to write it down! I have to write it down!"

Too stunned to react, he gaped, trying to make sense of her words.

She went berserk. Shoving at his arms, kicking at his legs, she went into full wildcat mode. "Get off! Get off! I need to write it down," she sobbed. "Please! I'm going to forget it!"

Hauling her upright, he yanked open the nightstand and tossed her a pad of paper and an old pen. With wild eyes, she flung herself down and started to write. Focusing entirely on the words, she seemed to forget he was there.

After ten minutes, she slowly sat the pen aside and lifted the pad. Growling in obvious frustration, she crumpled the page and threw it against the wall.

Watching her from the corner of his eye, he carefully unfolded the paper. What's this mean? He was more confused than before. There were only two words. Written over and over again, they covered the page from front to back.

"We should talk. Are you okay now?"

"Yeah. Let's talk. Why don't we start with who you are and where I'm at?"

Her tone was most unhappy. Bowing with a flourish, he said, "My name is Declan Manning. We've met before. I'm a little insulted that you don't remember me. You're in my company's penthouse near Gramercy Park. Don't freak out; we're not alone. My brother, Sean, is staying here. We didn't know what to do with you when we found you passed out in the flower shop, so we brought you here."

"Haven't you ever heard of a hospital? The last thing I remember is going to work... Wait a minute... You were at my building, weren't you? Did you follow me to the store? Why would you do that?" Her eyes drifted to the bed, narrowing as she tried to put the pieces together. "This is a little creepy for me."

"No doubt. But seriously, we weren't trying to kidnap you. We thought it was a good idea to check on you after what happened. I swear we were just making sure you were okay!" Gesturing towards the door, he suggested, "You'd probably be more comfortable in the living room. Let's go sit in there." He couldn't help smiling at the suspicion on her face. Didn't he look trustworthy? Unable to resist messing with her, he jabbed a thumb at the warzone on the bed, adding, "I promise you made that disaster all by yourself."

She flushed nearly purple at the implication and shoved him out of the way. He followed behind not looking at her ass… Once they were settled in the open space of the living room, he took a deep breath and hoped his mouth got the words right for a change.

"I know you don't have any reason to believe me, but I might be able to help you with some of your problems." There. Ball's in her court.

Sitting cross-legged on an overstuffed armchair, Rori gave him a top-to-bottom inspection. Help her? With what exactly? Who was this guy? What was in it for him? He'd saved her butt this morning. The timing had been perfect, but she'd assumed he and his friend were just walking by. A right place, right time sort of thing. But then he showed up at Angela's. Coincidence? Maybe he was telling the truth; they were only making sure she was all right. It sounded reasonable.

Even though she didn't know him from Adam, he didn't give her a creepy vibe. Probably she was crazy, but he just *seemed* trustworthy, kind. There was a strange sort of serenity about him that relaxed her. It could be his laid back attitude rubbing off. As she checked him out, he sat on the arm of the couch with one bare foot on the cushion, the other one on the floor for balance. He wore a pair of loose navy and white board shorts with a faded Hang Ten t-shirt. The shirt hugged his shoulders like he'd owned it forever. She noticed he had the same tan from his toes to his forehead. Surf, much?

The man in question was patiently waiting for her to respond, with an adorably sincere gleam in his eyes. His mouth curled into the barest hint of a smile while he studied a guitar pick he'd been toying with. Cute or not, it was probably time to go.

"I appreciate your help today. I really do. But other than beating up more gangbangers, what kind of help are you offering? I don't need anything else except maybe a ride home, if that's not a problem."

"Sure, love, I'll be glad to take you home whenever you're ready, but I think you should rest a minute first. Passing out isn't something to just blow off." With that, he tucked the pick into his pocket, slid from the arm to the cushion, kicked that smile to the curb, and got down to business. "You had a nightmare earlier. Do you want to talk about it?"

"Whoa! No foreplay first?" Her heart jumped a beat at the sudden flash of heat in his eyes.

Instead of making a sexy comment back, he covered his mouth to hide his grin and said, "This is important, Rori."

"Apparently so. Why do you want to know?"

He hesitated as if unsure how to answer that. After a second, he clasped her hands between his own, squeezing tightly. A soft tingle floated up her arms... Mmm, nice... her muscles relaxed, her eyes drooped... she caught herself swaying in the chair and stiffened before she fell on her face.

He smiled slow and easy as if she was doing exactly what he wanted. He squeezed her fingers and prodded, "The dream, Rori? Will you tell me about it, please? It might make you feel better if you tell someone."

"Sure. Okay."

Rori started to tell him about the fire and the wings, but the words wouldn't make it past her lips. Stuttering, she said, "Th... th... there's fire... and..."

Nodding with encouragement, he asked, "Fire? Okay, good. And then what?"

"Fire... and..." Damn it. She couldn't get the words out. Clearing her throat, she tried again. "Fire... fire..." She closed her eyes and the shadows and wings returned. She saw them clearly in her mind.

He searched her face and finally sighed long and hard with a groan tacked onto the end. Clearly he was irritated with her. Not that she could blame him! Why couldn't she just answer the question? The vision was right there! She saw the familiar traces of it lingering clear as day. But when she tried to tell him about it, the words wouldn't come. Why the hell not? It didn't seem like a big deal.

"Don't stress. I'm not in a hurry." Dec captured her chin between his fingertips. "Let's try something else."

He gave her jaw one last playful tap with his fingertip before leaning away. Smothering a yawn, she listed to the side, giggling softly as he caught her by the shoulders.

"Steady, darlin'. No need to fall at my feet now." The teasing tone was smooth as silk.

Silk? That's an odd description. True though... his voice was soft, silky, soothing... she wanted to tell him everything, tell him *anything* he wanted. She had a vague thought to laugh but didn't have the energy. Instead, she smiled, thinking she probably looked ridiculous. He murmured something encouraging before a faint woodsy fragrance tickled her nose.

"Okay, angel, you're really relaxed now. Your mind is open to you. Look deep inside and see if you can find that vision. Take your time and let it come to you. Can you see anything besides fire? Impressions?" The slight lilt in his voice relaxed her. Not Australian. Irish?

Was there anything else? She racked her brain but only the fuzzy image of fire remained. Everything else was just gone. This was part of her problem though, wasn't it?

"I'm sorry. I can't remember anything else. That's why I have to write them down. I forget them if I don't."

"Write them down? Why do you feel like you have to remember them? They're just dreams, aren't they?"

She shook her head, chasing away the lingering feeling of drowsiness. She could never explain this nightmare to him. How would he ever understand? Dreams, visions, nightmares--it didn't matter what you called them. They still came to her, out of the blue, startling with symbolism she didn't quite comprehend. Then there were the other visions... they were clearly real people, people who existed. Shuddering that old nightmare aside, she tried for a more sarcastic tone. She was finished with this crying bullshit. She had to get her emotions under some kind of control again. It was embarrassing.

"Sure, they're *just* dreams. Just like the Rangers is *just* another hockey team. Yeah, *just* a dream."

She wished to God they were only strange dreams. She'd begged God for them to be dreams. Begged, pled, prayed... whatever. She'd given up trying months ago. No one was listening to anything she said.

He frowned. "Okay, call me confused. *Aren't* the Rangers just a hockey team? Nothing special? Did I miss something last year? They didn't win the cup."

Rolling her eyes, she scoffed at his naiveté. "Whatever, man. You're not a true New Yorker if you aren't a Rangers fan. Anyhow, I don't know if they're just dreams. That's the problem. I... I don't remember enough and then..." She stopped, biting down on her lip to keep from saying the damning words out loud.

With his palm smoothing across her clenched fist, he prompted, "What happens? Tell me, Rori. Please."

She uncurled her fist and exhaled through her nose. "People die."

The pain came so suddenly she didn't have time to cry out before sliding to the floor. Clutching at her temples, she screamed, "No!"

Everything went black.

"Sonofabitch!" Shoving himself away from Rori's body, he sent a frantic call out to Raphael.

What the hell was happening with this woman? She'd collapsed again! He was at a loss. He'd even checked her for a brain tumor. There was some weird shit going on. He could use some help.

He paced the length of the island until the subtle shift in air pressure warned him that he had angelic company. Storming into the foyer, he practically hugged his maker for coming so fast.

"Thank God! I'm so glad to see you! I don't know what to do with her." He pointed to Rori who was lying on the couch. He'd taken her pain away and dropped her into a deep sleep.

Raphael simply raised his eyebrows and said, "I'm always here for you, Declan. Though I must admit I'm a little surprised at you. You have a *woman* on the couch." He actually cracked a smile. "And you're calling me for help?"

"Is everyone worried about my sex life? Seriously? Rori's not just a woman. She's a psychic. I know it."

"Ah. I see. No need to get snippy with me. What do you need from me? Is she ill?"

He paused to find the right words. "I believe her mind is under attack. I think she's got a demon on her tail. She's been having visions and unexplainable episodes of unconsciousness. She's just blacking out without any reason I can see. I caught a glimpse of one of her visions and it's not good. If this demon is sniffing around like I think he is, he's working his way into possessing her. The vision is a huge clue, but I don't know what it means yet. I was trying to get to the bottom of it when she grabbed her head and collapsed. I tried to heal her... but there's no injury."

The archangel listened while studying Rori's face. Squatting by her side, he rested a lean hand on her forehead before closing his eyes in concentration. After a moment, he said, "I'm not sensing wounds of any kind. You're certain she was in pain?"

"Absolutely. She scared the shit out of me. One second we were talking about hockey, the next she screamed and dropped like a rock." He lowered his eyes to the lady in question and asked, "Do you think it's demonic? It feels that way to me."

Raphael gave Rori's arm a light pat and stood. "It's possible, though I'm not sure why they'd target her. She *seems* ordinary enough. But there is something unusual about her. I'm sensing a restlessness in her soul that shouldn't be there. Let me do some digging. Perhaps there's more to your Sleeping Beauty than meets the eye."

He glanced at the clock and suggested, "You know it's still early. Perhaps you and your lady friend should go dancing. It's a beautiful night." With that, he dematerialized.

Et tu, Raphael?

"Declan? Hello?" Rori hesitated at the entrance to the roof top garden. Wow.

The sun had just slipped over the western horizon, leaving the sky a rich sapphire blue. A few misty mare tales raced across the sky, backlit pink by the last few rays of sunlight. She watched until the pink faded. Beautiful. As if it were waiting for a signal, the city burst into life around her. With 18 floors, their hotel was one of the taller buildings on the block. High-rise apartments loomed in the distance, their modern glass structures glowing with life as people settled in for the night. She was standing in a penthouse! It was crazy. How did she end up in this place? Apartments were astronomical anywhere around Manhattan, let alone a sweet penthouse overlooking

Gramercy Park. This gorgeous place must've cost a fortune! Who were these people?

Even as she watched, lights flicked on like so many lightning bugs. It truly was a magical sight. She envied them, just a little, for having this view every night. How nice it would be to see the beauty but not the filth down below. The sound of a male voice caught her attention and she pulled her eyes back to the garden in front of her. There was a brick wall surrounding it, topped with spikes. Apparently the wrought iron spikes were meant to discourage jumpers. That or maybe they were just for decoration. Either way, you couldn't sit on that wall. Not that she'd want to. It was a long way down. Simply thinking about that made her shiver. Oh, hell no. The two people leaning against it now didn't seem to mind the height. They seemed relaxed as they peered over the edge to watch the traffic below. The wind shifted, carrying their voices to her.

"Come on, Dec. She's got a major problem if you're right. What are you going to do about it?"

Problem? They had no idea. Her friggin' problems had 99 problems!

Declan answered, "I don't know, man. We don't know what's up yet. I'll keep an eye on her. I'll do whatever needs done. You know that."

"I can help if you want me to."

"I've got this for now. I'll let you know what you can do."

"Fair enough." The sound of bottles clinking echoed in the still of the night. "To damsels in distress."

"Ha. To *pretty* damsels."

"Exactly how many damsels have you brought to your, um, castle?"

They both jumped at the sound of her voice.

Declan actually seemed embarrassed. His dark-haired friend threw back his head and laughed.

Moving to her side, Declan cleared his throat and said, "Rori, meet my brother Sean. You sort of unofficially met him the other day, but you probably don't remember him. Sean, this is Rori."

Still leaning against the wall, Sean didn't bother to move. Instead of saying hello, he inclined his head and took a long pull of his beer, eyes traveling over her, missing nothing. A chill crawled down her spine. This one practically screamed 'danger.' By the time that sweeping gaze rested on her face, the force of it drew her in. The second she looked into his eyes, he nodded and she fell. Vivid cobalt, they pulsed with tiny gold lights. Beautiful, captivating... She couldn't tear her eyes away. Declan tugged her to the patio chaise. Sean's penetrating stare pinned her in place as the oddest feeling came over her.

An irresistible urge to share her thoughts, her memories, her past, swarmed over her. He wants to see my memories... why? But even with the question on the tip of her tongue, she didn't act on it. His incredible eyes pulled her in, and she was lost. After a moment of hesitation, the memories began to pour out like water leaving a dam.

Rori, no!

Chapter 6: Crazy Talk

"RORI, WAKE UP, DARLIN'."

Looking into a pair of worried eyes, she blinked to clear her fuzzy vision.

Those eyes crinkled with a scowl and Declan said, "Girl, you scared the hell out of us *again*. Do you mind not passing out anymore? My nerves can't take all the stress." Even as he scolded her, he massaged her temples with the pads of both thumbs.

She captured his fingers, crushing them against her chest. She should let him go, but things were escalating, and she was freaked out. "I'm so confused. What's happening to me? What did you do to me?"

Damn it. She'd blacked out again? Things were getting worse. She'd been handling it so far, but she was losing control. Feeling her eyes prick with tears, she bit her lip hard enough to draw blood. She needed some real answers. Breaking into tears and passing out were putting the brakes on those answers. She had to get a grip.

LAURIE OLERICH

Leaning away, Declan said, "I know you're freaking out now, but we'll figure this out. You're not alone anymore. Trust me, okay."

"What can you do about it?" Swiping at a tear that threatened to fall, she gave him a watery smile.

They gazed at each other for a full minute before he said, "You can cry if you want, but I have to warn you I might be forced to kiss you if you do. It's the only way to snap you out of it." He lifted one shoulder in a shrug as if he didn't care one way or another.

Kissing would put the brakes on getting answers too, but had much more appeal. She started to laugh, but her curious eyes dropped to his mouth. That fascinating mouth froze in mid-grin, one kissable dimple showing. Even though he wasn't touching her, she felt him tense. She licked her lips, trying to say something, anything, to break the awkward silence. Holy shit. He was really going to kiss her. Her? Gorgeous men never kissed her. She was dreaming again. This had to be another hallucination...

"Horrible timing aside, why wouldn't I want to kiss you? You're beautiful, love." His voice was barely a whisper over the pounding of her heart.

With infinite gentleness, he slid their joined hands up to her throat to cup the side of her face. "I can't resist touching you. You're so soft..."

He guided the pads of her fingers over her jawline. Slowly, carefully he moved as though she were made of delicate china... the touch of their hands was so sensual, so erotic; she sighed and let her eyes drift closed. Surely this was Heaven.

"Wow, Rori! That was some dream you had, huh? Oh, hey, you two need a room?" Sean's smart ass comment blew the moment.

She jumped up, nearly knocking Declan over. He backed out of range, catching her elbow in mid-swing. He wasn't even breathing hard, and here she was about to have a heart attack because he was *thinking* of kissing her. Dropping her elbow, he gave her a wink. She's an idiot. Seriously, what was she doing here? Gorgeous men played with women like her. He could pick and choose from millions of beautiful women who had actual futures ahead of them. She wasn't fit for even a loser like Hector. She had way too many issues. It was time to blow this Popsicle stand before she lost the last precious dregs of dignity she still had deep down inside.

Sean stopped grinning and considered her with those sharp eyes of his. He didn't miss a thing, and she had the distinct feeling he was reading her mind.

"Don't you think we should talk? I don't know about Dec, but I've got some questions for you."

With that, he strode off towards the kitchen without a backward glance. He expected her to *follow*? What was she? A puppy? Confident, sure, he was clearly used to getting his own way. Arrogant, conceited, obnoxious… she ran out of adjectives.

Dec nudged her and broke into her grouchy thoughts. "Sean's right. There are things you need to know. You're not safe."

After an hour of listening, she sat back, crossing her arms, glancing from one to the other's earnest faces. They were lucky she stayed through the entire hour. She'd almost tuned them out after the first five minutes, but to be fair, she stayed to hear everything they had to say. She had to admit they had some pretty convincing points. But it all boiled down to one blaring truth: It didn't matter how cute they were; they were both crazy. It wasn't simply the words they said; it was the devout belief in their eyes, their voices. They truly believed the insane crap they were telling her.

Demons? Uh, no, she wasn't buying that. Not even a little bit. It was way past time to go. She didn't know these men. They said they wanted to protect her. Ha. Yeah, right. Because that's what happens to women like her. Heroes just magically appear and make everything all better. For all she knew, these people were just more vivid hallucinations.

"You two don't seriously think I'm buying this story? You must be off your meds. First off, I don't believe in demons so I'm pretty sure there's not one sneaking around my bedroom. To tell you the truth, the fact that you guys think you know about them gives me the creeps. It's just too bizarre for words. Have you been watching "Supernatural"? You're cute and intense, but you're not Sam and Dean Winchester. Second off, I have too many other problems to lose my mind over this one. Dreams, visions, whatever... everyone dreams. I've always had a vivid imagination. And I'll add that none of this is your business."

The two men exchanged a meaningful look. Declan nodded before turning back to her. "We don't think your dreams are simply dreams. You said yourself that people seem to die after you dream of them. Have you ever thought you might be psychic? You have some of the signs."

Was he serious? How could he possibly know? They were really starting to freak her out now. It was time to go before they dug up anything else. But first... lie, lie, lie. Just one more sin to add to the list. If this kept up, she'd have to find a confessional.

"Look, I've been thinking about this. Yes, I've blacked out a couple of times, but this just started happening. Maybe I've got low blood sugar issues. If it happens again, I'll go to the clinic."

Dec circled her wrist, measuring it with his hand. "Blood sugar could be a problem. You aren't eating enough. You're too skinny."

The front door slammed hard enough to rattle the van Gogh hanging in the foyer. The painting settled into place with a final, subtle click. Neither of them moved for the space of a heartbeat. The sharp slap of Rori's sandals echoed in the marble hallway until she hit the elevator. With a final stab of a button, it dinged once and the penthouse was eerily silent. She was gone.

"Don't say a word." Unable to believe what just happened, Dec gawked at the door for another second.

Sean clapped him on the shoulder and mimicked, "'*You're too skinny.*' Seriously, bro, I have no idea how you ever get laid."

"My mouth moves before my brain forms the words. It's a gift." He scrubbed a hand through his hair, resisting the urge to dematerialize. This was a nightmare.

"Yeah, so now what? Are you going after her?"

Dec shook his head, thinking hard. Rori was not only pissed off, she was hurt. He wanted to take them back as soon as the words left his lips. She'd flinched away as though he'd backhanded her across the face. The pain in her eyes clawed at him. He was a complete asshat. What happened to his famous talent for setting people at ease? He'd have to try to make it up to her--later. He wanted to apologize, but he also wanted to keep his balls. Later would be better.

"Not yet. Probably I should give her time to cool off. My ears are still ringing from all the mean things she called me. Let's get out of here. I need some air."

Sean checked the magazine for his Sig P250 and untucked his shirt for easier access. After jamming the gun into its place, he said, "Good plan, Romeo. Let's go hunting."

Declan Manning was a dead man. If she ever saw that bastard again, she would kill him. It was 1:00 a.m. when she finally staggered up the sidewalk in front of her building. Walking 20 blocks in the middle of summer in New York City was a sweaty, smelly, painful venture. She could barely climb the stairs because her blisters had blisters. Her only sandals were probably ruined. The muggy heat had sucked the life out of her, but sleep would have to wait. As she locked her door, she took a good whiff of herself. The rank odors of sweat and something like burnt earth assaulted her senses. What was that god-awful smell? Another trash fire? Trying to close her nostrils, she limped to the shower.

Still angry, but mostly feeling defeated, she scrubbed herself with the last precious sliver of dollar store soap and leaned against the shower stall to rinse. She needed to go shopping. But how much could she really get with the $12.00 left in her purse? Soap? Toilet paper? Food? Yeah, sure, food would be good. The box that someone left was empty. She'd shared most of it with the little boy next door. He needed it more than she did. Poor little man. She'd probably have to wait to get food until she got paid again. That's assuming she still had a job. Angela had probably replaced her already. She was so screwed, and it was all Declan's fault. He should've left her alone. She would've woken up in the shop and gone home as usual. No problem. But noooo, he had to play hero. Man, she hoped she still had her job. She needed it more than ever.

The ancient light fixture flickered twice before finally sending the room into near darkness. Its last bulb clung to life; its illumination more of a wish than a fact. Awesome. Add light bulbs to her shopping list. Too exhausted to move just yet, she ran her hands over her body, closing her eyes against the memory of his face. Too thin? He didn't mean to insult her. He'd said it with great sincerity and pity in his eyes. That gorgeous man was disgusted with her body. Despite the fact that he was clearly delusional, the truth of that cut to the bone. Once upon a time, she had been pretty. She'd had breasts. Nice ones too. They'd been her best feature. It was ironic how those were the first parts to waste away. It wasn't fair really. Now her collarbone was sharp, her ribs beginning to show... she needed more food. She wasn't stupid; she knew what she needed. She just couldn't get it. She couldn't remember the last time she'd eaten red meat. There were other priorities for her precious few dollars.

The bathroom plunged into total darkness the moment she stepped out of the shower. Disoriented, she slammed her hip against the edge of the sink. "Great. Just friggin' awesome. Could this day get any worse?"

That depends on how you look at it, Rori. Are you a glass half empty kind of woman?

He watched from the doorway as she sank into oblivion on the peeling linoleum of her bathroom floor. Once she was out, he allowed himself the pleasure of shimmering fully into a corporeal form. Up until today, he'd stayed mostly in her head, but he was itching to play with her. For that, he needed working hands. Squatting down without touching the disgusting floor, he checked her pulse. Steady, sure. Good. She wasn't afraid; she wasn't even aware. Her mind was deep within its slide to complete submission. He lifted her arm and let it fall unchecked. It struck the floor with a snap and lay inert.

"Oops."

Scooping her up, he lay her on the futon and positioned her for the night. Everything needed to be just right. This was an important part of satisfying his needs. He'd waited too long to deny himself this treat. Now everything was coming together. After he curled her fingers into a delicate circle, he stepped back to consider his work. Rori's arms were spread, her legs pressed tightly together... she was the cross he'd bear.

Twenty-four years old--with magic number 25 only a few months away--she would be his after all these years. He could barely stand the waiting. Taking his time, he explored every curve of muscle, every knob of bone, until he came to the concave plain of her belly. Her golden skin gleamed as he ran his hands over her, summoning her blood to the surface. Close. Oh, so close. Inhaling deeply, he let her scent curl through his senses. Exquisite. Dipping his head, he ran his mouth over her, whisper softly, barely skimming her skin. Nipping into the delicate flesh just under her right breast, he savored the intoxicating cocktail that was her blood.

Only a taste for now, but soon she would be his until death do they part. Hers, not his.

A quick glance at the window spurred him into motion again. The sky was beginning to lighten. They were running out of time. Goddammit. He had to focus. They had work to do. Squatting near her head, he commanded, "Rori. Hear me."

She murmured, "Yes. I hear you."

He placed his hand over her heart. "Can you feel me?"

"Yes."

"Can you feel me protecting you? I'm keeping you safe, Rori. Do you understand me?"

"Yes. Safe."

With the back of his hand, he stroked her cheek, allowing himself a smile when she curled her mouth in response. "You are safe only with me. Do you want me to help you, Rori?"

She hesitated.

He sent her deeper into sleep and demanded, "Do you want my help?"

Still she didn't answer him. Her eyes darted back and forth beneath their lids as her heart raced under his palm.

How was she resisting him? This wasn't possible! Grinding his teeth together, he snapped, "Answer me!"

He gripped her shoulders, shaking her hard. "Say it! You want my help. Ask for it!"

She shook her head from side to side now. "No, no, please, no. Leave me alone!"

Reining in a sharp burst of rage, he purposely placed his palm over her heart again and said, "My offer won't last forever. Your time is running short."

Sean rounded the corner and headed deeper into the alley. Out on the main streets, the light was just beginning to brighten with the sunrise, but the shadows were thick as tar in between the buildings. Dark, light, it didn't really affect his mission. All Primani were blessed with excellent vision--day or night. He could see in the dark better than any human or animal on the planet.

His prey was a mid-level demon who'd been working with a local gang leader who called himself Tay-Z. Rumor had it that Tay-Z had a grand plan to gank the current asshole running drugs through the boroughs. Normally he would be on board with that. One more dead drug dealer was a good thing. Not this time though. In this case the results would be chaos. Tai Li wasn't the typical dumbass demon. He had significant connections and a grand plan of his own.

Palming his Primani blade in his right hand, he sent his thoughts to Dec. *You ready, Dec?* The long, slim blade was made of silver, with a crystal clear blue stone on the haft. The blue was the color of his eyes--Primani blue as Mica would say. It was more than a pretty rock though. The stone acted as a conduit for their *saol*, their energy. The blade was a demon killer, and his had seen more blood than most. Blessed by his maker, Raphael, the knife was an extension of his body, his will. He ran his thumb over the stone's facets as he stopped just behind Tai Li.

"Well, if it isn't my favorite fallen angel; Sean O'Cahan. Long time no see. We've missed you in Hell." Tai Li turned to face him, nudging the tip of the weapon off to the side. "No need to be like that. You're not going to kill me, are you?"

Not right this second... "What are you doing up here, Tai Li? You know you're fair game when you're fucking around topside."

Tai Li was wearing the same old unimaginative human façade they seemed to be drawn to. To anyone who saw him, he'd look like a cage fighter from New Jersey. This one had shaved his head and added a complex of tribal tats up and down each of his bare arms. Brown eyes under heavy brows completed his makeup. He tucked one hand into the pocket of his baggy jeans and pulled out a small plastic baggie.

Handing it to Sean, he said, "Okay, fine. You caught me. I was bored, man. I needed a break from all the drama that's going on down there." Lowering his voice, he added, "Irku's a motherfucking nightmare. You have no idea what it's like now. You're lucky you got out when you did."

He sniffed at the plastic. Pot? That's it? It smelled like high quality weed, but still... it was only weed. Not some creative lab synthetic that would kill kids the first time they took it. Not even coke. *Just pot?* As far as grand plans went, this one was a bust. Oh, how the mighty have fallen. Handing it back, he broke into a reluctant smile. "You suck as a demon. You're actually trying to tell me your idea of spreading chaos is to distribute *marijuana* to the masses? The only chaos you'll get is a mad rush for burritos at 2:00 in the morning. This is stupid even for you."

Relaxed now, Tai Li shoved the package into his pocket and grinned. "Whatever, man. It gets me topside and away from having my scales peeled off one at a time. I've got a sensitive stomach. That shit makes me puke. It's humiliating. So what are you and your boys planning to do about Irku? Going to banish him again?"

"Irku's your problem now. Your boss put him in charge. I've got strict orders to stay away. He wants my heart on a platter. It took months to heal the damage from the last time he wrapped his hand around it. For once, I'm following orders. I don't have a death wish."

"Yeah, but still, don't you want some payback?"

"Hell yeah I do, but I'm not an idiot." He considered the expression on Tai Li's face. He seemed genuinely worried about Irku. Not a shocker, that. Irku was one of the three biggies: Satan, Lilith, and Irku. All of demondom was wary of their new leader. He was more powerful than any of them and ruled with a cruel hand. Rumor had it the lower-level demons secretly hoped the angels would destroy Irku for them. Too bad the angels weren't strong enough.

Before Tai Li could say another word, Dec materialized and wrenched his arms behind his back.

"Congratulations, demon. You're lucky number 13. I'm having a good night."

Chapter 7: Fugue You!

THE STONE ANGEL SPRANG OUT of the mist right in front of Rori. She bit her tongue trying to scream and hyperventilate at the same time. Holy shit! Are you *trying* to give me a heart attack? With a galloping heartbeat echoing in her ears, she sucked in some calming oxygen and scowled at the looming statue. It stood about 12 feet tall including its large, squat base. The fierce angel was equipped with an eight-foot wingspread and a bronze sword. As far as she knew, it had been erected by pious men to oversee the Saint Anne's churchyard full of souls, lost and otherwise. She'd never asked for its bio. Not that it mattered, anyway. It was just another hunk of rock hanging out with hundreds of other rocks, representing a creature from the fantasies of people who needed to believe in such things. Angels didn't exist. Period. Now that her lungs were processing air again, she turned away to finish her errand and stopped.

What on earth?

This was New York. The summer weather could be weird sometimes, and it wasn't unusual for there to be fog in the morning. Even heavy fog happened now and then. She'd been here often enough to know that to be true. What *was* unusual was the glimmer of gold that caught her eye as she'd turned to leave. Frozen at the base, she stared upwards, but the glint was gone.

"I repeat. What on earth?"

If she didn't know any better, the angel's eyes were glowing golden in the morning sun. Impossible. It had to be a trick of the light, a reflection against the fog or something. She tied her thin hoodie more tightly around her to ward off the sudden chill. Tilting her head left and right, she squinted at the angel, but the phenomenon was gone. "Huh. Sure, that's not even a little freaky."

Maybe she needed to get her eyes checked. Determined to figure it out, she walked around the base three times, looking for some sign of the strange glow. But there was nothing weird to see. No glowing eyes, no gleam of light, nothing but the cold, kind of creepy stare of the stone angel. Upon closer inspection, she noticed bits of green moss clinging to the timeless hunk of rock. It seemed... fake somehow. It was almost like the angel was trying to be something it wasn't---ancient? How old was it? Hmm. Why hadn't she ever stopped to study the angel before today? Sure, it'd been there for as long as she could remember, but it never seemed alive before.

Alive? Now where did *that* thought come from? Snorting at her own overactive imagination, she mentally slapped herself in the back of the head. She didn't have time to dwell on the undead lawn art hanging around this plot of hallowed ground. Dismissing the angel and its mysteries, she headed towards the loneliest section of the cemetery.

Dec eased from behind the statue and winked at Saint Anne's guardian angel. All the corpses were still snug in their pine boxes. Hallowed ground was still hallowed.

There was nothing here but peace and quiet for the dead. Good job, mate! Keep up the good work.

The inanimate angel had nothing to add, so he went ghost to follow today's prey. She was infinitely cuter than the baker's dozen he stalked last night. He and Sean had vanquished a total of 25 demons between the two of them. That was really just a drop of water in an ocean seething with demons, but it was what they did, and it was damn good to blow up even a few of them. It was important to remember what he was. He was a dangerous soldier. He delivered justice. He was a killer. Well, that wasn't too flattering, was it? True, yes. Flattering, no. He sighed long and hard. He was what he was… there was no apologizing for it. Primani were needed, but that didn't mean humans would completely embrace them. They could be brutal.

After meandering along a crumbling asphalt lane, Rori finally slowed her steps. She seemed to be searching for something in the grass. He slipped behind a tree and gave up the ghost. Now fully visible, he lounged against the rough bark, wondering about the woman in front of him. Soooo, she didn't believe in angels or demons. She had psychic powers that she was trying desperately to deny. Aaaand, she had a demon sniffing around her like she was dinner. Things would come to a head at some point. And when they did, he was going to rock her world.

"Please, God, don't let her hate me for it."

The grave marker measured six by eight inches and was made of a cheap metal mixture that managed to be both shiny and tarnished at the same time. The plaque was inscribed with a name, dates of birth and death, and a heavily weathered sigil in the upper left-hand corner. That was it. No epitaph. No loving messages, no next of kin, nothing but the barest facts. This part of the cemetery was old, mostly forgotten. The grounds keepers focused their efforts on the sections that could be seen from the road.

After all, it wouldn't do for people to think the dead weren't resting under manicured lawns. This section was overgrown with stalky weeds, and thanks to the recent rain, dotted with dandelions and purple clover. As a result, the grave marker was buried nearly as deeply as the person it identified.

"Hey. It's me." Her voice sounded louder than normal in the last remnants of mist. "I need help. Something bad is coming. I see it... in my head. But I can't see enough! I can't warn him. I don't know what to do anymore."

The silence was broken by the shriek of a cat. She jumped, nearly falling on her butt. "Damn it!"

The skin on the back of her neck prickled. Spinning around, she scanned the trees, finding nothing. Something was out there. She sensed it watching her. After searching until her eyes were dry, she turned back to the grave, sinking into thought. While carefully choosing her next words, she idly traced the shape of the sigil.

"He's going to die, and I can't stop it. I'm useless."

Hello, Rori.

"No!"

Dec was already running when Rori sank to the grass. She lay sprawled in a tangled heap, her eyes open, staring, terrified. As before, her skin was chalk white, her mouth blue. Dropping to his knees, he checked her pulse in near panic. What was wrong with her? She was too cold, her skin icy against his hands.

"You're looking in the wrong place, Dec."

Killian materialized beside him with a slight smile on his usually stern face.

"Killian! Thank God. What do you know about this?"

"Enough." Killian knelt and gently closed her eyes with a fingertip. After a moment, he locked eyes with Dec. "What kind of psychic abilities do you *think* she has?"

The question seemed reasonable enough, but his tone was bordering on amused. Little red warning lights went nuts inside his head. Before answering, he thought about what he'd seen in her head. Dreams, visions, premonitions?

"She has visions, but they aren't clear," he explained. "She also has dreams, but I get the feeling those are separate from the visions."

Standing, Killian brushed grass from his jeans and asked, "And? Are they premonitions?"

"I think so. I haven't been able to get her to open up to me though." He stopped rubbing her icy fingers and asked intuitively, "But you don't think so?"

Killian ran his eyes around the graveyard twice before answering, "No, I don't. Neither does Raphael. He sent me to find you." He waved a hand over Rori's unconscious form and frowned. "Now this? This is something else entirely."

The earth shook. Banshees howled. Someone shrieked in pain.

He was coming!

Rori needed to move. Needed to run, needed to escape. She just needed to get away...

The shrieking split her head like an ax. It overwhelmed her, blinding her, deafening her... she rolled over, trying to center herself. The spinning made it impossible to get to her feet. She lay on the ground, clutching at the grass, willing the world to stop careening. Oh, my God, it's worse than before.

"Hey, baby! Whatcha doing under there? You want to party?"

Someone jostled her by the arm until she opened her eyes to find two teenaged boys dressed in... were those curtains? She blinked a few times to clear her vision. Not curtains... fringe. She studied their hair and shoved a groan out of her mind. Of course.

Not banshees.

Janis Joplin--again.

Her ears rang from the massive speakers blaring out music on the corners of the temporary stage.

"You'd think I'd recognize her by now."

Sonofabitch. It's like friggin' Groundhog Day.

Stumbling to her feet, she crawled out from under the stage after the two idiot boys woke her up. Did she want to party? Absolutely! Too bad this wasn't the place and damn sure wasn't the time. As usual, she was alone in this massive crowd. She'd give her right arm to have a friend to party with. She hadn't seen Raine in weeks.

On the slope above her, the sea of people was endless. Packed like pills in a bottle, there were half-naked bodies for as far as she could see. Most of them were stoned out of their minds. Thank God the party boys had wandered off in search of a more willing playmate. Gathering her strength, she edged away from the stage before her head exploded. The damn vibrations were so strong they made her teeth ache. Thanks to Janis, her hearing was nearly gone too. Note to self: Find a better landing zone next time. Okay, the world was standing still now.

She needed to move before he found her.

This morning had been a massive treat--better than her usual sucky days. After a night of nightmares, she'd woken up to find her wrist broken and her shoulder covered with bruises. If that wasn't freaky enough, she was also on the bathroom floor, staring into the beady, black eyes of a rat the size of Paris Hilton's purse dog. More surprised than she was, the rat took off like a cheetah, out the door and through the broken bedroom window. Lucky for her, she had an old stretched out Ace bandage stuffed inside her sock drawer. She'd wrapped her wrist and hoped for the best. Now, the crappy bandage was sopping wet with mud and pretty much useless in holding her wrist still. She tried to straighten it, but it was nearly impossible to do with her left hand. Hissing with pain, she forced herself to act nonchalant while scanning the crazy ass place she'd ended up. How friggin' long was she out this time?

As Janis belted out the final words to "A Piece of my Heart," Rori winced, squeezing her eyes against the pain. When she cracked them open again, her lost her breath.

"Oh, God."

Too late.

She'd know the tilt of his head, the defiant set of his shoulders, anywhere now. His blond hair reflected the weak sunlight like a halo. With the sun at his back, his eyes were deep in shadow, hollow, empty. She knew without light what color they were. She'd seen them other times. They bored into her now, demanding she listen, demanding she come with him.

"Go away! I can't help you!" she screamed over the music.

Shoulders slumping in defeat, he lowered his gaze to his feet as he picked his way across the muddy field.

Backing up against the stage, she searched for a way out. Frantically scanning the crowd, she spotted it.

At least she wasn't dead. That was a plus. What was he supposed to do with her? Killian flat out refused to let him move her. He said moving her from the store was a mistake. Probably moving her that day had exacerbated the disorientation that she experienced when she woke up, possibly even kicking off the horrible nightmare she had. In hindsight, that made perfect sense. He hoped she didn't have any permanent brain damage.

Dec tucked Rori's head against his chest and rested his chin on her, idly stroking her temples. Thick dark lashes brushed the bruises under her eyes. Purple now, they were a shocking contrast to the chalkiness of the rest of her face. She was so fragile, vulnerable. How had she been fighting this for so long? She had no one to help her, to teach her.

Living alone in that dump of an apartment... where was her support? Surely a beautiful woman like her had a boyfriend, friends, *someone* who would be there for her. The dread-headed guy jumped up and down waving madly. Nope, sorry buddy. You don't count. I don't like you. So, besides that guy, wasn't there anyone around?

Pressing his lips near her ear, he whispered, "Rori, come on sweet girl. I need you to come back to me. I need you to wake up. Come on, now. You can do it."

A car drove past with its radio blaring "Knockin' on Heaven's Door" and he chuckled under his breath. Not on my watch! I've fixed worse than this before. This woman was not going to be a casualty. Not going to happen. But... what to do with her? He couldn't just leave her lying in the grass and walk away. She was completely vulnerable. Leaving her here was a no-go, not even an option. He'd tried everything to bring her around. He'd even gone so far as to wrap her within the healing energy of his *saol*. He'd gently pushed some of his energy into her, hoping it would shock her into consciousness. All that had done was warm her up. Her white skin flushed to a nice rosy pink. He thought her lips had parted a little, but she didn't respond in any other way. Her eyes were closed now, but she was still catatonic.

"Stop that, Dec. Do you want to create another Mica? Raphael might kill you." Killian's tone was light in spite of the harsh words. None of them would change how things with Mica had turned out.

"Shut up, dude. She's not responding anyway."

"Be patient. She'll come around."

He huffed with impatience. He wished he was more like Killian sometimes. Patience was his middle name. At the moment, Killian sat cross-legged on the other side of Rori. He'd been staring off into the distance for the last 15 minutes. Every now and then, his mouth curled into a smile. He was talking to Mica again. The two of them were connected by love, true, but more importantly for the sake of the planet, they were bound by blood--Killian's and Raphael's. They had the ability to enter each other's minds. It was hilarious when they were on a mission and Mica would check in to yell at Killian. His face would go blank then he'd clamp his lips together and scowl at nothing. Normally it was amusing. Right now though, nothing much was funny.

"Rori! It's me, Declan. If you can hear me, I want you to see me in your mind's eye. Picture my face. I'm here for you. Let me be your anchor. Reach out to me. Call me if you need me. That's what I'm here for. I'll always come for you." It was worth the words. Nothing was lost by telling her the truth. He'd hear her when she called him. It was one of his special gifts.

Out of the blue, something changed. The air around them began to hum in a low tone, the decibel faint, barely within their supernatural hearing capabilities, building in intensity until the birds stopped singing in the nearest tree. The skin on the back of his neck prickled in warning and he snapped his eyes to Killian. Killian nodded once, hand on his personal weapon, *Sgaine Eiron*. Its ruby burst to life, lighting his face in its vivid red glow. He closed his eyes in concentration, listening to it, following its message.

A fine tremor started in Rori's feet, traveling slowly upwards. She trembled in his arms, her skin warmed to hot, flushing pink against his hand. He nearly dropped her and instinctively squeezed her tight against him. As their bodies connected, he saw a flash of something from the corner of his eye. It was a young boy, waving frantically.

"Incoming," Killian warned with eyes aimed a few feet above them.

He followed Killian's gaze and exclaimed, "Holy shit! What the hell is that?"

From a distance, it looked like a cloud of gnats, but as it came closer, the delicate particles glittered in the morning light. Killian backed away as it got closer. The swirl of gold dust made a beeline for Rori. As they watched in amazement, the tiny molecules swarmed over her flesh like another layer of skin and then disappeared as her body absorbed them.

"I believe that's her soul."

Rori came to more slowly than usual. She was aching; her head on fire. Something was different this time. Her skin was deliciously warm, tingly and soft. Her breasts were oddly sensitive, and her... well, her lady parts were demanding attention. Sighing with anticipation, she started to curl onto her side for the rest of what must be a good dream, when someone patted her cheek--hard.

"Rori! Wake up. Come back here."

Christ. Not a dream. She'd done it again!

Struggling to rise, she only succeeded in elbowing Declan in the groin before falling off of his lap. Jolting completely alert, she snapped, "What the hell are you doing here?" Whirling on Killian, she demanded, "Who are you?"

It was bad enough to wake up and have no idea where she was. She was starting to accept she was a freak. But an audience? Could the earth just open up and swallow her now? How long had she been out? How long had they been staring at her? It was too embarrassing to even think about. Damn.

"Come on, darlin', let me give you a hand. You're still feeling woozy. You're lucky we were walking by and saw you faint." Supporting her with an arm around her lower back, Declan helped her to stand.

She should have shrugged him off, but she didn't have the energy. Usually she slept for a day after these little trips of hers. Why had she blacked out here? Something had triggered it. This was a first, and she definitely didn't like it. She was too vulnerable out in the open. Damn it, things were escalating. It was scaring the living hell out of her. She wished for the hundredth time for Arthur's quiet advice. Pasting a weak smile on her face, she dragged in a couple of calming breaths. *He's gone. He can't find me here. It's okay.* She repeated the mantra a few more times before she believed it enough to say, "You're sweet, Declan. Give me a minute. I'll be okay."

"Take your time. I'm not going anywhere."

He gave her plenty of space but kept his hand resting on her, steadying her nerves, connecting them, warming her blood. Her heart stopped pounding as she inhaled his scent. She didn't know him very well, but she loved his cologne. Whatever he wore was absolutely spellbinding. Fresh, woodsy, a little musky… he always smelled heavenly. It was all she could to not press her nose against the warm skin on his neck and sniff him like a dog. His hand shifted as he made a small circle on her back, the motion soothing, maybe too intimate for now, but she didn't mind. She found herself leaning against him, eyes drifting closed. Her last conscious thought was *his chest was wider than she thought.*

As soon as she was out, Dec scooped her up and dematerialized. About 30 seconds later, they rematerialized in her little apartment. He carefully placed her on the battered futon, feeling guilty when she moaned. She'd be asleep until he needed her conscious.

"Sorry, sweetheart, I hate to do this, but it's for your own good."

She didn't have much to search. He chewed on his lip and considered the milk crate she had as a dresser. Her shirts and pants were neatly folded and stacked on top of an empty cardboard box. Socks and panties nested inside a smaller box. No drawers to rummage. No computer to hack. No safe to crack or locks to pick. Pathetic.

There was a small stack of mail lying on the cracked Formica counter in the kitchen. It was mostly bills plus a past due notice for the rent. Now this was interesting. He fished a dog-eared, yellowing business card from under the pile of other papers. There was only a name and phone number on the front. He didn't recognize either so he flipped it over and nearly dropped it. This was getting more interesting by the minute. He tucked the card into his pocket, moving on to the spotless bathroom.

The rusty medicine cabinet contained a toothbrush, a neatly crimped tube of toothpaste, and a tube of strawberry lip balm. She had nothing.

Sonofabitch! This was crap. This woman was special. She deserved so much more than nothing. How did this happen to her? He stood in the middle of her room, hands clenched into fists, and fumed over the unfairness of life. *Human* life.

Then he noticed the broken window... and the man staring into the room with murder in his eyes. Black-haired, black-eyed, cruelty etched in his every feature, the man seemed to snarl through the glass of his apartment window.

He met the man's stare, held it, and stalked to the window. The man refused to look away until Dec pointed his Sig directly at the ugly face.

"Bang!" The words carried directly into the man's mind.

The curtain swung closed and the man disappeared.

"That's what I thought." He shoved the weapon back into its proper place.

Rori was going to be royally pissed, but he wasn't leaving her here. He'd *drag* her out of here if she said no. There wasn't room for him to sit on the futon, so he squatted beside it and studied her serene expression. He'd given her that peace. It was the least he could do. Golden skin, exotic eyes, high cheekbones, pouty lips... she was the woman of any man's fantasies. His for sure. He'd thought himself immune to human beauty, he appreciated it, sure, but he'd never been so affected that it clouded his judgment. He wouldn't let that happen now either, but damn. She was sucking him in with every breath she took.

Something about her eyes was familiar... they reminded him of someone else. He couldn't put his finger on it yet, but it would come to him. He picked up her tiny hand mirror and studied his own reflection. How did she see him? He thought she was attracted to him, but she was afraid. People had let her down. She'd been on her own for too long to trust him easily. He'd have to work on that. She had to trust him if he was going to help her.

Reaching out to cup her face, he mumbled a prayer to Raphael, and let his energy flow from his fingertips. The pale light infused her face, and she opened her eyes.

"Don't be mad," he said. "I'm here to help you."

"OUT! Get out of here now!"

Rori shoved him so hard he fell on his ass. Leaving him sprawled with shock all over his face, she stalked away, pointing to the door as she moved.

"Who do you think you are coming into my apartment? You can't do that! You have no right to be here. No right to be in my life. You're freaking me out now. I want you out."

Declan's mouth was still hanging open. Clamping his lips together, he pushed himself gracefully to his feet. Twin spots of red dotted his cheekbones, the rest of his skin paled. Bracing for his rage, she crossed her arms, clinging to what little bravado she had left.

"I mean it. Just get out. I don't want to see you again! You've gone from helping to stalking!"

He flashed a dimple and begged, "You don't mean that, Rori. I know you don't."

"You don't know anything about me! Get out!" Her voice rose to a shout.

"No!" he shouted back, stalking towards her, his steps fluid and fast like a tiger striking. Backing away, she caught her breath. This was it. He was going to hurt her. She judged the distance to the front door and turned to run just as he stopped in front of her. She opened her mouth to scream and he covered it with his hand.

"Rori, stop this!"

Frantic to get away, she bit him then screamed bloody murder when he jerked his hand away. He shoved his other hand over her mouth; she kneed him in the balls. He shifted his hips at the last second so she only hit his thigh. He grunted in pain anyway and swore in some language she didn't know. He maneuvered their bodies so she was pressed into the wall and then tightened his grip on her. She tried to struggle, tried to kick him, tried to scream... he was too strong to fight. She couldn't budge his hands or his body. He was pressed against her from shoulders to feet, his legs around her so she stood between them with nowhere to go. Frustrated tears sprang to her eyes. She hated him as they ran down her face. He would probably kill her now... this was just the kind of year she was having. First the visions she couldn't understand, then the nightmares she couldn't remember, then the recent fugues she couldn't explain. And Arthur...

It was just too much. She was tired of being terrified, tired of being confused, tired of letting people die. Maybe this was best.

He held his breath when she surrendered but didn't dare let go. She'd probably rip his nuts off. The poor woman was completely freaked out now. What the fuck just happened? He knew she'd be mad but had no idea she'd be so upset. Rori sagged against him, his torso the only thing holding her upright. Her head lolled against the wall, throat exposed and vulnerable, pulse beating a hundred miles an hour. The waves of terror struck him like a shotgun blast to the chest. Damn it! He would never hurt her. Didn't want to scare her either. He was on her side! He just wanted to give her a better life. He royally fucked this up. He hoped he hadn't accidently hurt her. With that thought in mind, he unclenched his muscles and surveyed the damages.

The cheap material of her shirt had ripped along the shoulder seam and neckline. The delicate curve of her collarbone seemed to condemn him. To make matters worse, his hand bled through the fabric on her shoulder. The shirt was ruined. He bit down on his lip and stopped inhaling. The smell of blood made him nauseous. Now was not the time to puke. Puking would make him look like more of an idiot. Willing them both to calm down, he panted for oxygen. Eyeing her like she might explode, he uncovered her mouth and gently smoothed the redness from her lip.

"I'm sor--"

"Just make it quick."

Cupping her face, he growled low in his throat, "I'm not going to hurt you! Not now. Not ever." He placed a tender kiss on each cheek, kissing away the tears. "Look at me, damn it! You're special, Rori. Your life has a purpose."

Once her eyes had something alive in them again, he brushed his mouth to hers in a feathery kiss. He pulled back and gave her a lopsided grin.

"Would you mind if I did that again? I think I missed a spot."

It was working. She looked more stunned than suicidal now. He didn't like the defeated droop in her shoulders, though. She was still on the wrong side of happy. Tilting her chin up, he tried cajoling her. "I'm the good guy, Rori. I keep telling you that, but you're too stubborn to listen. I'd never hurt you, love."

He crossed his heart with an X. "Cross my heart!"

"You're killing me here. How can I be mad at you? You're too damn cute." She had herself back together and sniffed one last time. With a pointed glance at his hand still wrapped around her shoulder, she cracked a smile.

It was progress. He shifted his weight to move away and froze as he realized the position they were in. She was still standing between his legs. He should move away, God knew he should. But his brain refused to give the command to his feet. He closed his eyes against the feel of her pressed against him. She wasn't pushing him away so maybe she was as affected as he was. Holy Hell, he needed to move... things were about to be too obvious to ignore.

She tried to still the racing of her heart before it rang off the walls. He'd frozen when she did. Every inch of him steamed against the thin fabric of her clothes. Their shirts had risen up, leaving patches of abs exposed, rubbing against the other. How did she get into this position? She barely knew Declan... but she felt like she should know him. There was something about him that attracted her, and it wasn't just his gorgeous body pressed flush against hers. Now that she wasn't hysterical, she realized he gave off a good vibe. He'd done nothing but try to help her so far. She had bitten him. Dear God, she'd bitten the poor man, and he'd bled all over her.

She pulled his hand to her mouth and kissed the small wound. "I'm so sorry I hurt you. I don't usually freak out like that... it's been a weird week. My nerves are shot."

He raised his eyebrows, spreading his palm outward, voice dropping to a velvety purr. "I think you need to kiss it again. It hurts. A lot."

She brought it to her mouth and just when she was about to kiss it, he curled it around her nape, pulling her mouth to his. This was no feathery light tease. His mouth molded perfectly to hers, tasting, nibbling, before finally staking a claim. She opened her mouth to give him better access, and he took it. His tongue plunged deeper until an animal growl sounded low in her throat. She couldn't get enough of him. Plastering herself against him, she wrapped her arms around his neck pulling her pelvis up and across his erection as she did. Strong hands clutched her bottom, pressing her hard against him, sending starlight dancing behind her eyes and heat pooling between her legs. All she could think of was getting him naked. Her ability to think of anything else was gone. With a groan, he fisted her hair in his hand and tugged her head back to expose her throat.

"My God, you're like velvet." He dragged his mouth over her ear, nipping the lobe, and dipping the tip of his tongue around it.

She nearly exploded into a supernova right then. Reaching between them, she pushed his shirt over his head. Beautiful, sexy man! She couldn't help the groan that escaped the second she ran her hands over the bare skin of his chest. "You feel so good. I want you now." She froze in the middle of the assault and laughed. "I can't believe I said that! I can't help it. You're making me crazy."

He straightened from kissing his way across her shoulder and flashed a huge grin. "Don't hurt yourself trying to resist!" Even as he said it, he unsnapped her jeans and dipped his hand inside to cup her bottom. She was in the middle of yanking his zipper down when she cried out with pain.

"Where did these bruises come from, love?" He wrapped a blanket around her for modesty before snapping his jeans. He was still uncomfortably hard, but he'd survive. It wasn't the first time; wouldn't be the last. It was a guy thing. Rori was his only concern right now. He'd noticed the small black bruises right about the same time she hurt her wrist on his zipper. He would cut out his tongue before he told this story to Sean or Killian. They'd never let him live it down.

She looked away. "I don't know. I woke up with them this morning. My wrist too." She lifted one shoulder and added, "I must've fallen on the bathroom floor. I was lying there when I woke up."

"Did you have a nightmare last night?" Please say no. Please say no.

She lifted those sexy cat eyes to his and nodded. "Why?"

If that bastard touched her somewhere else... he'd tear Hell apart to find him. Keeping his tone even, he asked, "Any other bruises? Weird marks? Soreness?"

Now she straightened in alarm, dragging the blanket tighter. "What are getting at? You're scaring me."

"Do you or don't you have other injuries? Please. Answer me. It's important." It took every ounce of control not to yell. He was so pissed, his eyes were heating up. He had to calm down before he did something stupid and scared the hell out of her again.

She scooted to the other end of the futon. Too late.

Deliberately lightening his tone, he added, "I'm sorry. I just want you to be all right. Have you noticed anything?"

"No. I didn't see anything else. Do you... do you want to look at my back?" She pulled the shirt over her head.

He jammed his lips together so his mouth wouldn't run on autopilot this time. She was too friggin' thin. He could count her ribs. That's it. They were getting to the bottom of this demon, and then he was giving her a new life. Maybe their crime lab could give her a job. They hired humans for a lot of jobs there. They paid better than the flower shop did. They had benefits too. She could move out of the shitty neighborhood and into a decent place. She'd be able to buy healthy food and something nice for herself too. He was going to fix this.

"Can you lift your hair off your neck for me, darlin'?" He smothered another wave of anger. He'd hoped to be wrong, but he was too used to this shit to miss the signs.

On the positive side, she didn't have any more bruises.

On the negative side, she was royally screwed.

Chapter 8: A Matter of Trust

THE AFTERNOON SUN BLINDED THEM as they turned a corner and walked directly west on 28th Street. Dec slung a ratty backpack over his shoulder. It was pathetically light considering it contained most of Rori's worldly possessions. She carried a shopping bag stuffed with a few other things in her good hand. Together they looked like two day trippers hitting downtown Manhattan on a warm summer afternoon. Reality wasn't so sunny.

It had taken every one of his persuasive talents to convince Rori to leave that apartment today. Oh, she wasn't happy about it. She had a lot of good arguments, true. They'd gone back and forth over the reasons to leave and the reasons to stay. He'd patiently pointed out that her window was broken, and she had two scumbags paying too much creepy attention to her. The fire escape was conveniently located under her window--the broken one. She countered with the fact that they hadn't actually broken in--like he himself had. Yeah, hard to argue that one!

He'd offered the idea that she had a demon sniffing around which she flatly refused to believe. Again. Why was she being so stubborn about this? It wasn't that farfetched. They made horror movies about this all the time. She'd called him and Sean crazy when they tried to talk about it the other day. How could she not believe in demons? He'd asked her that question and she'd snorted. Snorted, scoffed, whatever! Tasting a sneaky victory, he'd demanded that she explain how she could believe in angels and *not* demons. Her reply had flattened him like an avalanche.

She didn't believe in angels either. Who didn't believe in angels? They were everywhere! Well, in statues and paintings and things like that. Live angels didn't usually announce their identity. So she was in for a shock. Wait 'til she got a good look at his halo…

Even worse than not believing in angels or demons, she was pretty sure God wasn't real, either. When he pressed for a reason, she'd clammed up and packed her bag.

She'd been quiet since they left. Walking beside him, bumping against him once in a while, she seemed sad. He squeezed her hand and she flashed a nervous smile. Damn. She was such a lost puppy. After weaving around a woman with an SUV-sized stroller thing, he stopped in front of an ice cream stand. A line of little kids wearing matching yellow t-shirts waited their turns, giggling and yelling like his godsons did. Man, he missed the little dudes. He wondered if Rori liked kids. It was hard to tell right now. She hung back against the glass front of a cellphone store while he braved the noisy kids.

A few minutes later, he bowed low, presenting her with a cup of Dippin' Dots. "For you, fair damsel!"

That earned him a real smile and he laughed out loud. About damn time! Note to self: Ply her with sugar.

Rori took the treat and remarked with less of a smile, "You don't have to do this."

"On the contrary, I do. It's my job to make sad women smile. And you, well, you should never be sad." He kissed her knuckles, winking up at her.

She didn't respond, but nibbled a tiny taste of the ice cream. Oh, yeah. Lost puppies were his downfall. The sun glinted off the curtain of her hair, spotlighting streaks of deep red. Unable to resist, he let it fall through his fingers. He'd thought it was black... but no, it was a blend of rich chocolate, burgundy, midnight... silky soft and straight as a blade.

"Declan, I'm scared."

"Don't be. I told you we'd take care of this. Killian's an expert in occult things. He'll know exactly what to do. Everything will be okay. I promise."

She rested a hand on his thigh before jerking it back. "That's not what I mean. I'm... I'm afraid to be near you."

"And here I thought I'd finally brainwashed you into believing I'm one of the good guys."

"I'm serious."

He couldn't resist. He ran his palm over her hair again. "I am too. I know you don't know everything about me, but I'm not going to hurt you. Are you still worried about that?"

She faced him and said, "No. It's not that." She paused, seeming to struggle to find the right words. "My visions... everyone dies. I see them die. I've never been able to save anyone." She sat the half-eaten cup of ice cream on the bench and looked out at the street again.

"And?"

An hour later, they stopped in front of one of the prettiest buildings she had ever seen. Even though she'd lived in New York most of her life, she hardly ever came to this part of Manhattan. Her foster families hadn't been this well off. The red brick with curling cream accents was old-fashioned and elegant. The glass doors had bright brass handles that gleamed from constant polishing. Craning her neck, she searched for the roof. Gargoyles glowered down at her nosiness.

"This place is beautiful. I can't believe you have a penthouse here. What business are you in again?" He'd never really given her a straight answer.

"Personal security. Let's go. They're waiting for us."

The entire lobby was a work of art. She wished there was time to slow down to admire it. The walls were covered with stained glass artwork and deep red draperies. Elegant crystal chandeliers winked in the oversized foyer. The black and white marble floors gleamed. Pretty seating tableaus were scattered throughout the lobby, inviting guests to sit with a cup of tea and a newspaper or two.

Declan steered them towards an elevator slowing, only to smile and say hello to the concierge.

"It's nice to see you again, Mr. Manning."

Giving him a quick handshake, he answered, "Same here, Jacob. Have a good time at the game tonight."

To Rori, he said, "Jacob's been here forever. He's a huge Mets fan. We gave him season tickets last year. He's a good guy."

The elevator spit them out on the 18th floor. It was just as pretty as she remembered before her hasty retreat. Black marble floors, rich blue walls, and vivid geometric paintings burst into view as soon as they left the car. Tasteful wall sconces provided dim lighting to show them the way to the penthouse door. There was a small niche next to it.

"Is this an angel?" She wanted to touch the gleaming gold but didn't want to seem gauche.

Plucking the small statue from its resting place, he offered it to her. "It's a cherub, technically. Think of it as our mascot. You can touch it. It's okay."

It was warm like human skin. A slight tingle zinged along her fingertips as she stroked the tiny, folded wings. The texture was soft, smooth, not at all what she expected.

Strange. Handing it back, she took a deep breath. It was time to go in and figure out what's wrong inside her head. Yay. This ought to be a great time.

Declan was in the process of opening the door, but hesitated. Her heart did a little flip flop and a bounce. Reaching out, he drew her into his arms and held her carefully. No passion, no tension, just warmth and comfort. Gone was the stress and fear of the unknown.

Tipping her chin back to look into her eyes, he vowed, "I promise that we'll help you, Rori. Please trust me. Trust my family."

She smiled and said, "I trust you, Declan."

He pressed a kiss against her forehead and replied, "Good. I'm ridiculously famous for being trustworthy. My Twitter handle is @TrustDec. One more thing, please stop calling me Declan. Only one person still calls me Declan, and he's not trainable."

The first person to greet them was the gorgeous brunette from the picture frame. Dressed in a gauzy purple and white sundress with strappy, gold heels, she practically tackled Dec in a bear hug. Dec whooped once, swung her around in a circle, and kissed her on both cheeks before setting her back on her feet. For a long moment they only had eyes for each other, and Rori tried to ignore a tug in her gut. Long wavy hair, huge blue eyes, wide smile and trim, muscular body... this woman was everything she wasn't. Damn. It figures. She wanted to sink into the floor. Staring at her ratty sandals and frayed sundress, her bravado took a nose dive. What was she doing here? These people were from a whole 'nother planet. She didn't belong with them. Edging back against the wall, she tried to blend into the plaster.

A deep voice rumbled quietly beside her, "Welcome, Rori."

She jumped with a smothered squawk. How did someone his size move so silently?

He held out a paw for her to shake. "I'm Killian. Remember? The amazing woman you're worried about is my wife, Mica. She and Dec are like brother and sister. Trust me. Dec would be dead if that wasn't the case."

Well, how do I take that? Looming beside her with an unreadable expression, he kept his tone nonchalant, but she got the feeling he was deadly serious. She took a step back and he sighed. So this was Killian? She vaguely remembered him from the cemetery. She tried to check him out without anyone noticing. He was much bigger than she remembered. Towering above her, he was easily 6'3"... taller than both Dec and Sean. His shoulders and chest were wider; he was more thickly muscled than Dec for sure. Dec was muscular but had a longer, leaner look to him. With his hard face and dark shadow across the jaw, Killian was attractive... in a stalking jaguar kind of way. Beautiful while capable of ripping her throat out... she backed farther away. Really big men intimidated her. Killian wasn't an exception.

So much for no one noticing her inspection... When she bothered to look at his face again, she realized he was staring back with a hint of a grin curling his mouth. He seemed to look right into her soul. Yeah, that wasn't a comfortable feeling at all. She shifted her gaze to Dec and admired the curve of his butt. He had a fine butt. A quick flash of their almost sex scene turned her knees to jelly. Damn, he was hot. She totally wanted to wrap her legs around him.

Killian cleared his throat. Oh, crap! She was so busted. His eyes sparkled until he broke into a laugh that drew everyone's attention.

Great! All eyes on me!

Dec practically flew over to them, demanding, "What did you do to her?"

She blushed even more impossibly red because Killian shrugged and replied, "Don't look at me. *I* didn't touch her."

Mica elbowed past both men, a friendly smile on her pretty face. "Hi, I'm Mica, and I'm so happy to meet you finally. Dec can't stop talking about you. He's been blowing up my phone for weeks."

"Dude! You have no filter whatsoever!" To Rori, he said, "Ignore the meddling wench. She can't help herself. So you've met Killian and Sean already." He nudged her forward to meet an older man. He dipped his head in a formal gesture of respect. "This is Raphael."

Raphael seemed to be in his 40s or so. Handsome without prettiness, he was tall and fit just like the others. He clasped her hand between his and said, "Welcome, Rori Austin. I'm told you're in need of some assistance. I believe you've come to the right place."

Flushing at her own awkwardness, she resisted the sudden urge to curtsey. He was as poised as royalty. "It's nice to meet you. I hope someone can help me. This is all a little creepy, but Dec's been really insistent. He seems mostly harmless." Did she say that out loud? Her face flamed even hotter. Dec coughed into his hand and looked away, shoulders shaking.

"Indeed he is." He squeezed her fingers gently and said to Killian, "I don't believe you have need of me after all." He and Mica exchanged glances before he turned back to Killian. "Mica can see to it."

Mica and Killian shared a long look and she finally commented, "Piece of cake. Stop worrying. The boys are fine. My dad's probably taking them fishing today."

Raphael smiled a little wistfully at that before touching Rori's arm. "All will be well, child. You mustn't fight what you don't understand, or you will never learn what you need. Have faith in Declan; he will see it through."

Mica pulled her husband into the back bedroom and closed the door. "Well?"

"Tell her you're hypnotizing her. Keep it simple. We need to test my theory. We'll wait to tell her until it's proven out. She's such a skeptic she won't believe us without some real proof."

Wrapping her arms around his waist, she rested her cheek on his chest, his medallion brushing her skin with its warmth. "I feel so sorry for her. She's a wreck, Killian. Guilt, fear, confusion! There's so much pain coming from her that it's giving me a headache. Can't you feel it?"

One of Mica's strongest psychic powers was her ability to sense emotions in others. She was a highly sensitive Empath. This gift, courtesy of Michael--*the* Michael--Archangel above them all--was a dubious one. Until she'd learned to rope off her feelings from others around her, she was a target for every emotion within spitting distance. At first it had overwhelmed her, gave her splitting headaches, made her embarrassingly weepy. But then Killian taught her how to shut herself off from the constant bombardment and how to turn it on again at will. She'd turned it on the minute Rori came into the hotel. What she sensed made her stomach churn.

Killian idly rubbed her back and replied, "She doesn't understand her visions, babe. She really believes she's seeing premonitions that she can't stop. The guilt of those deaths weighs on her soul. She needs to understand. You'll help her with that. I know you will." He tucked a lock of her hair behind an ear and kissed her, mouth lingering longer than time allowed.

She wiped a smudge of lipstick from the corner of his mouth. "And what about the other problem?"

"I'm working on it."

Two hours later, Mica and Rori were curled at opposite ends of the couch, sipping glasses of wine. Mica mentioned it was her favorite cabernet. Rori had nothing to gauge it against since she was a wine virgin. Mica had taken charge, ordering the men around until she had everything she wanted. Dec had fetched cheese and crackers. Sean picked up the wine. Then the men had vanished. Not literally. They were shoved out the front door. It was girls' night in.

Mica leaned over and topped off her glass for the third time. Rori buried her nose in the delicate crystal, inhaling the rich, fruity vapors. "How does something that tastes so funky smell so good?"

"Black cherry with a hint of cocoa. Mmm, and a note of smoke at the finish." Mica laughed before lifting her glass in a toast. "To new friends who have no taste in wine!"

She giggled and tried to tap her glass to Mica's. She swayed, and Mica's face swam in front of her. Her new friend carefully plucked the glass from her shaky hands and set it on the coffee table.

"I think it's time, Rori. Are you ready now?" Her voice was lovely, smooth, hypnotic.

She found herself nodding. Okay, sure, let's do this. They sat cross-legged facing each other on the couch. Resting on the top of their knees, their fingers were loosely entwined. Mica's touch was infinitely gentle as she carefully positioned Rori's wrist so it wouldn't be jostled. She gave Rori's hands a light squeeze, nodding with encouragement when she responded by showing a tiny pained smile. Holy shit, she was about to be hypnotized! She should've been more freaked out about this, but somehow she just couldn't find the energy.

Mica chided softly, "Lightweight. Sit back so you don't fall over."

"I feel weird."

"I'm sure you do. Probably you didn't need that third glass. Are you ready?"

"I think so."

"Okay, I'm going to need you to keep your eyes open and just relax. I'll see what's going on with those visions. I should be able to see what you can't remember. It won't hurt at all, but you need to let me in. Will you let me in, Rori?" She used the same coaxing tone. It was soft, warm, compelling. The sound drew Rori to her. She actually leaned closer. Mica smoothed a stray bit of hair from her cheek.

She nodded again. "Go ahead. Do it."

Mica studied her latest patient with satisfaction. Perfect. Rori was on her way to a bitch of a hangover, but they'd worry about that tomorrow. Right now, her tipsiness was just what the doctor ordered. They'd all agreed to leave the choice up to Rori. Sure, they had other ways to see her memories. They could've knocked her out and invaded her mind; or worse, just invaded her mind and ransacked it. None of them wanted to go those routes. If their suspicions were right, she had some pretty amazing psychic abilities. They wouldn't want to lose her trust when she clearly needed their help.

Of course, all of them had already done their usual unobtrusive readings--the Primani typically read a person's intentions through their eyes; it was a quick way of weeding out bad people right up front. It made their jobs easier to know what they were dealing with. In Rori's case, Sean had already gotten a butt chewing for digging too deeply into her memories. In his defense, he was only trying to help. His search shouldn't have bothered her, but it did. They suspected the demon shut her down.

Rori was struggling with more than one issue right now, and they all wanted to help her, not hurt her. Raphael was right. They didn't need him to heal her just yet. Mica had the touch. She'd be able to peel back the layers. She was getting very good at this sort of thing.

But that didn't mean she didn't want back up. Smiling serenely at Rori, she sent her thoughts to Killian.

I'm ready. Are you here?
Sure, babe. Let's do it.

To Rori, she said, "I'm going to count to ten, and you'll be asleep. Okay?" At Rori's wobbly nod, she started to count. Rori was under by six.

With practiced movements, she held her locket in one hand, waiting until it shone bright as a tiny sun before flaming out once more. The pale rune on the back of her hand began to glow as she allowed her sight to take control. Staring into the clear toffee irises, she breathed deeply and got to work. Each iris was a hundred different shades of brown, from the lightest of honey to the richest burnt sienna. Dec had described them as bourbon colored, but that was a one dimensional description. In Mica's view, all irises were formed of delicate puzzle pieces that had to be carefully separated to reveal the mysteries within the human mind. The colors fascinated her every time she did this.

The tiny click of recognition announced that Killian's mind was in synch with hers. Over the years, they'd perfected their technique. Intricately joined by their shared powers and Raphael's blood, they were able to do what no one else could. Through their shared psychic connection, Killian could project himself into her mind at will. She would allow him access to help her with the trip through Rori's psyche. As usual, his image, like an avatar, joined her inside the tranquil meditation room she'd created within her imagination. He gave her a nod of encouragement before she carefully peeled the last puzzle piece. True partners in every way, he'd never let her do this without being her safety net.

Time to focus. She was in. Visualizing herself standing in the center of Rori's mind, she got her bearings and began her journey. She pictured herself walking through Rori's life, moving backwards in time, seeing the images from Rori's perspective. Pictures, sounds, emotions, even scents, poured over her like a stream of water. Careful not to distress Rori, she let them float by as she slipped through them.

At first, they were simple images of the past few days... whoa! Making out with Dec was clearly a red letter event based on the clarity of every aspect of the memory. Her mind had captured every tiny detail in perfect preservation: the feel of his lips on her skin, the exact second his eyes went smoky with desire, and the heat of his hands cupping her. She slammed her eyes shut against the porn. Ewww! TMI, for God's sake! Killian chuckled at her horror.

I could've lived my entire immortal life without seeing that. Probably I'm scarred forever.

You'll live, Princess. It does explain some things, don't you think?

He was right, as usual. Dec's interest in Rori was starting to make sense. She wasn't just a charge to him...

And Rori's feelings were more than she let on. She seemed calm on the surface, but in here, her emotions didn't have any place to hide. She'd gazed at Dec with lust in her eyes and panic in her heart.

Rori seemed to be handling Mica's intrusion well enough for her to speed up the process. Walking faster caused the days to blur past. Days turned to weeks; weeks to years... It took almost no time to uncover years of memories because each day was nearly identical... Live alone, go to school, live alone, go to work, live alone, go to the library. The pattern was broken only by stops at the cemetery and rare conversations with a priest. Where was her father? Where were her friends? What about happy hour? No boyfriends? Who was this Raine guy? He'd popped up in more recent memories... Rori's emotions fluttered around him. Not love... friendship? Attraction? Well, he did have a smokin' body...

Seriously, babe? He's got dreads for crying out loud.

Dreads, schmeads. He's still hot. Did you see his eyes?
Ask her about it when she wakes up. You're wasting time.

Yeah, yeah, no need to get snippy. Moving on, she swept backwards through time, looking for clues to the lingering fear and pain that surrounded Rori's soul. Rori had lived in no fewer than five houses before she finished high school. These memories were faded, fuzzy, full of holes, filled with impressions of anger, conflict, and pain. The ragged memories scratched like brambles as she wove through them. They clung to her, tearing at her, drawing blood.

Foster homes. Damn. Killian's tone was sympathetic with an undercurrent of anger. He'd never admit it, but he had a soft spot for lost puppies too.

Damn it, Killian! No one should have to live without someone to love them! Her empath powers were happily soaking up the negative. Her heart was breaking for this young woman who had been so screwed already and now had to deal with a shitload of pain that was coming straight at her.

Something wasn't quite right. Mentally tapping her fingers together, she paused to regroup. Okay, she didn't see anything helpful to explain the visions. The point of this drill was to find some clue to her psychic powers. So far, all they'd found was a young woman's pain-filled past. That didn't prove Killian's theory. She carefully backed out, taking in all of the impressions she could along the way. More worry, more sadness… more fear. She hadn't seen any recent memories that should make her afraid. Where was the fear coming from? It seemed to be unconscious, an underlying part of her personality, deep inside of her heart, instinctive. What caused it? Was she even aware of it? Had Rori suppressed something that Mica missed?

Slipping ahead to the day they found her unconscious in the cemetery... now that's weird. She tilted her head for a better angle. Huh. Odd. The perspective was off... perpendicular to the ground... she was staring down at her body. She'd been disoriented. The memory was indistinct even inside Rori's own mind--mostly sensations, impressions of panic, of fear, of overwhelming despair.

What the hell?

Keep going, babe.

But--

Go.

She came to an odd shimmer, like a mirage, blocking her view. Nice try. Get out of my way, wall. I'm a pro. You're not keeping me out. Pushing through the wavering light, she popped up in a field. Where the hell am I? What memory is this? Studying the details, she came to the conclusion at the same time Killian did.

Woodstock.

1969.

Bingo!

Before either could say another word, they found themselves in a cavernous room with huge bare windows streaked by moonlight. The rest of the space was dark with shadows. Squinting to see better, she edged closer to the window just as a figure slid into the frame. The image started to crack apart just as she caught a glimpse of wings. They unfurled, stretching upward even as a body shifted to reveal a massive torso and the back of a head. The creature looked over its shoulder at her, the sound of laughter rumbling from its chest.

Rori suddenly stiffened, crying out with fear. In the deep recesses of her mind, she begged, "*Leave me alone!*"

The creature laughed even harder before snarling, "*Get out!*"

Stunned, Mica watched in horror as a solid black wall came crashing down just in front of her. Stumbling backwards, she bolted until she was completely free of Rori's mind. Shaking hard, she panted for air even as Killian rematerialized next to her. Wrapping his hand around her rune, he pumped his *saol* into her. Her breathing calmed immediately, and her heartbeat slowed to match the steady rhythm of his.

"I've got you. Are you okay? Anything hurt?"

Ignoring the nausea that was making her mouth water, Mica closed her eyes and answered, "I'm fine now. Really. Just a little freaked out. That was bizarre."

"Yeah, and not a good sign either." He'd seen those wings before. Rori was more screwed than they thought. This was getting worse and worse. How the fuck did she get sucked into this? Who was she, *really*?

"Are you thinking what I'm thinking?"

Rori woke to the sound of jackhammers destroying the street below them. At least that's how it sounded. She cracked her eyelids a hair to find a tiny hint of sunlight sneaking through the blinds. She dragged the sheet over her face in self-defense. The jackhammers continued.

"Good morning." Mica's face and a glass of water popped into the doorway. "Can I come in? I'll make you feel better. Promise."

Shoving her face into the pillow, she mumbled, "Sure, why not? This is your fault."

Apparently taking that as an invitation to come in, Mica slipped inside bearing gifts. "I brought you some aspirin. Take them and go back to sleep. You'll feel better in a few hours."

She did as ordered and crashed.

Feeling more than a little idiotic, Dec tiptoed inside Rori's room. The last thing he wanted to do was wake her up. Mica and Killian's trip down her Memory Lane had knocked her out for the last 12 hours. He'd be lying if he said he wasn't worried. Edging closer to the bed, he studied her face. She looked okay. No dark circles. No tension. Her expression was calm. No nightmares? He didn't want her to think he was sneaking around like some kind of perv. It hurt that she still didn't trust him. She said she did, but he knew those words didn't go soul deep. She seemed to *want* to trust him; that was a start. One day, he'd figure out where her fortress came from. When he did, he'd break down those walls. One at a time. She deserved to live, *really live*, the life she'd been given. He could give that to her. If she'd let him…

Pressing his palm to her cheek, he leaned in and kissed her, feather light and hardly a touch to her mouth. She turned into his touch and sighed, breath warming his skin.

"Will you dream of me, Rori?" he murmured near the delicate curve of her ear. She was beautiful and worthy. Why didn't she know that? With a last long look, he moved to the living room.

Mica spotted him first. "Really, Dec? You know we can see everything on your face, right?" She squeezed him in a hug, scolding, "I had no idea you and Rori were getting so close. Why didn't you tell me?"

That was a surprise. "We're not. What did you see? Does she like me?"

She just laughed and said, "You're such a dork! Of course she does. She's got the memory of your you-know-what on friggin' speed dial! Apparently you made an impression on her, and she's dying to take you for a test drive." She shrugged, adding, "Just sayin'."

Killian stepped between them with one hand raised to stop the bantering. "Okay, whatever, she's got the hots for you. Good job, stud! The bigger issue is still our main priority, right? Unless you're just trying to get laid and don't care about her problems?"

"Don't be a dick! I'm trying to help her. I am. But I've got to admit, she's twisting my guts in a knot right now. I need to stay about 1,000 feet away from her, but that's not gonna happen. I don't have that kind of control."

Mica winked at her husband and offered some advice. "She's a damsel, and you love to be the hero. Bottom line? You're two consenting adults. Why not just take it a step at a time and see what happens? You don't have to get serious, you know. Go out. Play. Show her a good time. Take her to see the city. Give her some happy memories, sweetie. She could use them to balance the darkness in her mind."

Killian smirked and commented, "She's playing matchmaker again. Don't let her fool you. Now can we get back to work? There's a lot to talk about, and then we've got to go. Abby's supposed to pick up the kids from Dani. That ought to be fun."

"What happened?"

Mica shot Killian a fierce glare and said, "Killian's overexaggerating. Nothing's happened. Abby and Dani had an argument a few weeks after you left. No big deal."

"And?"

"And what? Nothing. Dani is acting like you don't exist, and Abby's ready to choke the shit out of you. But hey, none of this is new." Mica laughed at the look on his face. "It's the way they always act when you're not around."

Jesus. This was a cluster.

"I never wanted to hurt Abby, Mica. You know that, right? I really do like her."

"Uh-huh. Yeah, I know you've done everything humanly possible to keep her out of your pants. Guess that one little taste is addictive. She's not over you."

Aaaannd, it's getting worse.

Killian crossed his arms and shook his head, a smile threatening to break out. Dec reddened and fixed him with a hard look.

"For the last time, nothing happened that night. I swear!"

"Well, Dani tells me she walked in on you and Abby naked in bed. Abby tells me she remembers kissing you and pulling off your boxers..." She let the sentence hang before bursting into giggles.

Grinding his teeth, he managed, "We didn't have sex. I, um, had to put her to sleep, though. She was... well, she didn't want to take no for an answer." He ran his hands through his hair. Not one of his shining moments. "It'd been awhile... I, um, almost didn't stop it. So I dropped us both into sleep."

"You knocked yourself out?"

"Well, yeah. It seemed like a good idea at the time. I was desperate."

His audience burst into laughter and then tears. Once laughter finally dissolved into snorts and chuckles, Killian wheezed, "To hear Abby talk, she had you every which way but upside down. Guess she's got a good imagination. Reminds me of her sister."

That got another snort of amusement out of Mica. "I don't hear you complaining."

Rolling his eyes to the back of his head, he grabbed hold of some patience and ground out, "I'm not sleeping with Dani or Abby. Ever. Can we please talk about Rori?"

After 20 minutes of explanation, Dec sat back, weaving his guitar pick over and under his fingers. He'd snatched it out of thin air at a Metallica concert back in '93. It was his most prized possession next to his Burton snowboard, and his soul, of course. The concert had led to one hell of an after party... the pick was a reminder. He was sentimental about it... whatever. It was his thing.

"Soooo... I get it. Not premonitions at all. Retrocognition. She's seeing snatches of the past... no wonder she can't save anyone. They're already dead. This

135

must mean something to us. Why would she wander onto my radar if she wasn't supposed to help me?"

"That's the question, isn't it, Dec? You said you connected to her more than once. Anything pop out at you? Recognize anything? Anyone?" Killian was not letting this go.

Dec turned thoughtful for a few minutes, all thoughts on Rori and the odd connection they'd shared. That nightmare wasn't familiar, but... At the cemetery, he'd caught a peek into her vision... Woodstock. 1969.

The boy!

Chapter 9: Love the One You're with

SIX HOTDOGS WERE GONE. It was impossible. Rori gaped at Dec as he smeared mustard on number seven.

As he jammed the second half of the dog into his mouth, he reached for her can of Coke. Swallowing visibly, he swigged the drink, burped with a surprising amount of restraint, and grinned at her. "What? Am I doing it wrong? Haven't you seen a man eat a hotdog before?"

"You are not a man. You are some kind of hotdog-eating god. No human could possibly eat that many in one sitting." She smoothed her hands over the hard muscles of his torso. There was absolutely no give to him. He was rock hard. Her helpful imagination provided all the detail of ridged muscles, taut golden skin, and a fine, silky, happy trail. It was sexy as hell. She loved her imagination. "I have no idea where you put them."

Easing back, he patted his stomach. "The usual place." Sprawling more comfortably, he rested his elbows on the step behind him and gazed up at the skyscrapers. Seconds ticked by until he finally said, "We should talk."

Uh-oh. Here it comes. Her stomach threatened to evict the hotdog she'd just happily eaten. His tone scared her. He was suddenly more serious than he'd been all morning. He'd played tour guide today, handling her gently, carefully, playfully. She wasn't stupid. She knew he was purposely keeping things light. His words had been upbeat, but every now and then his gaze rested on her... studying her? No, more like trying to sense her mood. He was gauging her readiness for this convo. Closing her eyes and wishing it away just wasn't going to work. She was a big girl. She could handle the truth, no matter how horrible it was. She already knew she was useless. What kind of friggin' psychic has visions they can't do anything about? What was the point in having them if not to warn people? Father Joseph was right about her. She was cursed. Useless.

Dec wore black Oakley sunglasses that completely buried his eyes. His wearing the glasses seemed like a wall going up between them. Was he protecting himself, or her? Crap. Bad news doesn't get better with waiting... kinda like leaving sushi on the counter...

Seeming to sense her reluctance, he tugged her closer to his side. His beautiful mouth quirked up on one side, and he removed the sunglasses. Those heavenly blue eyes looked into hers and seemed to find her soul. Suddenly unnerved by the notion, she lowered her eyes, but kept her hand in his.

"Go ahead. Tell me what Mica and Killian told you. I'm sure it's nothing good."

Dec pursed his lips and chose his words carefully. He had what he thought was good news for her and had been waiting for the right time to spill it. Her forlorn expression tugged at his heartstrings, though. Gently stroking her wrist, he sent a wee bit of his *saol* to calm her racing thoughts. Not enough to knock her out; just a little to relax her so she'd hear him. *Really* hear him. The soft vibration pulsed between them. Letting her head tip back, she rolled it around in a stretch before releasing a long sigh.

Leaning closer, he slid his free hand into the glorious silk of her hair, marveling at the colors as the strands poured through his fingers. He did it again, saying, "Relax, sweetheart. It's okay now."

Too much juice. Easing up a bit, he watched her face intently for the second her awareness came back into focus.

"I'm cold. Are you cold?" She shivered before wrapping her arms around herself.

"Come over here; I'll keep you warm." He spread his legs open so she could sit between them with her back to his chest. With his arms wrapped around her, he held her more tightly than strictly necessary. But she felt good; better than good. They were an exact fit. He rested his cheek against the top of her head and closed his eyes.

Bad idea, this. He shouldn't have brought her this close to him. His body was screaming 'hallelujah,' and his head was yelling 'abort, abort!'

Too late. They needed to talk, and this was going to help her relax. He'd just ignore his head and his body. For now, anyway.

"How long have you been having visions?"

"Years. I don't know... they started when I was... uh, maybe 13? My memory's a little fuzzy before that so I'm not sure."

Rubbing her arms, he said, "Relax. I have good news for you."

She tried to swing around, but he tightened his arms until she relaxed again. "What do you mean 'good news'? I'm a useless psychic. How can that be anything but bad?"

Stifling the growl in his throat, he ground out, "You're not useless! Damn it! Who told you that?"

Long silence. Rori was shutting down again. When she started to withdraw, he turned her to face him. He wanted to kill the person who put that pain in her eyes.

"Rori? Talk to me. Please."

Her mouth quivered once before she bit her lower lip and lifted her chin. "Never you mind, Dr. Phil. That's not important. Just tell me the verdict."

Whoa! Okaaay... She made his head spin.

"Have you ever heard of retrocognition?" She shook her head, looking more confused than before so he added, "You see snatches of past events. It's the opposite of precognition. Precognition allows you to see events before they happen. You're seeing things after the fact." More firmly, he said, "You couldn't help those people, Rori. They're already dead. It's not your fault. Ever."

Another long silence stretched as she stared first at him, then at the ground in front of her. Endless minutes passed before she asked, "When did you die?"

Clutching at his arm, she asked again, voice shrill with fear, "Tell me! I saw you die! I saw your neck broken..." Her voice cracked, ending in a whispered, "I saw you... How are you here if you're dead?"

Ah, hell. His turn to clam up. He couldn't tell her. *Couldn't* without her finding out the truth. That wasn't allowed.

She searched his eyes for the truth before starting to shake. Gathering her close, he tucked her face into his shoulder while she broke down and sobbed in his arms. Years of fear, pain, and shame poured out of her. She shook so hard he was afraid she'd bruise herself.

"It's okay, darlin'. Cry it all out. It's going to be all right now."

She needed to cry. She needed to let the pain out. He didn't need to be Primani to understand it. The man he used to be knew it... knew her needs. He let her weep, rubbing her back, murmuring those little words of comfort so she'd know he was there for her.

Time seemed to stop as they sat on those concrete steps. The sun disappeared behind heavy clouds, sending them into chilly shadows. People walked up and down the steps, circling around them like a boulder in the middle of a river. Probably he should move them. Probably he should tell her it was time to leave. Probably he should… damn. He had no idea what he should do just then. He held this amazing woman in his arms, listening to pain and sorrow pour out, and for the life of him, he had no idea what to do next.

She needed him. That much was crystal clear. So he sat. He held and protected her. He helped her heal. That was his job, right?

When her sobs had petered off to occasional sniffs, he let go long enough to fish a crumpled napkin from his pocket. Passing it to her, he kissed the top of her forehead as she mopped at her face and blew her nose. Grimacing at the wet sounds, he handed her the rest of the wad of napkins hidden under the hotdog wrappers. She coughed and laughed at the same time. It was a weepy sort of laugh, but a laugh just the same. It was a start.

"Ugh. My head's killing me now! I hate crying." She rubbed her temples and winced.

"Let me do that for you." Making tiny circles around her temples, he very carefully healed her aching head. His hands tingled as the healing energy seeped from his thumbs to her forehead. She closed her eyes in obvious bliss and sighed. Her lips were red and swollen from crying, her cheeks flushed bright. Suddenly those hypnotic cat's eyes caught his. Each gleamed with tears that accentuated the glorious bourbon irises. Beautiful eyes. Beautiful woman. They pulled at something inside of him, drew him in until he wanted to drown in them. With a mind of their own, his fingers drifted over her brow bone, circling her eyes, the tender flesh underneath them, the delicate skin of her lids until they both held their breaths at the spark flowing between them.

"Dec… I--"

He cut her off by kissing her. She opened her mouth in surprise and he took advantage, deepening the kiss, wrapping both hands in her hair and pulling her closer. He couldn't seem to help himself. Later, he'd probably regret this, but right now he needed to taste her, to feel her respond--respond to *him*. Rori moaned against his mouth, breasts pressing into him, hands tangled in his hair. He was breathing hard when he had the sense to end the kiss.

He sat back, shaken to the bone, surprised he wasn't on fire. His *saol* raced close to the surface, striving to be closer to her. His fingers tingled. He glanced at the tips of his fingers. They lit up with the force of the current. Ah, hell. This was not good. She licked her lip, eyeing him with surprise and more than a little hunger. Her pupils were dilated; she couldn't catch her breath. Yes! She wanted him. Too bad he couldn't get up now.

Sick old ladies. Baseball. Liver. Liver and onions. Raw sewage.

She watched Dec with more than a little wariness. Electricity still crackled between them. He'd just rocked her to the core on the steps of the Metropolitan Museum of Art. She'd never be able to come here again. People were still gawking. She peeked around his shoulder to check. Yep, the hotdog guy caught her glance and adjusted the package in his pants. Ewwww. Great. On the corner, a teenaged girl gave her a thumbs up while tucking her cell back into her pocket. Yay. Well, that's one video that'll go viral. Awesome. I'll be famous.

Dec's eyes were closed. He looked like he was in serious pain. She nudged him in the ribs, and his eyes flew open. "Did you just say 'raw sewage'? What are you doing?"

His dimples exploded with a flush of pink. "I had to think of something gross. We can't sit here all day."

What was he talking about? She started to ask when the light bulb went off. Oh! Now she turned bright red and mumbled, "Sorry."

Now he laughed out loud and said, "I should be the one apologizing to you. I don't know what I was thinking mauling you in the middle of broad daylight. I'm an animal." Springing up, he reached down to give her a hand. "Do you still want to go inside? There's time before they close for the day."

The Met was one of her favorite places. She'd been coming here, haunting the place really, for as long as she could remember. The Met and the library were the only two places she could go for peace and quiet. It was her day off, but the man refused to let her sleep in. She'd been sleeping at the penthouse for the past two days and dreaded telling him she wanted to leave. He and his friends were trying to help her. She got that. It wasn't like she didn't appreciate their intentions. But she'd been alone for so long, and they didn't really know her. She was overdue for another blackout and every second seemed to be a warning. She'd been filled with an unfamiliar dread since waking up this morning. Something wasn't quite right, but she couldn't put her finger on it. She'd slept okay... but woke with a lingering impression of fear, of a rage with its sights set on her. It was like a red laser beam settled between her shoulder blades the minute they'd walked out of the hotel's front doors. Something was watching her. She just didn't know what. Whatever it was, it didn't have anything to do with her retrocognition abilities. Dec's explanation made sense to her; she was relieved that she wasn't responsible for those people she'd seen. It was a huge weight lifted from her shoulders. Yet now she knew for sure this had nothing to do with the other bad shit going down in her life.

A sharp movement drew her attention to the corner across the street. The storefronts were in heavy shadow, crowds of busy people filling the sidewalks. She recognized the swish of black cloth as the man whipped around and stalked the other direction.

What was he doing here?

Dec followed Rori's eyes to the priest across the street. The good father spun about before melting into the throng of NYC-ers making their way to wherever they went at 4:00 on a Thursday. Rori had stiffened with fear when she'd seen him. Sighing mentally, he wondered, again, what she was still hiding.

"Friend of yours?" he probed, his arm automatically circling her tiny waist.

Clearly not feeling it, she forced a tight smile for him before answering, "Uh, no. Not really. I know him from St. Anne's. He works there."

The priest was long gone, but she stared at the spot where he'd been, her mind a million miles away. Okay. So she thinks I'm stupid.

Facing her, he asked, "How about you tell me the truth this time? Who is the priest, and why do you look like you're going to puke?"

She flinched and snapped, "You're pushing again. We had a deal, remember? Spilling my guts isn't part of it."

He spoke against her ear so she couldn't miss his next words. "You're right, sweetheart, we do have an agreement. I agreed to keep your pretty little butt alive. You agreed to tell me about your visions and dreams. Has it occurred to you that a priest would have the knowledge to summon demons?"

Resisting the urge to duck, he waited for the explosion. It couldn't be helped. There was no point in sugarcoating it. Facts were facts. The priest would be in a perfect position to summon the demon that was stalking her. He took a good look at her face and rolled his eyes at her stubbornness. All he'd managed to do was piss her off again. Her cheeks erupted into the most flattering shade of pink... uh-oh, they were bordering on magenta now.

"Demons again? Where is your proof? You've shown me nothing that changes my mind on that." Snatching her hand away, she grumbled, "Father Joseph isn't my favorite person, but that doesn't have anything to do with demons. He... he and I..." She stopped speaking and stared at her feet, indecision etched across her face.

His chest tightened as he put two and two together. No, no, no. Please don't be a creepy child molester priest... he didn't want to have to execute a priest. Probably it wasn't allowed, him being a man of God and all that. But if he'd touched this woman, if he'd *hurt* this woman... well, all bets were off. He hated, *hated*, child molesters. His list was filled with these monsters and one by one, he was hunting them down. It was the least he could do.

Sucking in a deep breath, he shoved his feelings into the back of his head. He'd dealt with his own demons a long time ago. Thanks to Raphael, he was able to move forward. That didn't mean he hadn't taken some side trips along the way. Vengeance might not be politically correct today, but the angels had been exacting it since creation. It was time to help Rori with her demons and maybe get a little payback of his own. Toning down his attitude, he asked softly, "Did he hurt you?"

The sounds of traffic and cooing pigeons seemed amplified in the silence that followed.

She struggled to find words to help him understand. She'd never spoken of this to anyone; anyone alive, that is. She couldn't begin to count the times she'd cried on her knees in front of her mother's grave. There was no one else to share the shame and fear with. Can't forget the pain, either. It followed her everywhere until one day it just stopped.

"It's not what you think. Just drop it, okay? I don't want to talk about it."

Those weren't the words she'd intended to say, but that's what came out when she opened her mouth. With a mental head shake, she tried again. "It's complicated."

Dec searched her face for clues. She wasn't lying, but she was leaving out the truth. He could force it from her, but that would be a shitty thing to do. He was trying to gain her trust and messing around inside of her memories would just piss her off. Soooo...

He hugged her. Just a simple, uncomplicated, friendly, non-sexual hug. She stiffened at first contact, but then let herself melt against his chest.

Breathing in the scent of her hair as it floated across his face, he fought the urge to laugh at this whole situation. 'It's complicated', she says. Oh, hell yeah, it was. More than she knew! The woman was beyond stubborn. Until she believed him, she was a target for the demon with a hard-on for her. She had no psychic armor against him and refused to listen to Mica's instructions on how to shield. This priest was a new twist to the story of Rori. Guess he had some detective work to do after all.

The sun was long gone when Rori came to a decision. With her heart like a brick in her chest, she picked up her bag and let the music lead her to the man who was making her crazy. She listened from the hallway. The haunting music sent a chill down her spine, but she wouldn't dream of asking him to stop. His music was part of him, a beautiful part that she loved. The 'L' word slipped out before she could stop the thought. Sure, she said it. She loved to hear him play. That didn't mean she loved *him*. Music. Man. Big difference.

Not wanting to disturb him, she hovered in the doorway. His eyes were half closed as his fingers danced over the strings, foot tapping ever so slightly to the beat of his own drum. Damn. He was something. Caught in the music, he tipped his head forward so those messy bangs fell across his forehead, hiding his gorgeous eyes. In the past month, she'd seen those eyes twinkle with laughter, crease with worry, and darken with want. He'd watched her sometimes with an intensity that made her jumpy, made her bold... made her want things from him that she knew would just complicate things. She knew he was attracted to her, but he'd been hands off until today when he'd kissed on the steps of the Met. She'd followed his lead, keeping her distance, even if she was more drawn to him every minute she was in his presence. Today's raw passion affected her more than she wanted to admit. She was left yearning for more, yearning for his touch, his heartbeat. That path would surely lead to madness.

"Are you going to stand there all day?" His soft accent sent a shiver of pleasure down her neck even if the words weren't sexy.

She swallowed an unnatural spear of jealousy of that guitar. The shiny, white instrument got to sit on his lap; it got to feel his fingers plucking at its strings. Man, she wanted Dec to pluck her. She'd trade places with the Gibson in a New York minute.

Her brain jumped in before her lady parts could make any decisions. He wasn't good for her. She knew it. He didn't want to be involved that way. He was protecting her while they figured out her problems. She knew that too. But her head and her body were in violent disagreement at the moment. She wanted him in ways that she was ashamed of.

Thank you, Father Joseph.

"I'm going out."

His smile faltered, but he slid the pick between the strings and started to rise. "Okay. Where are we going?"

She stopped him before he could stand up. "With Raine." She ignored the sharp glance and the twinge of guilt that almost made her change her mind. "I'll be spending the night at my apartment."

The smile vanished altogether.

Sean's eyes dimmed to a pale blue glow as his molecules settled into place. After flicking his eyes to clear the haze, he studied his surroundings in a 360 as he'd done for millennia. Noting nothing more threatening than a family of skunks eating bugs behind him, he re-sheathed the 10-inch utility knife he carried in the city. He was armed with his usual arsenal---you just didn't know when shit would go sideways--and ready to hunt. Dec materialized a nanosecond after him. Eyes blazing hot, he was more pissed than he'd seen him in decades. He'd started to screw with him, but there were just some things even he left alone.

"This is the place, huh?" He was underwhelmed. The cemetery was small and not kept up well. They'd come in next to a brick building and pressed themselves against its wall. He let his sight roam, picking up nothing more than a few restless spirits. Nothing demonic had been here in a while.

Moving like a wraith towards the back door, Dec jimmied the lock with a wave of the hand. Using a small flashlight, he went directly to the files in the tiny rear office. There were two rows of ancient metal file cabinets along one wall, a rickety-looking bookcase filled with binders on the other. A broken metal desk completed the furniture. The only upgrade since the 1960s seemed to be the fully ergonomic leather office chair. Sean dropped his ass into it and gave it a spin.

Grinning at Dec, he said, "Looks like the good father's got hemorrhoids. The pad on this thing's as thick as a mattress." He gave it a bounce and added, "We need one of these."

Dec cocked his head. "Something you want to tell me?"

He barked a laugh and started searching the desk drawers. "Hurry up. I've got plans for later."

Dec kept his attention on the files he was skimming, but asked, "You got a date?"

"Yeah, something like that. You want to come? She's got hot friends."

He leafed through the calendar, making mental notes about nothing since there wasn't shit written on it. The desk drawers were also a bust. Looking around for something else to search, he thought about Declan. The dude really needed to get out, really needed to get laid. For God's sake, how long had it been? Years? His testosterone was going to poison his dumb ass...

"Come with me tonight. Seriously, man, I'm worried about you. It'll be fun. Just fun. No strings. No guilt."

Dec put down the file folder and sighed. Rori was out God only knew where with that Raine guy doing God only knew what. He didn't like it. Not one bit. But... She didn't owe him an explanation. She didn't owe him anything at all. They weren't a couple. They weren't even dating. He'd done what he could to keep them from getting close, and she hadn't put up much of a fight. She had no idea what he was, but she sensed it wasn't a good idea. She'd stopped giving in to the chemistry between them and kept her distance. That distance bothered him on a lot of levels, but he'd shoved those urges to the back of his brain. He was there to help her, not sleep with her. Today's kiss was a huge mistake. He still ached from the hormones raging through his blood.

"Why the fuck not?" he finally asked. "Before we go, take a look at this." He handed Sean a file. "Do you recognize the name?"

Sean exhaled through his nose and slowly laid the folder on the desk. "Tammy Carmichael. Deceased mother of little Gary Carmichael, missing since August, 1969."

"And the plot thickens."

LAURIE OLERICH

Dump hadn't changed much over the years. True to its name, the crappy dive bar was one rat hair away from going out of business. Buried underneath an ancient brick apartment building, it had the atmosphere of a rat hole. The bullet damage had been mostly patched, though not much effort went into matching the paint colors. The result was an ugly patchwork of beige and not-quite beige. All of the furniture had been replaced since they'd blown the place to hell a few years back. Luckily, the old bartender was gone. Dead, from what Dec had heard. There was no way he'd have let them in. The new one, Julie, was just desperate enough for customers that she waved them inside without bothering to look twice. Clearly she didn't know about Primani. You couldn't miss the energy.

The music had changed since their last visit. Whatever happened to RockHard!? He'd given them some cash to replace all of their band equipment after the brawl. Even though he and his brothers hadn't started the fight, they felt bad about the band getting stuck in the middle. Well, he'd felt bad. Killian and Sean didn't give a shit about a few smashed speakers and one broken guitar. Tonight the music was just what he needed. Heavy, loud, guaranteed to juice him up--Disturbed and Five Finger Death Punch blasted from the speakers. It was shaping up to be a pretty good night. The beers were cold and going down too smoothly. The two women draped over him were neither heavy nor cold. Sinuous, lean, hot... their 'dates' for the night were also excellent pool players and had just won their third game. As he flipped out another Jackson, he couldn't help grinning. Sean was leaning against the bar, his date, Sara, was whispering in his ear. Supernatural hearing was cool. Dec shamelessly eavesdropped.

She whispered, "Why don't we go back to my place? Winning makes me horny." She ran her palm between his legs and purred, "I'm a very generous winner."

150

Sean stopped her hand right where it was and growled low in his throat, "I'm a sore loser, so you better be ready. Dec, let's go."

He choked on his beer. Busted. Flashing his best sexy smile at Haley, the blonde leaning at his side, he asked, "Are you up for this, darlin'?"

He couldn't resist stroking the silky skin of her bare shoulder. Her muscles were tight, curvy, and warm. She took care of herself. From the glimpses he'd gotten when she bent over to take a shot, she had beautiful abs as well. It had been a while since he'd seen such a sweet, tight package of woman. He wanted more than anything to peel her tank top off and bite his way up her six-pack. He just hoped she was game.

"Oh, I don't know, Irish. Let me think… stay here and play pool or spread you naked on my sheets?" She tapped at her chin in thought. "Hmm, are you as good as you look?"

"If you can still talk, you'll have to let me know later."

Letting his gaze rest at the junction between her thighs, he sent her a wee bit of heat. Just a taste of what might come her way…

Aaaand, score! Haley's eyes opened in shock, her lips parted with a gasp of pleasure, her back arched. When she licked her lower lip, he praised God.

It was good to be telekinetic.

Turned out the two women were roommates. Good news for the four of them since no one had any more patience. The second they hit the elevator, Sean turned Sara into the wall and buried his face in her neck. Her pixie haircut provided no curtain to hide behind. Dec watched her head loll back, eyes closed, as Sean kissed her throat. He used one hand to hold her face still, the other to cup her breast. Sara's hands moved frantically under his shirt, practically dragging it over his head even as the bell dinged.

He'd been primed from practically the second he set eyes on Haley. She was a honey blonde with sexy assets: green eyes, pert little nose, perky breasts, apple ass... and funny. She'd kept him laughing all night even with the tension building between them. She was hilarious. Smart, too. She was a quality kind of woman, true. Probably he'd appreciate that in another lifetime. Right now, he just wanted to bury himself inside her.

Grabbing his hand, she dragged him to her room, locking the door behind them. With her back to the door, she gave him a slow, sexy smile, murmuring, "I hope you can keep up with me, stud. I'm going to eat you alive."

Mr. Crowley nearly jumped out of his pants. "Start low; it's been awhile."

Her eyes dropped, and she hooked her fingers in the waistband of his jeans. "Low is good."

Backing her to the bed, he peeled the top over her head, pausing to pay respect to her breasts on the way by. Crawling onto his lap, she peeled off his t-shirt, kissing his neck, his collarbone, down his chest... lingering at his belly button...

He closed his eyes with the pleasure of her touch. Her soft hands and sharp nails seemed to hit every inch of his body. She was in worship mode---stroking him, exploring him, tasting him. It had been too damn long since anyone had touched him like this. His skin tingled. Goose bumps crawled across his belly. Her nails scraped along his biceps, up his neck, down... this was Heaven. He held his breath as she hovered above him. Her eyes challenged him to stop her, and he grinned slow and easy. Cupping the back of her head, he gave her a little nudge. Her smile lit up the room, and he lay back with his blood racing out of control.

"You just lay here and let me play. You'll get your turn in a minute." She'd scooted up to straddle his hips. Her clothes were gone, leaving her in nothing but silky smooth skin. That skin was rubbing all over him. If he could die from pleasure, he'd be gone in another minute.

The sound of Sean shouting brought his head up. "Sean?"

"It's nothing. Relax, baby." She wrapped her fingers around his shaft, stroking him slowly, setting him on fire.

He closed his eyes. She was torturing him one inch at a time. Sliding across his chest, she reached over his head, her breasts against his face. He opened his mouth and caught one tight nipple. Haley moaned deep in her throat, hips slowly circling against him with the age old rhythm. As he suckled her, she picked up his hand, nibbling his fingers one at a time, drawing them into her mouth. The entire world narrowed to the sensation of her hot, wet mouth on his skin, and he gave in to to the pleasure building…

He was about to explode. He tried to switch positions, but couldn't move his arms. Shit. His hands were tied above his head. What the fuck? He gave them a yank. Nothing.

The door opened, and Sara walked in. Flipping on the light, she surveyed the scene in front of her with a pair of ankle cuffs dangling from one hand and a bottle of honey in the other.

Holy Mary Mother of God! "Where's Sean?"

Her mouth curled into a sweet smile, eyes sparkling in the sudden light. She wore only a black lace thong and that sweet smile. The thong was barely a strip of material covering her creamy skin. A tiny pair of angel wings fluttered to the side of her right breast. The tat was beautifully done but didn't compete with the round globes of womanly goodness. Crowley started to weep. He was very fond of large breasts.

"Oh, he's just fine, Dec. Resting comfortably for now. He didn't want to cooperate though." Sara shrugged one bare shoulder and added, "He'll live. Now, you don't struggle, and we'll help you with that delicious hard-on you've got there."

He stared in confusion. It was hard to process with 90 percent of his blood pooled below his navel. What? "Exactly what are we talking about here? I'm a lot more fun when I get to move around." He smiled for good measure. He wiggled his hands, but the silk tie wouldn't budge. Part of him wasn't so sure about this... but Crowley had totally different ideas. He bobbed for attention. Look at me! Look at me!

With twin conspiratorial grins, Haley perched on one side. Sara knelt on the other. His hands and feet were bound. He was naked and sandwiched between two beautiful women. One of which just produced a peacock feather from a box next to the bed. A blindfold came next. The black silk covered his eyes. He was defenseless. Okay, not really. He could teleport. He could put them to sleep with a thought. But he hadn't had sex in three years, so he was shooting for at least one orgasm before making an escape. He really hoped no one pulled out a knife first.

"Okay, ladies. I'm all yours."

"You suck. You know that, right?" he grumbled as he limped down the sidewalk in front of Rori's building.

Sean strode along with his usual macho fitness. Oh, sure, he wasn't just wrung dry by two nymphomaniacs. Damn, his balls ached. He resisted the automatic urge to cup himself. Sean was already laughing his ass off. He didn't need more ammo.

Thoroughly unrepentant, Sean just grinned. "I love you, man! This is what real brothers do. They help each other. You needed some help. If you deny you had a good time, I'll call you a fucking liar."

Unbelievably, Crowley twitched with interest as Dec remembered the mouths, tongues, and other wet, warm body parts… uh, no. No way could he deny it was awesome. Now? He could hardly walk…

"Okay. We're here. Her lights are off."

Rori tossed and turned, struggling to get away. Massive, threatening, beautiful… they unfolded slowly, purposely in front of the glass window. Flames licked at her heels, forcing her to move towards the wings, towards him.

No! Leave me alone! She opened her mouth to scream, but he slammed his mouth over hers. Hard, demanding, rough… he used his fingers to pry her lips apart before plunging his tongue inside. His fingers dug into her shoulders as he pinned her down. She tried to thrash her head away, but it wouldn't obey. She was paralyzed, powerless. As the fire swirled inside her dream, she sank deeper into the void. She was cocooned in him. Lost.

She was almost his. He settled his energy into its human façade and watched Rori sleep. She was dreaming again--dreaming of him. He sent her those images, this night, and every night he could. Some nights she blocked him, most nights she couldn't. Her powers weren't strong enough. She had no armor against him. She didn't always remember the dreams. That was as he intended. He enjoyed these little games. It had been a bad week, so tonight he would play. He'd been showing restraint, waiting until the day he claimed her. On that date, she would be his whether she wanted it or not. No one could undo what had been done--not her, not the angels. Her weak Primani protector was so far out of his league. He didn't even know what he was dealing with. By the time the wingless idiot figured it out, it would be too late.

Rori opened her mouth to scream. Not yet, witch! There will be time for that later. He shut her up by slamming his mouth over hers in a brutal parody of a kiss.

She struggled against him, instinct, self-preservation driving her against the invasion, against the evil it sensed even during deep sleep. He hissed low in his throat as his cock responded to her pain, her fear. She fought him, her spirit screaming from within, head thrashing to the side. Good, Rori. Fight me. I like it this way. He pried her mouth open, forcing his tongue inside, taking hers, until she stopped struggling. With barely a thought, he willed her to go limp. Then he took his time, kissing her more softly, with more care. He wanted to taste her, feel her energy enter him. He wrapped his arms around her, cocooning her in his body in what was left of his soul. She cried out at his assault but was too far under to move against him. He held her for hours, soaking in her warmth, drawing away her soul.

Soon, she would be his. Always.

Chapter 10: Breaking the Girl

RAINE STOOD IN FRONT OF HER BUILDING gathering his courage. He was giving himself a rare day off. He had to work to eat, and he generally liked to eat every day. Normally he'd be working near Central Park since it was Friday and people would be out getting a head start on the weekend. It was warm for late September and the sun was blazing already. He glanced at his watch. Nine o'clock. Rori should be getting ready for work. Would she want to see him so soon? Last night had ended in a cluster. Dinner was Juliano's pizza. For entertainment he walked her through the park in the moonlight. Kiss goodnight? Disaster.

There she was. Clearly late again, she slammed the building's door before taking off at a fast walk. Sucking in a deep breath, it was now or never. He stepped out of the shadows.

"Hey, Rori! Wait up."

Damn, she looked beat. He should've brought her home earlier but he hadn't been ready to say goodnight. Man, he was an ass. Even exhausted, she made a pretty little package. She wore a yellow sundress with white sandals that had seen better days. She wouldn't appreciate his ogling her, but hey, he was a guy and she was a cute girl... what else was he supposed to do? It wasn't his fault she'd filled out over the past two months. She was still slender, but the gaunt look was nearly gone. Her breasts had grown enough to peek out of the neckline of her cotton dress. The lines of her exotic face were softer too. She'd gone from kind of cute to nearly beautiful since gaining some weight. Where was she getting the food? He knew she was still broke...

"Raine. What are you doing here? Aren't you working?" Rori kept walking but made eye contact with him so he knew she wasn't upset.

He casually draped an arm over her shoulders and loped along beside her. She didn't shrug him off so he took that as a good sign. The day was looking up already.

"Listen, Rori, about last night--" he began.

Without missing a step, she cut him off. "Don't. Hector is a menace. I'm so sorry you got caught in the middle of his bullshit." She slowed down to touch his cheek. "That bruise looks bad. How are you feeling?"

Sure it looked bad. Because it *hurt* like hell! Mornings after a fight always sucked. Today wasn't any different. His whole face ached. One eye was still watering... a molar was loose, and the cut on his right hand stung like a bitch. Fucking gangbanger tried to kill him last night.

Shrugging for Rori's benefit, he said, "I'll live, babe. This isn't the worst thing that's happened to me. I'm glad you're okay. If he'd hurt you, he'd be dead this morning. You know that, right?"

Rori pretended interest in a car driving by so he wouldn't catch her rolling her eyes at his macho attitude. He had every right to be pissed off. She definitely was. They'd had a perfectly nice date until he walked her home. Hector and his thugs were hanging out by the front door.

He'd stepped out with a switchblade and his ego to back him up. She was all for turning around and heading another direction, but Raine blew her mind by going all Vin Diesel on Hector. The fight went from knife waving to ass kicking in a heartbeat. All she could do was watch in shock as Raine beat the shit out of Hector. Sure, Hector landed a few solid blows, but in the end he was down for the count, bleeding from eyes, ears, nose, and mouth.

She'd been shocked and awed by the ferocity of the fight. Raine was always the easy going, fun guy. He wore dreads for crying out loud! His whole vibe was peace, love, and rock and roll. The Raine she saw last night was someone she didn't know. He'd scared the living hell out of her, but a bitchy voice in her head cheered him on. Hector had to go. Someone had to rearrange his attitude. Dec and Sean had kicked his ass once, but apparently that wasn't enough. He hadn't given up on her, but had been keeping his distance. Last night he'd clearly decided Raine wasn't a threat. Huh. Guess he wouldn't make that mistake again. *If* he regained consciousness, that is.

They were still heading towards the flower shop. Pausing at a red light, she asked, "So where did you learn to fight like that?"

Raine didn't answer. The 'walk' signal flashed to tell them to move forward or get run over by the crowd. He ignored her question and headed across the street. Throngs of busy people swarmed around them as they were swept along the sidewalks. The buzz of the city grew louder the closer they got to her store. Cabs zigzagged past, delivery trucks stopped with squealing brakes, street vendors shouted back and forth. Once they reached the flower shop, she unlocked the security gate and let them both inside. Angela wouldn't object to Raine's presence. He looked harmless.

She warmed up the cash register while he flipped the sign around to show they were open. Once the store was ready to go, she turned to grill him some more. He peered out the window, expression blank, eyes moving constantly as he studied the street. One hand curled casually against the glass, the other in his pocket.

"Raine? What is it?" She started to move to his side when he shook his head.

"Stay over there, Rori. Something's off."

He pulled a gun from under his shirt and circled back to the side door. Edging it open with the toe of his Doc Martins, he checked right and then left.

"Oh, my God, Raine What's with the gun?"

Before he could respond, the front door clattered open and something flew straight towards her head.

"Get down!" Raine roared.

The explosion blew her backwards just as he raced forward to grab her. Screaming in terror, she tried to scramble out of the way just as Raine threw himself on top of her. Glass and particle board chunks rained down on them even as he beat the flames out with his bare hands.

"Wakey, wakey, stud. We've got work to do." Sean flicked him in the ear.

It was too friggin' early for this. Not even going to try to pretend it wasn't. Dec yawned so wide his jawbones cracked. The involuntary stretch lifted him an extra six inches as his exhausted muscles tried desperately to process some oxygen. They'd slept about four hours since checking on Rori. Her apartment had been quiet so they'd traveled back to the penthouse for some rack time. He automatically healed himself while he was crashed, so at least he could *walk* normally again. Grimacing at the memory of *that* particular pain, he blindly poured sugar into his coffee and yawned again. It was too friggin' early…

"You're an idiot. You know that, right?" The coffee and cold wind gusts were helping. His brain was sending weak signals of reengagement to the rest of his body. The weather had turned ugly in the middle of the night. The sky was looking most unfriendly in the grey light. Clouds hung so low they covered some of the top floors of the buildings nearby. Rain? Maybe. Thunder rumbled in the distance, confirming his thoughts--a storm for sure. Guess Indian summer was a memory now. He yawned and stretched again.

Sean had already slammed his usual double espresso and predictably bounced from one foot to the other. It was annoying. He shot Dec a 'who me?' glance and flicked his ear again. "Come on, man. We've got a cold trail to blaze. We're so close! I feel it! Let's find Rori and get some answers. The kid's waited long enough."

He hated to admit it, but Sean was right. They were getting closer. The priest's records, the vision Rori had from 1969, the little boy he glimpsed in the background... these were related. They were sure of that. Today the plan was to get Rori to open up about that vision. They needed more info than just the face of the boy. A landmark would be useful. He just hoped she'd remember the meat of her vision. Even if she couldn't provide any more details, they had a priest to track down. Finally, some real progress! It was shaping up to be an interesting sort of day after an interesting sort of night. For the first time in days, he was optimistic about something turning out right.

Miss DeShante Jackson gestured with the pot to get his attention. She'd been vending on this corner for weeks now, and he was just a little bit in love with her... or at least with the muscle of the coffee she served. Some kind of Costa Rican blend... it was straight up caffeine. He softened his grouch, flashing a hint of a smile at her kindness.

Holding out the half-empty paper cup, he said, "You're an angel, darlin', pure and simple." Breathing in the bitter aroma, he sighed and added, "If you weren't taken, I'd sweep you away from here."

Miss Jackson tsked and poured more coffee. She might be all street attitude on the outside, but she couldn't hide the faint flush of pleasure his words brought. Instead of getting all gushy about it, she warned, "Yeah, yeah, my man would wipe his ass with you, skinny white boy."

Reaching out, he touched her wrist in thanks and smiled with all of the firepower within. "Oh, I'm sure he'd try. I'd give my life to keep someone like you!" Blowing a kiss, he grinned at her expression. Stunned would describe it.

It was a gift.

Sean cleared his throat and commented, "Glad to see you're awake. Let's bolt."

"All right. Give me a sec to find her."

He heard the explosion the second he tuned in to Rori's location. The sound of shattering glass echoed inside of him as his heart turned to lead.

They rematerialized in the center of massive confusion behind Angela's Flower Shop. Sirens screamed in the distance, people shouted, a stray dog howled... but all Dec could focus on was Raine's voice. Hoarse with burns and smoke, Raine prayed for a miracle. He begged for God to help Rori. Dec found her, and the bottom dropped out of his world.

She'd taken the brunt of the firebomb; her dress was burned to scraps. Her velvety skin scorched red, blackened in places, bloody in others... Her eyes streamed as her breath hitched with agony. Her lids fluttered as she lost consciousness in Raine's arms.

"No!" Raine's plea was drowned by the sirens, but hit Dec like a gunshot.

Sean grabbed his arm, took one look at his face and dropped it. "Go! Get her out of here. I'll cover you."

Raine cradled Rori, his own bloodshot eyes streaming steadily as he prayed for a miracle. He wasn't a religious man, but he'd try anything to save her. She was still now, her breathing shallow and halting. Her lungs struggled to work, struggled to keep her alive.

"Please, God. If you're really there, do something! Don't let her die like this!"

People crowded around. Someone stepped on his fingers, breaking more than one. The sharp pain took his breath away, but he refused to respond. He'd been through worse. Rori was probably dying. How did this happen? One minute she was laughing, vibrant and pretty, then the next she flew into him, broken and burned. "Get back, people! Give her some air!"

Rori coughed raggedly, the sound ending in a pathetic whimper. The smell of cooked meat washed over him as the initial adrenaline wore off. His hands were burned raw, skin hanging off his left thumb. The sickeningly sweet smell turned his stomach, reminded him of another time he'd seen such atrocities, other burned bodies. Jesus Christ. Where was the fucking ambulance?

Someone touched his shoulder, ordering softly, "Let me have her. I can help."

He couldn't see who'd spoken through the film of tears. The smoke had burned the hell out of his eyes. They'd been running constantly since he'd left the store. Who was talking to him? Was it a medic? Squeezing away the stinging tears, Raine looked into the face of an angel. The blond-haired man squatted where no one had been the second before. He seemed to pulse with a soft golden light, the blue eyes on fire in their sockets.

"What are you?"

The angel grimaced and said, "Not what. Who. I'm just a man. Now let her go."

He blinked again, and they were gone.

"Raphael! Hurry!"

Rori's eyes were closed. Thank the Lord she was unconscious. She had to be in agony. Moving carefully,

Dec laid her on a bed and got to work. Placing his hands on her chest, he started the healing process with her lungs. The warmth of his *saol* flowed like lava as he dumped the energy into her, desperation nearly making him insane. He shook from head to toe with the need to fix her. He'd healed some terrible wounds, but this was one of the worst he'd seen. Even Mica's broken bones had been easier to fix. Sucking in a deep breath, he put a leash on the panic and got down to business. Time for emotions later.

"Come on, sweetheart. Heal for me. I'm going to put you back together." He kept his voice low and soothing, but the strain was clear even to him. He was too close this time. He knew it, but there was no going back. There was no way in hell he was leaving this woman in this condition. What happened this morning? This wasn't the usual work of demons. No, they usually didn't toss bombs into stores. This was something else. What was Dread Head doing there? Clearly he'd been inside when the bomb went off. He was covered with cuts and burns. Probably he saved Rori's life. Shit. He didn't want to feel gratitude to this guy. But hell, if he saved her, he'd get Dec's gratitude… and then some.

Her breathing sounded normal again, so he let his hands drift over her abdomen and watched as the bloody flesh knitted and returned to pink health.

Raphael joined him without announcing his presence. He stood on the other side of Rori and ran his eyes over the destruction. With a soft growl in his throat, he laid his hands over the delicate bones of her face. The archangel's healing power flowed, a soft vibration of energy that made Dec's hands tingle. Neither spoke as they worked from the top of her head to the tips of her toes. There was so much damage, so much to heal.

"How's she doing?" Sean spoke softly from the doorway.

Raphael glanced up, answering, "She'll be okay physically. I am unsure how she'll feel about this when she wakes up. Her nightmares are full of fire and darkness. The demon still haunts her sleep."

Dec lifted her hair, pointed to the tiny sigil that was branded into her skin, and said, "Raphael, this needs to go-- now. Maybe we can break that demon's connection? Maybe something good can come from this disaster?"

Sean stepped closer, his eyes hooded along with his thoughts. "I've seen that mark before. It's on her mother's grave."

The clock struck 1:00. Raine stared stone-faced at the hands as they inched forward into another hour. Very, very slowly, he closed his eyes. He'd been sitting on his kitchen floor for hours but he couldn't make himself move a muscle. God, everything hurt. He'd been burned, cut, and bruised. Every time he moved his left elbow, something grated inside, sending fresh sweat beading over him. The perspiration stung the hundreds of cuts that dotted the front side of his body. Fuck. It hurt to breathe. Funny how you don't feel pain when you're running for your life... or saving someone else's. The body just does what it needs to do to survive the moment. But after? Yeah, afterwards, the chemicals vanish, and you're left feeling like shit. Like right now. There was nothing but pain: Pain in his body, pain in his heart.

Memories tumbled over one another from today, from yesterday, from years ago in another lifetime. He wished he could change his life. His past... his future. He'd been so close... so close to escaping the nightmares, but they were back. The explosion, glass shattering... the ringing in his ears, today and a lifetime ago, ran through his head. Screams echoed. Eerie cries for help crawled over his skin, sending him spiraling into this pitiful bloody waste he was right now. He shivered, opened his eyes, and noticed two of his fingers were purple. Broken. Not the first time. He knew he should go to the hospital, but no one would treat him. He was a nobody. Had nothing, meant nothing. Death just followed him, but refused to claim him. Resting his head against the wall, he concentrated on being still. He was too tired to move now. He'd just lie here…

A light swung across his eyelids like a flashlight beam. Squinting against the blinding light, he struggled to wake up. His muzzy head refused to cooperate so he lay as still as possible, trying to force his brain to function. A prickling of electricity tingled through his limbs. The skin on his face and chest tightened and relaxed. The pain receded. He tried to open his eyes, but a voice whispered to keep them shut. Someone picked up his wrist, and the piercing pain in his fingers vanished with a burst of heat.

"What the--"

"Shh. Don't talk. Don't open your eyes, or I'll leave your dumb ass just like you are."

More whispering. More than one person? Some of the words were clear enough to hear, but in some foreign language. What the hell was going on? He seemed to be paralyzed; he tried to sit up, but his muscles didn't respond to his brain. He must be in the hospital. That's got to be it. But how? When? Rori? Did she look for him? Did she find someone to help him?

"Rori?"

"Rori's fine. She's healing someplace safe. I'm going to wake you up now. Don't fight me, or I'll knock your ass out again. Deal?"

He managed to mutter, "Yeah, sure," before a sharp burst of adrenaline crashed through his chest, flinging him upright like a jack-in-the-box. Squinting against the energy zinging through him, he could only gape. He must be losing his mind. Maybe he was in a coma and having really lucid dreams.

"Holy God… you're that angel."

The blond-haired angel sat at the foot of his bed. His eyes burned, literally, with a brilliant blue flame, and he held a thin silver blade in one hand. The metal gleamed in the glow of his halo as he let it rest on his thigh. Strangely, the angel was dressed in jeans and a long-sleeved button up shirt, sleeves shoved up his forearms. A frayed leather bracelet circled one wrist.

"You won't remember any of this, but I'd be a complete tool if I didn't talk to you." He nodded his head as if agreeing with himself. "Yeah, it's the least I can do."

He'd been saved by an Irish angel?

Were all angels Irish? The nuns failed to mention this. He was thoroughly confused. He must've hit his head. He reached behind, checking for lumps. Nope, no goose eggs on his noggin. No crusty blood either. "Uh, sure. Okay. Am I dead?"

"Not today, Raine." His mouth curled into a hint of a smile. Those terrifying eyes faded to a clear blue, the brilliant halo vanished. He looked just like any other guy now except for the aura of power and strength that ebbed around him.

No way this guy was human.

"Okay. So what do you want with me?"

The angel stood and dragged his fingers through his hair, shoving it away from his face. "You pulled Rori Austin from that building before I could get to her. If it wasn't for you, she'd have been toast. Because of you, she's going to be okay. For that, I have to say thank you. I owe you a debt. I don't like the position that puts me in. So I just took away your pain."

My pain? He took a few seconds to look over his body. The burns were gone. The glass was gone. His broken fingers were healed. It was a miracle.

Choking up, he swallowed hard and whispered, "I don't deserve this. I'm not a good man."

The angel narrowed his eyes and fingered the hilt of his weapon for an entire minute before re-sheathing it and taking Raine's face between his two hands. Staring straight into his eyes, he commanded softly, "Let me in, Raine."

Time had passed. He knew it in his gut, but he had no idea how much. He was so tired. He wanted to sleep forever. Someone squeezed his hand.

He cracked an eye and sat up straighter.

With sad eyes, the angel sighed next to him. "You're killing me here, dude. I don't want to like you, but you're making it tough. I've just seen your entire life, and I'll be damned if I can fault you anything. But you fault yourself, don't you? That's got to stop. Because I'm such a nice guy, I'm going to take away your self-loathing and guilt from Afghanistan. Those deaths were not your fault--you have no reason to feel responsible or guilty. The fact that you survived to fight another day is your destiny. You were a good soldier, Raine. You still are. When you wake up, you will be able to remember all of the events clearly but without emotions clouding your perception. This will help you move forward and live the life you're supposed to be living. Get off the streets. Find your family. *Now* we're even, you and I."

What the fuck? How did he know about all that?

"I know everything, and I am always right." He actually winked.

Was it possible? Could he move on with his life? Could he forgive himself? He searched his heart for the familiar weight of guilt. It was gone. Maybe the angel was right. If that was true, he'd not only been blessed; he'd been saved. Raine swallowed the flood of emotions washing over him. He wasn't going to cry. Not now. Not in front of this powerful creature who looked like he would like to strangle him. Changing the subject seemed the best way to manage.

"You healed Rori too? Thank you for that. She doesn't deserve what happened. She's beautiful and--"

The angel's fist tightened around the hilt of his wicked-looking blade, and he bit off his words. The angel snarled, "About that…" and leaned into Raine's face.

Two days later, Rori woke to the familiar walls of Dec's penthouse. The flood of memories struck her hard, and she fell back against the pillows, panting with fear, waiting to feel excruciating pain.

Dec poked his head into the doorway and said with irritating cheerfulness, "Good. You're up. How are you feeling?"

Throwing off the sheet, she yanked the t-shirt over her head before frantically taking inventory. How was this possible? No burns? No cuts? Not a single sign she'd been in the middle of an explosion.

With eyes drilling into him, she demanded, "What the hell happened? Why am I not dead? Where's Raine?"

Dec sighed, long and heavy, annoyance clear. "You're not dead because it's not time for you to die. Raine is also not dead. Jesus, what is it with you two? Are you in love with him?"

"What? No!" She narrowed her eyes, suddenly sure he was actually jealous. "Why do you care?"

"Never you mind, sweetheart. Just get up and get dressed. Today's an important day. There are some of Mica's things in that dresser. I think they'll fit you." With one last lopsided grin, he closed the door.

Thirty minutes later, she was showered and dressed in Mica's clothes. The jeans were a little loose on her narrow hips, but they were flattering enough. She'd chosen a purple Henley with tiny pearl snaps. A rummage in the closet turned up a pair of well-worn black leather combat boots. These were the last things she'd ever want to wear, but there weren't any real options. It was either the boots or nothing. Her sandals were nowhere to be found. Since her heavy hair took forever to dry, she twisted most of it and secured it to the top of her head with a simple plastic clip. A couple of long locks fell out to frame her face. Huh. Not bad.

She was surprised to find others in the kitchen when she rushed in. She'd been expecting only Declan, but Sean was there too.

"Glad to see you're up and moving, Rori." Sean gestured for her to come in and have a seat. "You scared the hell out of us."

Dec shoved a plate of waffles in her direction and said around a mouthful, "Help yourself. The hotel makes awesome waffles, and I know you're starving. There's juice and coffee too." He shoveled another huge forkful into his mouth and caught a bit of escaping syrup with the tip of his tongue.

He was entirely too cute. With his streaky blond bangs brushing his eyes, that adorable smile, and those eyes... he was a triple threat to her hormones. She drank him in despite her plan to get information and then leave post haste. She was more than a little freaked out by all this. She didn't really have time to lust over him... but the body doesn't always follow the mind's instructions, does it?

"I'd like some answers. I think I deserve them."

The two guys shared some extended eye contact before Dec nodded and turned back with resignation written all over his face.

"You're right. You do deserve them. The problem is I'm not supposed to tell you. It's a family secret."

"I can keep a secret, Dec. God knows I've got enough of my own. What's one more?"

He exhaled hard through his nose and started to pace. His version of pacing was really more like stalking... his long legs ate up the space as he moved between the foyer entrance and the French doors leading to the patio. Clearly this wasn't easy for him.

Sean studied her from under half-closed eyes. After a minute, he said, "Go ahead, bro. Tell her about your abilities. She's not going to tell anyone."

Dec started, opening his mouth to protest, but then seemed to change his mind. A slow grin teased his dimples into a full appearance. "Fine. But you have to swear not to tell anyone else."

"Fine. I swear as long as you don't try to tell me you're some kind of guardian angel like Castiel. That would be totally nuts." She joked because that's what she did when she was nervous.

That comment seemed to sober everyone but herself. Sean gave her an intense stare and said, "I've met Castiel. Dec's nothing like him."

Dec elbowed him in the gut and rolled his eyes. "Not helping."

"You two are beyond weird. Can we just get to the truth telling?"

Dec reddened and said stiffly, "I have some psychic abilities like you do. That's how I know what you are. I sense you. We all have some degree of abilities. I can heal people. I healed you and Raine."

Her mouth fell open.

He reached over and gently tapped it shut. "There. Now you know my big dark secret. Happy?"

"That's it? You can heal people?"

"You sound disappointed. What's the matter?"

"Nothing. It's nothing. I'm just surprised. I guess I should say thank you or offer up my first born son?"

He waved a hand in dismissal. "No human offerings necessary. It's a little disturbing that you'd come up with that. If you want to pay me back, I need your help with something."

Sean had been standing over by the doors, looking out onto the patio. She guessed he was giving them a little space, but now he sauntered back to them and sprawled across a loveseat. The man moved like a panther. It was sexy as hell. Dec's eyes narrowed a bit.

Surely he couldn't read her thoughts too? One quick glance at his angry expression, and she flushed hotter.

"Are you reading my mind?"

Snorting rudely, he snapped, "I don't have to read your mind; it's written all over your face. If you were any redder, you'd be on fire." He pushed himself upright and glared down at her. "I'll call you a cab."

He dialed the cab company before dialing back the uncharacteristic wave of fury that threatened to knock him on his ass. Rubbing his fingers over his jaw in total frustration, he ground his molars together and hissed at the wall. Damn her! Damn *him*! He shouldn't give a shit who she looked at. She wasn't his. He didn't want her to be. He closed his eyes and fumed, trying to breathe normally, searching for his Zen. It was nowhere to be found. He was just... just... pissed. Who was he kidding? He wanted her to look at him like she'd just looked at Sean. Her face was an open book. She had no idea how transparent she was. She'd undressed Sean with pure womanly appreciation.

Fuck.

This sucked ass. What the hell was he doing? Hiding in the bedroom? Sending her home in a cab instead of sucking it up and taking her? She was his charge. He had to get to the bottom of the firebombing. And the demon. And Woodstock. Usually, he was stronger than his emotions. Rori was twisting him into someone he didn't know, someone he didn't want to be. He didn't need this in his life! How the hell did she worm her way under his skin?

He was so screwed.

Chapter 11: Bad Timing

HECTOR RAMIREZ WAS SO FUCKED UP. A single candle flickered in the open window, sending eerie shapes dancing across Rosalie's black walls. The entire room was painted black. The sheets were black. The carpet was red. The single candle was the only light she'd allow at night. As the walls melted into the floor, he thought it looked like a giant puddle of blood. Even the floor undulated, giving the impression of a current running through the pool of crimson. Moving in slow motion, he shook his head like a wet dog, blinking into the orange light and swimming shadows. Rosalie clutched his back, digging her nails into his skin, breaking it… tearing at him. She was just as wasted as he was… her eyes were unfocused and staring into the ceiling as he fucked her again. He'd lost count of how many times he'd climbed up on her, or she'd climbed up on him. Who cared? He was getting his.

"Harder!" she whined into his ear. "I can't feel you!"

He kept pumping against her, sweat dripping into his eyes, splashing onto her tits. The hallucinations were cool, but the acid made his dick numb. They'd been fucking for hours, but he couldn't come. Close now, he was so close to coming. The ringing in his ears ratcheted to a crescendo as his sac tightened painfully. Yes, yes!

He was about to explode when someone grabbed him from behind, one arm around his throat, one hand gripping his dick like a vice. Both body parts burned like fire. His eyes saw nothing but red.

"Ho*la*, Hector."

Rosalie started screaming, but the sound abruptly stopped. Hector stared stupidly as her mouth opened wide, but no sound came out. The candle blew out, plunging the room into darkness.

"You want to be real quiet now, miss. I'd hate to have to hurt you. Sit still. I'll be done in 30 seconds."

She clamped her mouth shut and scooted all the way back to the headboard.

"Better. Now Hector, I'm going to tell you this once and only once. Are you listening?"

Hector tried to get out of the hold he was in, but this motherfucker was like a monster or some shit. He had superhuman strength, and his skin was on fire. Was that steam coming off the arm wrapped around his throat? Hector clawed at the arm around his neck but it only pressed harder, cutting off his oxygen. He tried the same thing with the fist wrapped around his dick.

The monster twisted it backwards until Hector howled like a dog.

"I will rip your dick off and make you eat it if you even look at Rori Austin again. Ever. Do you understand me?"

Hector grunted.

"That includes sending another motherfucker to firebomb her house. If she even gets a paper cut, I'm coming after you. Do you understand what I'm saying to you? Nod if you do."

Hector couldn't see the bastard behind him, but the fear on Rosalie's face told him he wasn't dealing with anyone he knew. The strength of his hands was wrong, the heat, the fucking glow coming off of the parts he could see... This monster wasn't human. He was in Hell. That Rori bitch was a demon. He should've known she'd be trouble.

He nodded as hard as he could.

"Good, you pathetic piece of shit. Now, why don't you take a little *siesta* while you wait for the police? I hear they're very interested in your stash."

Sean greeted him with a raised eyebrow followed by a quick look-see over his rumpled clothes. "Sooo... You look like dog shit. Rough night?"

"Fuck you. I don't want to talk about it."

He pointedly turned his back on Sean. He wasn't in the mood. Probably he didn't need to yank the refrigerator door open, but he was still pretty juiced up. After chugging a glass of milk, he slammed the empty glass into the bottom of the sink.

"Couldn't have been that bad. You're still eating." Sean's tone was light, but Dec knew he was digging.

Huge, huge sigh. He didn't want to admit this to anyone, especially not one of his Primani brothers. He let the silence linger as he thought over his options. He could keep his trap shut and figure it out on his own. He was an adult. He didn't need advice. Option two: He could unload on Sean, and let him dog him for days.

Sean finally broke the awkward silence with a long sigh of his own. "Dude. You know I'm not all touchy feely about shit, but I'm not a complete asshole. You know better than that. How much do we need to survive together before you get it? We're brothers. I've got your back and you've got mine."

"It's nothing. I'm just tired. I'm going to grab a shower and head out to St. Anne's. Let's go hunting."

Sean gave him the hairy eyeball at this obvious lie. "Yeah, sure. I'll go sharpen my spikes."

Two hours later, he swung the Challenger into the crumbling asphalt parking lot of St. Anne's Catholic Church. It was old and forgotten by the archdiocese, in dire need of a new roof and a coat of paint. Most of the wooden trim was either warped or rotten. The window sills were missing on two of the windows closest to them. The stained glass was clouded by years of dirt; the disapproving saints blackened into obscurity. Leaves from a massive maple tree littered the ground, their fiery hues exploding in the brilliant sunlight of the late morning. The ground itself seemed to burn around the church. Probably a horrible omen. A raven called from the tree. And… *that's* not eerie at all! Letting the vibe of the place wash over him, he fingered the haft of the silver blade.

"Friggin' creepy for a church."

Sean nodded grimly, his eyes missing nothing as he scanned the grounds and building. "Not all churches stay holy. This place looks like crap. Think the priest is here?"

The sign on the front doors proclaimed the church was closed for renovations. From the looks of it, progress was moving at a crawl.

"Nope. No demons either. Let's have a look around. The good father might have an office here."

"Or a nice dark basement with chains and bloody power tools."

"This isn't a horror movie." Still, he shuddered at the thought. They'd seen worse things.

Sean chuckled and replied, "Yeah, yeah, you keep telling yourself that. I've got a bad feeling about this."

He itched for a face-to-face convo with the priest, but this would have to do for now. Making quick work of unlocking the deadbolt, he slipped inside with Sean right behind him.

"Do you feel that?"

A cold stream of air flowed over them the second they crossed the threshold. It lingered around them, chilling them to the bone, stiffening muscle and freezing blood.

"Keep moving," Sean grunted next to his side.

"Yeah, yeah," he muttered as he armed himself against an attack.

The air was numbing, but they simply drew on the energy within their *saols* to counter it. In full protective mode, their *saols* automatically pulsed harder through every cell, filling them with light and heat, forcing the evil energy out. It would keep this up until they were safely out of the church.

If the exterior of the building was falling apart, the inside was ready for a complete demolition. Once finely polished pews had been tossed around like Legos, split into kindling, some even burnt to ash. There were psalm books and bibles littering the floor, pages ripped out, molded and burnt. The fonts that once contained the blessed holy water were crushed into twisted metal, the precious water long since evaporated.

The altar stood as the lone survivor of the force that had leveled this place. Sean and Dec skirted the rubble to check it out. Its adornments were torn away, leaving only the heavy wooden framework. The surface was covered in ash… the final remains of the priest's holy bible.

A crucifix lay twisted into a knot just beside the ashes.

They stood in silence, each lost in their own thoughts. Dec finally said, "Let's find that basement. This place is making me sick."

Rori closed the new window with a satisfied smile. "What a great window! I feel tons safer now." She flipped the lock in place. "It even has a lock!"

The perv across from her gave her a creepy little wave through his window. She gave him the finger and snapped the curtains closed. Not exactly curtains, but the green wool blanket would block out the sun, the noise, and the peeper a lot better than the old sheers. It was yet another reason to thank Raine. Not only did he save her life, he got her window fixed and gave her the blanket. It had U.S. Army stamped all over it, but hey, she wasn't picky. Her place was a dump--nothing could really make it any worse.

"Well, look, I should really get going. I've got to make some calls, and it's late." Raine stood awkwardly by the front door. He'd just installed a deadbolt and a security chain. After testing it out, he pronounced her secure.

"Are you sure? It's not that late. It's been weeks since we had a chance to talk, and you just got here."

He wasn't going to stay. He wanted to, but it wasn't fair to her. In the past few weeks, they'd both tried to get their lives back on track. He'd woken up--healed--on the bed in his apartment. He had no idea how he'd been healed. He just woke up that way two days after the fire. His clothes were burned, charred, reeking of petrol and barbeque. He'd ripped them off in a panic only to realize he was completely intact. His body was perfect. Better, his *mind* was perfect.

Confused, terrified, and then abruptly aware, he knew he'd been blessed. He didn't know why, didn't know how, he just knew he'd been touched by something holy. The cross he wore hummed with an unfamiliar energy that barely registered to his senses until he'd touched it. The vibration headed straight to his heart, unleashing a flood of emotions that he'd buried during the war.

After sobbing himself into exhaustion, he fell to his knees. He'd been given a second chance.

Thank you, God, for giving me my life back. I swear I won't disappoint you.

"Raine? Hey, are you all right?" Rori touched his arm, bringing his thoughts back to the present. Her golden eyes creased with worry.

"I'm fine. Stop worrying. I should be worried about you. You're the trouble magnet."

She tossed her hair and huffed. "There's nothing to worry about. Hector's gone. His lieutenant's in jail for the fire, and word on the street is they've crossed me off their list. I've got a nice solid window to keep the perv out and door locks to keep any other random scumbags out. I'm as safe as possible! Now, I just need a J.O.B. before the rent's due next month."

Dropping a quick peck on her cheek, he yanked open the door and stepped into the hallway before he could change his mind. "I'll see you at the library on Thursday, okay?"

She gave him a smile and said, "Absolutely. You know that's my day."

Rori slid the deadbolt and chain into place. Raine was acting twitchy. What was going on with him? She looked around the tiny apartment and sighed when she spotted the splotchy brown rat sitting in her kitchen again. He'd chewed through her box of cereal.

"Shoo, you nasty thing! Out! Out!" She chased it into the hallway and right into a man.

Dec had just set a box of supplies outside of Rori's door when it flew open and something warm and heavy hit him in the shin. Whatever it was kept going like a bat out of Hell.

Running at a good clip, Rori hit him next. Both went tumbling backwards; he caught them just before he fell on his ass. Her face was flushed pink, her hair a curtain over them both. Bouncing upright in a flash, he set her on her feet so fast she wobbled.

"Whoa! You don't have to throw yourself at me, love. I'm easy."

"Dec! What on earth are you doing here?"

He sidestepped in front of the box, but she spotted it anyway. Her mouth made an 'O' before clamping shut in a furious line. "I can explain."

"Explain what? That you think I'm a charity case? You're helping to feed me because I'm too skinny?" She backed him into the hallway.

He backed her into the apartment and closed the door. "That's not it. You know I care about you. How come you always assume the worst about me? I've never done anything to hurt you!"

She stuck her finger in his chest and started to answer him. But he cut her off by snatching her finger and firmly lowering her arm. "Don't do that. It's rude."

She stared in surprise.

"Yeah, I said that. Get over it."

Unfortunately, she found her voice again. Probably the neighbors three blocks over heard her. "I don't need your help. I can buy my own food. I was fine before I met you. You're not responsible for me."

"Yeah? You were doing just fine? You've put on 10 pounds since I've been leaving you food. That tells me you were starving. You want to deny that?"

Her face blanched, and she stumbled back. He followed her. "I'm sorry, Rori. I didn't want you to find out like this. Please don't let your pride keep you from taking what I can give you. I'm begging you." He reached for her, but she shook her head, shoulders stiff, jaw set.

"Don't. Touch. Me." Pointing to the door, she ordered, "Get out."

Sean hit the mats with a muffled curse and rolled to his feet, clenching and unclenching his right fist. Shaking it out, he sucked in some oxygen before giving Dec the signal to wait. He slammed a few gulps of water and asked, "Rori?"

Dec shot him an evil glare and ignored the question. He swallowed half of his water before crooking his finger at Sean.

He nodded and sat the bottle down. "She's still not talking to you?"

Dec lunged, hitting him in the torso and sending both skidding back a few feet. He retaliated by wrapping his arms around Dec and flipping him over his shoulder. Dec landed on his back but rolled smoothly to his feet, swinging a right hook that Sean ducked easily. Sean countered with a roundhouse kick to the chest that landed him on his ass. Before Dec could gain footing, he gave him a kick in the ribs--pulled back of course--and declared himself the winner of the round. Finally! Dec had whipped the shit out of him for the past four rounds. Guess he had a lot of pent-up anger.

Dec threw his arms under his head and closed his eyes.

Sean flopped down beside him and waited.

Dec had been looking peaked for two weeks now. He hadn't said much which wasn't like him. Out of the three Primani, Dec was the chatty one. He was the one who actually talked about things. He was definitely the only one who talked about feelings. But since he'd taken responsibility for Rori, he'd changed. Sean didn't like the new Dec. He missed his brother. Dec wasn't lighthearted anymore. He'd lost his will to play. That meant Sean had, too. Dec was the only one who kept him balanced. If it wasn't for Dec's happy personality, he would be all work, no play, all the time. Dec reminded him they could actually enjoy immortality--lately though, Dec was not himself.

"Maybe you should just tell her."

Dec flipped over and gaped like an idiot. "Tell her? We're Primani? You've lost your friggin' mind!"

He shrugged off the protest. "It's been said before. Possibly true, but we'll never know for sure." Even if it was crazy, it was a good idea. Bending to stretch out his hamstrings, he set out to convince his depressed brother. "Maybe she'd stop running from you if she knew you were one of those nosy guardian angels." He used air quotes around the word 'guardian.' "You could even tell her you're good friends with Castiel. Maybe that would help? Then she'd believe in the demon too, and we could get her to cooperate so we could get rid of it once and for all."

Thursday finally! Rori swung up the sunny sidewalk a couple of blocks from her home away from home. The library waited for her, a welcome beacon of truth in a city of lies. She hadn't been to visit in weeks and bubbled with excitement as she approached the corner. One thing to do on the way though... where was Raine? Slowing and moving out of the crush of pedestrians, she shaded her eyes and scanned the corners for him. There you are. He was a beacon himself. The brightness of his hair shone like a spotlight among the dark coats of the people streaming past her. Fall was here with a vengeance; the temps had dropped, giving everyone the excuse to drag out wool coats, leather jackets, and stylish scarves. Rori shivered in the thin hoodie she wore all year long. This was the best she could do. When winter hit hard, she stayed inside as much as possible. She'd lost her only pair of gloves years ago.

Raine finished making change for a tourist and hammed it up as the young woman took a picture with her cellphone. Trying not to laugh, Rori shook her head and enjoyed the view. Oh, yeah, Raine was a hottie; one of these days, someone would discover him and make him a star. She waited for the flirting tourist to move on before coming over.

"So can I have your autograph before you get famous?"

He aimed that million dollar smile her way before swinging her around in a bear hug. Frowning, he pulled away and said, "You're freezing."

He opened the front of his leather jacket. "Come over here and warm up."

He was like a furnace. Ooh. Ahh. Maybe she'd stay here instead of going to the library. She must've moaned out loud because his chest rumbled with laughter. He held her like he wanted her to stay put so she did.

The gentle pressure of Rori's heartbeat thudded against his chest until he couldn't resist tightening his arms. The lemon and coconut scent of her shampoo lingered, and he breathed her in with a contented smile. She was one special woman. He'd miss her. He rubbed his chin over her hair and sighed. Her skin was chilled even under the hoodie she wore.

"Okay, enough hugging. Get moving, lady, so I can sell some cheesy tourist crap. I have a hot date tonight. I need to buy some wine so I can get lucky." He shrugged out of his coat and coaxed her arms into the sleeves before she had time to protest.

"Raine! I'm not taking your coat! You'll freeze out here today!"

Taking her shoulders in both hands, he locked his eyes to hers and said, "You'll take it, and you'll wear it. Don't be too proud to accept help. I mean it. Give it back to me after our date tonight."

Even though he could tell she wanted to protest, she put her arms around his neck and kissed him softly. Her lips were smooth with strawberry lip balm, but stiff with the cold. He cupped her head and warmed her lips for a few extra seconds before dropping one last peck on her mouth.

He zipped up the jacket and pulled the collar up to protect her from the wind. "Come get me when you're done." He watched her walk away with a heavy heart.

Across the street, a movement caught his eye. Standing mostly in the shadows, the man was camouflaged, but a wink of blue sparked once, and then he was gone.

Rori paused to say hello to one of the lions that guarded the entrance. Patting it fondly, she hustled into the warmth. Her eyes immediately went to the place where Arthur always waited. The space was filled with other people today. As much as she hoped it would be different, Arthur wasn't there. He was gone and never coming back. She swallowed a lump in her throat as his smiling face filled her mind. He'd been there forever... been part of her life for years. She missed him, the sweet old flirt. Oh, Arthur, I hope you're happy wherever you are. Dabbing at a sudden tear, she sniffed and headed straight to the computer lab. There was work to do and only a few hours to do it. After logging on to the computer, she went to People Search.

She was up to her eyeballs in details when the power surged. Flopping back in the chair, she rubbed her eyes and groaned. Damn it! She'd been making good progress. The lights flickered again and went off. The library was usually quiet; now it was deathly so as everyone held their breaths. After a moment, the lights flickered back to life. The computers did not. The clock on the wall flashed at 12:00. Judging by the fading light outside, it was time to go anyhow. Raine always packed up at dusk. It wasn't profitable to be on the corners at night.

She gathered up her notes and stuffed them into her backpack.

"Leaving for the night?" A familiar voice stopped her in the middle of zipping it up.

"Yes, ma'am, it's that time again. How are you feeling, Mrs. Anselmo?"

Mrs. Anselmo was as ancient as Arthur had been. A retired librarian, the sharp little woman haunted the halls of the building, drifting through the stacks, touching her favorite tomes. No one really knew how old she was, and she wasn't sharing. A lady never discussed her age... or money. These topics were gauche. Rori gave the thin shoulders a lingering pat. Was she sick? Did she look more tired than usual? Was she breathing funny?

The older woman cleared her throat and said firmly, "I'm not dying. Do stop looking at me that way. We all miss poor old Arthur, dear." She patted Rori's hand and chuckled. "Just because I'm aging, doesn't mean I'm dying. Don't count me out just yet! Now, did you get your research done? You were very intent this afternoon."

Done? Not yet. Progress? Yes. More progress today than in the past few months. It was looking promising until the power surged. Maybe she'd stay a little longer... a crack of lightning made her jump. The lights went out again. Okay, maybe she was done for the day.

"I have to do some more digging, but I found an old property deed." She couldn't stop the excitement from showing. "I'm getting closer."

It was pouring cats and dogs when she heaved the heavy glass door open. Ugh. This was a nightmare. No way did she want to hoof it all the way to Raine's corner. He'd probably ducked into the Thai place to get out of the weather. A rummage in her pockets turned up a wrinkled five dollar bill and two quarters. Damn it. This sucked. Where did this stupid storm come from? No one told her it was supposed to rain today! She didn't have too many options unless she wanted to shower in her clothes. She'd just have to wait it out. How long could it last? A taxi pulled up to the curb and honked. No way!

"I can't believe you got a taxi for us! Come inside. I need to change." She shrugged out of Raine's jacket and dashed to the kitchen for a towel. Patting the leather dry, she draped it over a hanger hooked on a drawer pull.

"There. It'll dry better now. I hate to say this, but I think we'll have to stay here and skip the romantic pizza dinner. Did you bring wine?"

Rain spattered loudly against her tiny windows causing them both to jump. The lightning was gone now, but Mother Nature was still throwing a tantrum. Gusts of wind rattled the glass every few seconds. The new window was holding up nicely. She glanced from the window and back to Raine. He grinned like a little boy. Before she could run, he shook his head, scattering water on her.

"Stop!" She broke into helpless giggles until he stepped away from the wall. Something in the way he moved, the heat in his eyes... she froze in mid-laugh with her hand raised. Raised in welcome? In defense?

"Rori...I..."

As his lips moved over hers, she let herself sink into him. The kiss was tender, sweet, sad. He slid his tongue along her bottom lip, teasing, tantalizing, until she opened her mouth for him. With a harsh groan, he cupped her chin and dove in. Lights danced behind her eyes, heat pooled in her core, her knees went weak. It was almost too intense. She tried to pull away. He pulled her closer. She clutched at the back of his head, standing up on her toes, taking control of his mouth with a growl.

For the second time since meeting Rori, Raine was on fire. He'd come here for one last night with her. One night to talk to be sure she'd be okay without him--one night to say good-bye. He had to leave, and if not forever, at least for a long time. There were things he needed to do, and they weren't in the city. Damn it! He knew it would be hard to say good-bye, but he hadn't planned on this. What was he thinking? He knew he shouldn't touch her, knew she'd ignite him. He wanted her so much even his teeth ached. She wanted him too--but that wasn't the point. He wouldn't make love to her knowing full well he was leaving in the morning. That would be a shitty thing to do, and he wasn't *that* guy.

These thoughts raced in the back of his brain as he stroked her tongue with his… the silky sensations shot straight to his groin… the voice of reason grew dim. When she ground herself against him, he was already rock hard, already tipping past his fragile control. Her heart pounded, magnifying the thud of his own. Blood pulsed hard and fast into every place south of his brain. With eyes closed, hands fisted in her hair, he gave in to the demands and slammed her against him.

One last kiss. One last kiss. One last kiss.

Flinging himself away, he put the futon between them like a wall, one hand clenching the back of the futon in a death grip.

There are millions upon millions of nerve endings in the human body. Right now, every one of hers was screaming for Raine. She pulsed in places that shouldn't have sensors. She couldn't catch her breath. "Raine? What's wrong?"

He was bent over, breathing harshly, eyes squeezed shut. She touched him and he flinched. "Baby, don't. Please."

Hunger? Sorrow? Regret? Love? When he finally raised his eyes, she couldn't read his expression at all.

"Do you have a dream, Rori?"

"Don't answer. I've been dreaming of making love to you for months. It's been on my mind constantly. *You've* been on my mind constantly. I care about you in ways I never thought I'd ever feel. But our timing is all wrong. I'm not free to take your beautiful, sexy, body."

This was the last thing she expected to hear. Stunned, she sank to the futon. "I don't understand. Are you married?"

He moved closer, but didn't sit. "No! I swear that's not it. I'm leaving. Tomorrow."

"What?! Why?"

He cringed at the volume, so she lowered her voice. "Where are you going?"

He lowered himself gingerly to the other side of the futon and reached for her hand. "I've got to find my family. After the war, I wasn't myself. I was wounded in here." He tapped his chest with two fingers. "I was... damaged. I was too ashamed to face my father. So I didn't. I didn't go home. I didn't call. I didn't write. I just went off grid until I finally drifted to the Bronx."

Clearly he'd been struggling with this for a long time. She kissed his fingers and gave him a sad smile. "I'm so sorry, Raine. I wish you would've talked to me. I'm a good listener. You've been here for me; you know I'm here for you."

"Yeah, I know. But I didn't want to dump any of my bullshit on you. It's mine to deal with."

"Why now? What happened to make you change your mind?"

"Do you remember the day of the fire? You almost died right in my arms. I was pretty messed up. Third degree burns on my hands and arms. My throat was seared. My face, too. I had a couple of broken fingers. I was a wreck." He paused before plunging on. "I never told you about the angel. At first I thought I was hallucinating, but the more time goes by, the more I clearly remember him. He took you from me and vanished." He snapped his fingers. "Just like that. He appeared out of thin air, told me he would help you, and then vanished with you. I guess I stumbled to my place and passed out."

"If that wasn't freaky enough, I woke up two days later--completely healed. How the hell does that happen? Angels? Voodoo?" He flashed a quick grin. "I've got no answers. But I know one thing for sure. I was blessed. *You* were blessed. Someone upstairs thought enough of me to make me whole. I need to honor that by living my life the right way. That means letting my parents know I'm alive."

He lowered his eyes, carefully choosing his next words before stroking her cheek with the backs of his fingers. "That means letting you go without sleeping with you. I want to, God knows I do, but it wouldn't be good for either of us. I won't leave you like that."

He tried to drop his hand, but she pressed it against her face once more and held it still. Her eyes glittered, but she didn't cry. She gazed into his eyes, connecting to him, letting him know she accepted him. Instead of weeping, she pressed her lips to his palm.

"I think that is the sweetest thing I've ever heard. Now I really want to jump your bones! Will you keep in touch at least? I don't want to say goodbye forever."

It was nearing midnight when the front door opened and Rori stepped outside into the cold air. The rain was long gone, but the wind still gusted. She laughed when it whipped her hair into her mouth. Dec straightened in the shadows. Was she going out? All set to follow her again, he started to step away from the building. Whoa! What's he doing here?

Raine faced Rori in the open doorway. She wrapped her hands around her bare arms, hugging herself against the wind. She smiled up at the man in front of her. They were talking quietly, their voices muted from the distance. He could tune into them if he wanted, but he was afraid of what he'd hear. He'd been tailing Rori ever since she'd banished him weeks ago. He'd resorted to ghosting after her... pathetic kinda, but there it was. She was still his charge, still in trouble. Just because she didn't want him around didn't change things. He was responsible for her in ways she'd never understand unless she knew what he was. That little convo wasn't happening any time soon. He'd done his absolute best to keep her in the dark about Primani. And his best had been good enough--she couldn't stand him. He was banished. She didn't care about him. She definitely wasn't in love with him. Sure, he'd done a great friggin' job.

That's exactly what he wanted. Right?

He could keep her safe without any emotional attachment. So why did her rejection hurt so much? He wasn't even going to pick at that particular scab. There was nothing there but pain. Instead, he'd do his job. Tonight that meant he'd stand here, stalking the woman, with one hand on his Sig and the other one clenched in a fist. Probably no one would bother her now, but he was nursing a flame of hope that Dread Head would fuck up so he could shoot him.

The target in question stepped closer to Rori, gathering her into his arms even as she eased up on her toes. He wrapped his hands behind her neck, capturing her flying hair in one. They both smiled just before he kissed her. And kissed her. And kissed her some more. Rori clung to him, touching him, pressing against him from head to toe.

His heart actually broke. The slash of pain took his breath away before rolling over him in waves. Flipping the safety back on the weapon, he slid it into its holster. Rori's voice drifted over him, her throaty words whipped away in the wind. He edged farther into the shadows and closed his eyes.

He was an idiot.

Chapter 12: Innocence Lost

HE WAS GONE. Rori crawled under the blanket with more than just a heavy heart. Her chest hurt, her head ached, her soul wept for the loss of her only friend. She was beaten into nothing again. "Oh, Raine. I hope you find what you're looking for."

She wanted him to be happy, truly. So she'd done nothing to get him to stay. He was a good man. He deserved time to reconnect with his family. She wouldn't hold him back. But that didn't make her feel any better just now. Tucking the pillow against her chest, she let the tears come before slipping into a restless sleep filled with dark angels and fire.

He shimmered into her room, molecules settling into his solid form. He'd been away for too long. He'd been missing her, their little chats, his nighttime visits.

She lay asleep, but restless. She tossed and turned in the grip of a dream. Nightmare? Her breath came in short gasps, her fingers grasped at something only she could see. Time was running short. Her birthday was coming. It would be a very special day for both of them. Until then, though, he'd chip away at her defenses, ease his way inside... by the time he owned her, she'd be thanking him.

He knelt by her side, his black leather boots creaking in the quiet. He touched the side of her face to enter her dreams. The bolt of energy knocked him to his ass. With arms flailing behind him, he landed hard. The power lingered in the dim light, a crackle of bluish electricity that dissipated quickly. His hand stung from the force of it. What the fuck was that? She turned over and mumbled in her sleep, unaffected by the energy exchange.

"What have you been doing?" he hissed. He sent his thoughts to her, willing her to open her dreams again. Nothing. Instead of the usual slide into her subconscious, he saw nothing but a darkness that hadn't been there before. It was like a wall... no, not a wall... a barrier! He tried again. And once more. Nothing. She had blocked him out.

He circled her, using his sight to search for lingering psychic energy. Any residual power would linger. Faint traces tickled at the edge of his mind. No! This wasn't possible! She didn't have the knowledge. She couldn't keep him out! She didn't even believe in him. He stalked across the room and back again. What in the name of Satan had happened since he'd been gone?

"You've been a bad girl, Rori."

He stared down at her, hands clenched at his side, thinking hard. Grabbing her hair, he jerked her around, looking for his mark. It was gone!

Primani!

A vicious stab of pain roused Rori with a cry of protest. Still groggy from sleep, she was confused for a split second before adrenaline jump-started her. He was there! The dark man from her nightmares was there--for real this time. He straddled her waist, hand twisted cruelly in her hair, eyes glowing yellow in the gloom.

"Go ahead and scream, bitch! No one can save you. I'll take what I want now, and then I'll be back for the rest of you when it's time."

"Get off me, you sonofabitch!"

She struggled to shove him off, but he swung his fist into her face. Her thoughts splintered into a thousand fragments. Before she could respond, he hauled her upright and slammed her into the wall. The plaster cracked. She tried to cry out, but he was on her before she could utter another sound. With strength that couldn't possibly be human, he flung her across the room into the window. It shattered from the impact, glass raining everywhere. She sank to the floor, numb.

"Where is your Primani now, Rori? Where is your protector?" he growled softly in her ear. Twisting her chin around, he hissed, "You are mine! Do you understand me?"

The words barely registered in the haze.

"No! I'm mine... only mine. No one owns me..." Her voice trailed off into a whisper.

He slapped her across the face. "Wake up! I'm not done with you yet." He yanked her upright before shoving her onto the futon again. "I've been patient. I've been nice to you."

He held up his hand. She screamed as three inch claws sprouted from each fingertip. She tried to scoot backwards, but he simply grabbed her thigh to hold her still. "But you don't want to play nice."

The claws sunk deep, forcing another cry from her. The yellow snake eyes gleamed when he smiled. A set of fangs dropped over straight white teeth.

"Vampire?!"

"Sorry, but no."

"Then what?" Her words came out as a whisper. The effort sapped her strength.

"Demon."

A cold black wall cracked deep inside of her. "But you don't exist... can't exist..."

He curled a claw around her ear, almost tenderly stroking the delicate skin. "Looks like Father Joseph was right after all. You should've paid better attention during confession."

This isn't happening! Demons don't exist! I'm not evil.

The forgotten mantra tripped and stumbled across her mind as she tried to make sense of it all. The crack widened, red light beginning to seep through as memories came tumbling to the surface after so long in the dark. If demons really exist, then what else was true?

For all those years, Father Joseph had told her it was her fault. He'd told her she was bad, evil... something inside of her would draw the demons. He said she would welcome the touch of evil. She'd prayed he was wrong. God, how she'd prayed till her knees bled! But each week, he heard her confession and damned her. She was a special child; her absolution required sacrifice. Her path to redemption was always the same. When the dreams started, she begged Father Joseph to help her, to save her. She was afraid of the fire, the wings... Surely God was merciful?

He'd said in a voice dripping with sorrow, "You know the sacrifice the Lord requires. Are you ready to make it, my child?"

After months of terrifying nightmares, she'd finally agreed. The nightmares had stopped.

The price had not been worth it.

That wall was now a crumbled pile of debris that didn't slow the rushing memories she'd so painstakingly buried away. Squeezing her eyes closed against the abomination in front of her, she desperately tried to sink into oblivion. But she couldn't drown out the harsh rhythm of his breathing, or his claws tapping the floor beside her head as he waited, enjoying her terror.

They say your life passes in front of your eyes when you die. It's not life that passes--it's a jumble of frantic images that your brain throws up in some kind of psychic defense against the overwhelming terror of the chase and the final certainty when you're trapped without hope of escape. She was about to die.

Every muscle flooded with adrenaline, the constant pulse hurt as it raged through her, demanding *run, run, run*. She'd wished for death many times, but now she didn't want to go. There were reasons to live. Raine's smile winked into her jumbled thoughts. She'd never see him again.

The monster regained her wandering attention by gripping her jaw. "Don't worry. I'm not going to kill you. You and I have a shared destiny."

"No! Don't touch me! Let me go! I'm nothing to you!"

The cruel smile widened as he dragged a claw up her leg to rest in the crease of her groin. With a little more pressure, he popped the skin. He shoved her legs apart with both hands. "Oh, but you mean everything to me. Call your Primani now! They won't come for you!"

With that threat, he lost whatever passed for restraint. His skin disintegrated like a molting snake. The scales underneath reeked of burnt earth, gleamed with black fluid. He arched his back and groaned as the skin sloughed away. Rolling his neck one final time, he ran his black tongue over his fangs and reached for her.

Holy God!

She screamed for help and struggled to crawl away. Snarling at her resistance, he tossed her around like a rag doll, clawing her to shreds before slamming her into the futon and throwing himself on top.

Primani? Primani? What is that? She didn't understand him. The words echoed inside of her head even as she started to shut down. She was in tatters. She was sinking into shock. Primani? Demons? Raine's voice whispered to her now... an angel saved her. Declan? Her vision was red around the edges as he set the walls on fire. The flames slowly licked at the plaster, undulating as they climbed higher.

Fire. Flames.

"Look into my eyes, Rori Austin. I own you. You belong to me. You fight me now, but soon you will have no choice. Your soul belongs to me."

"No... I'm not--" Her protest died in her throat. Evil. *I'm not evil.*

The winged creature crouched over her. Powerful wings spread wide, tips touching the walls. Black as midnight, they filtered the fire's glow. Beautiful... she blinked up at it. Its face was carved from marble with glittering yellow eyes and a cruel slash of a mouth. It smiled down at her, long narrow fangs winking in the orange glow.

Wings.

Rori's scream for help hit Dec like a lightning bolt between the eyes. With a horrified shout to Sean, he dematerialized directly from the patio. A nanosecond later, the two Primani rematerialized inside Rori's apartment. Blood was everywhere, splatters and puddles of it. Glass sparkled across the floor, plaster dust floated like snowflakes in the air. The demon was massive. He turned to face them the second they appeared.

"So the wingless wonders finally showed." He let Rori's head loll to one side and unfolded himself to his full height. "A little late, don't you think?" With an icy stare, he began to retract his claws one at a time.

Click. Click. Click.

Blood dripped from his chin, and he casually wiped it off with the back of his hand before licking it clean.

"Waste not, want not."

"Get away from her!"

Dec started to lunge with his knife, but Sean grabbed his arm. "No! He's too strong for our weapons."

His instincts screamed for action, but he knew Sean was right. Well, let's just do it the old-fashioned way then. How about a little fireball up your ass? It hit the demon in the chest, leaving a smoking hole but not slowing him down. He took a step forward with a grin splitting his face. Sean hit him with another blast which took a chunk of his shoulder out. He stopped smiling.

The demon created a protective barrier with a casual wave of his hand. The next three fireballs bounced off. The fourth, he caught in his fist and hurled back at Sean. Sean dove and rolled out of the way. The small explosion only added to the heat and smoke in the burning room.

He folded his wings into a neat bundle between his shoulders. "Weak Primani. You can try to protect her. But in the end, her soul belongs to me. There's nothing you can do about it. A deal's a deal."

Tick-tock!

With those words ringing inside their minds, he shimmered out.

Sean cursed and followed him. Dec raced to Rori's side. Dropping to his knees, he swallowed the urge to chase the demon himself. Rori was covered with blood. She'd been clawed to ribbons. Shoving his emotions into the bottom of his mind, he went into healer mode and checked for life-threatening wounds. A quick look showed most of the cuts were shallow, except for a large gash in her groin. She was bleeding steadily from a cut in the femoral artery. More a rip than a cut, it was the most pressing wound at that second.

"Will she live?" Killian's voice came quietly behind him.

Dec didn't look up. He sealed the deadly tear before answering. "Too early to tell. I just started looking. My God, Killian, there's so much blood."

Killian studied the scene. The poor woman lying in a puddle of her own blood was tiny, untrained, *defenseless* against a monster like this. The place looked like a bomb had gone off. The demon had obviously lost his ever-loving mind. As he noticed the shattered window and cracked walls, he knew this demon had exploded. Something had set it off, and he had a bad feeling about what that was.

"This place isn't safe. We need to move her to the penthouse." He waved a hand to emphasize the general disaster that was the apartment, and added, "I'll grab what I can and meet you there."

As soon as they rematerialized in the penthouse, Rori's eyes opened a tiny slit. Dec forced a tight smile and said, "You're okay now. I've got you."

Screaming bloody murder, she went berserk. He nearly dropped her in surprise. Before he could say a word, she swung her fists and tried to kick him. He did drop her then. She landed flat on her back. With pupils dilated with blind terror, she tried to scoot away, shrieking, "No! No!"

Every time he tried to touch her to calm her, she screamed even louder, swinging weakly. She was breaking his heart. He tried to reason with her. "Rori! Please calm down. I just want to heal you. You're hurt!"

Her eyelids fluttered as some reason returned. She stared for a minute before shaking her head, the hysteria building again. "No! Don't touch me. You're not human! None of you are human! Keep your filthy hands off of me!"

Killian walked in on a scene he'd never thought he'd see. One of their charges was on the floor, back against the wall, covered in blood, crying her eyes out and shrieking at Dec. Dec? He was the healer--the gentle one, the nice one. He and Sean did most of the killing; Dec did most of the healing. No one *ever* said no to him. He had to blink to be sure he was seeing this right.

"That's enough." He cut her audio so her screams wouldn't bring the police down on them. More softly, he added, "I'm so sorry, baby girl. But you've got to stop screaming."

She closed her mouth but kept crying, eyes darting from one of them to the other, her fear out of control. Huge tears rolled over her swollen cheekbones. She didn't bother to cover her face. She just leaned her head back and wept. Something shifted inside of him, and he shoved a hand through his hair.

He needed Mica. He was way out of his element with this one. Rori was not simply hysterical. She was having some kind of breakdown. She'd drawn her knees to her chest and was beginning to rock back and forth. Damn it. She was heading off a cliff. God only knew it wouldn't be unrealistic after what she'd just been through. He'd go get Mica and bring her back. Before he could bolt, Dec pushed himself to his feet.

Dec said, "Don't. I'll handle her."

"How?"

Dec pulled him off to one side so Rori couldn't hear them. "I know what she needs, brother. I've got this. I need a favor from you though."

He nodded. "Anything."

Once upon a time, Dec had been the sensitive one. The time spent being dead had done things to him, though. Michael didn't only heal him--he'd changed Dec. He'd expanded his healing powers with no explanation. He'd hardened him into a finely-honed weapon. Dec had always been a powerful warrior, but he'd hung on to his innocence, his optimism for millennia. His primary power had always been his ability to heal, to connect with humans on a physical level. He could sense wounds that no one else could. People instinctively trusted him. It was impressive.

The new and improved Dec had added strength that had served him well over the past few years. When Mica had been savagely tortured and killed by a powerful demon, Dec had been devastated, barely able to contain his grief.

Now faced with Rori's mutilated body, he ticked off the list of items with a hard clip to his voice, no sign of the compassion or anger Killian knew were both just under the surface of his control. He was damn proud of him.

"I need the name of that demon. I need a history on her mother. The demon is linked to her mother and her mother's dead. Probably not a coincidence. He kept talking about a deal. 'The clock's ticking', and that kind of bullshit. Deals are usually related to events or significant dates like birthdays. Rori's turning 25 in March. That's only five months from now. We need to track this down and nix the deal before then."

Killian agreed and added, "I'll talk to Raphael too. He's been snooping on his own." He slid a sideways glance at Rori. "She's completely freaked."

"Yeah, well, she just found out demons are real. Her safe house of denial is toast."

"Will you tell her about us?"

Rolling his shoulders to ease the tension, he replied, "Probably, yes. I don't see any other way to get her to trust me. She has to trust me so I can help her."

"And will you let her keep that memory when this is all settled?"

Chapter 13: The Long and Winding Road

"PEEK-A-BOO. I SEE YOU."

The neon orange sun popped out from its hiding place as Dec pulled the Challenger off of the interstate and onto a two-laner deep in the Adirondack Mountains. It winked for a split second before vanishing behind yet another peak. They climbed steadily higher for another couple of miles, playing peek-a-boo with the blob of gas and singing along with Tool's "Sober". He checked the dash clock. Awesome. They were right on schedule. They should be inside before nightfall. He flipped the headlights on as the next curve flung them into a pitch of full night. Another curve brought a slash of blinding sunlight. The next curve threw them back into darkness as they entered a particularly murky stretch of road where a thick canopy of branches loomed overhead. Creepy? Yes, but in a good way. He loved this place! He really appreciated Mother Nature hanging onto her party clothes for a wee bit longer than usual. Rori would love these trees.

Thanks, Mom!

A million shades of red, gold, brown, and the occasional orange, would show their beauty in the warmth of daylight. Fall was one of his favorite seasons to explore the mountains. The curves of the road brought amazing views that the heavy foliage of summer kept hidden. The sparkle of the narrow waterfall they just passed would've been impossible to see through the usual dense greenery. Man, he wished there was time to stop and explore. He knew exactly how the rush of freezing water sounded; how it would feel on his hands if he stopped and cupped them. It had been awhile since he played in these mountains. He missed the earthy smell of rotting leaves, the smoke from campfires, the sweetness of apples stacked up at the farmers' markets. Would he admit to Sean that he liked the smell of apples? Probably not, but there it was.

He slowed waaaay down when the road disintegrated to a gravel lane. His baby wasn't excited about bouncing over the ruts. Shit! That did *not* sound good. Screeching and clunking were not sounds he wanted to hear. They were barely moving at a crawl, but he tapped his brakes for a small herd of deer that decided to hopscotch across the road. Two does stood closely together and were as beautiful as a song. Their eyes seemed to stare right through him for a split second before they ambled by, looking back over their muscular shoulders as they moved in search of another buffet. How long had it been since he'd hung out in a forest? How long had it been since he ran his fingers over the tawny pelt of one of these creatures? In his most humble opinion, it had been entirely too friggin' long. He was overdue for some wildlife. He let the motor idle, in no hurry now. No reason to run Bambi over. He rolled the window down, stuck his head out, and took in a lungful of the fresh air. After consulting the GPS inside his skull, he edged past the last pokey deer.

He glanced at Rori in the rearview mirror. Her silence was unnerving. Her eyes were closed in an unnatural sleep.

No doubt she would be pissed when she woke up, but it couldn't be helped. He'd apologize later. Probably he should dig up some body armor. There was a slight break in the brush line to the left, just after a massive gnarled oak tree. A splash of color drew his eye to the right of the grassy driveway. Perfect. A few remaining blooms of wild pink roses dotted the brush. This was a good sign. Delicate they might be, but they refused to give up, refused to be blown away by the stormy fall weather. They clung to life, filling the air, the world around them, with color and scent.

"Come on, darlin', let's get inside. The light's fading fast, and I'm sure you're ready to stretch your legs." He scooped her into his arms and carried her inside. She didn't protest since she was conveniently still asleep. That was about to change. He was pretty sure she'd protest her ass off in a few minutes. He swallowed with more than a little regret as he thought about her reaction. He prayed she would be cool with his plan.

'Cool' would be awesome… grudgingly accepting would be okay too. Anything other than pissed off and ready to kill him would work at this point. Back in the penthouse, she'd looked at him and Killian like they were monsters. He'd do just about anything to change her mind.

Her face was serene. When she wasn't covered in bruises, she was lovely. Her smile, when she deigned to give him one, was a punch to the gut. Would she ever smile for him again? He smoothed some stray hairs away from her eyes and frowned at the scabbed cuts on her face. Maybe he'd just take care of a few things before disturbing her. Sure, he would be a terrible protector if he didn't make sure they were all safe and secure, right? A few more minutes of rest wouldn't hurt her.

The cabin was a safe house for any Primani with a need. Most of his fellow operatives didn't really like being so far off grid, but he didn't mind. He and Rori would have this place for as long as it took. The cabin had all of the physical security they needed--alarms, cameras, bulletproof windows and walls, perimeter sensors. A redundant generator system would keep the lights on and supply heat if they decided against the fireplace. He checked the alarms and cameras. They were state-of-the-art tech and all working fine. He flipped on the lights and checked the fridge. Killian and Mica had traveled in with some supplies for them. There was enough fresh food to last a week. Mica had even brought two bottles of wine. She was a shameless matchmaker, that girl. The sight of two glasses and a bottle gave him hope, though. Maybe things would work out.

Moving to the bathroom, he checked the water pressure before giving the porcelain throne a couple of flushes. Finally ending his walkthrough in the living room, he checked out the small area. Great, there's firewood ready to go. He lit the kindling with his hand, watching as the tiny splinters caught and smoldered. Once they were stable, he added some bigger pieces of dry wood. Maybe the pretty fire would put Rori in a good mood...

All right, there's only one more place to check out. There was an arsenal of spare weapons and ammo in the basement. He grabbed a flashlight before heading down the steps. As required, someone had been by to rotate the ammo and clean the guns. Wracking his brain for details he might've missed, he used his fingers to add everything up: food, water, power, fuel, weapons. Check, check, check. Perfect. They could live here for months without having to see another person. He was going to need the time for what he had planned. One last thing. He dragged out some sheets--they smelled okay--and made the bed. The king-sized bed was ready for Rori. He'd rack on the couch.

How long had he been standing there staring at the couch? Rori winced in her sleep. He hadn't healed all of her injuries. She'd gone completely ballistic when he'd tried to heal her in the penthouse. He'd managed to heal the most dangerous wounds before she gained consciousness and refused to let him help. She was covered with claw marks, bruises, and probably had some broken bones. She would never understand how lucky she was to be in one piece. Clearly the demon wanted her alive and unbroken for future use. Most vics ended up missing parts they found useful... like their heads!

He and Killian tried to reason with her, but she wasn't hearing them. They backed off for fear she'd have a complete breakdown. Guilt punched him straight in the side of the head now. She looked horrible. Both eyes were swollen and black with bruises. Her skin was peppered with cuts from the window she'd smashed. Most of them were clotted, but he picked up the metallic scent of fresh blood. Some of those clots had been disturbed when he picked her up. She had to be in agony. This was the first time ever he'd purposely chosen not to heal someone. Every instinct screamed to heal her now while she's out cold. Let her be mad later...

Sure, then she'd never trust him again. Or Killian. Or any other Primani. Once lost, trust was nearly impossible to regain. He had to tread very carefully here. She was allowed free will, and her will was clear on this. Crystal! She didn't want his hands anywhere near her. Period. Soooo, he'd brought a nice big first aid kit too.

It would be interesting to watch her stitch herself up.

Sucking in a huge deep breath, he laid his hand on the top of her chest with every intention of waking her, but hesitated. The steady thud of her heart vibrated against his hand, its voice strong and true. It was a beautiful sound. Leaning carefully across, he kissed her forehead, just once. At the touch of his mouth, she visibly relaxed, sliding even deeper into rest, trusting him even in her sleep. Likely *because* she was asleep... Ah, hell. She was dragging him under again. He gave in to his need to touch her and traced the shape of her face with a gentle sweep of his lips. With eyes closed, he could see her laughing again.

"Please don't hate me."

The forest was quiet at this time of day. With sunset only a few minutes away, the critters were settling in for the night. On the bank of a small creek, a fat grey squirrel scolded him because he got too close to its tree. With one last censorious glance over its shoulder, it scampered up the tree and glared down from 20 feet up. He flashed it the peace sign.

"Chill out, furry dude, I'm on your side. Look, I've got a halo and everything!" He let his *saol* seep out of his skin. The little animal leaned down for a closer inspection, nose twitching madly, chattering with questions.

"Told you."

The dusky light was fading into nothing since there was no moon on the horizon. Easily carrying Rori, he worried about her. She was losing all of the weight she'd gained back. Barely 95 pounds now, she was getting dangerously thin. It had been a week, and still she hadn't regained consciousness. She wouldn't wake up, wouldn't respond to him, his touch, his powers. Her eyes had opened and closed a few times, giving him hope that sent him straight to Hell again when she sank back into oblivion. The first few days, he'd done everything to bring her around. He was on the verge of invading her mind and dragging her back out when Raphael had appeared.

Luckily, Raphael had stopped him from taking such drastic measures with a touch on his hand. Looking up in misery, he had asked, "How can I fix this? This isn't right."

Raphael had shaken his head with a frown. "She will come around when she's ready to face the world again. She's been damaged very badly, Declan. The hurt she feels is more than you can heal with a quick smile and kind words."

He had mulled that over and finally said, "I'm what she needs. Isn't that true? Something about this feels predestined to me. It somehow feels right."

"Don't let your ego give you direction. Understand that this woman is caught in more than she knows, more than she's ever imagined. Her life was hard... impossible before. Now her reality is nothing as it seemed, her memories are tainted with questions, and her heart is shattered."

With concern shining in his eyes, he placed his palm over Dec's heart. "Do you think we brought you back only to kill demons? This may truly be your biggest challenge; your biggest mission yet. This woman, this tiny, fragile woman, has a purpose. She's necessary. *You* will heal her." He paused for a breath after the intense speech. "And you will do it alone, listening to the forest, and guided by the beat of your own heart."

He faced his maker with a renewed sense of awe. Raphael's touch filled him with purpose, a sense of direction. It gave him strength to do the impossible. He was unbelievably blessed. Dipping his head, he tapped his chest twice in acquiescence. He would do anything for this archangel, his maker. He'd done many things in their past, but now he knew he'd give anything, do anything. That's what you did for someone you loved, right?

Raphael had given him a few minutes to process his orders before crossing to Rori's prone body. With his usual fluid motion, he rested his cheek against hers. After a second, he stood and said, "There's something about the demon that she knows but has been blocking... for a very long time. She's trying to shut everything out to protect herself because she's terrified, but she's vulnerable to you. Tread gently, my son, and she will come around."

He stopped in the center of a trail to pick a direction. Left looked good. The last thing he wanted to do was go trail blazing through the brush with Rori in his arms. Probably she'd be unimpressed with branches slapping her in the face.

"No scenic route today, love. Lucky for you, I'm a considerate sort of guy."

Speaking of slapping… He tucked the loose end of the blanket between them to keep it from flapping around and hitting her in the face. Every time it did, she wrinkled her nose, and he tried not to laugh. When this was over, he was going to rent "Weekend at Bernie's" again. Before moving on, he pressed a chaste kiss on the tip of her nose and frowned for the millionth time this week. Rori. When will you come back to me?

"I miss you like crazy."

By now most of the tiny wounds had healed on their own. She had tiny scars dotting most of her body, but they would fade with time. He'd resorted to stitching up the larger wounds without magic. She wouldn't be happy with the scars, but hell, she'd ordered him not to heal her. He would argue that she'd healed herself--totally natural like. All he did was give her first aid, right? She couldn't be mad about that. He washed out her wounds, dressed them with salve and bandages. Shot her full of antibiotics via her glutes. Stitched up the bad wounds; even gave her a sponge bath without peeking. Lastly, he'd wrapped her up in a robe that Killian had brought with a bag of Mica's things. He'd done everything possible to ease her mind… to comfort her.

And still she refused to respond. Well, it was her call, after all. She'd come back to him when she was ready. He knew it in his heart. He sensed it with his mind and every nerve in his body. She was in there, hanging on, holding on…

He'd be right here.

He chose the right fork to explore more deeply into the forest. Stopping near a small creek, he planted his butt on a downed tree and settled her against his lap. She fit perfectly in the curve of his arms, if he did say so himself.

The forest was silent around them. The dayshift critters were tucking in their babies for the night while the nightshift was clocking in. He shivered in a sudden gust of wind. With any luck, the skunks would hang out someplace else tonight. Even though he'd forgiven them for the, uh, *misunderstanding* on Saturday, he wasn't ready to forget about it. How the hell he was supposed to explain skunk spray to his comatose patient, he had no idea. She didn't fully appreciate his powers. Finding a bathtub full of tomato juice at 2:00 in the morning isn't hard if you can *teleport*. He sniffed her hair and grinned. Still smelled like spaghetti. Good thing he liked Italian. The little bastards were lucky he didn't make coats out of them. Yeah, that was one story he was never telling Rori. Probably, she'd kill him.

Was he weird for digging the smell of rotting leaves? He didn't think so, but maybe he was a wee bit weird for holding a mental conversation about it... It would snow soon. God, he hoped she'd wake up for that. He wanted to share the first fat flakes with her. He wanted to *talk* to her. All of this peace and quiet was making him mental. His brain was running in a thousand directions. He really missed conversation.

"So, darlin', here we are again. Can you smell the woods? It smells like fall. I know you'll love it when you wake up. I don't know if you can hear me or not, but I can't stand to think of you drowning inside your own head with no one to anchor you. I'm your anchor, Rori." He stroked the curve of her jaw, leaning down to whisper in her ear, "Follow my voice. Let me pull you back. Follow me."

She sighed but showed no signs that she'd heard him. He tucked the tips of her ears under the purple cap he'd pressed over her head. She was beyond adorable, and he couldn't stop the smile that snuck over his face. If only she was willing…

"Yesterday I promised to tell you more about my childhood. You know you should feel pretty honored to hear this story. You're the first human I've told. Mica'd be pissed if she knew. Oh, she knows I was born in 426-ish, but I've never given her the whole sordid tale. Obviously I think a lot of you, but don't let that go to your head."

Probably Rori couldn't hear a word he said. Probably wouldn't remember any of this, either. He kind of hoped she didn't. It wasn't a pretty sort of story, if truth be told.

Settling into bard mode, he began with, "Once upon a time, when I was ten or so, my mother took me to another village to visit my cousins. Back then, the villages were pretty small, nothing like the towns and cities we have now. Anyhow, we climbed up on the family donkey and went on this grand adventure. Keep in mind the time I lived in. Back then, people didn't go wandering about just for fun. You stayed put and lived your life one day at a time. I was ten years old and hadn't ever been to another village!"

He paused to picture the softness of his mother's face. She promised him and his little sister a treat if they'd hurry up and get ready to go. She wanted to get back before dark, and they'd been cranky at being dragged from sleep before dawn. He'd long since given up on wishing he could change what had happened that day. Life taught him there was no going back, no way to right those wrongs, no way to bring the dead back to life. Oh, he'd tried over the years… until one day Raphael had given him other options.

But that was another story for another day.

"The day was bright, sunny, and full of promise. I was so excited I wouldn't stop babbling. My mother was so unbelievably patient with me. I was always talking, always asking questions, nosy and goofy. I was a happy kid." He flashed an exaggerated toothy smile that stretched his whole face. She couldn't see his gesture, but he was in storytelling mode. Drama was called for here.

"Okay, so I'm smiling like an idiot right now. It would be cool if you'd throw me a bone and laugh at me." He waited a beat before adding, "Nothing? Wow. Tough crowd."

"So I helped my little sister, Brigid, onto the donkey and led the way as the young man of the house should do. Brigid was a tiny little thing, barely three years old then. Named for the goddess, she was... she was a sweet, sweet, child. The sun rose and set on her pretty dark head. She was dark where I was light, you see. My father always joked she wasn't his, but he didn't mean it. He treated her like a princess. We all did. She was special."

It seemed like yesterday. Brigid. Big blue eyes, hair as black as a raven's wing... innocent smile, deep dimples in her chubby cheeks... he swallowed hard and sighed. She was tiny, defenseless, just a toddler. Just a baby...

A rustle in the dry leaves caught his attention, pulling him from the dark memories he'd kept buried for over a thousand years. It was only an opossum digging for dinner. Nothing to worry about there.

Nothing to worry about, true, but his mood was turning south. Time to head home.

"To be continued."

The next morning dawned cold and grey. Wind rattled the window frame every few minutes and whistled over the chimney. Probably wasn't the best weather for a miracle, but he'd take whatever he could get. He was easy that way. Shivering with the abrupt temperature change, he stepped out of the glass shower with a towel in his hand and a grimace on his face. The hot water tank left a lot to be desired. He dreamed of a much longer shower. He bent to rub the water out of his hair and snapped upright again, listening for anything that shouldn't be there. The cabin was quiet as a tomb. It was making him jumpy. He needed some noise, something to break up the quiet. He'd been talking to himself again. God, he hoped she didn't wake up when he was in the middle of that! He cracked the bedroom door. Maybe today would be the day? She was lying on her back, hands tucked under the covers, exactly as he left her the night before. Naked and dripping, he squatted beside her.

"Good morning, sweet girl. I'm in the mood for a miracle. What do you say you hook me up? We're going hiking again, and it's cold as a witch's tit out there. Maybe that'll wake you up?"

No response. No surprise.

He pumped out a couple hundred pushups and sit ups before dragging on his favorite jeans and a navy thermal shirt that he left open at the throat. Socks and beloved leather boots completed his look. He ran a comb through the tangles of his hair before shaking it out so it could just fall however it wanted. Deciding it was too cold to shave, he left the two days growth alone. After all, no one was checking him out, were they?

Now came the fun part. Rori. He wanted her to wake up more than anything, but he really hoped it wouldn't happen when he was taking her clothes off. That would be, um, awkward. He sang "Sex on Fire" while undressing her as quickly as possible. Not going to look, not going to look. Every day he made that promise… right before he broke it. He had such good intentions, but hell, he was a man. Bare breasts were a work of art. Hers were masterpieces--small and round--perky with pale rose nipples. If he wanted to torture himself, he'd close his eyes and conjure up the memory of his hands cupping those soft mounds that day he'd kissed her last summer. That sort of memory made bad things happen inside his pants.

"Not looking. Not looking," he murmured under his breath.

Damn. Her nipples were hard in the chilly air, practically begging him to bend over and warm them with his mouth.

Instead of helping her out, he grumbled, "I am Iron Man," and hummed a few bars of the song.

Mental note: Call Mica for a bra.

And maybe a chastity belt.

Just to be sure she hadn't sprouted any malignant tumors since yesterday, he ran his eyes down her belly to the concave playground right above her...

"Nope, no tumors. That's a relief. Good to check, though. Just to be sure." She was beautiful all the way down. He gently lifted her knees to slip on clean panties and a pair of heavy sweatpants. They were too big for her, but they'd keep her warm. After slipping her arms into a sweater, he wiped her face and brushed her hair.

"Come on, love. Let's commune with Mother Nature before she gets bitchy."

The wind had died down a bit by the time he'd trudged through the heavy leaf cover and found the granite niche he was hunting for. The last Ice Age had conveniently scattered massive chunks of granite all over the region. Time and Mother Earth herself manipulated them into interesting works of art and the occasional handy cave. He'd found this spot two days ago and couldn't wait to explore. Directing energy into the palm of one hand, he used it as a flashlight to check out the interior. The front opening was a good six feet across with the back wall only sitting about four feet deep. Not really a cave; more of an alcove created when these house-sized boulders tumbled like dominos. Perfect. It just happened to overlook a creek that had several downed trees spanning across in a natural bridge. The crystal clear water gurgled and hissed as it bounced over the rocks that littered the bed. A grassy clearing was visible to the right, and he crossed his fingers for some deer to show up. After spreading a thick blanket on the ground, he propped Rori into a comfortable sitting position against the wall. A sudden sense of rightness tingled down his spine. Leaning in, he thumbed the feathery softness of her eyelashes as they swept across her cheekbone. He dropped his lips to her temple and sent his thoughts to her.

Follow my voice, Rori. Come on baby girl, follow my voice. I miss you.

He nearly lost his balance when she murmured in response. She stiffened before going limp once more.

Chafing her hands between his, he felt hope for the first time in days. "That's it. Follow the sound of my voice. I'm your anchor. Reach for me! I can protect you. The demon will have to go through me to get to you, and I won't let him do that."

No response.

I'm your anchor. Reach for me!

He squeezed her hands one last time before letting them go. It was back to square one. There was, however, a tingle of recognition this time. He saw the spark of Rori's soul glimmering inside of her. It would be soon.

After wedging himself behind her, he settled her between his legs, caging her with his arms so she would stay warm. Cranking up his inner thermostat, he cocooned her in the warmth before resting his cheek against her hair.

"Stubborn wench."

A grey squirrel hopped across one of the makeshift bridges, nose twitching, ears cocked. Unafraid, he ventured closer until he was a dozen feet or so in front of their resting place. It stopped and stood on its hind legs, eyes flicking between them and the grassy clearing.

"Lose your nuts?" He tossed a chunk of apple from his pocket. It bounced a few times before rolling to a stop in a clump of dead leaves. The squirrel crept towards it, stopping every few inches to check for booby traps, tail twitching back and forth.

"What? You don't trust me?"

After a bit more creeping and a lot more staring, his stomach got the best of him. Rushing the last few steps, he snatched up the fruit, sniffed, and took a nibble. He closed his beady eyes in bliss before taking off like a rocket. Huh. Animals were a trip.

"It's going to rain today, so we have to make this quick. I'll tell you the next chapter of my life story before we head back. I don't want you to get wet." That would be bad. She could catch a cold... he couldn't have that, could he? He'd be forced by common decency to take steps to keep her from getting sick.

His imagination drummed up a tasty scene showing him stripping her naked and laying her gently into a steaming hot bath. Her hair would be piled on the top of her head, curling tendrils lying against the smooth skin of her nape... those cat's eyes of hers warming with passion. They'd darken for him when he slid into the water, lifting her over him, onto him...

What the hell was he thinking? No! She was absolutely NOT getting a bath. She'd better wake up soon, or she'd be crusty dirty. He'd given her a couple of sponge baths so she'd be comfortable and her wounds wouldn't get infected. The wounds were mostly healed now, leaving him fresh out of valid excuses. He'd never touch her while she was in a coma, for God's sake. He wasn't a pig. But that didn't mean he could stop his imagination from spinning out of control. He couldn't help getting aroused. If she was any other female, it'd be easier to deal with. He'd just shut his sex drive off for the time being and finish the job. Piece of cake.

Not so with Rori. The longer he held her, the more pieces of the universe dropped into place around him. Even asleep, she brightened his existence. Cheesy? Maybe. But there it was. There'd been a twinge of connection the moment he'd healed her the first time. Barely there, the sense of awareness had almost slipped his notice. He chalked it up to her latent psychic abilities. They acted as a silent bell that rang for Primani to hear. He'd definitely heard that bell, but shrugged it off. He was beginning to realize there was more going on than he'd ever dreamed. Their connection was being woven more tightly every day. The strands of their lives were being pulled inward, drawing them together, drawing them towards an end that would be a true beginning. He sensed it when she'd been dreaming at the penthouse. Dreams of flames and black demons... dreams that he was caught in, dark visions he understood all too well. The window, the shattered glass... those wings. Her nightmare, his life.

Her retrocognition was another thread. He knew it in his gut. She'd seen Gary Carmichael's spirit, calling to her from the past. Woodstock. She didn't understand the little boy's importance, but he did. He and Sean had been working this case for decades, but the trail was ice cold. The boy's remains were never recovered. His mother died a few years later under odd circumstances, too. The official autopsy report listed the cause of death as a drug overdose. Hell, it was the 70s... Everyone did drugs, right? The police didn't do much digging into it, and there was no family left to press for an investigation. He never believed the autopsy was right, but they didn't have permission to stay on the case. Because of this, her death haunted him for years. Still did, if he was honest. Now they had a lead: Father Joseph.

Thanks to Rori.

Everything about her fit him perfectly. Her energy called him in a way he'd never experienced before. She made him hum from head to toe. His blood raced every time he kissed her, touched her, just friggin' leaned against her... it wasn't lust, wasn't just sexual. He wanted to hold her, protect her, love her. Wait! Hold up. Where did that come from? Closing his eyes, he grimaced at the crazy idea. Love? Ah, hell. This wasn't part of the plan. He opened his eyes and groaned out loud. He was so screwed.

A flicker of motion interrupted his inner monologue. What he saw took his breath away. One day he would swear this was the defining moment of his entire existence. It was the one moment when he knew without any doubts whatsoever that he was doing the right thing. He was in the right place, the *exact* place he needed to be at that precise second of time. Every thought in his mind? Validated. Every feeling in his heart? Validated.

Terrified it would disappear if he moved too quickly, he pressed Rori's fingers to his mouth, kissing them hard. Raising her chin so she could see too, he whispered urgently, "Look!"

Directly in front of them, a sunbeam pierced the canopy of branches before plunging straight into the creek. The playful spray refracted the white light like a prism, separating it into clearly defined rays of brilliant colors. The effect was a rainbow exploding at their feet. Every creature in the forest stilled. Not a single sound distracted from the beautiful sight.

The finger of God...

Even the massive trees bent ahead of the storm. Their leaves clung desperately before being ripped away by the howling gale. Bruised clouds tumbled and surged across the heavens, their energy gathering, building into something more terrible, more destructive than Mother Nature herself could imagine. Lightning knifed across the churning mass before stabbing the earth below.

All of God's creatures bolted for the safety of dens and caves. They knew better than to stay in the open. None thought to risk the onslaught, opting for survival instead, except for one.

Rori huddled behind a rock. She crouched low, shivering in the cold, wishing for the nightmare to end. She'd traveled these woods for countless days and nights without food, without sleep, without a compass. Lost. Exhausted. Starving.

She had no idea what was going on. How had she gotten here? Was she asleep? Was she even alive? Maybe this was purgatory? She couldn't escape the constant stream of images that bombarded her day and night. Were they dreams? Memories? Her subconscious sorting out the last minutes of her life? She didn't know, didn't understand any of this. So she ran, and ran, and ran.

Pursued by the demon, she never saw its face, never touched its body. Like a shadow, it followed her, filling her with panic, terror.

"Leave me alone!" she screamed over her shoulder every day.

"You're mine. Mine! Run now. Run fast. But in the end, you will welcome me." The demon's velvety voice made her skin crawl, made her nauseous, even worse, sent arousal curling through her veins.

Relentless, it came for her until she crawled on her knees, desperate to escape its call, too exhausted to run. As the daylight in her dream faded, she'd collapse, waiting for the claws to rip her apart again.

But it didn't attack.

Each sunrise she'd wake up to find it standing over her wherever she'd fallen asleep.

"Say yes, Rori," he demanded every dawn.

Every day, she scrambled to her feet and ran until her body gave out. The forest surprised her with hiding places at the most unexpected times. They simply showed up when she needed one. She threw herself behind the boulders or massive trees, crouching and panting like a terrified rabbit.

Danger was everywhere. She wasn't safe. *She wasn't safe*. The demon was always there. Her heart beat like a jackhammer in her chest making it impossible to hear footsteps. She closed her eyes, refusing to cry, willing her damn heart to settle down so she could rest. One day she heard him.

Follow my voice.

The command was faint, distant, but she heard it clearly. The words lingered inside her mind. She'd sat up, straining to hear them. The voice was gone. The next morning, she woke to the shadow and the demon's demand. Sprinting into the trees again, she prayed, chanted really, "I'm here. I'm here. I'm here." She ran blindly, but this time she saw his face in her mind's eye. Blue eyes, curved lips. Worried frown.

Declan!

Follow my voice, Rori. Come on baby girl, follow my voice. I miss you.

"Dec! I'm here! I can't get out! I can't get out!" she cried out between gasps of breath. "Where are you?"

Spinning around, she peered intently into the shadows. The foliage was dense, pressing in from all sides as she frantically searched for him. She saw nothing in her nightmare. Nothing different from any other day… storm clouds, dark forest, chattering birds… Wait! That was new. Birds?

I'm your anchor. Reach for me!

"I'm trying! Oh God, Dec! Where are you? Help me! Help me!"

Lightning struck the ground in front of her, sprawling her flat on her back, stunned by the force. Squinting against the blinding light, she barely noticed the weight of the shadow settling over her.

Look!

Dec's command rang louder than the clap of thunder that echoed in the mountains. The shadow froze in mid-stride.

A brilliant prism speared the ground, widening to form a wall between her and the demon. She threw her hands over her eyes as the light sucked her in.

Rori snapped upright like she'd been electrocuted. Her breath came out in a harsh gasp as she swallowed a scream. He nearly jumped out of his skin.

"Rori!"

She tumbled out of his arms, landing on her elbows and staring in horror.

Her terror rapidly evaporated when she realized who he was. Dragging her into his arms, he held her hard enough to leave bruises. She clung, weeping all over his chest while he stroked her hair and dropped kisses on the top of her head.

"Oh, thank God! You found me."

The clouds shifted to diffuse the rainbow into natural white light. The vibrant colors were gone, but the sensation of glorious peace remained strong. He would never be certain, but he thought he heard a soft chuckle drifting on the wind.

As her tears slowed, he held her even tighter. He wasn't taking any chances with this one. No one was ripping her out of his arms. She wrapped her arms around him, pulling him closer, and his heart settled into a happy beat. All was right in the world.

She finally gazed into his eyes, searching, probing. "Are you an angel?"

He couldn't look away from the question. She had a huge tear dangling from her lashes…

"You're back from a coma, and that's your first thought? You haven't eaten in over a week. Aren't you hungry? Thirsty? Itchy?"

Still groggy, she gnawed her lower lip before wagging her head to clear it. "You saved me." She reached out, cupping his cheek in her palm, closing her eyes. As she caressed him, every layer of armor fell away. Clink. Clink. Clink. She left him with no place to hide. Exposed. Naked.

Moving carefully so he wouldn't startle her, he pulled the shirt over his head. Turning to the side, he dropped his eyes over his shoulder. At his nod, she reached for him. Slowly, softly, she explored him with feathery strokes that tickled yet sent his blood racing.

"Go ahead, darlin'. Look. Touch. Find your answers."

Rori was treading on shaky ground, she knew that. He was beautiful. Perfect. His face was like a painting, a sculpture. The hard planes could seem cruel, but right now were softened by his emotions. Love? Patience? She didn't know, but she knew one thing for sure. He wasn't trying to hide now. He'd taken his shirt off, and she'd lost the use of her vocal chords. He was beautifully made; muscular without being massively huge, golden skin that begged for kisses... he turned so she could see him, and she froze. What would she do if he had wings sprouting from his shoulders?

"No wings?"

Grinning like a naughty little boy, he shook his head. "Sorry. No wings." He captured her roaming hand and kissed it. "I have other mad skills though if you'd like me to demonstrate. For instance, I can make you hot."

He placed her hands on his shoulders and busted out laughing when she snatched them back with a horrified gasp. What the hell? He was glowing! The harder he laughed, the more obvious the light became. She was trying to put some distance between them, but he wouldn't let her. Instead, he reclaimed her hands and forced them flat against his chest.

He scolded, "Uh-uh. You wanted answers. Man up and get them. The light is my *saol*. It's our life force, technically. You might consider it the source of my powers. You have one too; but yours isn't strong like mine is. Yours is human." The teasing smile vanished. "Mine isn't. Anymore."

He wasn't human? This was getting better and better! She seriously needed to put some space between them. She couldn't think straight.

He pressed her hand harder against his chest. "Do you feel that? That's my heart beating just like yours does. Don't be afraid of me, Rori. I'm here to protect you. It's what I do. I tried to tell you that before, but you didn't want to trust me then. Do you trust me now?"

That was a good question. Did she?

She studied the trees in the distance while she considered her answer. After all of the crazy things that had happened in the past few months, she had to admit he'd been there for her without asking for payment. Strangely enough, she didn't think he was insane anymore. "I do."

"I'm sensing a 'but'."

He was really, really hard to resist. She brushed his bangs back from his eyes. His mouth curled into a lopsided, sexy as all hell grin. The impact slammed all the way to her toes.

"You could melt butter with that smile. How do we mere mortals resist you?"

Flushing an adorable shade of pink, he choked on his snappy comeback before clamping his lips together in a line. Was he embarrassed? How cute was that? Grumbling under his breath, he reached for his shirt, and she shocked them both by stopping him.

"Wait! I want to look at you." Did I say that out loud? Crap.

He shot her an incredulous look before dropping the shirt and pushing gracefully to his feet. He moved so fast she scooted backwards with a girly cry of alarm. The grin he wore this time was all heat, no humor. Slow, sexy...

forget butter, her entire body might combust. Before she could squeak out a protest, he unsnapped his jeans and dropped them in a pile. Kicking out of them in a movement that was so smoothly done he must've practiced it, he hauled her upright with her mouth hanging open.

Not an ounce of material in sight.

"Uh... uh, Dec... I'm not sure--" She kept her eyes pasted on his chest. His muscles were nicely shaped, hard, tanned... flat nipples begged for a kiss.

Oh, yeah, he certainly looked human!

He stood in full naked glory, daring her to look lower. He gave her that sexy grin again. She backed up. He stalked forward until her back came up against the granite boulder. His bare chest brushed her breasts. Something hot and velvety brushed her belly. With her heartbeat pounding in her ears, she swallowed hard and placed her hands on his forearms. Stopping him from moving forward? Keeping him from moving backwards? The hard muscle blazed at her touch. He had fine golden hair dusting across skin that she couldn't resist caressing. Soft...

"Admit it. You wanted to know if I had all the correct equipment." He was teasing her. She could tell by the humor in his voice, but he was so right. At that moment, she wanted to look down more than anything in the world.

He turned around and said over his shoulder, "I've been told I have a nice ass. What do you think?"

"Dec! You're horrible! I am *not* looking at your ass!" But she couldn't resist bursting into giggles at the lift of his eyebrows.

"Are you sure? I can stand here all day."

"I'm sure you can." A wistful sigh slipped out when she snagged a peek at his butt. Yum!

He was beside her so fast he was a blur. Lifting her chin, he winked before dropping a sweet kiss on her open mouth. "Don't be so obvious. There's time for us to get naked and hump like bunnies later. Right now, you need to recover your strength so you can keep up."

With that he stepped into his jeans while she focused on his hands. Capable. Smooth. Hard. Those hands had nursed her, held her. How would they feel making love to her?

Chapter 14: Snow Angels at Play

"I CAN'T BELIEVE YOU STITCHED ME UP." She studied her fresh scars with a critical eye. The stitches had been evenly spaced and small. The scars would fade into flat, silvery lines eventually. "You did an amazing job. Where did you learn to do that?"

He gave her an absent glance and answered with a frown, "Oh, I learned to stitch wounds from a Chinese Primani about a thousand years ago. His name was Tsang Tso."

Something was bothering him. For the past few hours, he'd been distracted. She'd asked a ton of questions, trying to get caught up on what she'd missed. He'd answered her, but seemed to be lost in his own thoughts. And he was fiddling with that guitar pick again. The tortoise shell triangle seemed to be a part of his hand. He passed it over and under his fingers when he was thinking, tapped it on any hard surface if he was feeling impatient, and occasionally used it to actually pick out a song on his guitar. At the moment, he was sprawled across one of the recliners in the living room, one knee looped over the arm, combat boot bouncing to the slow beat he was creating in his head.

"Really? There are more Primani? How many are there?"

"Oh, not too many. A few hundred of us at the most. We've got small ops cells set up over all major population zones, keeping things in balance."

Switching the sexy musician hat for the lovable bard hat, he sat up a little straighter and got into storytelling mode. In the past few days, she'd seen him change personas one right after another. He could also be 'bossy doctor,' 'scary bodyguard,' and 'adorable playmate.' He was a man of many faces. She wasn't sure which one she was falling in love with, but the slide was happening every time her eyes met his. There was something between them… a spark, a connection. It was more than attraction. Her heart warmed the second he spoke to her. She got all fluttery and mushy inside. It was a little disconcerting. Even more alarming, every time he touched her, she had to fight the urge to throw him to the floor and screw his brains out.

Damn. She was really, really glad he couldn't read her mind.

After adding some more wood to the dying fire, he settled beside her on the leather couch. With one arm carelessly draped around her, he said, "You smell amazing. Too clean, I think. Maybe I need to dirty you up?" He dragged those finely-shaped fingers of his down the side of her face and under her jaw. "Are you purring? Really? How long has it been since you had a proper shagging?"

She snorted a laugh before chastising him in her most prim and proper tone, "A lady doesn't talk about such things. Shame on you, sir!"

Before she could say another word, he caught her mouth with his and all thoughts of bantering flew out the window.

He hadn't planned on kissing her just then, but damn, she was beautiful. Laughing up at him, eyes glowing with joy, a rosy flush on her cheeks... he couldn't resist the impulse to taste her. The second he touched her, he wanted more. She slipped her tongue around his, and something inside went up in flames. Gentle. Gentle. Don't rush. Don't scare her...

He trapped her face between his palms, holding her mouth against his, taking his time, feeling every part of her mouth. She was so soft, sweet, like honey... Her lips, her tongue, the tiny indention in her lower lip...

"Dec!"

The banging on the front door rattled the hardware. "Dec? I know you're here. The car's out front. Come on, man, open up. I've got news."

He dropped his head onto Rori's chest with a groan. His vision was blurry; his heart pounded like a racehorse. He didn't think he could move just yet. "I hate him."

Rori, bless her heart, just fizzed with half-smothered giggles before finally breaking into an astonished grin.

The banging continued. Idiot. He yelled, "Stop pounding! I'll be right there." To Rori, he asked, "What?"

"I think I just came."

"Without me? How could you? Selfish wench." He sniffed the air and sighed long and hard. Yep, those last involuntary twitches gave it away.

The story of his life.

"Rain check, baby?" He resisted the instinct to slide his hand between them and smear her scent all over his body. Maybe he could beat his chest and roar while he was at it. Probably this wasn't a good idea with Sean standing on the porch.

"No guarantees. You're cute though. I'll keep you in mind."

"Now that's just mean." He tugged his shirt over his melon and passed her sweater to her. How they'd come off, he had no idea. Apparently he'd been blinded by lust. He couldn't help staring as the last creamy curve of breast was smothered under the heavy material. Damn. They had the worst timing.

Friggin' Sean. There were some days when he'd happily strangle him, partner or not. Sean was long gone now, but he was still annoyed. Sean reported a few interesting things so that made up for the cold shower. Raine was gone. He'd left the city with all of his stuff. It didn't seem like he'd be coming back. Dec wasn't *un*-happy about this. This Raine guy was honorable and worthy of the new lease on life he'd been handed. He wouldn't ever regret making that decision. Raine earned it so he got it. Period. Dot. End of story. He sincerely hoped Raine would find his family and settle down some place nice. This 'some place nice' should be on the other side of the country if he wanted to enjoy it. Bottom line, it would be healthier if he never came back to see Rori again.

He was beginning to be a little... territorial about his damsel. He'd be damned if he'd let that friggin' Dread Head waltz in and sweep her away again.

Oh, hell, no. Not happening.

"Why the evil eye?" Rori elbowed him as she slipped into a pretty good imitation of his scowl. Her ability to imitate people was a cool surprise. It was yet another thing he loved about her.

Was he that obvious? Rearranging his mouth into a smile, he tugged her up the trail behind him. It wound upward, turning into nearly vertical stone stairways that were awkward to navigate. Both were quiet as they picked their way over the odd sized rocks that made walking more than three steps impossible. Rori was breathing hard behind him so he slowed his pace to let her catch up. Even though her cheeks were windblown and her lungs had to be screaming, she didn't whine. No, she kept her eyes on the ground, carefully evaluating the rocks and selecting the most stable ones to step on.

"Are you doing okay?"

Without missing a step, she replied, "Sure! This is awesome! Just don't want to break an ankle so I'm taking my time."

That's my girl! She was stronger than she ever thought she was. There would be no babying her after today. It was time for her to grab her destiny with both hands.

The trail disappeared once they reached the top of the small mountain they'd been circling. Thousands of years of wind and rain had scraped it to a bald granite dome. To get to the actual summit, they needed to scale an eight-foot chunk of rock that jutted crookedly from the ground. Hefting himself easily to the top, he leaned over the side with his hand held out. "Take my hand. You've got to see this view!"

After hauling her up, he gestured at a jagged peak in the distance. Storm clouds hovered around part of it, making it appear more sinister than it really was. "See that? We're going to snowboard down the side of that gorgeous hunk of rock. You and me, sweetheart."

"Say what?"

"Don't look so shocked! If I can do it, you can do it!" With a sweep of his hand, he declared, "Today you climbed a mountain. This is the first step to the rest of your life. This is what you've been missing, what you crave: Peace. It's what you need."

She gazed at him like he'd lost his mind.

He threw back his head to laugh, the sound whipping away with the wind. "Welcome to your life, Rori Austin! It is guaranteed to be one hell of an adventure, with some life-threatening moments tossed in just to keep you on your toes. But in the end, you will have the peace you crave." He bowed over her hand, "My name is Declan, and I'll be your official tour guide and sex toy if you'll have me."

She stomped down a sudden wave of dizziness that smacked her between the eyes when Dec practically launched her over the top of the big-ass rock. Clutching his arm for an extra second or so, she drank it in. Wow! This was the most beautiful sight she'd ever seen. Even with heavy clouds filtering the sunlight, the mountains were heavenly. It was like standing in the middle of the universe. There was nothing for as far as she could see. Nothing but trees and rocks and the occasional black ribbon of highway... There were no buildings, no telephone lines, no people. Not even a bird chirped up here.

Her calves ached. Her lips were frozen numb. Her eyes were drying out. She closed them and let her mind drift, soaking in the sound of the wind, the sharp pine scent... the feel of his hand wrapped around hers.

Heaven.

All of her life she'd searched for this, ached for it, *longed* for it. In and out of foster homes, she'd been surrounded by people, yet always alone, always so lonely. Haunted by a childhood she didn't ask for, never understood, and couldn't run away from... she stood in the grip of a man who wasn't even human. This *man* promised her answers, promised her safety, promised her freedom from fear. Who was she to deserve such a blessing?

"Do you believe in a higher love?" he asked, voice hushed, mouth grazing the curve of her ear.

Seconds ticked like hours as she stared without seeing. Such a simple question, but she wasn't sure of her answer. Did she?

The answer came as a surprise to her, but he deserved to hear it.

"I believe in you."

His plan was working. After she'd woken up, Rori had bloomed like an orchid--slowly, carefully, one day at a time, she filled out; she got her color back, became stronger and more confident. Any day now, her bud was just about to pop.

Okay, so that sounded a little gross, even inside his head. Maybe 'popping' wasn't the right word... she was very slowly blooming into a rare and beautiful flower with every beat of her heart. That sounded better.

"What are you grinning at? You look pretty satisfied over there. It's dinner, not an art project."

He tossed her the radish he'd been fiddling with. "What do you think?"

She studied it with great interest before answering, "Is it a dog?"

"You never told me you were blind. That explains a lot." Snatching it back with an injured air, he joked, "It's a heart!"

Before he could stop her, she plucked it from him and popped it into her mouth. Around the crunching, she mumbled, "Yeah, I totally see that. A perfect heart."

"Everybody's a comedian. Sure, laugh now. Someday I'll be a world famous vegetable sculptor, and I'll pretend I don't know you."

Rori thought she had finally perfected the single brow lift and displayed it now. Some people, like Sean, could pull this off, looking very cool when they did it. Rori wasn't that coordinated. When she did it, the other brow crinkled off to the side, giving her a mental patient sort of look. It was pretty friggin' adorable. No way was he telling her she looked ridiculous. She shot him that look and he burst into laughter.

Dinner was hands down the best meal she'd had in years. Everything was simple but delicious. Between them they managed to pan sear some strip steaks, toss a salad, and throw a couple of potatoes in the oven. Once the steaks were a memory, they lingered at the table, sipping the last of the cabernet. She was pleasantly buzzed after finishing two glasses. Her tour guide had gotten more and more thoughtful as they ate. The silence was comfortable though, as if they'd known each other for years. It was nice sitting here with Dec. She was on the verge of clearing the table when he drained his glass and sat it down with a clink. Startled by the sound, she caught his gaze resting on her face.

"Why are you staring? You know that makes me nervous. When I'm nervous, I babble. Do you really want to put us both through that?"

Snapping out of his thoughts, he said, "We need to talk. I wanted to wait until you were stronger, and I think you are now. It's important, Rori."

Poof! And there goes her buzz...

"You look so serious. What's wrong?" She glanced automatically at the window as if monsters were about to climb inside.

He could've kicked himself when her expression flipped to panic. Crap. He was such a moron around her. Trying to backtrack, he took her hands and said, "There's no one here. Don't worry. Come on, let's go for a walk. It's starting to snow!"

"Seriously?" Racing to the door, she jerked it open and caught her breath. "Oh! Look at it!"

The huge, fat clumps made a soft whispering sound when they hit the ground. The wind was calm for a change so the snow looked like a curtain as it fell straight down. The front of the property was working hard to resemble a Christmas card. The pines were already drooping with a thick coating of frosting while the driveway was a smooth trail winding towards the fence line. Bits of taller grass stuck out, but they'd soon be buried under a blanket of white. It really was pretty to look at, but if he had his way, he'd much rather mess it up with a snowmobile. Since they didn't have any of those handy, he'd just have to enjoy it the old-fashioned way. "Come on, grab your coat."

His sneaky redirection worked. She wasn't freaked out anymore. Of course now, her attention was on everything but him. They really needed to talk. It could wait, but not for much longer. If he was right, they'd have company soon.

She pirouetted in the middle of the yard, arms spread wide, head back, and tongue out. Her laughter warmed him from the inside out. She had shoved her hair into the purple hat and wrapped a matching scarf around her throat. Floppy purple mittens swallowed her hands. She reminded him of another enchanting snow maiden.

"You remind me of Mica right now. She is a total snow fiend. She taught me how to make a snow angel once."

"Before or after she knew what you are?"

"After. Definitely after. It was our first Christmas together."

"Together?"

"Not *that* kind of together! Mica's always been like a baby sister to me. Trust me--I've never thought of her in any other way. She's not my type."

"Oh, really? 'Beautiful' isn't your type?"

He laughed once and tugged Rori into his arms again. "*Beautiful* is absolutely my type." He bent to kiss her, hesitating a centimeter away from her mouth. Pushing her hat away, he murmured, "No particular woman has ever been my type." Until now.

A branch creaked under the heavy snow, breaking the spell, leaving an awkward silence. He pulled back and led the way to the narrow road. "Come on, snow goddess, let's walk."

She bit back a sigh but didn't press him to finish his thought. He meant to say something more but checked himself. He wanted to walk with her instead. This man could lead her to Hell, and she'd happily follow. She'd stopped questioning him days ago. When had she started to trust him? Why was she blindly following him? Snorting at the pointless, rhetorical questions, she mentally pinched herself. Oh, she knew perfectly well why; she just wasn't going to even think the thought. Her life was complicated enough without that.

Snuggling close, she stuffed her hand into his jacket pocket to keep him pressed tight against her as they walked. They headed down the lane into the swirling snow. Without moonlight, it should've been dark, but the snow illuminated it into a fantasy of white. Had she ever played in the snow? Surely she had... but the memory was out of reach.

"So... You wanted to talk about something?" she ventured when the silence began to weigh on her.

"I want to talk about a couple of things. As much as I'd like to stay in this cabin with you, we can't stay here too much longer. The real world is out there, and it's more dangerous than you could possibly know."

He squeezed her waist in question and she nodded, fully understanding his point. "I get that. But I thought you were going to protect me?"

"I am, but it's time for you to learn to protect yourself. I can't be with you 24 hours a day, every day for the rest of your life. We'd both feel better if you had some mad skills of your own."

"Okay, that makes sense to me. What do you want to do?"

"First off, I'll teach you some basic self-defense moves, and then we'll work on weapons. How do you feel about guns? Knives? Spears?"

"Spears? Holy shit! Are you serious?"

He laughed and said, "Nah, I'm kidding about the spears. But we all carry guns and knives. I'm not asking you to become an assassin, Rori. I just want you to be able to disarm an attacker if you need to and be able to hit someone without breaking your hand. How do you feel about that?"

There were so many times a gun might've been helpful, starting at about age nine. Sure, she'd learn. She'd be damned before she let another monster hurt her simply because she was vulnerable. Not going to happen again. Next time some asshole decided to target her, she'd be ready. They might still take her down, but they'd bleed in the process.

"Yes to all of the above. Teach me whatever you think is best. I'm tired of being weak. I think it's time to yank the target off my back once and for all."

"That's my girl! We'll leave here in a week or so and head to Plattsburgh for your training. We have a full gym in the basement that's perfect. Mica wants to help too. She runs a self-defense studio for women. She donates the hours to women who can't pay and charges a low fee to everyone else. It's her dream that no females become victims because they're untrained."

They had come to the main road. By unspoken agreement, they made a U-turn to head back towards the cabin. The wind pressed down on them now, scooting them along the snowy road. She slipped and grabbed at his jacket. Her boots weren't exactly made for tramping through heavy snow. She used Dec for support so she wouldn't fall on her butt. He was as steady as a statue. It wasn't fair. After a few minutes, she realized she was warmer than she should be. The heat radiated from his arm that draped over her.

"Are you doing that?"

He grinned and said, "What? I have no idea what you're talking about."

Punching him playfully in the chest, she continued, "You're using your powers to make me warm, aren't you?"

A definite jolt of energy sizzled along her back, heating her skin, buzzing in her mind... like laughing gas... euphoric and lightheaded, she burst into giggles.

Sweeping her into his arms, he kissed her with a thoroughness that stole her breath. The bubbles in her head popped one at a time as he used that sexy mouth to turn her inside out. The man could kiss God from a nun...

Carrying her easily, he crossed the driveway. "Next subject. Your visions. Can we talk about them for a minute?"

"Whoa! Hey! You can't just kiss a girl into a puddle and then switch gears. No way can I focus on that until the blood comes back to my brain."

He stopped and locked his eyes to hers. It was disconcerting. Every time he looked at her that way, she was lost in the sensation of falling, drowning, vanishing... he seemed to see into her soul, and found it beautiful. Her instincts screamed to run, but her body begged her to stay. She could still taste him on her tongue.

"Maybe we should forget talking altogether and just focus on the kissing part. Like this?" He kissed the curve of her neck. "Or like this?" He dragged his bottom lip over hers in a playful nudge. "Or maybe like this?"

She shuddered when the tip of his tongue stroked the sensitive spot just under her ear... she didn't even bother to smother the moan that broke the silence. "Oh, more of that, please."

"Your wish, my command."

He did as requested before sliding around to her mouth again. Unhurried, he moved seductively, barely touching her, but still grazing every nerve ending in his path. Warmth surrounded her as he held her more tightly against the broad muscle of his chest. The rest of the world vanished as his mouth moved over her, nipping, stroking, making her dizzy with need. The faint zing of the current flowed under her skin, pulsing with the rhythm of his heartbeat. Her blood quickened, her heart picked up his beat... her head swam with the overwhelming urge to throw herself against him. Animal, primal... the urgency shocked her to the core. Without using his hands, he'd set her on fire.

He jerked away, eyes glowing cobalt, boring into hers, questioning, searching... before he growled, "I need to be inside you. Now."

His raw hunger snapped her control. She nodded only once before the world spun out from under them.

Rori squinted at the sudden bright light. How did they get into the cabin? She started to say something, but he cut her off by stripping her coat and tossing her onto the king-sized bed. With a wave of his hand, the lights flicked off, and he was kneeling beside her.

Her heart pounded with more than a twinge of fear as she looked into his face. Gone was the playful man who'd chased her around in the snow. The boyish grin, the sexy dimples, were nowhere in sight. The man who sat stripping his clothes off was a stranger: A smoldering hot, sexy, spellbinding threat to her orgasmic dry spell. Her mouth went dry as all liquid pooled in a much lower spot. Speechless, she could only stare as he stood naked and rock hard. Every gorgeous muscle was taut with the strange energy that flowed through him. She scooted to the center of the bed and patted it. Without taking his eyes from hers, he dragged her into his arms. That energy pulsed between them, soft as a heartbeat, spiked with adrenaline, surrounding them like a web. The more they touched, the stronger the bond grew. She arched her back against the pressure, but it held her steady as an invisible hand pressed her down.

His brain disengaged the second her *saol* jumped the barrier to wrap itself around him. The shock of that connection blew his mind, but his senses erupted before he could question it. With their *saols* entwining them, there was no way he could stop what was happening. The energy flowed too hard, was too demanding; they could only cling to each other while it swept them away.

He'd planned to take it slow, but they were too far gone, too far into the zone for anything other than raw, animal sex. Her eyes were closed, lips moving. Praying? Begging? No, she was calling his name... over and over again, the sound finally penetrating the deafening roar of blood rushing in his ears. The binding of her *saol* had finally loosened enough for her to move, and she rocked her pelvis unconsciously to the rhythm of their hearts.

"Hang on, baby," he warned while sliding a hand between her thighs to spread them wider.

She locked her legs around his hips even as he plunged straight to her womb. With Dec surrounding her inside and out, her world vanished to nothing but the two of them. The feel of his skin, the taste of his mouth... the scorching heat as he held himself still inside of her... she was lost. There was no going back. She barely saw the golden web. Instead, she only saw the blue of his eyes an inch from hers as he claimed her mouth in a long tender kiss before the wild animal sex took over.

An hour later...
"Oh, God," she said.
"You're welcome," he said.

Two hours later, she stretched languidly as he dropped sweet kisses over both pink nipples. He rubbed his stubbly chin over them, making her squeak in protest. Grinning tiredly, he smoothed over the pain with a soft sweep of his tongue.

She shivered and sighed. Everything he did was perfect. *He* was perfect. Damn.

Sniffing the air, he rose up on an elbow, proclaiming, "Good Lord, this place smells like sex." He sniffed her neck, nibbling all the way around it in the process. "*You* smell like me. I like it."

Wild monkey sex? No way. Too tame. What they did was off the charts. She'd actually screamed. Loudly. More than once. He'd brought her to the most mind-blowing orgasms she'd ever had. She'd practically launched herself off the bed during the second... or third one.

The flashback was so strong, her lady parts shuddered, and she couldn't stifle a gasp.

"Did you just come?" he asked with a massively satisfied expression. "I didn't even touch you this time." He ran the back of his hand over her belly until it rested on her hip. "You are so soft; I can't stop wanting you."

Flushing hot pink, she couldn't help the smile that burst through her embarrassment. "Are you using your powers on me? Surely this can't be normal! I've had orgasms before, but this was... mmm, *super*natural." She erupted into giggles, gasping the last word out.

"Flattery will get you nowhere. But no, I'm not." He tenderly kissed her bare shoulder and added, "There's some wicked powerful chemistry between us, love."

He was too friggin' exhausted to move, so he didn't bother to try. Instead, he cuddled his woman close. She wiggled her bitable butt, and Mr. Crowley actually opened his eye and stretched.

Oh, hell no! Go back to sleep! There's such a thing as showing off.

She felt the twitch and moaned, low, throaty, and just a little amused. "Don't even think about it. I'm slipping back into a coma..." Even as she protested, her breath quickened the second he trailed his fingers over her breast. The nipple hardened as he caught it gently.

Yep, he was all in. He was sure he could pull off another round. "Mmm, but maybe if we go really slow this time?"

Rori chuckled, "How can you be hard again?"

Stroking against her silky skin, he blamed her in the rough sexy voice she'd come to love tonight. "How can I not? You feel so good."

Dec's hand palmed her breast as if it was made for it. Her nipple hardened with a disturbing eagerness that had her wondering fuzzily if she'd lost control of herself. Her undersexed body didn't seem to care that her brain was shutting down with exhaustion. No, it was already juicing up and moving on its own. Even as he fingered that traitorous nipple, her thighs parted and welcomed him back inside.

Curled on their sides, they made love in a slow dance this time. His mouth and tongue played over the nape of her neck in a lazy motion until she stiffened once more. Seeming to sense her fall, he bit down hard, sending them both over the edge.

This time, when he cuddled her close, they slept like the dead. Neither noticed their gleaming *saols* crisscrossing around them or the face watching in the window.

Chapter 15: Those Three Little Words

RAPHAEL BLEW ACROSS THE TOP OF HIS TEA before daring a sip. His natural immunity to cold temperatures didn't reduce the pleasure of a steaming cup of Earl. If he had to pick a favorite tea, Earl Grey would be it. Mica always had some on hand especially for him. He appreciated her thoughtfulness; it was one of many qualities that made her a favorite.

Although it wasn't yet Christmas, winter had settled in with no intention of leaving any time soon. It had been snowing steadily for two weeks with another 12 inches forecast for the weekend. If he was human, he might've found the cold temperatures and barely passable roads troublesome, but he didn't. No, he found the majesty of acres of snow something to rejoice in, not complain about. The farmhouse sat nestled between a copse of beautiful tall pines on one side and a leafless deciduous forest on the other. Its two acres of rolling lawn was a perfect playground for his three rambunctious grandsons. Those three miracles were presently dozing in the nursery after an hour of snowman building. No, he wouldn't trade the snow for anything.

Declan was in the middle of debriefing him on all that had happened with his latest charge. The young warrior spoke with his usual animation, waving his arms to make his points, changing the inflection in his voice to stress particularly worrisome problems. All he needed to do was nod his head and make some sounds of understanding at the correct times. Declan would continue without expecting more interaction until he was completely finished.

Vastly amused at Declan's attempts to hide his feelings for Rori, he sipped at his tea and finally commented, "It seems our Rori is a woman of many secrets. Have you told her?"

Dec scrubbed a hand over his shaggy hair, shoving his bangs away from his forehead for the thousandth time. Cocking his head to listen for Rori, he shook his head at his maker's question. "Not yet. This is too massive to just dump it on her. I want to have all the facts first. Will you help me?"

Before Raphael could respond, they were interrupted by Mica's delivery of lunch. It looked like turkey, avocado, and Havarti sandwiches--with a dill pickle on the side. There were many reasons he loved this woman. Her spoiling him with food only synched the deal.

She dropped a couple of napkins on the table and said, "Here you go, guys. Need anything else before I go back downstairs? Rori's waiting for me."

Dec answered for both of them. "Thanks, sweetheart. You know we don't want to put you out, but I'll never say no to lunch. How's our girl doing?"

He and Rori had arrived just before this latest storm hit two days ago. After spending some time helping Rori get reacquainted with everyone, he'd set up a training plan. Today was the first day of said plan. Mica agreed to start with some basic muscle-building exercises before he started throwing Rori around the basement--her words, not his.

Mica was dressed in black yoga pants and a loose long-sleeved t-shirt with black and red Sketchers. Her hair was braided into a long tail that she pinned haphazardly to the top of her head. Her cheeks were rosy, eyes sparkling. She was in her element. The complete lack of sweat stains was a testament to her level of fitness. The ladies had been downstairs for an hour already. Rori was looking pretty rough the last time he'd poked his head down the stairwell. Of course, he would cut out his tongue before mentioning that little factoid to anyone.

Mica rolled her eyes and replied, "*Our* girl is doing perfectly. She's got a lot of natural grace and strong bones. Once we build her some muscle, she'll be fine. You're not worried, are you?"

"Nope. Not even a little bit. She's a lot stronger than she seems. She just needs to learn the skills to protect herself. My life is dangerous on a good day. I don't want to worry about her when I have to be out of town."

Both Raphael and Mica stared with surprise before breaking into nearly identical grins.

"Ah." Tapping at his chin, Raphael spoke thoughtfully, "I see."

Dec flushed beet red the second the words left his lips. He might have tried to take them back, but his brain didn't cooperate. Instead, his mouth opened and closed twice before he clamped it shut. Shit.

Mica burst out laughing and gave his shoulder a squeeze before saying, "I see too. No wonder she was stiff this morning. She blamed it on the bed."

He tossed Rori a towel and pretended to tie his shoe so he could scrutinize her from the corner of his eye. Was she doing too much? Pushing too hard? She swiped at the bead of sweat slipping down her face. Did she need more water?

243

Her face was red. Maybe she was doing too much. He was teaching her to drop and roll today. Her eyes were bright, happy. He searched for signs of strain, but she seemed to be hanging in there all right. She'd laughed when he asked if she needed a break.

"Dec, I'm not fragile. Yes, I *am* breakable and yes, it *hurts* when I'm broken. But, and this is a huge 'but', I'm *not* a wuss. I *will* learn how to stay alive. I have something to live for."

What was that 'something' she had to live for? Her tone made it seem like a recent discovery. Was it him? Was it the mystery of her mother and that demon? Curiosity was a big motivator. So was vengeance. She'd been eerily focused on their lessons for the past week. She'd pushed herself harder than he would've done. Mica worked tirelessly with Rori. The two women spent hours every day working on Rori's skills. It was a little scary.

Of course, he was used to Mica's intensity... Rori seemed so delicate compared to her. Mica had always been athletic, strong. She took to their Krav Maga training with perfectly natural enthusiasm. Rori wasn't nearly as 'natural' and had the bruises to prove it. She'd nearly ripped his head off when he offered to heal those bruises. She boggled his mind. On one hand, she believed in demons and Primani now. On the other hand, she flatly refused to let him use his powers on her. They'd gone toe to toe on this until he finally lost his temper. Yeah, that was a low point for him. He wasn't proud of himself for going all alpha male and scaring the hell out of her. He saw the fear in her eyes, but he stuck to his guns.

He would use his powers to save her life each and every friggin' time he needed to. Period. End of story. If she wanted to suffer with minor injuries, fine. But no force on earth would stop him from keeping her alive.

She was stubborn, but so was he.

He called time. "We're almost done for the day. It's Friday night. I think we need to go out."

"That sounds amazing. I need a shower first."

She bent at the waist to drop her hands to the mat. Breathing slowly as Mica had taught her, she stretched her muscles with a satisfied groan. Ow. But a good kind of 'ow.' Bending backwards, she closed her eyes and let her spine unkink. Oooh, so good. No, make that great. She'd been training for a week and was already thinking about kicking some ass. Sure, she wasn't an expert, but she was getting more comfortable with the idea of violence. Next week, Dec was going to start really sparring with her--with gloves--and she couldn't wait. Hopefully she wouldn't hurt him too much!

An hour later, she stepped out of the shower to find the man leaning against the bathroom door. He'd slipped into the room as silently as smoke. Her heart nearly jumped out of her chest and she dropped her towel. Moving in a flash, he was in front of her before she could pick it up.

"Do we have time for a kiss?"

"More than that if you hurry!"

The Angry Lizard was a pool joint. It didn't try to be anything else. There were tables scattered around with tall black pleather-topped seats and a modern jukebox in the corner. Dart boards hung here and there for people who liked to throw things. The eight pool tables were the main attraction. She craned her neck to check out the funky scowling lizards covering the walls. One looked like a dragon, but it was so faded now it was hard to see its tail.

"Do you like it?" Mica asked with a smile and a wave of her hand.

She grinned across the table at her new friend. "Sure. It's cool. I've never been inside a bar before."

Mica slurped the foam from the top of a beer and said, "Well, it's not much of a bar, but it's our fave here in town.

We've been coming here forever." She tossed a glance at Dec and hinted, "You can get him to dance with you if you ply him with enough alcohol."

"Oh? Okay, I'll, um, keep that in mind."

Mica leaned across the table. "Don't tell me you don't dance either? Holy shit, girl, we've got to find you a life. Before you go back to The City, I will teach you to dance. It's the least I can do for you."

While they went back and forth on the pros and cons of dancing in public, the guys deserted them for some dude time at the bar. She was about to die of curiosity. What were they talking about? Every now and then, one of them would shoot a glance in their direction. This was usually followed by a shake of the head, a laugh, and a shrug. Killian's expression was mostly watchful, neutral--he kept a good poker face. That made his occasional bark of laughter even more suspicious. Dec, on the other hand, was a whole different story. She loved watching him around other people. He was definitely gorgeous, but it was the way his eyes flashed and his mouth moved that drew her in. He had a million expressions, and she was falling hard for every single one of them. Killian said something just then. His mouth twisted up on one side, the dimple flashing, and lips thinning a bit... joined by a slight shake of his head. It was his 'annoyed' look. And it was so damn cute she wanted to kiss him.

It reminded her of someone...

"Dean Winchester," she mumbled absently. Exactly. Well, not *exactly*, exactly... but his face was just as animated.

Mica's brows shot up, and she asked, "Sorry? Who?" Turning on her stool, she swept her eyes around the small crowd until she spotted Dec. "Dec?"

"Yes! I'm not saying he looks like Jenson Ackles, the actor who plays Dean Winchester on "Supernatural", but he makes the same faces when he's talking. He's got the cutest expressions."

"He always was the cute one."

"What do you mean?"

"Well, Sean was the brooding serious one; Killian was the terrifying bossy one, and Dec was the adorable cute one." She stopped smiling and said, "Declan is the healer, the fun one. He loves people. He's sensitive and intuitive. He loves to play. Rori..." She let the sentence hang as she chewed her lip.

Lowering her voice, she said, "Rori, I have to say something to you--woman to woman. Can you hear me out for a sec?"

Oh, great. Here it comes. The speech. A giant knot formed in her stomach. It took a huge effort to swallow a pithy remark and simply say, "Sure, go ahead."

Mica's sincerity rang true when she picked up Rori's hand to hold it tightly. "I love Dec almost as much as I love my husband. He's saved my life; he's made my life. I can't even define how much he means to me. He's warm and kind. He's sweet and good. He's funny, and he's clever. But you need to understand him for who he is... what he is." She took a sip and made sure the guys were still occupied before continuing. "Primani are not do-goody guardian angels--they're killers."

Rori's mask of composure slipped. "What?"

"They exist to destroy demons to keep chaos in check on our plane. They follow a loose code of honor, but they will kill a human without batting an eye if they need to. Greater good and all that."

"But Dec told me they protect humans; they help people like me stay safe. I don't understand what you're telling me. Are you saying he might kill me?"

Mica shook her head and said with not a little sympathy in her tone, "He didn't lie to you, sweetie. Protecting humans, like you, like me, is a big part of what they do. By the way, I'm pretty damn excited to see what you turn out to be. But that's another convo. My point is you've only seen him in his protective 'saving the damsel' mode. He's sweet. He's gentle. He's healing you, helping you to learn and to grow. But that's only one side of him. Dec and the others are terrifying when they're in what I call soldier-mode. When they're on a mission, when their bodies prep for combat, they will scare the shit out of you. He's extremely dangerous when he's going to fight. You can't ever forget they have supernatural abilities. Don't underestimate them. They're simply not completely human."

Mica shared more than a little kinship with the pale-faced woman whose fingers were like ice now. After all, she'd been on the receiving end of a Primani protection detail once upon a time. She was Sean's charge. He'd done a terrible job of keeping her safe. She got beaten half to death a few times. When she considered things from that angle, she stopped feeling guilty about breaking Sean's leg in half. In any case, it was usually Dec who patched her up again. Rori was in very good hands--literally.

At the moment though, Rori's emotions flowed completely unchecked Fear, confusion, worry, and... ah, there it is. Perfect.

"Don't panic. I'm telling you all of this for a reason. Declan is one hell of a good Primani. He's smart. He's powerful. He's deadly. But he's got a beautiful soul. Are you strong enough to accept him for what he is?"

"Warts and all?" Rori's voice shook even though she tried to crack a joke.

Dec's eyes met hers from across the room, and he refused to let her go. Could she accept him for the killer he was? She truly didn't know. His jaw tightened as though he read her thoughts, but he didn't break eye contact. A beautiful soul? Well, he was certainly beautiful on the outside. But then so were leopards... and they ate people.

She shivered as she remembered the feel of his teeth on her neck…

She turned back to Mica and said, "I guess we'll find out. Will you help me?"

"Probably more than you'd like. I'm an excellent meddler." She raised her glass in a toast. "To dangerous men!"

"I'll drink to that." Life just couldn't get any stranger.

Dec rolled over to watch the door for movement. Tense, ready… something had pulled him from a hard sleep. Listening intently, he searched for the source of the sound. A scratching at the window? No. The sound came again. It was the irritated exhale of the resident canine coming from under the bedroom door.

Domino.

He cracked it open for her. She used her snout to push her way inside and waited for him to close the door again. Once all was in order, she hopped up on the bed, sniffed his pillow, and curled up into a ball. She gave Rori a dismissive glance before resting her chin between her front paws.

I missed you.

"I missed you too, pup. Come on, scoot your butt over so I can slide in." Careful not to wake Rori, he peeled the covers back enough to squeeze underneath. He curled around the dog and kissed the top of her silky head. She let out a long sigh and kicked her leg out a couple of times. She really did miss him when he was away. Sometimes she moped for days. Needing to ease his guilt, he stroked her ears until her breathing evened out.

Rori turned to snuggle against his back as soon as she sensed his presence. Mumbling something indistinct, she settled deeper into her dreams. When her breasts pressed softly against him, he thought he'd never been more content.

"So this is your latest charge?"

Maybe she'd go away if he closed his eyes. A heartbeat later, he cracked an eye.

Shit. Still there.

Standing stiffly beside him on the stairs, Dani showed no signs of teleporting back out the way she'd come in. Below them in the basement, Mica was fitting Rori's gloves and showing her how to tie them. Rori was so focused on Mica's instructions that she hadn't spotted his pain in the ass ex yet. He sort of hoped she wouldn't. This wasn't going to go well. He should've expected Dani to show up, but he thought she'd have more class than that.

"You're not going to make a scene, are you? She's still healing."

Dani sneered, "I'm sure she is." Pushing past him, she threw her trademark sunny smile over her shoulder and called out to Mica.

"Hey, Dani. Come on down. This is my friend, Rori. Rori, Dani. Dani's a good friend of mine. She's the one I told you about. She's helping me with the studio and with the kids. I don't know what I'd do without her!"

He straightened a bit at Mica's warning tone. She'd stressed the word 'my' when making the introduction. That's my Mica. Mothering all lost puppies and wandering souls. Warning or no, he wasn't a dumbass. No way was he leaving Rori alone with an angel with a shitty attitude. She could blast Rori to another country, and they'd have no idea where to look! So he jumped into the ring to keep the peace.

"Come on Rori. I'll spar with you. Mica, why don't you and Dani go do your business? We're G2G here."

As soon as the two women cleared the top of the stairs, Rori gave him the hairy eyeball with hands on each hip. "Let me guess. Your ex?"

"Not really. It's complicated."

Before they got moving, he plugged in his iPod and set the playlist to start. He was in the mood for some old school alt rock today. The list was full of The Cure, Jane's Addiction, Green Day, and Nine Inch Nails. While "Been Caught Stealing" kicked off, he strapped on his favorite gloves and started to loosen up. He hadn't been sparring in months. It was kind of odd to work out with someone other than Sean. He rarely sparred with anyone else. Over the years, he'd worked with Mica some, but she was waaaay more intense than he was thrilled with. She was an excellent fighter, but he didn't feel comfortable slamming her with his full strength. He was much heavier and stronger. He could seriously hurt her, so he pulled his punches and avoided moves that were dangerous. The problem was she got carried away and actually broke him a few times. One time she'd cracked two ribs and another time she got a lucky shot and hit him in the nuts. *That* happened more than once. Probably he needed to wear a cup around her! He could heal himself, sure, but that didn't mean the pain hurt any less! He avoided her like the plague these days. He and Sean sparred well together. They just happily beat the shit out of each other until they were tired or there was too much blood to see. It was a guy thing.

"Complicated? That's a bullshit word and you know it. Come on, now. Spill it." She didn't look unhappy, but he wondered if he needed a cup...

He tossed a right jab at her in slow motion. She blocked it and then swung a right jab of her own. Good form. Impressed, he grinned down at her and repeated the movement a few more times. Once she had gotten comfortable with that, he switched to the opposite hands. She kept up pretty well except for once. He gave her a light tap on the jaw when she failed to block him.

"Bam! You're on the ground."

"Funny! Ha. Ha." She attempted a roundhouse that missed when he easily leaned out of range. Scowling now, Rori asked, "Who is Dani to you?"

They exchanged a few more blows before he shrugged and said, "She's someone I cared about once."

Rori hesitated with hands raised in front of her chest. "And now?"

"Now?" He paused for a split second before adding, "Now, she's someone I know."

"That's it? You don't love her?"

He moved in close to look her straight in the eyes. "Yes, that's it; and no, I don't love her. And before you ask, no, I never did."

Well, that's short and sweet. She wasn't stupid. The tension between Dec and Dani was thick enough to cut with a sword. She didn't miss the veiled warning from Mica either. This Dani person had hurt him. She heard it in his voice, saw it on his face. He might say she was nothing to him, but his eyes said differently.

Dropping her arms, she offered her lips for a kiss. A little surprised by the gesture, he pressed his lips lightly to hers. She eased up on her toes to fit herself against him.

"I love you, Declan Manning." Her words were barely a whisper, but he heard them. He blinked with surprise and then smiled slow and easy. Her lower half turned to jelly.

With gloves still on, he put his hands on either side of her face and pressed their foreheads together. After what seemed like forever, he responded, voice hoarse with emotion, "I've waited lifetimes for you," before slanting his mouth over hers once again.

Those words hit Dani like a spear to the chest. The pain took her breath away. Holding herself up with the railing, she watched as she lost Declan forever. He held Rori in his arms and kissed her with longing and passion and real love. There was no misunderstanding the tenderness in his touch. No way to excuse it as just a little fun before casual sex. His eyes promised forever when he broke the kiss just long enough to say, "I love you too."

She'd waited too long.

Chapter 16: And the Plot Thickens

"WHERE IS THIS PROPERTY?" He was in full detective mode. Serious words, serious expression... there was no evidence of the happy-go-lucky guy she fell in love with. This new face of Dec's was intriguing though. He looked like a sexy FBI agent. Note to self: Ask him to wear a suit with a bad tie sometime... just for the fantasy.

She shot him an amused glance before peering more intently at the laptop screen. For the millionth time this week, she wished for her stuff. She had a notebook full of research but it was long gone now, along with most of the things she owned. After that rat bastard demon, or RBD for short, set her apartment on fire, Killian managed to grab her purse and an armful of clothes before the place was too hot for him. The big man had apologized the next time he saw her. He'd actually felt bad that he wasn't able to save her things in spite of the fire raging out of control. It was very kind of him to even try. She was starting to understand why Mica was so devoted to him. Still waters and all that...

"Thank God for the internet! Here we go. The deed was registered in the name 'Robert Austin'. I figured that must be my grandfather, though I don't know for sure. My mom died when I wasn't quite three yet. The property is located near Albany. It's out in the woods."

Dec slid his butt onto the bench neatly pushing her off the end. He didn't even notice that she'd moved. His face was practically pressed into the screen as he appeared to do math in his head. Resorting to his fingers, he counted off a couple and mumbled to himself. Both eyes were mostly closed and he chewed his lower lip between his front teeth.

Don't laugh. Don't laugh.

He gave a sure nod and started in on the keyboard. With fingers flying at warp speed, he sent out several messages to God only knew who.

Snorting with laughter, she finally asked, "What on earth are you doing to that poor keyboard? I think I see smoke."

Barely slowing down, he replied, "We have an awesome lab of techies. It's time for them to earn their paychecks. I just sent all the deed info. They can access much better data than we can here. They'll be able to trace the property AND your mother's info. With any luck, we should know if this is your grandfather's property or not by the end of the day. We'll also know what happened to your grandparents and confirm a lot more about your mom's life." With one final click, he shoved his hair back and yawned hugely. "I'm ready for a break. Want to take a ride?"

Twenty minutes later, they rolled into the parking lot at The Broken Wing. The closet-sized shop bragged about having the best chicken wings in the state. She had her doubts--it couldn't possibly be better than Buffalo's in Brooklyn. Johnny Mencini was from Buffalo, for crying out loud. The man was a genius with sauces. The garlic teriyaki was sublime. It didn't really matter much at the moment. They could be eating cardboard, just as long as they were not home. They were on a mission to get away from the house, computer, and Dani the Nanny. Dani was working with Mica today. She hadn't been rude exactly, but the air was frosty.

They sat at one of the tall, round tables and relaxed, while the freckled-faced teenaged girl threw their wings in some red sauce. Somewhere between the farmhouse and the restaurant, Dec's oh-so-serious detective face had morphed into sexy man-candy.

She couldn't resist burying her face against the side of his neck and nibbling him. He gave her an encouraging sort of groan. Apparently biting his earlobe was taking it too far. He decided to take charge by dragging her onto his lap. Clutching at him, the table, and the air, she barely stayed off the floor. Her hero easily snagged her and plopped her on his knee. Catching her breath, she glared in mock anger. "You are so wrong! You know that, right?"

"Really? I don't see you trying to move. I think you like sitting on my lap."

Drawing back, she laughed, "You smell amazing! I can't resist you." With that, she gave his biceps a squeeze.

"Do me a favor? Don't try. If you start resisting me, I'll have to beg, and that would kill my badass reputation."

"You have a badass reputation? Really?"

With an oddly dark chuckle, he said, "More than you want to know, Rori."

He caught himself before he said too much. Huh, there was a first time for everything. To keep himself out of trouble, he stuffed a wing in his mouth and let her do all of the talking. No hardship, that. Rori's big doe eyes sucked him in big time. She had no idea how pretty she was. As he drank her in, she chattered on about wings and things and how cute and adorable he was... yeah, sure, whatever. He would listen to her talk about nuclear reactors if that was her thing. Just the way she said words tied him up in knots... all Brooklyn-ish and shit. Oops. She was waving a wing to get his attention. Busted.

"Hey! Are you listening to me?" she demanded around a bite of wing. A smear of sauce stuck to her cheek. She rubbed to clean it, but just smeared it even more. She was adorably clumsy.

"Yeah, yeah. I'm listening. You're in love with me. I know. But you should hold back a little. It'll go to my head." He stripped a wing bare to gesture with the bones. "You, woman, have no pride."

Totally dismissing his lame attempt at a joke, she nodded towards the window. "Do we have time to have a beer over at The Lizard? It's nice out. I'm not ready to go back yet."

Nice? Was she mental? He had to double check the window to be sure they were looking at the same view. It was snowing like mad--again. It wasn't even Christmas yet and they'd had feet of snow already. Personally, he had mixed feelings about snow. On the slopes? It was perfect. On the roads? With his baby still brand new? Not so much. He'd sweet talked Mica into letting them borrow her SUV so he could leave the Challenger in the nice, safe driveway. Luckily the SUV was ready to drive because, unlike his baby, Mica's truck had a place in the garage. It got to sit right next to Killian's badass ride. Since coming back from England, the McLaren NEVER got out in the cold of winter. It was warm and happy under a custom cover inside the garage. Man, he was so jealous of that garage.

"I want a house." Did he just say that out loud? What was wrong with him? He had no filter whatsoever.

Rori tripped over the door seal, gripping his arm to keep from falling. She looked confused. Okay, back peddling... "A house would be nice. You know, with a yard and a dog, a Dalmatian..." He was making this soooo much worse... he clamped his big mouth shut as they zigzagged behind a building on the way to the bar. The narrow alley gave them some protection from the blowing snow. As they neared the end, a figure stepped from a doorway to their left. The light was weak so the man's face was shadowed, but the challenge in his stance was clear. Dec pushed Rori behind him, drawing his knife at the same time.

Only the knife wasn't there. He'd left his gun and knife at the house. You'd think you could get some friggin' wings without getting mugged in this town. Unarmed, in the dark, with one, no make that three, assholes lining up in front of them. Awesome.

He didn't dare take his eyes off of any of them. They fanned out to block the entire road. Rori clutched at the back of his jacket, sidling closer.

With voice just loud enough for her ears, he ordered, "Turn around and run. Get back to the main street and get inside. I'll come for you."

"No way! I'm not leaving you here! They'll kill you!"

The cockiest of the men casually swaggered to about ten feet in front of them. About the same height and weight as him, the asshole was bundled up for the cold, so naturally he had a handy black ski mask pulled over his face. He clearly thought he was dealing with an idiot since he said, "We just want your wallet. We're not going to hurt anyone." The telltale glint of metal flashed in his right hand.

"Rori, go now." He gave her a hard shove. Even without weapons, this would be a piece of cake. There were only three of them. He wanted her out of here before the violence started. She would freak.

She took off at a sprint, putting 30 yards of distance between them before hiding behind a dumpster to watch. Dec might need her help. No way was she leaving him all alone. She'd just jump in if things went sideways.

What the fuck was that? Asshole number one sailed into the brick wall with a hoarse cry and a sickening crunch. Ewww. She kinda hoped that was only his nose and not his entire head! That did *not* sound good. Dec stood with his back to her, so she couldn't see his hands clearly. One was held out in front of him, moving weirdly. Was he egging the guy on? Was he nuts? The man answered the call with a grin, swinging as he came. In a practiced move, Dec ducked out of reach and swept his legs. Asshole number two went down hard, but quickly shoved himself to his feet as number three moved in for the kill.

Number two dove into Dec's legs, taking him down on his butt. Before Dec could move, number three landed on top of the pile. She screamed, multiple times before slamming her hand over her mouth. Oh, my God, she sounded like such a damn girl! She would probably be embarrassed by that forever. She ran forward and hovered to the side, wanting to help, not sure what to do. Dec and the two men were rolling around in a pile of vicious swearing and blood splattering blows. Dec was up. Then he was down. He was on top. He was on bottom. Just when she thought he was really hurt, he laughed and threw asshole number two into the closest wall, just missing Rori. The man didn't move.

Number three wasn't doing any better. Dec had him on his stomach, one arm wrenched behind his back. He shoved the guy's face into the snow with his free hand and snarled, "I could kill you right now. Maybe I'll just break your shoulder." He pulled the arm back and the man screamed.

"No! No, don't!"

"Yes, please don't break him. He's useful to me." The arrogant deep voice with a Southern drawl came from just behind Rori's head.

Dec swore but didn't release the human beneath him. The demon held Rori in front of him. His filthy hands covered her face, scaring her to death. Her eyes were frantically begging him to do something. Dressed for topside, the demon wore the façade of a black man in jeans and a dark leather jacket. His eyes gleamed greenish in the dark alley. Thank God Rori couldn't see behind her. She'd flip out.

"What do you want, demon? This your bitch?" He gave the man's arm a turn. He squealed again. "You can have him back. We're done here."

The demon grinned over Rori's head. "Tsk, tsk. The Primani has an attitude? This is new for you, isn't it, Declan?"

His cocky grin faltered. "Do we know each other? I don't recognize the meat suit."

Rori whimpered for air. She tugged on his forearm to get him to move it from her throat. The demon's expression turned oddly regretful. He leaned into her ear, asking, "If I let you go, are you gonna scream? You can't scream anymore. The police will come."

She shook her head, mumbling something negative. He flashed next to Dec's side, leaving Rori to sink to her knees in shock.

He straightened for a fight before the demon got to his side. Now, they stood just feet apart, each judging the other, gauging strengths. Finally, Dec's face split into a grin.

"Holy sonofabitch! Is that you, Kyrrin?"

The atmosphere was significantly warmer when he and Rori returned to the farmhouse. It was late, but not too late to take care of some business, especially when that business was lighting him up from the inside out. Back in the alley, Kyrrin hinted at some usable intel. If he was right, they were about to blow the lid right off of Gary Carmichael's case. Rori had no idea how awesome it was to find Kyrrin in such a traitorous mood. The demon was one of the few who was actually in the know about the plans and politics that went on down below. Since he was well aware of how demons treated betrayal, Kyrrin refused to talk so close to nosy ears. Not a problem, unless Killian threw a wrench in the plan.

Knocking on Mica and Killian's bedroom door, he called out, "Hey, you two, I need to call a family meeting. This is a big deal. Can't wait."

Looking like he had actually been sleeping, Killian opened the door with a hard tug. The crease from the sheet totally took the scary out of his scowl. "Can't wait 'til morning?"

"No, man. It can't. It's about Rori."

Checking over his shoulder, he whispered, "Give me five. I'll meet you in the living room."

Rori was curled up on the couch when he came downstairs again. She had to be exhausted. Her eyes were drawn nearly closed until he disturbed her dozing. She wasn't going to like her orders, but Killian was very clear.

He tried the easy way first. There was always a chance that she'd be reasonable, right? He hugged her, rubbing her back, and kissing her temple. "It's really late, Rori. Why don't you go on to bed? I'll catch you up in the morning."

Aaand of course, the easy way wasn't going to cut it. Damn stubborn women. He was surrounded by them. Nope, it was too much to hope for. The second he started to talk, she was magically alert and suspicious as only a woman could be.

Sitting back with crossed arms, she gave him a pointed stare. "I'm fine. I want to hear what's going on too. I can sleep later."

"Sorry, love. You can't sit in on the meeting. It's ops only. You're not cleared."

"Are you serious? It concerns me, doesn't it? I have a right to know what's going on."

With perfect timing, Mica rounded the corner and broke up the argument. "Get used to it, Rori. You don't get a say. Sorry. I know you don't want to hear that, but that's how it is. These guys have a protocol. You aren't a member of the team. Think of them as military spec ops. They protect you, but they don't let you in on their super-secret plans. Same thing."

Rori flushed, started to argue, but stopped abruptly when Killian walked in. She demanded, "I want to stay."

With exaggerated patience, Killian growled through his teeth, "Not your call, babe. We're the ones who run the missions. My team, my call. Period."

"But--"

Mica took her by the elbow with every intention of leading her away. Rori dug her heels in. Mica rolled her eyes and yanked her down the hall. "Yes, it's really his way or the highway. Suck it up and get used to it. When it comes to their work, they get to make the calls. Come on, let's go to bed. They'll be up all night."

Three hours later, Sean was back from hunting. Dec and Killian sat sprawled out in their chairs while he dunked his head in the kitchen sink. He'd been rinsing for five minutes, but the water was still black as it raced down the plumbing. The last demon had exploded way too close to Sean. He'd ended up with a shitload of ash on his face. Yeah. It was gross. He plunged his head under the stream again and scrubbed. Taking a breath, he asked, "So how did Kyrrin look?"

Dec snorted a laugh, but it was Killian who answered with more than a little humor in his tone. "He's redecorated."

He spit and asked, "He's wearing someone? Really? That's odd. He usually goes *au naturel*." Ouch. Ash in the eye sucked. He rinsed his face again, shook his head, and finally dragged a kitchen towel over it. Mica would yell. He got grey soot marks all over the yellow cloth. That's four this month.

Dec grinned from ear to ear. "Yeah, you could say that. Think 'Terry Crews' and you'd be in the ballpark. He says he's tired of being fucked with by other demons, so he's taken to wearing a black football player-slash-actor-slash-Old Spice dude. After I picked my jaw up off the ground, I had to admit he's much more intimidating than in his skinny little demon body. I'd think twice before fucking with him." He paused to scratch at his chin. "He's got a Southern accent now. That's some funny shit, though. Man, I can't wait for you to see him."

After one last rinse and dry, he grabbed his own chair. With long legs sprawled, he asked for an update. Dec filled him in on what he'd missed.

Killian took the ball and finished up with Kyrrin's intel. "So your guy Tai Li was right. There is a faction of lower-level demons who want to break away from Irku's grip. There's a ton of finger pointing and killing going on as they try to save their asses. It's a bloodbath. But I say more power to them. It's better to let them kill each other."

Sean agreed, "True, true... but what is Irku doing about it? If he's keeping them under control, I don't see a problem for us. Anything we need to worry about yet?"

Killian shrugged. Not much got him worried so he was probably the wrong Primani to ask. "The usual. He's got feelers out collecting his own intel; killing off the ones who are too stupid to live; basically keeping things stable as far as Hell goes. He's got Kyrrin running more than his personal business now. Kyrrin's managing the collection points and directing snitches. He's in way over his head, by the way. He's going to wear that body out. He's got an ulcer already."

"Well, you can change the outside... can't change the heart, or whatever passes for hearts in demons anyway. Kyrrin's always been a wuss. He's not going to change. He doesn't have the stomach for all the shit Irku wants done."

Killian nodded and continued. "Exactly. That's his angle. He wanted to pass some info to us in exchange for a way out. He wants to vanish. I told him I'd work on something for him. Not sure what we can really do. Raphael's probably going to kill me for trying to deal with him."

Dec barked a harsh laugh. "Since when did we start witness protection for demons?"

Killian chuckled too. "I hate to say it, but I've started to like the little idiot. He's grown on me the past few years. I don't mind helping a brother out."

Dec snorted his water through his nose and hacked up a lung. Once his face turned a fascinating shade of purple, Killian whacked him between the shoulders.

"So all of this is very interesting, but Dec sounded like he'd just won the fucking lottery when he called me earlier. What's the excitement about? Why did I have to cut my night short? I was on a roll."

Dec sat up straight, grinning hard enough to bust a lip. "Dude! As a gesture of good faith, Kyrrin told us everything he could about Gary Carmichael's case. Guess whose name popped up with some interesting connections? Turns out this Father Joseph douche is really a soul broker for a demon named Azrael. Azrael is pretty big shit in his world. He's an old Knight of Hell. Nearly impossible to vanquish."

Another like Irku? Yay. "Impossible? Okay, so why the crazy look in your eye? What the hell is a soul broker? Why is this good news?"

Dec tucked his hands behind his head and explained. "Father Joseph used to be a real human. Still is, possibly, someplace under the demon's powers. He's been possessed by this demon for more than 40 years. Kyrrin thinks the demon's name is Ikini. Anyhow, apparently he slid into the priest and took over his life. The parish has gone to crap over the years and very few parishioners bothered to show up until they finally closed the building for remodeling. Before that, though, he was a big deal--quite the popular priest. You know the drill. Collected donations for the poor, brought food to the homeless, counseled people, performed funeral ceremonies… all your typical priest jobs."

Dec slugged another gulp of water before continuing. "The Carmichael family attended the church back in the 60s. The bastard even performed the baptism on Gary. When the kid vanished, he led the search to find him. There are pictures of him holding up Gary's mother in a press conference."

Sean nodded. "Yeah, okay. I got that. We already know they're connected. How is this proof he killed the boy? Did Kyrrin say anything about that?"

They already suspected the priest. They needed actual proof before they could execute him. It would be really, really bad to whack a priest, at least without a damn good reason. Karma and all that… Not to mention Michael's reaction… he shuddered at the thought of spending any more time in the stone garden. He still got the creepy-crawlies around stone angels. It wasn't an experience he ever wanted to repeat. Oh, hell no.

Killian interrupted Dec. "He didn't give specifics, Sean. He wanted to be able to tell the truth if he was tortured. So he shared some *suggestions* for us to explore. His words, not mine. We were right about Rori's visions. Woodstock is a clue. I suspect the boy's body is somewhere in the field. We should take her there to have a look around. There are probably other clues in her subconscious. That's what Kyrrin was getting at. I'm positive."

Sean took some minutes to wrap his head around this news. Not too surprising, really. The Woodstock vision seemed symbolic already. It wasn't a leap to tie the priest to the boy's death, or the mother's suicide either. If the good father was responsible for counseling her and hearing her confession, it would have been simple to twist her grief into something lethal, leading to her overdose. Why would

Kyrrin tell them this? It wasn't anything they wouldn't already be able to figure out.

Dec leaned forward and knocked on the table. "What? You've got that look on your face. We're missing something, aren't we?"

"Give me a sec. Something's bothering me about this." He tipped his head back and closed his eyes in thought. "What did Kyrrin say a soul broker does? It sounds like a rock star job. There have to be perks. Why else be some demon's bitch?"

Killian replied, "The broker scouts out people who are desperate enough to make a deal with a demon. They typically barter their souls for whatever they want--money, fame, love, sex… typical genie wishes. The demon ends up owning their souls."

Sean picked up the thread. "So the human gets their wish granted; the demon gets the soul and says 'hallelujah' before torturing it for eternity. That makes sense. What's in it for the broker? There's got to be a bonus of some kind. What's his cut?"

Dec froze with his hand halfway to the glass on the table. The blood drained from his face so fast, Sean thought he was going to faint. He and Killian leaped forward at the same time, both grabbing Dec's shoulders to keep him from keeling over. The transformation was instantaneous. In the wink of an eye his face lit up like a Roman candle, and he leapt to his feet. "That sonofabitch! I'll kill him with my bare hands!"

Killian grabbed his arm and snapped, "What? What do you know?"

Dec sucked in a lungful of oxygen and tried to calm down. His chest heaved with the force of his *saol* raging through him. His vision had gone totally white.

He stood with Sean and Killian, face on fire with a fury he could hardly control. They watched him like a loose grenade. He was about to lose it. He'd been listening to

Sean and Killian talk through the same intel he'd heard while Kyrrin was still here. He'd been listening with one ear and thinking hard. He'd been replaying all of Rori's actions, expressions, and comments concerning Father Joseph. Clearly they had a history. She was afraid of him. Even worse, she'd looked ashamed when he'd asked about the priest. When he'd pressed her for details, she shut him down, totally refusing to talk about it. Then there was the mark on her neck that matched the sigil on her mother's grave marker. She didn't know what it meant. She thought it was just a decoration. Then there's the night she was attacked. That friggin' demon said she was his. He owned her soul.

It made perfect sense now.

"Dec?" Sean kicked his foot to get his attention.

He didn't trust himself to speak without screaming.

"Dec, we need to hear it. What are you thinking?" Sean wasn't going to let him get away without telling them every filthy detail he'd just put together.

Taking several breaths to calm down enough to find his voice, he steadied himself by slamming both hands on the table. "Rori's mother sold her."

Chapter 17: Forgive Me Father for You Have Sinned

"THAT MAKES NO SENSE AT ALL. You're talking crazy. Why would she do that?" Rori refused to look him in the eye.

He tried to take her hand, but she jerked away and stalked to the other side of the room. She sent him a wary glance from the corner of her eye. She wasn't there yet, but she was on her way to accepting their theory. It *was* an insane idea. But stranger things had happened. This wouldn't be the first time a parent made horrible choices.

"Dec, I'm going to the grocery store. Will you guys watch the kids for me? They're all racked out so you've got a reprieve for an hour or so." Mica hurried to the garage door, juggling her purse and a pair of gloves.

She'd already promised to talk to Rori if he couldn't get her to see reason. Like him, Mica had a way with people. He would take her up on that offer if he couldn't figure out a way on his own. She stopped to wave before vanishing through the door. "Love you!"

"Rori, I know it sounds absolutely nuts. I get that. I do. But let's try something else." He laid a gentle hand on her shoulder and squeezed. She didn't flinch away. Good sign. He continued, "Can we agree that something suspicious happened between your mother and this demon? The sigils point to a clear connection. Would you at least agree to that?"

She was silent for a few heartbeats. Nodding, she said, "Fine. I agree that's weird. I don't agree she sold my soul to Azrael."

Clamping his hand over her mouth, he hissed, "Shh! Never say his name aloud! Don't even think it!"

She blinked over his hand and shoved at his chest to make him let go. "What's the matter with you?"

"There is immense power in the name. He's in-tune with you already; saying his name just attracts his attention. And that is *never* a good thing. This demon is powerful; more powerful than I can stop." He bent to kiss her before folding her against his chest. "He can get to you, love. We're doing all we can to hide you, but if he finds you, he'll come."

"But something is holding him back, right? Otherwise, he'd already be possessing me… or whatever he wants to do. Why isn't he here now?"

"There are always limits to these deals. People get their wish for a specific number of years; 10, 20, even 25 years is common. Or the debt is due on a certain birthday, or some other date the demon comes up with. In your case, I think it's a date versus a number of years. I'm thinking it's your next birthday. That explains why he's been coming around the past several months. He's trying to soften you up, play with you a little… they love to torture, get off on it. He can't take you completely; he doesn't own your soul yet, but he can twist your mind until you're dying to go with him."

She blanched, sagging against his arm. "Father Joseph said something… a long time ago. Oh, God, he was right? He must've known what was coming. He must've known about this." She bit her lip and whispered, "This isn't happening! Demons don't exist! I'm not evil."

The abruptly childlike voice sent a shiver of real fear over the back of his neck. She repeated the phrases with her eyes squeezed shut.

"This isn't happening! Demons don't exist! I'm not evil."

"Shh, it's okay now. You're not evil, darlin'. No power on earth can make you that way. Take a deep breath and tell me about this priest. What did he say to you? You'll feel better if you get if off your chest."

She studied him with her huge eyes before shaking her head. "I… can't tell you. It's worse than you can imagine. I… don't want you to look at me differently. I can't handle that."

He was going to skin that priest alive. He didn't give a flying fuck if he was still in a human body. That demon was toast. The shame in her eyes ripped a hole in the middle of his chest. It nearly killed him to see it even though he pretty much knew what was coming. He didn't want to hear it, didn't want to force her to re-live the shame, the pain. But she had to talk to someone, had to get this off of her conscience if she was to heal. And she *would* heal, if it was the last thing he ever did.

Pulling her over to the couch, he took her hands in his. "I want you to listen to me, and listen hard. There is nothing you can say that would change how I feel about you. I love you. All of you. Scars and all. We have to get to the bottom of this if you ever want to have a normal life. Tell me what he said to you. Tell me what happened. I swear on my own mother's grave, that I won't think less of you."

She didn't want to tell him. God only knew he'd never be able to look at her again. It was probably her fault. She had been a pretty child. Needy, trusting, delicate. She hadn't understood what he wanted until she was older. Then, she understood exactly what he asked of her. She should have been horrified. Instead she was resigned. It seemed to be the only way. And things could have been worse.

"It was the nightmares. They started when I was young. I'm not sure exactly when. I didn't remember them much at first. I'd wake up with a lingering feeling of fear, but it disappeared by the time I was fully alert. As I got older, they stuck in my head. I'd wake up screaming, out of control. Ranting about monsters and fires... crazy talk. I started to see them when I closed my eyes, even when I was awake. I withdrew, got depressed, stopped smiling. That started the cycle of foster homes. When I was cute and sweet, it wasn't a problem. I was a smart kid, nice, kind. It wasn't hard to place me; I stayed in the same house for three years. It was nice. Then the nightmares ruined it."

She had been happy there. But the screaming, half-crazy kid was more than the family could take. Her siblings started having bad dreams... the parents had enough. By the time they'd sent her away, they no longer looked at her with gentle eyes. They looked at her with fear. And pity. Don't forget the pity.

"What did Father Joseph have to do with all of this? How did you know him?" Dec asked in a kind, encouraging tone that made her smile. He was really good at this. He should be a shrink.

"I went to church at St. Anne's. My mother did too. I remember playing in the pews when I was very young."

"How did your mother die? You've never told me."

She turned to look at him. He kissed her nose. "You know what? I don't know how she died. She was there one day, gone the next. I remember Father Joseph saying words… must've been her funeral… the memory's fuzzy now. A few of the old ladies from the neighborhood hugged me, and then I was sent to live with another family. They went to the church too."

She didn't know how her mother died. For some reason, that really bothered her now. What had happened to the woman? She just didn't have any clear memories. Too much time had gone by. She had too many other memories filling her head now.

"Do *you* know how she died?"

Dec frowned before answering, "Unfortunately, no. The death certificate states 'natural causes', but nothing more specific. No one requested an autopsy. My guess is there weren't any obvious signs of *unnatural* causes so they didn't look any deeper."

"It doesn't feel right to me. She had me… died young… then her priest…"

Dec broke the lingering silence. "It's okay. You don't have to finish. I want to know so I can help, but I can't stand to see you hurting. Forget it, we can figure him out another way."

"No, I need to do this. You're right. It's just festering inside of me. I need to get free of this demon in every way I can. So here you are. The whole disgusting story."

Taking a deep breath, she ripped the bandage off and dove right in. "I talked about the nightmares in confession. I didn't know what else to do. Everyone always said to go to the priest if you have a problem. It seemed like the right solution at the time." She curled her fingers into a fist and slowly released them, staring at her nails for several seconds, wishing hindsight wasn't really 20/20. "Now I see how he manipulated me."

"How could he do that? I was young, terrified, alone! I was just a little girl… He didn't care about that. I see that now. I can't believe I let him play me! Dec, he was so good at it. He listened patiently; said all the right things, drawing me in, gaining my trust. But then, after a while, he started insinuating that the dreams were of my own making. I *wanted* to have them. I *wanted* to be closer to the creatures I saw. I was *searching* for the demon. He said I was destined for great evil; that one day I would beg the demon to take me and... *fuck* me. Yeah, those were his words. I was ten years old then."

Now that she thought about it, she saw it all so clearly. It was right there in front of her face the whole time, and she had no idea. She created the mantra in her mind to block it, to shut out the overwhelming fear, the sense of inevitability that swallowed her up every time she dreamed. *This isn't happening. Demons don't exist. I'm not evil.* She created these phrases out of desperate denial--denial of the dreams, the priest's words, and worse, of her own feelings of excitement, of a strange hunger.

"By the time I was 12 or so, he'd started hinting at ways I could make the nightmares stop. It required a special sacrifice. I needed to feed the beast..." Choking on the last word, she hung her head and broke down, the memories nearly blinding her as they came swarming back.

Rori was crying again, sobbing in his arms. He held her while she shook, smoothing her hair back, murmuring soothing words in her ear. She sniffed against his shirt and kept talking, voice harsh, words tumbling over each other as if she was afraid to slow down, afraid to stop lest she choke on the pain. He kept a grip on the rage building in his heart with every word she said. As he listened to her story, images of another tiny girl flashed across his mind. Her bloody body left for wolves...

"Feed the beast! That's what he called it. At first I didn't understand what he meant. It felt wrong, though. I said no! God, for weeks I said no. For months! The nightmares came every night. They were worse each time. The fire, the wings... the fucking black demon with his beautiful face. The monster smiled at me. He called my name… over and over… he called my name and demanded I answer. He came to me every night, Dec! I felt him touching me, kissing me! And God help me, it felt good! But I woke up feeling filthy, tainted, used. Finally I stopped sleeping for days at a time. I tried to stay awake until I collapsed with exhaustion. I begged Father Joseph to help me and each time he said in a gentle voice, 'You know the sacrifice, my child'."

She barked a bitter laugh and sneered, "Oh, I *thought* I knew the sacrifice! But I was so wrong! My imagination couldn't conceive of what he really wanted. I thought I knew. I thought he wanted to have sex with me. But I was wrong. When I'd finally been broken enough, I gave in. The moment I said I'd do it, he pushed me to my knees, right in the confessional. That night, I cried myself to sleep and slept like a rock. Each week I went to confession. Each week, he taught me the pain of true sacrifice. I learned there are an astonishing number of places to feel pain. He was more interested in hurting me, in breaking me, than in having sex with me. My mind could barely understand what he wanted. I was so innocent. But you know what? The nightmares stopped. I could sleep again! But then the psychic visions started. When I told him about them, how I couldn't save any of the people, he said I was useless; that the visions were just another example of how evil I was, of why I should keep away from other humans. I wasn't like them. I wasn't fit for them. I was destined for evil… He said this while he beat me like an animal."

Out of breath, she stopped talking, stopped crying. The bitter silence simmered between them, Rori trying to cope with her emotions, while he prayed for restraint. The red film of rage nearly blinded him as the truth of her words sank in. Her head lay limp against him. Her heart fluttered like a butterfly. He felt her fear, her pain, and her anger coming in waves. That's my girl. Let that anger in. Time to get rid of the shame.

Kissing the top of her head, he spoke slowly, choosing his words very carefully. "I love you, Rori. What that bastard did to you is not your fault. He's a demon. They play with humans. They like to destroy pretty things. He preyed on you like he did a hundred other vulnerable people. You were a victim--a child! You finally stopped him, right? You stood up for yourself and took your life back. That's no small feat. You're much stronger than you think. I'm so proud of you."

Her mouth curled into a tiny, pained sort of smile, but a smile just the same. Her eyes lost the dead expression; she was finding the good. He let her finish. She needed to see this through.

In a much stronger voice, she said, "You're right. I *did* stop him… it was Arthur. He saved me. He showed up out of the blue and struck up a conversation on the steps of the library. I was sleeping on a step… he sat down and talked to me like I was the queen of England. He asked me to visit with him every week. He needed someone to help him find things in the shelves. His eyes were weak. That was the start of our friendship. He was an angel."

He chuckled and said, "You know, babe, he just might've been a real angel. I'll have to do some digging. Let me guess. He was kind, caring? He was a good listener? He encouraged you to share your pain with him and then encouraged you to stay away from St. Anne's?"

She looked startled for a split second before laughing weakly. "Exactly. How did you know that?"

"It's what I would've done. He passed away just when I came into your life. That sounds like odd timing to me. I'd say you were blessed."

The storm had passed. With arms wrapped around him, she snuggled closer and relaxed. He held her more tightly than strictly necessary, but he needed the contact. He tried to focus all of his attention on Rori, but old wounds nagged at the back of his mind. Memories harassed him even though he'd long since moved on. That wasn't exactly true though, was it? Enough millennia hadn't passed to dull the pain, the guilt. He would find that demon and rip him to pieces. No child should have to suffer like she had.

Ever again.

The lanes gleamed like black satin ribbons as they travelled down I87 towards Kingston. The sun was blindingly bright against the tons of heavy snow that blanketed every tree, river bank, and mountainside. There was so much snow that it looked like Mother Nature simply lost any sense of restraint. Despite the strain of the past few days, Rori craned her neck to see over the guardrail to the river meandering through the valley on the opposite side of the road. The edges had already frozen so much that there was only a narrow strip of water flowing down the middle of the river. It was the most beautiful sight she'd ever seen. It was a wonderland of white. Wow! Just wow!

"You look like a little kid over there. What are you looking at?" Dec glanced over with a grin, one wrist casually looped over the top of the steering wheel.

"It's amazing out here! I've never seen so much snow. It's like a painting."

"You're so cute. You've never seen this much snow? Well, just you wait. I'm going to take you to the top of a mountain where the view will take your breath away. You'll love it."

"Can you fly us there?"

He burst out laughing. "Sure, if you grow some wings."

"You can't fly?" Well, that was disappointing. She'd been having fantasies of winging over the snowy mountains and zooming low to just skim the rivers below.

"Ah, no. No wings, remember? Sorry, love. The best I can do is teleport. Guess you'll have to hold out for Superman."

"Huh. Well, that sucks."

Maybe she'd need to adjust his position on the pedestal a bit. He draped his arm casually around her shoulders, thumb idly stroking the back of her neck. She leaned closer so he could reach her more easily. Mmmm, just the touch of his hand affected her in ways that made her blush. This man was a wonder. He brought her peace she desperately needed. He'd been amazingly patient with her since the day they first met. He was unbelievably kind when she needed it most. More though, he loved her in spite of secrets so black she'd all but buried them herself. He heard the shameful things she'd done, watched her fall to pieces, and somehow, he'd still held her with love shining in his eyes. Instead of condemning her, he wiped her tears and put her back together. He healed her.

Thinking back to that day when she confessed everything to him, she marveled at how much he changed her in just a few months. Later that night, he'd made love to her with such tenderness, such sweetness, that she'd cried in his arms as they lay in the afterglow. He'd gently stroked every inch of her skin, feathering kisses, tonguing the sensitive dips and valleys. He'd alternated kisses with light pulses of his *saol* from the tips of his fingers until she'd hummed from head to toe. Her muscles had melted even as her back arched in demand for the hard pressure of his fingers between her thighs. As the last shudder stilled, he'd kissed those tears away and swore he'd always love her.

She smiled at the memory of his beautiful body covering hers. If she closed her eyes, she could see the hard muscles in his shoulders flexing as he moved, trickles of sweat snaking along the side of his face... the heat in his eyes that took her breath away. She could still hear his

voice whispering in her ear as she exploded beneath him...
Mine!

His? Oh, hell yes. She was all in now. By all measures a woman could use, Declan Manning was a keeper.

The perfect man snapped her from the delicious daydreams by asking with an annoyingly smug expression, "Are you thinking about me?" He sniffed the air like a bloodhound before cracking up at her horrified expression.

As if that just explains everything... she blushed and gave herself an experimental sniff. "I don't smell anything."

The rat laughed harder before finally settling those dimples into their cutest position. "Sweetheart, a man knows when a woman wants him. It's obvious by the glazed look in your eyes, the way your mouth opens for a kiss, and most importantly, and I can't stress this one enough, the scent of your, um, juices flowing. I have supernatural senses--all of them. I can't miss it. Besides that, *your* pheromones are the best perfume I've ever smelled. Just knowing you're sitting here dreaming about sex makes me hot as hell. We might have to pull over."

Apparently the 'girls' thought it was a grand plan since both nipples stood up and cheered. The rest of her newly oversexed body wasn't far behind. She fought the urge to say 'yes, yes, yes!' A girl's gotta have *some* dignity.

She must've taken too long to answer because he gave her a long, sexy once over and said, "Rain check, love. It's snowed so friggin' much there are no empty shoulders to park on. So I guess you'll have to wait for me to rock your world."

She actually felt like sulking... shaking her head at both her disappointment and his arrogance, she said, "Your ego is becoming a problem for me." That was total bullshit, and she knew it. If she was honest, she'd admit his cockiness was 100 percent earned. He was beyond fabulous between her legs. Still, he didn't need to know that.

She stuck her nose in the air and turned her head to stare out at the scenery again. It was too pretty to ignore. Somewhere in this vast wilderness were the answers she'd been searching for. She'd spent hours researching her mother and her grandparents. At first, she'd been completely overwhelmed by the idea. How on earth was she going to find her family? Where would she start looking? She had no clue. Eventually she learned to use the library computers and started digging around the internet. It was Arthur who helped find her grandparents' property information. The sweet old man had been amazing. He knew all about property records and other public information. She dug around in every place he suggested until she found the deed for the land in the Catskills. Funny how that was really the only tangible evidence she had that her family existed. That and her mother's death certificate, of course. So she had proof a dead person had once lived, and proof that the person had parents; parents who were also dead. Awesome. Not much to go on.

She stared out the window, letting the scenery blur past. Dec popped in one of her favorite CDs, Kings of Leon's "Only by the Night" and turned the tunes up just loud enough to fill the car with sound. The bass thumped through her veins as they cruised along. It was oddly comforting to see the emptiness of the mountains again. The vast beauty was soothing. Maybe it did call to her soul as Dec had hinted. She definitely felt at peace here. Peaceful or not, she didn't know what they thought they'd find. She hoped they'd find something to clear up her mother's mystery. Maybe she'd left a journal buried under the floorboards or hidden inside a wall. Was it too much to hope for? Probably. Her heart ached to think that her mother had knowingly sold her soul to a demon. Her own mother? She just couldn't believe that. It had to be a mistake. From what she knew, her mother didn't have any rewards to show for this deal. She wasn't rich or famous.

She hadn't had a fabulous life. The opposite was true. They'd been poor even before her mother died. And she had died tragically young without happiness. If she *had* made a deal, she hadn't gotten the good end of it. That was for damn sure!

"Earth to Rori. You're a million miles away again."

"Just thinking. I still can't believe my mother could do this. I know my memories of her are pretty fuzzy now, but I don't remember her as a bad person. I don't remember feeling unloved. That just doesn't synch with her randomly selling my soul. The whole theory feels funky to me."

"I really hope we're wrong about this. I really do. You've got to be prepared that we might not find anything at the cabin. We might never know the truth."

The interstate had been cleared, so driving was easy so far. With no snow or ice, they'd kept a good speed and made it to the Catskills in record time. They turned onto a smaller highway to head more deeply into the mountains. This road was a snow-covered nightmare. Dec slowed down to a crawl to make the turn onto a one lane road that led to nowhere. The lane was narrow, rutted beyond comfort, and lined with bare trees. Crap. This thing was no better than a snowmobile trail! Her rational brain knew there was no way they could possibly die if they slid off the road. They were barely moving at all... but that didn't make her feel any safer. Clinging to the armrest to keep from bouncing into the door handle again, she shot Dec a sideways glance. Nope, not even a shift of his butt in the seat. How was it she was flung all over the front seat, but he sat in perfect comfort and control? She smothered a yelp as the SUV bounced over what felt like a meteor crater and slid to the side with a jerk before he brought it back to the center of the road again.

"Hang on! This road sucks." Dec reached across the console to squeeze her thigh in what was probably supposed to be reassurance.

It wasn't helpful.

"Ya think?"

With more amusement than called for, he flashed a grin at her grouchy tone and said, "Stop scowling. You'll wrinkle. We're almost there. It's not much farther."

It wasn't as sunny under the heavy tree cover and the temperature seemed to drop. A thin layer of ice formed on the windshield, and she could see puffs of her breath.

Dec blew out a stream of air like cigarette smoke before frowning into the windshield. "Weird. It feels colder to me. I hope we aren't going to get stuck in a storm. I have no idea if the cabin has any supplies at all. It would go way beyond shitty to be stuck here. You might get your first trip by teleport if that happens."

Humming nonchalantly under his breath, Dec turned up the defroster and winked. She wasn't fooled. Did he think she was blind? Rolling her eyes to her forehead, she smirked before leaning across to drop a quick kiss on his cheek. He was so obvious. He alternated between clenching his jaw and gnawing on his lower lip. His knuckles were tight where he gripped the wheel. He drove slowly, cautiously, over the ruts, while keeping up a constant 180 degree sweep with his eyes. She could almost hear the wheels turning in his head. He was searching for something. It was freaking her out a little. She found herself squinting into the gloominess of the trees, looking for demons, or aliens, or Bigfoot. All she saw was an endless landscape of bare tree trunks and lots and lots of snow.

Hugging her arms around herself, she asked, "What do you see? Is there something here? Bears?"

"Nah, not bears. They're sleeping." He shrugged. "I don't think it's anything. We just need to be alert. You never know." Pointing at a clearing in front of them, he announced, "Okay, looks like this is it. Are you ready to check it out?"

"Absolutely! Let's get this over with."

Something was off about this place. His spidey senses were tingling, but he couldn't see anything. No heat signatures jumped out of the trees. The forest was eerily silent, but that didn't bother him. It was the middle of December, the forest was buried under three feet of snow, and there were very few people out in this area. The silence wasn't an issue. He parked the SUV in front of the cabin and studied the woods around them one more time. Nothing. Rori perked up and looked around with excitement in her eyes. If she was nervous, she didn't show it. She was curious, anxious, and maybe a little sad. Hopefully this wouldn't be one big waste of time.

The rustic little building was craptastic. The brown wooden siding was faded and warped. The roof was missing a large swath of its metal sheeting, and the front deck was partially caved in on one end. On the upside, the two front windows were intact, filthy with years of dirt, but unbroken. There were no sheds or other buildings around. Just the cabin. The front door lock wasn't a problem for his B&E skills. It turned easily with a wave of the hand. Taking the lead, he stepped into the front room with Rori right on his heels. She started to laugh at his little show of magic, but the sound died in her throat.

"Your mother and I used to come here before she died. You could say it was our little… love nest."

The man stepped into the main room from what was probably the tiny kitchen. He wore baggy jeans and a NYU sweatshirt. White haired, with deep lines around his mouth and sallow skin, he was probably in his 70s. He looked like anyone's grandfather. The mocking voice was at odds with the homey plastic spatula he held in front of him. The aroma of bacon and eggs drifted from his clothes.

Rori gasped and grabbed onto Dec's jacket. "Father Joseph!"

Dec eased her back against the door, saying, "Stay put," before drawing his Primani blade with one quick movement. "Not Father Joseph. Ikini. Isn't that your real name, demon? You're the soul broker for Azrael."

The demon called Ikini tossed the spatula into the kitchen. Bowing at the waist, he shared his best priestly smile. Gentle, serene, it was designed to comfort distraught parishioners of all ages. "Guilty. But I do so prefer the name 'Father Joseph' after all these years of wearing him. Joseph Alexander: born in Brooklyn in 1939. Raised by sickeningly devout parents in a faded yellow duplex. Forced to attend all boys private school where he was teased for being too skinny and beaten by nuns so ugly even Christ wouldn't touch them. Despite all of that, he heard the call of his God and marched off to the seminary to learn how to be a good priest. And he *was* a good priest... that's what made him so useful."

Sweeping a hand apologetically over his clothes, he commented with a wry smile, "You'll have to forgive me for being out of uniform; I wasn't expecting company. All that black becomes monotonous, and the collar was getting too tight." He patted his rounded paunch. "The good father's been eating too much. He's put on some weight." Pointedly ignoring Rori, he gave Dec the once over before adding, "But you're not here to talk about an old priest's fate, are you Primani?"

Leaning casually against the door, Dec didn't bother to hide a feral smile. This couldn't be more perfect. They'd come for answers and answers they would have. He'd get every answer they needed from this cocky prick. Inch by scaly friggin' inch if that's what it took. He had learned a few tricks over the years. They'd just have to play this out and hope he wouldn't have to butcher the asshole before he talked.

"Actually we came to check out the property. Finding you here was a bonus, probably a sign that my karma's in good shape. I've been looking for you for a long time. Today's your lucky day. I'm in a good mood. If you cooperate, I'll blow you up nice and fast. You won't even feel it--much. If you want to be an asshole, I'll take you apart piece by piece." He shrugged, adding, "Your choice, really. Either way, you're not leaving this place in that meat suit."

In a lame attempt at dominant posturing, Ikini crossed his arms and straightened to his full height, several inches shorter than Dec. Over time, the old man's eyes had clouded to a murky, olive green. They were bloodshot and runny now. Between the oversized sweatshirt and sickly eyes, he wasn't really all that threatening. Still, he was a demon under all the geriatric window dressing. His shitty attitude came through loud and clear. It was almost too predictable.

"Playing the hero again? You Primani are always trying to save people--a ridiculous notion since most humans don't deserve to be saved. They're greedy and stupid. They all want more than they have and are happy to make a deal to get the dream life. Funny how they're all so surprised when it's time to pay the price. *Everyone* thinks they can get out of it." He dropped his eyes to Rori and observed coldly, "And you're entirely too late to save that one's broken soul. She's bought and paid for. She will pay her mother's debt whether you intervene or not. You can kill me right now, but that doesn't change her fate. She's already lost."

Rori lunged from behind Dec with a hiss of anger. Snatching her back, he wrapped his arm around her to keep her still. She snapped at Ikini, "You sonofabitch! You don't own me! I'm not property."

"No? You're wrong, Rori Austin. You *are* property. You've been Azrael's since before you were born. Your slut of a mother gave you to him just as easily as she gave herself to any creature with a cock. Angels, demons, priests, she wasn't all that picky." He smacked his lips and sighed. "I remember it like it was just yesterday. She came to me, crying about how she'd killed your father. She was positively distraught about the whole thing. Delusional too; she swore he was an angel, had a halo and magic powers. Crazy bitch... She thought confession would save her soul. As if I gave a shit about her guilty conscience!"

"She killed my father? You're lying!" Her voice rose with a sudden rush of anger, but she didn't lose control.

The only outward sign of her emotions were her nails gouging holes in the top of his forearm. He winced but didn't move away. She was handling this better than he expected. Still, maybe it would help to calm her down a wee bit. With this thought in mind, he sent a trickle of *saol* to calm her down.

She jerked her arm away. "Stop that! I'm not losing it!"

"Just chill and let me handle this. I know what I'm doing."

To Ikini, he said in a conversational tone, "Let's back up. I hate to admit this, but I'm not exactly sure what a soul broker does. Want to enlighten me for future reference? Seriously, what's so great that you'd let yourself be some other demon's bitch? What's in it for you?"

Booyah! He'd hit a nerve. Clearly he didn't like the word 'bitch'. He stared coldly at Rori until she dropped her eyes and sidled closer to Dec.

"Since you're so curious, let's use Rori's mother as an example. She came to me in confession with this insane claim that she had sex with an angel. Even crazier, she was convinced she had killed him. She was inconsolable over it. She was terrified for the child. She was sure God would kill her and the baby as punishment for her crime."

Shifting his eyes to Rori's white face, he laughed softly before crowing, "Imagine my surprise! A human woman getting knocked up by an angel? If her story was true, it was oh so very rare. What an opportunity for me! Getting her to agree to give us the child was really too easy. I simply explained that she couldn't possibly kill an angel. Real angels can't be killed by weak little women. Of course, then she wanted to find the father. After all, he should know about his child. I humbly explained that I was a simple parish priest without the power to contact angels. Perhaps we could pray together for a solution. And you both know the power of prayer, right? Within minutes, an angel came to help."

"Your boss."

He nodded patiently before continuing, "Yes, exactly. You're not as stupid as you look. Azrael appeared in a glorious flash of light. He was magnificent! Bold, fearsome, and powerful! And those wings! Fully spread against the stained glass, he was the perfect avenging angel. She fell to her knees before him, head bowed like an obedient little Christian, weeping so piously. It was sweet, really." He chuckled and sighed. "Azrael did the rest. He ranted and raved about how much trouble she was in. Humans and angels weren't supposed to create children. She had committed a grievous sin and should be severely punished." He stopped to scrub at the back of his head. His words lingered painfully in the space of a heartbeat before he finished his story.

"By this time, she was hysterical. Sobbing and begging him to help her. It was kind of pathetic. So the boss waited for her to get nice and worked up before reeling her in. He said he had spoken to God on her behalf. Since God was merciful, he wouldn't kill them if she agreed to give her daughter to his messenger, Azrael, on her 25th birthday. He wanted her to experience human life so she could share the knowledge with his angels. Once her birthday came, he would welcome the angelic child into Heaven as was only right."

"What's the significance of 25?"

He shrugged. "Azrael likes patterns. Annalisa would be 25 when she had the kid, so that seemed like the appropriate age to take the kid. She'd suffer for 25 years, watching her daughter grow up, knowing she'd be taken in the prime of her life. You asked what I get for brokering the deal. I play with the ones who interest me most."

Three months? She was going to die in three months? She closed her eyes and drew in a deep breath. The damn air was too thick too inhale; she couldn't seem to get any of it into her lungs. Breathing deeper, she counted to ten. Don't faint! Come on, come on. She was swaying on her feet, leaning into Dec's side. Biting her lip hard, she steadied herself by sheer force of will. The demon's story rang true, heartbreakingly so. Her poor mother! She had been so eager to do the right thing, and it had gone so horribly wrong for her, for both of them. She swallowed a lump in her throat. Now wasn't the time to put this story under a microscope. No doubt she'd relive this conversation more times than mentally healthy over the next three months of her life. Dec and the demon were still talking, trading insults and barbs while Dec set him up. He was up to something. His expression was relaxed, almost amused as he bantered back and forth with the one demon he had to hate with a passion. This was the monster that had killed eight little boys, aside from the other atrocious things he'd done. He was on Dec and Sean's list. They'd been hunting him for decades. He'd shared the history with her one night. Now he was so close to punishing this freak. The casual approach hid his true feelings. He was fiercely angry underneath that cool attitude. Yeah, he was up to something.

The clock was ticking in more ways than one. She might only have three months to live, but this horror would be dead in the next few minutes. Father Joseph, Ikini, or whatever he called himself, would be gone when Dec decided the time was right. There was no doubt in her mind about that. She'd seen him in action already. She watched Dec's body language and relaxed a little more. His muscles were taut, fingers gripping that wicked-looking knife with deceptive ease. He killed demons for a living. So this one should be easy, right? He's a rock star.

Even so, it was getting harder to ignore Ikini's mocking voice. It chafed her nerves, dredging up memories better left buried. She could almost smell the mustiness of the basement, the stale water... the stench of his breath. He burst out laughing at something Dec said; the inappropriate sound jolted her into action.

"Shut up!"

Ikini aimed those filmy green eyes at her with such malice that she took a step back. While she struggled to find her voice again, the green eyes flicked to red.

He studied her like something stuck on the bottom of his shoe. The disgusted expression shifted to a feral smile that she remembered too well. It was intimate, knowing, hungry. The same expression he'd worn when she showed up for confession. She froze as the memories threatened to swamp her.

He took advantage of her hesitation and said, "Save your speech, bitch. I don't care how you feel. If your feelings were any concern to me, I wouldn't have chained you to a table and taught you all about pain. You should be thanking me for not taking your virginity. You'll get over the rest."

"I said shut up! Stop talking! You ruined my life!"

He raised his brows and replied, "Did I? It wasn't me who came to you at night. Do you even realize he's with you? He's been softening you up for months. You're almost ready for him now. The next time he comes to you, you'll say yes. And then you'll scream. You'll howl in agony as the clock strikes midnight, and he rips your soul out. I promise you'll beg for a death that won't come; you'll scream inside your head as you lose all control. Your body and soul will belong to Azrael. But cheer up; he doesn't take very good care of his toys. They tend to have a short lifespan, even in Hell."

"Stop it! I'm not afraid of you anymore! We'll figure out how to fix this. I'm keeping my soul!"

"Too late, honey, your soul was broken the minute the deal was made. Think of it as a bomb. The timer's running, and you can't stop it. Your attempts to try will probably be amusing, though."

With a slight incline of his head, he asked, "I trust you're satisfied now? The big mystery's solved? As much as I've enjoyed this little trip down Memory Lane, I really must be go--"

"Going? I don't think so. Have a seat." Dec's tone changed in the space of a heartbeat. A minute ago, he'd been purposely conversational, keeping Ikini talking, keeping things calm so he could get information from the demon before he killed him. Now? Icy shivers crawled down her spine as his words sunk in.

Before she could blink, Ikini flew backwards into a chair, mouth hanging open in shock. She stared at Dec in surprise, too. She didn't see him move. How on earth did he do that?

"What did you do to me? You can't do this!"

Peeling himself away from the wall, he prowled closer. The cold look in his eye sent another shiver running down her back. Was this what Mica called soldier-mode? He wasn't glowing... but he was definitely getting there. Every movement was controlled, purposeful, tight, yet he was clearly feeling the adrenaline. She felt a wave of heat, even from across the room. Things were about to get interesting.

He winked at the stunned demon and asked, "I can't do what? Oh, you mean keep you from shimmering? Huh."

He squatted a few feet in front of the chair with his chin on his fist. "Looks like I just did."

Rori blinked, and Dec stood behind Ikini with the knife pressed against his throat. "So. What shall we talk about now that you've bragged all about your sick job as a soul broker?"

"You'll never get away with this! Azrael will hunt you!"

The feral smile was back in place, his lips curled to show his canines. "So predictable. Every demon says the same thing. And yet, somehow, I always get away with it." He rapped the knife against the top of his head. The demon winced but couldn't move away. "Funny how that works. Must be all my clean living."

"So here's how this is going to work now. You're going to sit nice and still while I drag your sorry slimy ass out of that priest. Then we'll have a little chat about Gary Carmichael and the other kids you've killed."

"You don't have the power to compel me!"

Ignoring the demon's protests, he continued without missing a beat. "Then I'll do the whole fucking universe a service and put you down once and for all. One..."

"Go fuck yourself!"

"piece at a time."

"Dec?"

Meeting her eyes over Ikini's head, he ordered, "Go wait in the car."

"But--"

"Don't argue! Wait in the car." He softened his tone and amended, "Please."

He waited until Rori closed the door before turning his attention back to the scumbag in the chair. Time to put some ghosts to rest. "How many were there?"

"I can't count that high."

Dec considered the abomination at his mercy while idly fingering the finely-etched runes that circled the haft of his knife. A hundred heartbeats passed before he trusted his voice. When he spoke again, his voice was deceptively soft.

"I remember you. You wore a different face, but it was you, wasn't it?"

"I get bored. I travel. Sometimes I travel back in time... sometimes I explore the future. It's entertaining." He paused for a split second before sneering, "Your sister died quietly. Just bled out in the grass, those big blue eyes staring up at me. You shouldn't have left her alone. It's no wonder your mother hated you."

Chapter 18: Scars on the Soul

SHE NEARLY BIT HER TONGUE OFF when Dec eventually tapped on the car window. She'd been staring into the trees, letting the stereo speakers drown out the screams... a quick glance at the dash clock showed only an hour had passed since he'd asked her to leave. It felt like decades. She swallowed the saliva pooling under her tongue and unlocked the doors. He'd survived; that was all that mattered.

"Is it over?" God, she hoped so. Her nerves were shot. Her stomach was sick. She wanted to puke and then curl up in bed and sleep for a week.

He didn't try to smile. He rubbed tiredly at his eyes before finally saying, "If you want to search the cabin, now's the time to do it. We can't stay here much longer. It's not safe."

It's funny how things can change in a couple of hours. Not too long ago, she'd been searching for answers, digging for the truth about her mother, about her life. She had certain beliefs that had shaped her existence. Now those beliefs were shattered. For the past ten years, she'd known without any doubts that Father Joseph Alexander was an evil predator. He preyed on the weak, took advantage of vulnerability, hurt innocents. She'd been damaged by him, changed by his actions. For years she hated him, praying for his death, sometimes even dreaming of killing him with her own bare hands. But never in her wildest dreams did she think she'd feel sorry for him. What a difference an hour made.

Dec ushered her inside. She hesitated at the entrance, not sure what to expect. The room reeked of burnt earth. The chair was overturned, empty except for small clumps of grey ash still clinging to the wood. The same substance spattered the walls around the chair in an arc pattern, much like blood castoff at a crime scene. She looked up at the ceiling and stepped closer to Dec. A three-foot diameter of scorched wood smoldered with wisps of acrid smoke. There was no sign of the demon.

She reached to take his hand, but he jerked away, warning, "Don't touch me right now. The ash will burn your skin, and it's all over me." He forced a weary smile and said, "He's gone. He won't be able to hurt anyone ever again. One down, one to go."

"Dec? Are you all right? You don't look so good." He was swaying on his feet even as he grimaced at her question. It was hard to see his color under the dusting of grey, but he seemed pale. Something was off. No cuts or bruises. Nothing ripped or bloody either. He appeared to be untouched--except for bloodshot eyes. That was new. A blood vessel had burst.

Completely ignoring her concern, he flapped a hand at the mostly empty bookshelves that were built into one wall. "You go ahead and look around. I'll take care of him."

What was once Father Joseph Alexander lay curled on the floor. His body had aged the moment the demon had left him. The wrinkled, shrunken mess was barely recognizable as human. She turned away with a twinge of sympathy that brought a lump to her throat.

"I used to wish him dead. But now I see he already was." She dragged an old raggedy quilt from a rocking chair and covered him with it. "Will he go to Heaven, do you think?"

"He's already there, love."

The stockings were hung by the chimney with care--as were three sets of mittens, three miniature hats, and three pairs of wet winter boots. All were fire engine red because that was their favorite color. As an added benefit, no one argued over what belonged to whom. God knew there were enough arguments about other super important things, like who got to sleep with Domino, who got to race the purple Mustang Matchbox car, or who spilled the cereal all over the pantry.

Mica finished sopping up more melted snow from the brick hearth. A peek out the window confirmed that, yes indeed, it was frickin' snowing again. She scowled at the ceiling and muttered at Mother Nature. "Jesus, woman, when are you going to run out of juice? Enough already!"

They were practically swimming in the fluffy crap. Once upon a time, she loved snow. That was before she had three kids who were pretty sure they were polar bears. They spent most of their free time in the yard. They were lucky Dani liked snow too, or they'd be corralled in the house all winter long. Dani watched the kids during the day while she taught classes and managed the studio. Since Dani was a nanny versus a housekeeper, Mica usually ended up washing 80,000 loads of clothes and mopping the floor a 1,000 times a week just to keep up with the mess.

Dropping a peck on Killian's cheek, she flopped on his lap hard enough to make him grunt. "We need a maid. I'm exhausted."

Her handsome man was sitting cross-legged on the floor in front of the coffee table. He was trying to fix her 101 Dalmatians music box. For some reason, the tiny Perdita figurine stopped turning. As soon as she landed, he dropped the miniature screwdriver and pulled her in for a more serious kiss. Drawing back to study her face, he caressed her cheek with the backs of his knuckles and pressed a soft kiss on her mouth. "You look tired, babe. You're doing too much. I'll ask Alex to find us a housekeeper to come in once a week. He'll know who's been vetted to work with Primani."

She rubbed her cheek against his and sighed. He was the best husband in the world. No doubt she was very lucky. There was another reason she needed help, but she wasn't sure how he would take the news.

"Mica? Babe? Are you asleep?"

Laughing against her hair, he scooped her up and carried her to their bedroom. She was so tired... she wasn't sleeping; she was resting her eyes.

The sound of pounding and yelling dragged her out of a solid sleep. Her brain couldn't get it together enough to make sense of what was happening, though. Groggy, she leaned up on an elbow and strained to hear. Was that Rori? Just as she lurched off the bed with every intention of flying (or tumbling) down the stairs to see what was going on, Killian Jr. threw the door open and ran inside, his face glowing with excitement.

"Daddy says to come quick! Uncle Dec's really hurt!" He took one look at her and said, "Hold my hand, Mom. I'll help you down the stairs."

Was he really only three? Such a little man already... still feeling wobbly, she smiled for him and let him help 'cuz that's what he did. Exactly like his father, he took charge and fixed things. The apocalypse was in very good hands.

The living room was filled with people when they finally made it down. Killian, Sean, and Raphael were huddled up by the front window. Dec was prostrate on the floor with Rori hovering by his side, strangely *not* touching him. He was awake, but not trying to sit up. He looked horrible. He turned towards her as she entered his line of sight. Uh-oh. Bloody eyeballs can't be good.

Rafe and Michael were watching from the kitchen doorway where their very smart father probably banished them. Taking a deep breath, she sent the rug rat still by her side to keep his brothers company. "Go on, little man. I'm okay now."

She took three steps into the room when her vision went dark around the edges. Unable to stop the momentum, she watched the floor hit her forehead with entirely too much force.

Consciousness came back with just as much force thanks to the smelling salts stuck underneath her nostrils. Snorting out the obnoxious fumes, she blinked awake and regretted it immediately.

"Ow!"

"There you are. You scared the hell out of me." Killian frowned from a position just above her nose. He laid an ice pack across her forehead where it arched over the goose egg that throbbed like a mother.

She had an audience. Everyone, minus Dec who was still on the floor, must've scurried over when she face planted. Yep, Sean, Raphael, and Rori all stared down at her from way up above her. It was kind of like looking into a forest...

"You guys are creeping me out. Help me up. I'm okay."

Killian didn't trust her to know whether she was okay or not, so he helped her up and steered her to the couch.

Something you want to tell me, babe?

His eyes gleamed with knowledge that his wife was up to something… she swallowed hard.

Not at the moment.

His eyes dropped to her belly, one brow lifted in question. Damn him. She couldn't keep anything from him.

He patted her stomach and said, "As of right now, you're off laundry duty." He handed her the ice pack and ordered, "Stay here and rest. We need to settle things with Dec and Rori."

Rori was back to kneeling beside Dec. He was covered in ash. That's why she wasn't touching him. He must've already warned her. For someone so new to their world, she was holding up pretty well. Killian pegged her as more of a girly girl, but she wasn't wigging out over the fact that her boyfriend was covered in demon ash that came from killing said demon in the most brutal way possible. He knew what Dec had done. He'd felt it through their psychic connection. Stripping the meat from that bastard had taken more than 45 minutes. Dec had been thorough in his retribution, but not without damage.

Did he let Rori watch? Since she was still willing to be in the same room with him, the answer was probably no. Good call, Dec. That's not a side of you for your woman to see. No, definitely not. She caught him watching but didn't say anything. All of her attention was on Dec. Her brows were knitted with worry. Her lips moved in prayer. Once she said there was no God. Now she trusted Dec's life to Him. Maybe the girl would be all right after all. Leave it to Dec to fix the broken ones. It truly was his unique gift. Time to help the healer heal though. The broken blood vessels in his eyes weren't the only ones they needed to worry about. Fresh blood snaked from his nose and slowly followed the curve of his cheek. He was out cold.

Wedging between Rori and Dec, Killian gestured to Sean for help. Between the two of them, they helped him to the bathroom, stripped him, hosed him down, and then stuffed him into his bed. Rori hovered in the doorway watching every move they made. She was clearly still worried but stayed out of the way. Smart girl. He liked her more and more every minute.

"What's wrong with him, Killian? I'm so sorry; I didn't know what to do. He told me to drive us here so I did. I just thought he was tired, but now…"

"You did the right thing. I don't suppose he told you everything about his Primani powers yet, did he?"

"Not much, no. Is this one of them?"

Sean chimed in. "Hemorrhaging after ganking demons? Uh, no. As far as powers go, that would definitely be lame."

Killian didn't hide his grin for a change. "Yeah, glad I don't have that one! Seriously though, he's got to rest now. His *saol* will heal everything while he sleeps. He's used a massive amount of energy to do what he did today. He's bleeding inside his melon. We need to leave him alone for a day or so."

"Are you crazy? We need to take him to a hospital. He can't stay here! He'll die!"

"Keep your voice down!" he snapped. "Listen to me. We don't need hospitals. We can heal ourselves. You should know that already." Guiding her by the arm, he towed her towards the door. "Leave him alone for a few hours so he can get better. He needs to focus."

Sean suggested, "You can sleep with him if you want to. He'll know you're there even if he doesn't respond. It'll help you both."

Rori tugged at her arm until Killian let her go. After smoothing the bangs away from Dec's eyes, she kissed him and whispered fervently, "I'm not leaving you."

Floating in a brilliant blue sea, Dec relaxed in the gentle swells, letting them work their magic. The healing place in his mind was this endless sea. The warm water lifted him above pain, numbed his body so his *saol* could focus on knitting him back together. Although anyone staring down at him would think otherwise, he was aware of the outside world. Rori watched him now. He sensed her, felt her energy settled comfortably beside him. She had been lying there for hours, not crying, not worrying... no, surprisingly she was calm. Her arm was draped across his bare waist, face turned into his side. So sure of his immortality, she slept like a rock. Funny how she accepted he was indestructible when she'd once seen his death.

Nearly completely healed, he stayed still as he conducted a mental inventory of his body parts. All of the pain was gone now. The blood vessels drained to their correct capacity again... his headache had finally dissipated. He could open his eyes any time now. But he wasn't quite ready. His body was healed, but his soul was forever scarred by what he'd done. If he was going to find a lasting peace, there was someone he needed to see. Something he needed to say to her...

Concentrating hard, he searched the vast expanse of Heaven. His eyes roamed over sweeping vistas of mountains and plains. Rivers and streams snaked through fields and forests like so many satin ribbons. Sun-drenched deserts rioting with spring blooms popped up here and there. As beautiful as they were, he wasn't looking for a desert. That wouldn't be her idea of Heaven. No, he was looking for something more green, more like home. There! Gathering wildflowers from a lush, green meadow, she wore a vivid yellow smock that shone like a miniature sun. The clothes didn't matter; he would recognize her anywhere. Her hair was braided; her feet were bare. She straightened from her task, looking around, looking for *him*. Frozen in time, she was beautiful. Perfect and unbloodied.

Brigid.

Her face lit up the second she spotted him. Laughing, she tossed the flowers and raced to meet him. Flinging herself against his legs, she squeezed hard, crying, "Declan! You've come to see me!"

"Of course I have! I've missed you, sweetheart!"

Scooping her up, he swung her around, laughing and then weeping at her squeals of delight. Holding her tightly after all these years, he thoroughly and completely lost it.

The lullaby was one their mother always sang before bed. He hadn't heard it in more years than he could say. She'd stopped singing after Brigid's death. She stopped talking, too. Brigid cuddled on his lap, singing softly and patting his shoulder, mothering him as best she could. He hugged her again, cherishing the lightness of her bones, the baby softness of her skin. It would be a long time before he saw her again.

"Shall I sing with you, little one? Maybe together we can get the words right?"

She giggled, but then studied him intently. "You should not be here, brother. You are not ready for Heaven. Why have you come?"

"Mostly to see your pretty face again. But there's another reason. One that's very important to me. I need you to try to understand something that's kind of complicated for a little girl. Can you try?" When she nodded soberly, he continued, "I've come to ask for your forgiveness."

"Forgiveness?" She wrinkled her nose in puzzlement and asked, "What did you do?"

He kissed the back of her tiny hand. "I... I found the bad man who did this to you. He won't ever hurt anyone else."

"Did you stab him like he stabbed me? It hurt a lot. I cried hard. Did he cry?"

"Not *exactly*, no. But it's done, and I wanted you to know that."

She lifted round blue eyes to peer into his for so long he had to look away. "So why are you so sad?"

"I'm sad because I couldn't save you. I would give anything to turn back time. If I could re-do that day, I would stay with you instead of wandering off to look at those stupid horses! It's my fault you were alone. My fault that bastard grabbed you. If I was doing my job, you would've had a different life; you would've actually *had* a life. Can you ever forgive me, Brigid?"

Her eyes, so like his own, sparkled with mischief as she dabbed at his cheek with the hem of her dress. "Do all big people weep this much? Papa never cried. Are you sure you are all grown up?"

Papa never cried? He was glad she had that memory of their father. His memories were very different. Racked by guilt and shame, he watched as his parents collapsed under the weight of their grief. Papa cried for months. Mama cried for years.

"Brigid, please don't tease me now. You'll break my heart all over again." He pressed her palm to his chest and said with a slight smile, "See how it beats? I think you've broken it."

He sighed as her attention wandered to the sky. After watching clouds drift by for several minutes, she seemed to fall asleep. He dropped a light kiss on the top of her silky little head. She was too young to understand such concepts as vengeance, justice, forgiveness. She'd certainly not understand what he'd done to that demon. She asked if he stabbed it. Stabbed? Not quite. He always thought he'd feel better afterwards. After all, he was stopping a vicious predator, avenging the deaths of so many children. But all he felt was a tearing in his soul. He'd crossed lines, and he wasn't proud of it. But it was done. There was no way to make her understand his need to avenge her death. She was just too young. He got that. But even so, he needed to see her now, after all this time had passed, to tell her the monster that ended her life was gone. She wouldn't know the words to ease the guilt he felt even today. He needed to move on. To do that, he would have to find a way to let the guilt go. She was happy here. He would leave her alone with her Heaven.

Waking as abruptly as she dozed off, she yawned hugely and stretched her arms. After climbing down, she patted his leg and said, "You are not a monster, brother."

Then she was gone.

The meadow shifted back to his sea just as something soft danced across his stomach.

Rori.

God, he was beautiful. She'd come awake with her nose pressed against his ribs, the smell of lemongrass soap teasing her senses. That stuff was amazing. While she inhaled the fragrance of soap mixed with *eau de* Declan, she peered down at his sleeping form. He was better. His breathing was slow and regular. His chest rising and falling as it should. The golden color was back in his skin--all of his skin. She was thrilled to realize his brothers had put him to bed naked. They had thrown a blanket over him, and that was it. Carefully, soft as a feather, she caressed the delicate skin across the ridges of his abs, exploring a random scattering of tiny freckles and the happy trail on the way. She practically had her nose pressed against the damn thing as she checked out the hollow of his belly button. It was an adorable innie that begged for her to taste it. After tickling it with the tip of her tongue, she couldn't resist running her lips over his belly too. Relaxed in sleep, he was warm and cuddly… and entirely too sexy. Just as she was considering her next move, the blanket twitched next to her ear.

Dec's fingers curled around the back of her neck, rubbing lazy circles while watching with heavy-lidded eyes. He propped himself on his elbows and chuckled as she jerked her face away from his stomach.

"Are you feeling better?" The question came out in a throaty whisper she didn't recognize. She flushed and cleared her throat.

The slow smile and dimples said he was. Dragging his hand through her hair, he played with it, watching the strands slip between his fingers. Such a simple touch, nothing erotic about it... but it stoked the fire that was already smoldering. She must've moaned or swayed or done something else obviously blissful because he tightened his grip with enough pressure to make her gasp.

"I *was* feeling better, but now I'm all hot and bothered."

Smuggler's Notch. Rori had heard of it, of course, but being there was not something she'd ever imagined. For a city girl raised by dead broke foster families, the idea of going to a ski resort in Vermont was as farfetched as flying to Siberia for a latte. And getting on a snowboard? Never in a million years. Yet, somehow, here they were. She was so nervous she was about to implode. Dec was 100 percent convinced he could teach her to snowboard... she was 100 percent sure she would end up in the hospital. Had he not noticed she wasn't especially coordinated? Really... she walked into walls, for crying out loud! No, for some reason she didn't get, he was sure she'd take to boarding like a fish to water. He was ever the optimist. Hey, if he wanted to teach her, she'd at least *try*. She'd seen a few miracles since they'd met--maybe he would conjure up another one.

The mountains seemed taller here in Vermont. They'd been steadily climbing, the tree line changing the higher they drove. The bare deciduous forest thinned to snow-dusted pines. The winding roads were coated with a fresh few inches of powder. Both Sean and Dec got really jazzed about that--she wasn't nearly as thrilled. The tires of the SUV hadn't slipped yet, but she couldn't help clutching at the armrest and pushing down on an invisible brake pedal.

Sean turned around from the front seat. He'd called shotgun and jumped in before she could protest. Jerk. Now he flashed a cheeky grin. "You do realize we're immortal, right? I can 100 percent guarantee you're not going to die in a car accident with one of us. If you don't ease up on that poor floorboard, you'll be doing the Flintstones shuffle."

Dec burst out laughing and peered into the rearview mirror. "Relax, darlin'. I promise I've done this a million times. It's just a little snow. Now, you might bust your ass on the mountain today... but that's out of my hands."

It was called Magic Learning Trail. The name was perfect because it would take magic to get her ass on it. It started at the top of the biggest mountain she'd ever seen. From where they stood, she couldn't even see the beginning of the trail. What she *did* see scared the bejesus out of her. It was a sheer vertical drop if she'd ever seen one. And there were trees beside the trail! Hitting them did bad things to your head. People died from trees! No friggin' way. Nope. She wasn't coming down that horror. It was certain death.

Sean wagged his head with a disgusted, but very amused expression, and said, "Rori, it's the bunny slope. Look at that kid over there. What is he? Three? He's not crying about it." He shook his head again. "Man up, sweetheart!"

"You're kind of a jerk. You know that, right?"

"It's been said."

It was time to appeal to the kinder, gentler Primani. "Dec, you can't possibly expect me to handle this, can you? I'll die!"

"Don't be such a girl. You'll be fine. Sean, no video!"

Crap. So much for kinder and gentler.

After clapping her on the back hard enough to send her careening into Dec, Sean saluted with his cellphone and deserted them for a black diamond. She watched him walk away, wondering how long he'd be alone today. Dressed in solid black pants and jacket, with a dramatic splash of red from his Oakleys, he attracted attention from every woman in his path. Heads swiveled. It was that walk of his.

And maybe his fine ass...

"Come on, chicken. It's time for you to spread your wings."

Was it her imagination, or did Dec's smile turn just a little malicious? Shit. She was busted again.

"You know I don't like him, right? It's just hard not to look." Why on earth did she just say that aloud?

"Whatever," he muttered with a frown.

According to the guys, there were three main hurdles she needed to jump to master snowboarding: Getting on the chairlift, learning to control the board, and getting off the chairlift. Ideally, all of the actions should be done without falling on her face, hitting any trees, or killing any fellow humans. They made it sound so easy.

Clearly annoyed, Dec stalked around her, heading to the lift. Like checking items off a to-do list, he walked her through the boarding process without his usual jokes and teasing. The second the lift moved, she bounced into the back rest with an embarrassingly girly squawk. As the lift jerked and shuddered on its ascent, trees blurred past. Was it supposed to go this fast? Oh, my God. One stiff gust would dump her out. Her board flopped around as she struggled to rest it on the bar. The ground was impossibly far below. Was there enough snow to break her fall? She'd probably break a leg... minimum. With a death grip on the safety bar, she closed her eyes and tried not to panic. How the hell was she supposed to get off now?

That little problem was solved in the most humiliating way possible. The entire way up, Dec gave her instructions, tips, reassurances, whatever. The second her board hit the landing, she fell on her ass and slid over the side in a pile of body parts and a lot of screaming. Several of said body parts unfortunately belonged to a family of four who she managed to take down like bowling pins. Three little kids went flying into the bank.

He watched Rori struggle to get back to her feet with mixed feelings. On the one hand, she had to learn to get up by herself. On the other hand, she was so friggin' cute sprawled on her back, trying to push herself upright and failing miserably. She looked like a baby turtle... with something really long stuck to one of its legs. Probably he should be helpful and go do something. But... he was still stinging over her comment about Sean.

One of these days he might have to strangle Sean just simply for existing. What was it with him and women? Dark and mysterious? Huh. Dark? Yes. Mysterious? Not so much. Try emotionally unavailable, volatile, dangerous. Nothing mysterious about him. Maybe it was the danger vibe women were drawn to. Hmm. If Rori wanted dangerous... maybe it was time to let her see that side of him.

"Dec! Help!" She was on her feet, finally, but had no idea what to do next. The board began to slide with the pull of gravity. With a whoop of surprise, she waved her arms madly to keep her balance. The purple hat slipped to cover one eye; the other eye glittered with excitement and more than a little fear. Rosy cheeks, pink lips pursed in an uncertain smile, she was friggin' adorable. There was no way he could stay irritated with her. The only solution was to kill Sean. Damn. He'd fallen to the point of no return. That was for sure.

An hour later, she mastered getting on and off the lift. They celebrated with a long, lingering kiss on the side of the Lower Morse lift line. The wind picked up, blowing hair into his eyes, interrupting their kiss with a rudeness only Mother Nature could get away with. Frigid blasts pushed between them practically shoving them apart. Rori held his arm in a death grip to keep on her feet. Her board slid one way then the other as she tried to keep her balance. Unwilling to give him up so easily, she used him as a shield and tugged his head down for another kiss.

"What's up? Something wrong?" she asked while nibbling on his bottom lip.

"Maybe." He studied the sky. It wasn't odd to see grey clouds hanging low above these mountains. The heavy nearly black ones weren't harmless though. The storm was moving in fast. It was time to go before they got caught up here. A sudden gust of wind got everyone's attention at the same time. It was almost funny to see the entire group of people around them look to the north at exactly the same time. After a collective silence, they all headed for the trail. It was bad juju to stick around this mountain top. Rori was ducking to avoid a sudden shower of snow, when she abruptly froze, eyes wide with fear.

He sensed it the same second she froze. Deep inside the gloom of the trees, a shadow shifted, gliding around the trunks, moving closer. The shadow was featureless, but its malevolence radiated in waves of frigid air.

The wind roared straight at them, trees bending with the force. Icy snow slapped at them now, stinging like bees. The few people who were still hanging around bolted past, yelling to get off the mountain. He was torn between tearing after that demon and staying with Rori. Looking back and forth between the two, he realized there wasn't really an option.

Rori started shaking, eyes rolling up, lips turning blue. Catching her by the arm, he shouted, "Rori! Stay here!" She went limp before sliding down his side, dead to the world. Ah, hell. Not now!

A tingle of recognition crawled down his spine. The shadow had moved. It stood less than 20 yards from them. Worse, it wasn't a shadow anymore. The demon stood in his natural form, wings folded against his shoulder blades, eyes seething with fury. Dark energy hit Dec like a lightning bolt, sending him flying backwards to land hard on his back. Rocketing to his feet, he flashed to Rori and threw her over his shoulder.

Azrael simply spread his magnificent wings, head lowered in a mockery of prayer. His familiar voice echoed inside of Dec.

You cannot fight me, Primani. The woman is mine.

"Over my dead body!"

Yes, most likely.

He nearly dropped Rori when she started to struggle in panic.

"He's coming for me!"

Chapter 19: Through the Looking Glass Darkly

THEIR REENTRY WAS JACKED UP. With snowboards still strapped on, they landed awkwardly, staggered around a second or so before crashing to the floor in a tangle of twisted limbs.

"What the hell happened?"

"Where's my truck?

"Where's Sean?"

"Are you hurt?"

Mica and Killian hit him with a barrage of really relevant questions the second they hit the living room. Unfortunately his brain was on hyper-drive, and he was too busy yanking the Burton's straps open so he could bolt after dick with wings. Rori was safe. Time to fly.

"Whoa! Hold up! Where are you going?" Killian pinned him with the WTF glare just before shoving him towards the basement door. "What's up?"

Spinning back around, he fumed, "Motherfucking Azrael--that's what's up! Sonofabitch showed up on the mountain. Scared Rori half to friggin' death. She was a heartbeat away from vanishing again. I managed to hold her back--no idea how--but it was too close. We got out of there just in time. I'm going back. He's bound to leave a trace, right?"

"No, probably not. Sorry, man, but this demon is no amateur. You're wasting your time. He's not going to leave you a crumb to follow."

"But--"

"Dec, it's a blizzard over there. The weather is getting worse here, too. That snow's going to bury any trace of him. There's no way I could convince my girl to let us go anywhere in this nightmare. Let's calm down and think this out. He's holding all the cards. We need to come up with something other than jumping on him and trying to beat him to death."

The last part was said with a smirk that showed just how intuitive Killian really was. That was exactly what Dec's brain was cooking up. Jump on the bastard until he's a big puddle of black mush. Okay, so that's not a realistic plan. But he could do so much more...

"Don't even think about it. I know what you did to Ikini." He locked eyes with him, daring him to deny it. "Your melon was melted when you got done. I'll knock you out myself if you try going after this asshole alone."

"Damn it! I'm not letting him take her! This isn't her fault." He was still steaming inside. He wanted to hit something, wanted to break a tree in half. He peeled out of the jacket and dragged the thermal over his head. Still too hot...

While he was busy stripping and pacing like a caged lion, Killian flipped on the stereo, threw in some Disturbed, and cranked up the volume.

"Let's go."

He spun around. Killian stood with a huge grin splitting his face, flexing his hands and rolling his shoulders to loosen the muscles.

"I'm still pissed," he offered in fair warning. Killian wasn't *quite* a tree, but he might be able to break him in the mood he was in.

Killian shrugged one shoulder, but kept that cocky grin in place. "Are we going to yabber or beat the hell out of each other? I've still got things to do tonight."

Rori was still trying to drag her boots off when a sudden blast of music came through the floor. What the hell? Mica frowned at the floor. Before she could ask what was going on, Mica took off. She reappeared with a tray. On it was a bottle of Jim Beam, three shot glasses, and a first aid kit. Not much of a snack.

"I don't know what to say about that." She waved a hand at the tray with absolutely no idea what it was all for.

Seemingly resigned to whatever drama was unfolding, Mica enlightened her. "When they come back up, they'll need some TLC and a couple of shots. What happened out there? Dec is more pissed than I think I've ever seen him. You look like death warmed over. And I mean that in a good way!"

"Uh, sure. That RBD showed up at the ski resort! I don't know what happened really. One minute we were getting ready to finish the last run; the next minute, all hell broke loose. We stopped so I could catch my breath; that led to some kissing... we got a little carried away, I guess. A storm rolled in, and then, out of the blue, the demon was there. I don't know what else happened. I... I sort of blacked out again." She rubbed her arms to chase away the goose bumps. She felt too exposed even here where she was safe. "He spoke to me, Mica... inside my head. He said he was coming for me."

Mica pondered the bottle for a minute before pouring Rori a shot. Handing it to her, she ordered, "Drink it. You need it." She tossed her a quilt from the back of the couch. "You're shivering. I can see it from here. Listen, sweetie, this place is pretty well protected from demons. You can relax. No one can get to you here. Killian won't allow it."

She curled her knees up and tried to relax. Between the screaming metal vibrating the floorboards and her lingering fear of the demon, relaxation wasn't a sure thing. She hoped Mica was right about that. Killian seemed to have a strength the other Primani didn't. She couldn't put her finger on it; there was a power in him that intimidated her to no end, but also left her feeling strangely protected.

Mica handed her another shot and smiled knowingly. "Dec is the one, isn't he? I can see how it is between the two of you. He loves you, Rori. He loves you with every ounce of his being. I feel it when you're together. The intensity makes my head swim. And a few other parts too!" She laughed softly before adding soberly, "That's a rare, rare thing. There's no one else like Dec. He's more special than you know."

Despite the residual shakiness, she beamed at Mica's words. "I've never felt this way. He's done so much for me; saved my life, protected me... but it's more than that. When we're *together*, I feel like my soul connects to his; like we're bound somehow."

Mica didn't comment. Her eyes went wide in surprise, just before she laughed so hard she ended up crying. "Bound? Did you say 'bound'?"

"Er, yeah, it was, um, sort of freaky and mystical..." She closed her eyes to picture the first time they made love... the intensity, the raw hunger, the delicate filaments of gold. At the time, she was too into Dec to wonder about that. She thought it was a figment of her imagination... but she'd sensed the binding every time they made love. It was more subtle each time, but the sensation was there. Every cell in her body seemed to reach for him even as he plunged into her.

Mica fizzed with barely restrained humor, trying so obviously not to laugh. Her face went through a series of expressions before finally bursting into an ear-to-ear grin. She shook her head and said only, "Oh, my."

Before she could jump on that cryptic comment, the doorbell rang and the excited chattering of little boys filled the room as they burst inside. Mica jumped up to greet them and swayed abruptly.

She said, "Oh, crap," and sank back to the chair again. Ashen faced, she put her head between her knees, muttering, "breathe in, breathe out."

Michael was the first to reach her. And though he might have been in the lead, Rafe and Killian were right behind him. The three of them climbed onto her lap, all talking at once. Was she sick? Did they need to call Daddy? Was she going to read them a story? Were there any cookies? The noise was overwhelming. Rori couldn't help laughing at the look on Mica's face… she obviously felt ill, but the boys were so damn cute and worried that it was impossible to be annoyed with them. Instead, Mica wrapped them all in a hug and shushed them in between giggles.

After the volume came down, Mica fixed her with a hard stare and said, "Don't breathe a word about this to Dec. He's got enough to worry about."

"Cross my heart. Can I get you anything? Water?"

"It'll pass." To Dani, she said, "Hey woman! Come in and sit down. How was the movie?"

Dani had been waiting by the door so quietly that Rori hadn't noticed her. Once the boys had settled down, Dani came over to talk to Mica, while pointedly ignoring her. The stiff set of her shoulders spoke volumes. She was still not over Dec. Huh. From what he'd said, they hadn't had a real relationship--hadn't even slept together. So what was her problem? The more she thought about it, the more she just didn't give a shit. Dani could go screw herself. She fucked up with Dec. Snooze, lose, etc.

Two could play the bitch game. She was just as good at ignoring people. In fact, she'd start right now. She crossed to Mica and said, "I need to get out of these clothes. When I come back out, I'll make dinner. You should rest."

Dec and Killian stumbled up the stairs feeling exhausted and exhilarated. Bloody and bruised, they limped and winced their way through the house. Blowing off steam was just what he needed. All that clawing frustration was nicely tamped down for now. He didn't feel driven to tear down the forest, so that was a good thing. Nothing like a good ass whooping to burn off anger. Yeah, he felt much, much better. He needed a shower though. He smelled like ass. The last thing he needed was Dani. And that was the first thing he saw when he staggered to the living room. She rolled her eyes over him before turning away.

Fuck you very much, witch.

Mica smothered a laugh behind her hand and pointed to the tray. "Grab the bottle and go see your girl. She's taking a shower." She made a big display of sniffing the air and added, "You two reek. Maybe you need a shower too."

The guest bathroom was small and tidy. It was decorated very simply with pale blue towels and throw rugs over gleaming white tiles. All of the faucets and towel bars were polished chrome. No potpourri or knickknacks, no magazine baskets full of Good Housekeeping magazines, no candles. No one would ever consider it a fussy room. It had an efficient sort of feel to it. Mica's only feminine touch was a small watercolor painting of a flower market set near the Eiffel Tower. Even though the room was small, it had a huge glass shower that practically screamed 'have sex here' and a marble vanity topped by a huge mirror. Rori and Dec had been gracious guests and christened that shower in ways that would surely shock Mica. She hoped

Dec would finish whatever he was doing and get his sexy ass in here.

The room was chilly so she cranked up the shower, setting it to just below scalding, loving the heat as it pounded between her shoulder blades. Closing her eyes, she rubbed the lemongrass body wash across her arms and breasts, enjoying the slippery soap and the heavenly scent. She just lathered her hair with shampoo when she heard the bathroom door click closed. About time! "Dec?"

No answer.

The scalding water had steamed up the shower stall. She couldn't see anything clearly. Rubbing shampoo away from her eyes, she peered into the glass. Nothing. Did she hear something or not? Cocking her ear, she strained to listen above the running water. After standing that way for several seconds, she scoffed at her twitchiness and started to lean back into the water. Just as she closed her eyes, a shadowy shape darkened the glass. "Is that you, Dec?"

An uneasy feeling wormed through her gut. With way more stupidity than bravery, she yanked the door open and nearly stopped breathing. The room's temperature dropped at least 50 degrees. The steam on the vanity mirror had frozen to frost; frozen except for a section that had been scraped clear.

Two words were scratched into the mirror below it.
Hello, Rori.

Dec was halfway to the bedroom when he heard her scream. Taking off at a full sprint, he cleared the door just in time to see her being dragged through the bathroom mirror. Her head and shoulders vanished, the rest of her still inside the room. She was clinging to the marble sink, knuckles white, fingernails broken, legs kicking behind her.

She was screaming at someone, the sound warbled as if under water. "I don't want you! Leave me alone!"

"Killian!" He grabbed her around the waist, trying to pull her back. As strong as he was, he couldn't hold her against the force. Wet, soapy, naked, she slipped forward, inch by inch, as he dug in his heels and hung on. Desperate to pull her back, he reached for her hair. The mirror was solid where he touched it. He tried to put his hand through it and it bounced off, yet she was still sliding through the glass as easy as water. What kind of magic was this?

"Hold on, Rori!" Where the hell was Killian? She was half way through now, her body arched like a bow as she strained to resist the momentum.

From the corner of his eye, he caught a movement in the mirror. From infinite darkness, a hand reached for her, grasping at her face. Like a living statue, the hand was hard and black as onyx, gleaming like a burning ember. It opened, spreading its fingers wide, a fiery sigil branded on the palm, moving to her face. The voice shouted with fury inside his head.

She's mine! I'm coming for her.

"Let her go!"

Killian burst in with *Sgaine Dutre* blazing in his fist. He took one look at the mirror and shouted, "*Sgaine Dutre seao demonae. Eiron es finiate!*"

The sigil burst into flames before vanishing into smoke. Rori tumbled backwards into Dec. She was completely hysterical, clinging to him like a life preserver, chanting, "Don't lose me! Don't lose me!"

"Here, take this and put her to bed." Killian draped a towel over her, tucking the edges in and actually patting her back. His eyes were troubled as he inspected the mirror. He muttered something to the blade and held it to the glass. The silver gleamed until he crossed the part of the mirror where Rori had been grabbed. When it passed the section, it was covered with frost. The blue stone flared at the same time. He ground his teeth together and hissed, "Stay the fuck out of my house, Azrael. This is my turf. I'll bind you so fast your fucking head will spin."

Dec lifted an eyebrow. "Can you do that?"

"Shut up."

The sun was long since gone when she opened her eyes to find herself in bed. A single white candle burned on the nightstand. The flame leaped in the darkness sending shadows jumping against the gauzy white curtains. Something had woken her from a fitful sleep full of fire and shadows. The flames were so real she felt their blistering heat on the backs of her legs as she ran. But it was only a dream, a nightmare. One she was both familiar with and tired of.

As her mind began to clear, she felt heat again. Mmm... Not fire; a different kind of flame, but one that would consume her more completely. Dec. He was gloriously naked, gloriously hard, and oh, so very hot. They lay facing each other, barely touching, yet connected from head to toe. The pale strands appeared one by one as she watched in astonishment. The lines began to undulate and grow, wrapping themselves around their bodies, joining them more tightly. They didn't have to work so hard. She wasn't going anywhere. Purring like a cat, she rubbed her cheek against the sandpapery shadow that darkened his jaw. The scruffiness made him look more dangerous, more mercenary. He lay perfectly still with eyes closed, face serious.

Rubbing her lips across that shadow, she went just a little limp at the idea of danger. Danger and Dec. That had sexy, sexy appeal. She teased his jaw with her tongue, dipping along his throat, before murmuring, "You are so damn hot. I can't control myself around you." His only response was a groan and hard inhale when she nipped his earlobe. She could feel his tension building and it made her bolder. She looked into his face and swallowed the instinct to run. His eyes gleamed with hunger that sent her heart skittering into overdrive.

"Rori, you had that dream again." His hand shook as he caressed the side of her face, spreading gentle kisses across her jaw. His lips were gentle but the rest of him was tense, poised, ready to pounce.

She nodded. "Yeah, but it's over."

She shivered as he smiled into her eyes. It wasn't simply a smile; it was more of a promise, maybe a warning.

"It's not going to happen again." His voice was husky with strain, almost sad. He fingered a lock of her hair and brought it to his nose with a sigh.

She started to tell him it was okay, she didn't fear the dreams now. She knew he would keep her safe.

He put his finger to her lips and shook his head so close his eye lashes brushed her nose. "Shh. I'm trying to work a little miracle and get laid at the same time. Cooperate, wench."

He leaned in and tugged her bottom lip between his teeth. At her yelp of surprise, he sucked it in with gentle strokes while drawing her closer to him. The second his tongue met hers, she lost any kind of will to resist. Letting him take control was her wildest fantasy… she'd been nursing the dream for months.

"Do what you need to."

He blinked in surprise. "What I need might be more than you can give. Trust me?"

"With my soul."

He held her with one hand around her waist while he took control with his other hand. Moving intentionally slowly, he dragged his hand up her the back of her thigh, squeezing gently, following the curve of her butt, before resting it on her waist. The gentle pressure was an order to stay still while he used the other hand to set her on fire. With the lightest touch, he skimmed his palm over her thigh, between her legs, and across her belly. Exploring everything he wanted, he watched her melt. She whimpered and pressed his hand against her breast.

"Patience, love. Let me do this my way."

Her entire world tunneled to nothing but the feel of his mouth on her neck, his hand kneading her breast, the velvety heat of his cock pressing against her core. Tiny lights sparkled behind her eyelids. The scent of the forest filled the air as her body dissolved into a puddle. Clutching at his hair, she held his mouth to hers, taking everything from him. Rocking her hips forward, she stroked him with her body, urging him to put out the fire. He pulled away, still touching her, but not enough to ease her hunger.

He kissed her hard before growling, "No more nightmares of him. I want to fill your head." He cupped her breast hard enough to make her gasp aloud. The twinge of pain sent ripples of desire curling through her veins. He worked the nipple between his fingers while capturing her mouth in a kiss that was nowhere near tender. His mouth plundered hers... demanding her response, sending her control into pieces. He took everything in that moment, her mouth, her body, her soul. Her back arched as his fingers sank deep, pressing harder, twisting... until she cried out, the explosion brilliant as a star.

Breathing harshly, he held her face between his palms, thumbs caressing fragile cheekbones, eyes glowing cobalt. "When you close your eyes, you'll dream of me."

Like a fan slowly unfolding, her mind opened to the vision he created... The first thing she saw was the candle flame flickering over the walls, blurry, indistinct, wavering in the darkness. As the images grew clearer, she found herself looking down at the bed, seeing them from above. A vision? A memory? Yes. A memory that was more vivid as she relived it again. She watched the scene below her... her legs wrapped around his hips, head flung back... his strong hand clutching her breast like a treasure, his beautiful mouth sucking at her throat, the muscles bunching in his arms as he held her tightly… The explosion left her dazed, but he wasn't done yet.

Turning her onto her stomach, he rubbed her aching shoulders and legs. Stroking surely, firmly, he massaged away her aches and pains. Stopping to stroke her more sensitive areas along the way, he feathered kisses across each vertebrate, over each cheek, across the backs of her knees, down to each toe. Drawing them into his mouth one at a time, he teased her until she squirmed with pleasure. Surely she was in Heaven. She was more relaxed than she'd ever been in her life. Just as she thought about dozing off, he buried his face against the nape of her neck and nibbled. At her moan of approval, he draped his body over her back and cocooned her beneath him. Holding his weight from squashing her into the pillow, he worked his mouth around to her lips and back to her neck.

"You're so beautiful… I didn't know how much I was missing until I met you. Making love to you is a miracle. We're meant to be together, love. See the beauty of us?"

As before, her mind opened to fill with the memories he created. Everything was crystal clear. The muscles in his shoulders and back flexed as he covered her, his ass was tight and bitable as she looked down at it. His thighs wrapped around her hips, spread to hold her between them. Just the sight made her mouth water with anticipation, causing an involuntary shiver. Instinct took over and she tilted her hips for him. This time, there was no urgency, no roughness, he lifted her hips, kissed her back softly and slowly pushed inside. As the pressure built, she closed her eyes to see the images flow.

"Remember the beauty, Rori. Always remember."

He looked into her sleepy eyes with a feeling of satisfaction he didn't recognize. He'd never thought of himself as an alpha male; he was a surfer, a boarder, a sucker for babies and sad women. Something about Rori changed him. He didn't make love to the woman; he'd claimed her as his to the universe. Just the thought of her belonging to that demon made him mental, pushed him past the edges of his civilized self. He knew what her life would be like--knew what the demon would do to her delicate body, her fragile soul. Those nightmares were one step away from his taking control.

Over his dead body.

Oh, he meant that when he said it, and he meant it now. He was throwing up every weapon he could think of. He'd be damned before he'd let the demon win. God, he handled her roughly... he should feel ashamed, but she surprised him with her passion. He'd brought her to the brink and stood by her side while she fell. She embraced his touch with complete abandon. Not only did she go along with him, she pushed him to go harder, faster, rougher. This woman brought out every alpha instinct hiding in his DNA. He wanted to protect her, true. But more than that, he was driven to claim her. There was no doubt in his mind that they were made for each other. Their hearts knew it; their *saols* knew it. The binding didn't lie. That alone spoke volumes. Where on earth had she come from? Who was her father? There were a lot of mysteries to wrap up, but he was all in.

Sighing with contentment, she curled into his arms, rubbing her cheek against his chest like a kitten before saying, "I can't get the images out of my head. I keep seeing us. Not that I'm complaining, though it might be distracting when I'm trying to drive. On the other hand, having an orgasm at a red light does have some appeal. Did you do that?"

He smirked over the top of her head. Mission accomplished. "I have no idea what you mean."

Chapter 20: A Serpent Coiled and Waiting

"WHY DOES IT HAVE TO BE KILLIAN?" She was trying to be reasonable, really she was. But they had to understand where she was coming from. She didn't feel even a little bit comfortable with this latest plan. Killian? No thank you!

Using the same patient expression she used to placate the triplets, Mica squeezed her hand and dropped another marshmallow into the top of Rori's untouched hot chocolate. The woman was clever. She'd give her that. Mica seemed to have a theory that food or alcohol could break all resistance. She used both to get the men in her life to do whatever she wanted.

Before she could say another word, Mica cut her off. "Look, Rori. It's simple. Killian has psychic abilities that none of us have. He's got *other* powers that no one else has. Period. Dot. If anyone can teach you to project safely, it's going to be him."

Safely? How could zinging off to random places and times ever be safe? She didn't want to learn to control it; she wanted to learn how to stop it altogether! It was terrifying. Over the past six months she'd been forced to accept a lot of things that she'd never believed before. Angels, demons, psychic abilities... All of it blew her mind, but she was grateful for the knowledge. It freed her from the lingering fear that had shadowed her life for so long. Once she'd gotten over the shock of it all, she felt something click in her head. Accepting these crazy notions answered so many questions, steadied her in a way. She was still afraid, but now she knew what she feared. Now the faceless terror had a name. Azrael.

Along the way, her new friends helped her learn more about her abilities. For that, she was also grateful. Mica taught her how to shield from psychic attacks. Dec taught her all about retrocognition and how it could actually be helpful. It was a big relief to know she hadn't really let people die. That was a huge weight from her shoulders. She wasn't useless after all. She was abso-positively thrilled to learn the fugues weren't random breaks from sanity. Astral projection? Never in a million years! She'd never even heard of it. Oh, she understood it now. Thanks to Dec and Killian, she had more knowledge about it than she ever wanted. The projections might be uncontrolled, but they weren't random. She was projecting to protect her soul from that RBD. Self-defense for the soul. Crazy how the mind works!

Okay, she needed to learn to control it. She'd agree to that. But going off alone with Mica's gigantic husband? She shuddered at the thought. He could be a friggin' saint for all she knew. He still scared the shit out of her. And apparently he was reading her mind again. Note to scary dude, the scowl isn't helping your case.

Across the table, Killian studied her with barely concealed annoyance. He tapped his fingers on the table top and rubbed at his jaw every few minutes. Finally he stood up and said, "Here's the deal. If you don't learn to control your projections, you will die. Simple as that. Your soul can't just wander around the universe every time you're scared."

Leaning into her face, he slapped his palms on the table and snapped, "You want to live or not? It's your choice, but it seems to me you're being pretty selfish here. Dec nearly died trying to save your chicken ass. I know for a fact he's killed for you already. Do you think this is easy for him? Just another day at work? No. He has to deal with the things he does. We all do. Sometimes it eats us half to death before we get numb to the guilt. If you love him like you say you do, you need to step up and take care of your business."

Twenty minutes later, Dec and Mica waited to see them off. They were both struggling not to laugh. Oh, sure, ha ha. There was absolutely nothing funny about this.

Mica squeezed her in a tight hug and warned, "You need to be in and out of Eden fast or weird things might happen. I'm warning you now, if you kiss my husband, I will slap your face off."

Dec burst out laughing and tried to glare at Mica. "Dude, that's just wrong. Rori doesn't even like Killian."

Rori's face went up in flames. Why does the man have no filter? "I'm sure it'll be fine... right?"

Mica leaned up to give her husband a kiss and slapped his butt. At his wince, she threatened, "I know what magic happens there, remember? Six hours. Max. Be back here, or you'll be cut off."

"Yeah, yeah. Don't worry, babe. I'm a one-woman man." With that smiling declaration, he bent her over his arm and kissed her so thoroughly she was glowing by the time he straightened her back up. "Keep the light on for me!"

Playfully jabbing her finger into his chest, she said, "It's two days until Christmas. I'm actually looking forward to having this house packed with family and food. Don't be late!"

Before Rori could say goodbye to Dec, Killian took her hand. There was no sensation of movement at all. One second they were in the living room, the next they were here. Well, that was easy. They reappeared in a windswept landscape next to a seacoast. A slope of stubby clumps of grass and purple heather ended at the top of a sheer cliff. Though she could see for miles, the horizon felt closer than usual, contained in a defined space. The sky shimmered in the brilliant sunlight, cloudless except for a few wispy mares' tails zipping very high above them. It was warm here. Not winter… maybe spring? The grass was green, the plain dotted with bright wildflowers. The roar of water was the only sound. Curious, she dropped his hand and walked over to get a better look. The cliff ended abruptly in a 100-foot drop to piles of blackened rocks and angry surf. Suddenly lightheaded, she stumbled back a few steps.

"It's a long drop. I'd stay away from the edge if I were you."

He loomed behind her, larger than life, eyes shadowed and dark. In her wild imagination he was a giant roaming the empty lands of…. wherever the hell they were.

"Ireland. This is the Ireland of my past. No houses, no cars, no electronics. Nothing but the sweeping hills and powerful sea." He flashed a genuine smile that caught her by surprise. The smile transformed him into someone much less intimidating, attractive even. "Welcome to Eden."

If anyone had told her she'd be standing in the middle of an alternate universe that was a dead ringer for the Irish coastline, she would've told them to go visit the methadone clinic. But her life had definitely taken more bizarre turns than she ever expected. This was just another of those twists. The wind shifted, tossing her hair around, scooting her back a step even farther from the edge. Wait a minute. He said there were no houses… did that mean there weren't any people either? They were alone here? Completely alone? Resisting the urge to gulp, she scanned the landscape and confirmed that, nope, not a single building in sight. Crap.

The boyish smile vanished. Annoyance was stamped all over his face again. All business now, he turned on his heel, shouting over the wind, "Let's move. We're on a schedule here."

After tramping through the grass for a half mile or so, they ended up next to a partially collapsed stone shelter. It was built into the side of a hill, sort of. The thick walls seemed sturdy enough, but they were leaning ever so slightly inward, probably holding each other up. Killian waited in front of a narrow entrance. A squat rock stood guard beside it. Thousands of years of wind and rain had worn the edges to form a small, shallow depression filled with water. The surface shimmered slightly as the air currents brushed it. The air itself vibrated with life, humming with energy. This place was old. Ancient. Holy.

Planting her feet, she wondered for the millionth time how Dec got her to agree to this. This was nuts.

Still all business, her host nodded at the water. After dipping his fingers in it, he said, "Cleanse yourself before you enter. It's respectful."

She followed his example, and then looked up expectantly. What now? This place gave her the creeps. Her skin crawled from the odd vibrations coming from the stone. They got stronger the longer they stood outside. The raw power set her teeth on edge.

"Come inside. We'll do it in here." Judging by his tone, the scenic tour was over.

Impatient to leave? Impatient to get rid of her? He looked over his shoulder and shook his head with another annoyed frown.

"Hasn't anyone told you that it's rude to read minds?"

He didn't crack a smile. "No one's ever dared. You might want to tone that attitude way down since I'm about to do more than *read* your mind. I'll be joining you inside of it. It might be uncomfortable for you."

Whoa! What?

Dragging her through the narrow entrance, he snapped, "I'm not going to hurt you. Relax for God's sake. This is *my* temple. It's been in my family for more generations than you can possibly comprehend. I'm the last of my people. The energy here is powerful. More powerful than I've ever found on any plane--human or otherwise."

He lit the room with a wave of his hand and looked around. Apparently satisfied that all was in order, he pinned her with his gaze and said very precisely, "I scare you. I understand that. But you need to get over that silliness. I'm the good guy. I have no reason to hurt you, and I don't want to screw you."

She blushed like a tomato. Jesus. That little mental image sent her nerves running for cover. So not helping. He was right, though. She was being an idiot. Dec and Mica wouldn't agree to send them off alone if there was any danger. She needed to focus. Taking a deep, steadying breath, she said, "I'm sorry. I know you're trying to help. I'm just... um, nervous. You're too intense."

And holy shit! Is that an altar? What the hell was that doing here?

Killian cocked an eyebrow and sighed. She was going to be a problem. This woman was more skittish than Mica ever was. Even when they first met, Mica had been more comfortable with him. He knew damn well he was intimidating; he got that. This wasn't a new problem... he could practically hear Mica snickering inside his head. The 'I told you so' echoed loud and clear. This experiment was his idea. It would work if Dec's girl would just chill. He'd have to try some more interesting ways to get her to let her guard down.

"Sit down and relax. Let me tell you what we're going to do today. The goal is to teach you to control your projections, right? We want you to choose when and where to project. No more flying off to random places. That's a no-go. It's unsafe and you'll kill yourself doing that. So the first step is control. The second is to create a safe house--a safe place for your astral body to hide. Think of it as a little panic room. You have to construct that place in your mind. You can make it whatever you want--a room, a little cave, a protected island, whatever works for you. The point is, it's your place to go. You're safe there."

So far, so good. She was actually focusing on his words and paying close attention. She seemed to be following his explanation, nodding in the right places. Good. Progress. "Something you should know. You're extremely vulnerable when you're out of your body. I'm sure you can understand why. While you're projecting, I need you to be 100 percent aware of who's around you. Look around and see who's there."

Shivering in the chilly air, she wrapped her arms around herself. "You think the demon can find me, don't you? He'll show up?"

Without a doubt. He'd keep that to himself. She'd never go through with this if she knew. Instead he said, "It's possible. That's why you have a safe house. Ready to try?"

Her attention was gone. She flicked her eyes back and forth between him and something behind him: the altar. Sigh.

Instead of answering his question, she asked, "You're not going to cut me, are you? Those knives are freaking me out. What are those squiggly carvings?"

With so much patience even Raphael would be impressed, he ground out, "They're simply runes, Rori. They honor the old gods, invoke protection within these walls, and give me the power I need to do what I do. Look.

You can either trust me to help you, or we can go back to the farmhouse, and you can take your chances."

"I'm not very good at blind faith. It hasn't worked out for me much."

"Seems to me that blind faith is all you've got right now."

Reaching her was going to be harder than he thought. She really only trusted Dec right now. That was problematic. Dec couldn't do what needed to be done. He watched her fidget, resisting the urge to roll his eyes. Clearly she wasn't comfortable. Okay, plan B.

"Have a seat."

Rori watched warily as he went behind the altar and knelt. After rummaging around for a minute, he produced a couple of clay pots. A small brazier glowed nearby. He carefully crumbled something into the embers. They hissed and popped sending tiny sparks into the air.

"Herbs. These'll help you relax. We need to get moving."

A bitter herbal fragrance drifted in the air. Her nose wrinkled in protest. After a few minutes she was used to it and breathed it in normally. As she breathed, the hard walls of the temple softened and blurred before narrowing to a small cozy den. The orange glow from the brazier tinted the grey stone while sending dancing flames across the altar. Flames...

Too weak to stand, she started to sink to her knees but Killian caught her elbow in a surprisingly gentle grip. He led her to a heavy blanket on the floor.

"Easy now. Lay down here."

When she did without arguing, he smiled with real warmth before sinking to the floor. Sitting cross-legged near her side, he held her hand loosely. "I'm going to hold your hand. The physical connection will help us. Look into my eyes, Rori. Look and see. You can trust me to help you. Trust me to keep you safe."

Her vision was fuzzy. The room swirled and shifted oddly, but the ocean blue of his eyes stayed steady. He locked his gaze to hers until there was a soft click deep inside her mind. He squeezed her hand, still so gentle, carefully leading her to trust. As she peered more deeply, she heard his voice coming sure and strong.

"Focus on my eyes. I'm coming to join you. I'll be with you the whole time. Is that okay?"

She nodded, never taking her eyes from his. The room continued to shift, but his eyes stayed steady. "Do you feel my presence?"

"Yes. I think so."

"Okay, that's good. Now, I need you to close your eyes and get ready to project. Concentrate on rising just above your body for now. Once you can control that, we'll expand to the other side of the room, then outside, and so on. We'll do this as long as it takes for you to learn control. Okay? I'll be right here in case you need help."

Even in her drug hazy mind, she was nervous. He was sitting too close; he loomed over her... he was too big. His body heat was stifling. What would he do if she couldn't do this? Would he be mad? Would he give up on her? Worse, would he insist on putting his hands on her? It was bad enough she could feel the roughness of callouses against her palm. His fingers were loose around hers, but they practically oozed strength and power. Why couldn't he be Dec? Dec's hands were strong, but only touched her with care. Was it her imagination or was Killian getting hotter? He was making her sweat. She fought the urge to move away, struggled to focus on what he wanted her to do.

Killian studied Rori. Good. She was finally relaxing. She stopped fighting everything he did. She was... what the hell was she doing? Her soul floated a few inches above her body, hovered a nanosecond, then bounced back inside. Up and down, up and down... He smothered a smile with the back of his hand. Well, shit.

Sweat ran down the side of her scrunched up face. Her eyes were squeezed tight enough to burst blood vessels. Her mouth was pressed in a frown that looked painful. She was focusing so hard *his* head hurt!

"Uh, Rori, stop for a second."

She rolled her eyelids open and pushed herself up on her elbows. "What?"

Her face was so red she looked like she was about to explode. He couldn't stop the laugh that burst out. She was a freakin' wreck. It wasn't funny, really, but... okay, yeah, it was funny.

"Stop laughing! I can't help it. I have... performance anxiety! You're scaring me to death!"

Laughing harder, he sat back on his butt, pondering the woman in front of him. What the hell was he supposed to do with her?

"Maybe it would help if you didn't sit so close?"

"Whatever it takes to keep your head from exploding."

Four hours and eight different tactics later, Rori finally learned to project to a specific place. She could pinpoint herself to any place within the temple, just outside the walls, and eventually to the middle of the plain. They didn't dare try getting any closer to the cliff edge. He didn't have that much confidence in her coordination. Still. It was progress, and he was impressed. Once he'd gotten her to relax, she demonstrated more control than they thought she had.

Control she had, but stamina was in short supply. She didn't look good. She was weak, exhausted, nearly spent. After each attempt, he insisted she sip water to stay hydrated. As usual, she sipped from a cup of water, but this time most of it ran over her chin. She didn't notice. Her face was very pale; her lips still bluish from the last projection. That wasn't supposed to happen... what was going on with her physically? It almost seemed like seizures, but he'd be damned if he could figure out what caused them. She seemed all right once she returned to her body... though each time it had gotten worse. The last time was pretty bad, but she insisted on trying again. One more time she'd said. He let her. Now he was second guessing that decision. After dropping the cup, she collapsed back onto the floor, breathing shallowly.

"Take it easy now. You're doing great."

She lifted her bloodshot eyes with such a look of fear he nearly grabbed his weapon.

"What is it?"

"Killian... I can't do this anymore. My brain's scrambled. I need to sleep..." Her voice trailed off as she passed out.

"Rise and shine, darlin'! We've got work to do."

"Dec?" she mumbled into the blanket. The blanket didn't respond, but someone shook her shoulder until she snapped fully awake. "Dec!"

Launching into his arms, she squeezed him like a tube of toothpaste. He grunted at the impact, laughing at the same time. Man, he was the answer to her prayers. She'd passed out wishing he was there... and somehow... he'd showed up this morning. Wait. Was it morning? It was dark inside the temple...

"I hate to ask why you're so happy to see me. You've only been gone about eight hours. What did Killian do to you?" This question was followed by a softer warning, "He's standing right here."

"It's not his fault. At least I don't think it is! To tell you the truth, I'm not really sure what he did to me... there was some kind of herb... and I was stoned. Then he held my hand and... it was really hot... then I think he watched me go in and out until I passed out. It took a really long time since I couldn't get it to go up."

Dec and Killian both burst into laughter. Dec wheezed, "So let me get this straight. You smoked a joint and had mind-blowing sex with my brother? I'm going to have to kill him now. It'll ruin Christmas."

Killian's laugh disintegrated to a coughing fit that left him red faced and breathless. He finally managed to say, "She's confused."

Dec grinned hugely. "You don't say?"

"Why are you here, Dec? I thought Killian wanted us to be alone so there wouldn't be any distractions for me."

Killian answered her. "That's true, but you were so nervous around me that I thought this would help you. Dec can sit with us and hold your hand. I need you to build your safe house now. Then we'll see about sending you out to another place, if you feel strong enough. I don't want you to do too much. You're still weak from earlier."

After a quick walk around the area to stretch legs and wake up, they snacked on some bagels Dec brought in until she was ready to try again. This time when she lay on the blanket, she rested her head in Dec's lap. The familiar warmth relaxed her more than any drug Killian could find. Dec was there. Nothing would hurt her.

"Good to know you're superman now," Killian observed dryly.

"Stop reading my mind!"

Killian chuckled and said, "I don't have to read your mind. It's all over your face. Seriously, you can't hide a single emotion. Okay, let's get busy. Mica needs us back ASAP."

"He's right." Dec gave her shoulder a reassuring squeeze. "Let's do it."

Killian said, "Okay, let's talk about your safe room. Most of the time your astral self should be able to snap back to your corporeal body because they're tethered. But there might be a time when you run into trouble and don't want that trouble to follow you back to your body. That's when a safe room is good. It can be anything you want--but you need to build it how you want it."

"I understand. I've got something in mind already. Mica talked to me about this a few days ago. I think I can figure it out. It's similar to the meditation room she opens in her mind, right?"

"Very good. That's pretty accurate. It needs to be something you feel secure in. Close your eyes. Imagine what you want, and then construct it step by step. We'll be with you. Dec will anchor you. I'll keep an eye on things like I've been doing, so please don't daydream about Dec. I'll have to bleach my eyes."

Rori let her mind drift to the quiet countryside she'd begun to imagine as her special place. The rolling hills grew higher until they became the forest-covered foothills of a soaring mountain range. She would build a small cabin on one of those beautiful green hills. It would be her safe house if she needed to run and hide while in her astral form. Gradually and very precisely, she created the foundation and then raised the walls. Not simply logs, they were re-enforced concrete, lined with iron sheeting, and then covered with logs for appeal. Windows? Windows would look nice.

Windows are a weakness. It's a way in.

Killian's comment made sense. Damn it. She virtually erased the windows she was already picturing. Now the walls looked weird. Who builds a house without windows?

It's a safe house, not a vacation home. Get over the windows for God's sake.

Fine. Don't yell at me. I'm new at this.

The final step was constructing the roof; no chimney because that's a way in too. Once that was done, she considered her handiwork. Was this good enough? Was it sturdy enough? Could another astral body get inside?

Looks good, Rori. Why don't you go see how it feels?

Switching gears to project out, she focused her attention on gathering her energy, gasping softly as her astral body shot through the temple roof. It was too easy! It took several tries, but eventually she ended up at the cabin. She settled inside and looked around. The walls were plain white, windowless, dimly lit by an unseen light source. Not bad. Even Killian couldn't fault the results. It was safe and secure.

Just as she was patting herself on the back, an odd sound intruded on her thoughts.

Tap, tap, tap.

What the hell? Straining her ears, she held her breath.

Tap, tap, click, click, click.

Swiveling around in every direction, she saw nothing but the plain white walls, but the hair on the back of her neck stood up. Again, what the hell?

The clicking grew more insistent, louder, faster, until it sounded like machine gun fire. It was coming from the walls. Before she could react, the clicking turned to scratching, horrible scratching like... like claws on a blackboard, scratching and tearing...

You can't hide from me, Rori!

The scratching turned to pounding, a thousand sledge hammers beating away. The noise was deafening, disorienting... she clutched at her ears and tried to think. Concrete crumbled away, leaving her unsafe in the middle of her safe house. Frantically looking around, she froze when the first piece of the ceiling broke loose and light shone in.

I'm coming for you.

She bolted.

And reappeared under the stage at Woodstock... Janis sang her heart out while Rori huddled under the bleachers, ears full of bass. Oh, my God! This can't happen! It was my safe house!

Dec drilled his eyes into Killian's face. Something was wrong. Rori's heart just jumped to an impossible rhythm. Killian was intense as he focused inward. He was with Rori. What the fuck was happening? Damn it, wake up! He could only watch helplessly until Killian's eyes flew open and he shouted, "He found her!"

"Where is she? What happened?"

"Azrael. He breached her safe house."

"Sonofabitch! Is she--"

"She's gone."

She huddled under the bleachers trying to breathe, trying to think. Think, Rori, think! He wants you to be scared, wants you to panic. It's part of his game, part of his sick fucking game. You have to focus. Breathe. Think. Stop talking to yourself and move! Yes, right. She needed to move. While Janis closed her set, she hunched over to lurch out from under the platform towards the back of the stage. There were usually fewer crowds on this side. She'd been here enough she knew the entire friggin' festival by heart. She would slip away and try to get back to her body. Dec would be worried.

No… no, not now.

The tiny boy frowned as they made eye contact. Damn it. She didn't have time for him. The RBD would be on her ass any second. The boy raised his hand solemnly. She turned away, pretending not to see. When she turned around he was right in front of her, tears rolling down his cheeks.

"Please. You're my only hope. Bring them to me. Bring them to me so I can rest." His voice cut her to the quick. Pleading, begging, he cried as she was about to blow him off for her own protection.

With her heart pounding like a drum, she hesitated, the one thing she knew she shouldn't do. She who hesitates is lost… but as she looked into his big sad eyes she knew she couldn't walk away, couldn't leave him to wander, lost and alone for eternity. His killer was dead, but the ending was not happy. It wouldn't be happy until the boy was buried in holy ground. The skin on the back of her neck prickled, a shiver ran down her back... he was coming. Coming for her!

A tug on her hand dragged her attention back to the kid. He pulled to the right, determined little face set. He wasn't taking no for an answer. Searching over her shoulder one more time, she let him lead even though her soul screamed in warning. After wending their way through heavy crowds of half-naked partiers, they ended up outside the farm near a patch of woods. The woods weren't particularly heavy, but there was a small stream cutting through the trees that was still here in her time.

"Is this where your body is?"

He nodded soberly, moving forward. Carefully picking her way around fallen trees, tangled brush, and what was probably the largest poison ivy plant on the planet, she finally stopped next to him. He pointed to a lichen-covered boulder, left by the ice age that was long since gone, and said simply, "I'm under there."

The lump in her throat threatened to strangle her. Poor little guy didn't deserve this. The last thing she wanted to do was look at his rotting corpse. But she had to be sure. She studied the rock and the ground around it. She wasn't any CSI, but even she could tell the dirt and leaves weren't where they should be. The area at the base of the rock was definitely disturbed.

"Rori! I found you!"

"Damn it, Killian! Where is she? Where would she go? Where would she vanish to if she was totally freaked out? What would be familiar..."

Killian grabbed his shoulder, shouting, "Woodstock! Go!"

"How?" Could he find that connection to her again? The one time he'd seen her there was a fluke. He didn't know how to consciously connect to her visions.

Killian grabbed his shoulder again and said in a tone that brooked no argument, "Let your *saol* find hers. It knows her. Go!"

She flew into his arms with a cry of relief. Her astral body melted into his projection, creating a weird mash up of the two of them that... itched a little. Still, he tried to hug her. He was so damn happy to see her he would've done a friggin' cartwheel if there was time, and he was sure he was solid enough to not fall on his head in the middle of it. Grabbing her hand and losing it again, he said, "We have to get out of this place. He's coming."

"Wait! There's someone you should meet before he goes away. Come on out, Gary. This is Declan. He's the one who's been trying to help you forever."

It couldn't be! Gary Carmichael. Killed so young; destroyed by a demon that did it for kicks. Gary Carmichael... the little boy whose mother committed suicide, succumbing to grief so overwhelming it ate her alive... Gary Carmichael. The little boy whose death he avenged with pleasure more wicked than righteous. That pleasure would scar him forever, but the boy's death was avenged. Not one single part of him regretted his actions. Now that tiny boy watched him with an expression of such understanding, of knowing, that Dec felt tears prick his eyes. He knelt in front of the boy and tried very hard to smile. Failing mostly, he grimaced and said, "I'm so sorry for what happened to you, Gary. I promise to take care of you so you can move on. There's a special place in Heaven for you."

The boy nodded soberly and took Dec's hand in his. The cool touch was odd in the heat of the projection, but he didn't pull away. Gary searched his eyes and said, "There's a special place in Heaven for you too, Declan Manning. Thank you."

The slight body shimmered in the hot August sunlight and vanished forever. They would send the police an anonymous tip and make sure the bones were buried properly. It was the best ending Dec could think of. His soul finally released from the restless existence it endured for the past 40 years, Gary Carmichael would rest in peace at last.

"Let's get back."

He started to pull away from Rori when something caught his eye. He tensed for a fight. A shadow? No... what the hell? Who's that?

It can't be!

Chapter 21: A Family for Christmas

CHOCOLATE? Yes, especially when it was that time of the month. She was a peaceful sort of woman, not super comfortable with violence, though the more she hung around Dec, the more that changed. There were few things she'd consider killing over... chocolate was one of them. Another was the warm man curled up around her back. Buck naked, heavy with sleep... his arm draped over her waist, hand lying open on the sheet. The leather wristband he always wore was frayed now; even so, the brilliant blue teardrop gleamed with an inner light in the dimness of their room. It was still dark outside, but it felt like morning. The heavy blinds were closed against the night. His doing, that. He was intuitive that way. She didn't have to ask, didn't have to say the words; he seemed to know the dark haunted her. The reflections from the window made her jittery. He knew her better than she knew herself.

It still made her head spin. Less than six months ago, she was alone, lonely. She was afraid of her past, her present, and totally in the dark about her future. She'd been stumbling through her life, searching for answers, digging up her family tree by its gnarled and tangled roots. Now? So many things had changed. Her *entire life* had changed.

It was weird to have someone in her life like Dec. He hadn't proposed or anything crazy like that, but he looked into her eyes and promised he was hers. Hers? It was more than a little vague. What did that really mean? She had no idea... and she wasn't going to pressure him to make that crystal. He was beyond amazing, and if he turned out to be a temporary lover, well, she'd just have to deal with it. The annoying romantic voice in her silly head thought that was a stupid attitude.

Shut up, voice. It's called self-preservation, for crying out loud. We can't just assume that happily-ever-after will come in a fancy box gleaming under the tree. No, her long-term expectations were grounded in reality. Life wasn't a fairy tale and happy endings weren't guaranteed. In the meantime, though... he made her feel alive. She was going to enjoy the hell out of him until one of them died, or he stole her chocolate.

Her daydreams must've woken him up because he rubbed his chest against her back and nibbled his way across her shoulder blade. Now *that's* better than coffee. Before she could say a word, he dragged her on top of him, her back against his chest, thighs sprawled open across his groin. Cool air crawled between her legs and sent her mind straight to the gutter.

"Merry Christmas, love." The heat of his breath on her neck promised more exotic presents to come.

Both hands were doing wonderful things to her breasts when the door flew open and slammed into the wall.

"Uncle Dec! Hurry up! Santa--"

"Michael!"

"--came. What are you doing to Rori?"

Dec practically rolled her onto the floor before dragging the sheet over his naked and very awake body.

Michael didn't leave, nor did he close his eyes. Oh, no, the little boy gawked like he found treasure. Oh, yeah, Santa had nothing on two naked adults. There was no possible way she could turn any more red. Instead, she buried her face in the pillow. The image of her lying sprawled out, naked and open with Dec's hands roaming over her, washed through her mind again. Oh, yeah, this is going to be Michael's red letter Christmas. He was entirely too young to have such an eyeful. It was just so wrong...

Dec grinned at the pillow. Rori buried herself like an ostrich. Ah, hell, his godson just saw way more of him than he should've. Well, this oughta bring on some serious penis questions later... hopefully not in the middle of Christmas dinner. The boys had already compared their equipment and were pretty sure that even though they were identical everywhere else, their weenies (Mica's choice) were clearly different sizes. The argument about who had the biggest was just about the funniest thing he'd ever heard. Killian, Jr. put him on the floor when he demanded a ruler.

Ah, yeah, good times...

"Santa came, huh? Well thanks for letting us know. How 'bout you go check out your loot, and we'll be down in a few minutes? Miss Rori's got a boo boo I need to fix."

Michael nodded soberly before lighting up like a tree bulb. "Okay, Uncle Dec! Bye!" With that, he flew out the door, slamming it hard enough to make Rori jump.

While he pondered the innocence of four-year olds, Rori slipped her hand between his legs.

"Merry Christmas, Mr. Crowley."

The noise was deafening. It was shocking how much noise three over-stimulated young boys could make. It only got louder the closer they got to the living room. Awwww... She wouldn't believe it if she didn't see it with her own eyes. Bad ass Killian sat on the floor, under siege by the triplets. They were all trying to climb him at once. Identical

342

and adorable, the boys were sturdy and strong; there was no doubt who their daddy was. They dog piled their father who collapsed under them before dragging each into some kind of daddy tickling machine game. Bloodcurdling war cries drowned out occasional grunts of pain as a knee or elbow connected with a soft spot. Rafe worked his way to the top and waved cheerfully at her before diving in again. They were a hot mess.

The real canine perched on the couch with head cocked, tongue lolling in a doggy grin. She thumped her tail as soon as she noticed Rori. The dog was a pretty, petite thing. Her delicate features were picture perfect. She was dressed up for the holiday with a soft red leather collar. At Rori's attention, she nodded once. Dismissed.

This was the first Christmas spent with other people in more years than she could say. If you counted the few times she went to mass and the one time she spent the holiday in a homeless shelter... this was probably only the fifth time she was around people since her last foster family ditched her. She was a regular Little Match Girl for a few years until she shrugged it off as *just her life*. Not everyone has a Hallmark Christmas. That was just how it was.

She had no real idea what to expect, but holy shit, Mica had turned this place into a movie set. The massive tree held court a picturesque but still safe distance from the cheerfully burning fireplace. Dripping with colored lights and simple gold ornaments, it was topped with the most gorgeous angel she'd ever seen. Its wings spread wide to give it balance, its hair flowed down its white-robed back. It held a golden sword in one hand. The fierce expression looked so real it might have been alive. But the beautiful top of the tree couldn't compete with the flash of color exploding from its bottom. The underside was bursting with piles of brightly-wrapped presents. Odds were pretty good that most of them were for the kids... but Dec had already warned her that they were going to have a ton of people here for lunch, so maybe some were for them.

She drank it all in with a huge sigh. It was magical. The gorgeous tree gleamed softly; Trans-Siberian Orchestra rocked the house; a cheery fire burned and wind howled past the windows. It was more than she could stand without getting all choked up. The tender kiss on the back of her neck sealed the deal.

"I knew you'd like it," the kisser teased before turning her in his arms. "Are you all right? You look like you're going to cry."

"It's just… so much! I've always wanted a family. I've always wanted to have Christmas. It's too bad it's my last one."

"Look at me. Do you see these people? This is your family now. We're here for you, Rori. You're part of us now. We accept you for who you are, for what you are."

She gave up on swallowing the lump in her throat. It was trying its best to strangle her. Instead of shoving it away, she drew in a ragged breath. With tears in her eyes, she said, "It's too good to be true. All of this is more than I've ever dreamed. You… you have to know how hard it is for me to believe in a happy ending. I… I don't know what's going to happen tomorrow, let alone next year or forever. I'm trying to live one day at a time. It's the best I can do."

Lowering his voice, he pulled her against him, pleading in her ear, "Don't walk away from me, Rori! When this is over, I swear we have a life together. Give me a chance to show you what your life could be. You deserve a life without fear, without pain. Let me give it to you. We'll start fresh; start from the beginning. A man meets a beautiful woman and magic happens. No more nightmares. No more demons. Just you and me… You and me. Give me a chance to love you."

Her voice was gone. She didn't trust herself to say a word. Instead, she nodded and buried her face in his shirt. He wanted a chance? She wanted what he offered so badly she could taste it. But was that kind of happiness really possible? God's truth? She didn't know.

Dropping a sweet kiss on her forehead, he lifted her chin and said, "I'm actually insulted by your lack of faith in me. I'll have you know my track record with saving damsels is almost 100 percent. I haven't lost a woman in over 1,000 years. So the odds are in your favor."

"Oh, really?"

"Yes, really." All joking stopped. A few seconds drifted by before he spoke again. "There is no way in hell I'm letting that demon take you. It's not going to happen. Period. We're already working on a way out of this. I swear on my life to keep you and your pretty little soul safe. Do you believe me?"

"It'll take a miracle."

He shrugged and grinned down at her. "Oh, is that all?"

Mica poked her head out of the kitchen. Wearing flowing black pants and a silky ruby blouse with diamond-shaped cutouts around the neck, she looked more elegant than Rori had ever dreamed of being. Her heavy chestnut hair was piled on the top of her head in a messy, yet somehow still artful pile. Her cheeks bloomed, and her eyes glittered with more firepower than that tree. Clearly she was a Christmas person. The decorations, the music, the smell of cookies... but there was something else lurking behind the grin on her face and the twinkle in her eyes. She had a secret.

"Hey, lovebirds!" She shot Rori a knowing glance and winked. "There's coffee if you're tired."

Pulling Dec into a hug, she rubbed her nails over the scruff on his jaw before saying, "I'm so happy for you both. Come in and relax while we open presents." Ignoring the chaos in the middle of the floor, she gestured for Rori to follow, yelling, "Boys! Let Daddy up so he can play Santa!"

The herd of children magically rose from their prey, stampeding to the living room where they waited with absolutely no patience. The noise level hit a high note as they argued over who got to go first and who got the biggest present. Killian dusted off his butt and grinned at Rori's shocked expression. "Yeah, yeah, I know. Loud."

"Hey! There's Uncle Sean!" Rafe announced before throwing himself between his two brothers.

Sean had come in so quietly Rori missed it. He didn't look happy. His jaw was set like he was grinding his teeth. His usually mesmerizing eyes were glowing, literally glowing with a faint blue fire. Dec followed him into the kitchen. She strained to hear, but that was pretty much impossible.

"It's Aisling." Mica caught her expression and filled her in. "She's pissed at Sean again and wouldn't commit to bringing Sean Michael here for his visitation. She's in London. Sean traveled to see them, but she wouldn't let him bring the little guy back with him." She frowned and added in a harder tone, "She can be such a bitch sometimes. It wouldn't kill her to give Sean a break once in a while. He's done right by her in more ways than she knows."

The two guys came back a few minutes later. Sean took one look at his godsons and beamed a real smile at them. It had to be so hard for him to spend Christmas without his boy. What kind of woman was Aisling? She sounded like a piece of work. After everyone found places to sit down, Killian went over the rules with the boys while Mica and Rori talked. Rori was jealous. Pure and simple. Mica's face was soft with love for her boys. Her happiness was so obvious. Man, she wanted kids too. She wanted a family of her own.

If Mica noticed her envy, she graciously overlooked it and nodded at the Primani standing together by the tree. "They don't really celebrate Christmas like we do. For them, it's a human tradition. I've convinced them to humor me, so they let me do all the traditional things. I'm warning you now; this place will be overrun with people in a few hours. I thought you might be more comfortable knowing that ahead of time."

Dec asked, "Who's coming?"

"Everyone minus Monica. She's spending the holiday break with her boyfriend down in Cancun. Other than that, the whole family will be here, including Trevor's pretty new girl, Helene."

"Did Raphael say he'd be here?"

Mica shook her head. "Killian says he's in Thailand on family business. No idea how long that will take." Handing Rori a mug of coffee, she explained, "Monica and Abby are my step-sisters. They're twins. Fraternal, not identical. Monica models in The City. She's busy with some new guy, as usual. The woman goes through men like bottled water--thirst quenching disposables."

Mica wasn't kidding. By 2:00, the house was swarming with people. Rori vanished to the kitchen, using that as an excuse to hide from the crowd. Dec watched her from the corner. She stood at the sink, up to her elbows in sudsy water, cleaning up some pots and pans from lunch. Most of Mica's family was in the dining room, setting the table, getting food positioned, and rounding up the kids. Ten minutes 'til it was time to feast. Rori stared out the kitchen window for so long he knew she didn't see the snow. Her mind was definitely someplace else. He let her daydream while he scoped out her butt. Once upon a time, he would have thought this was disrespectful. Now? Not so much. She was like a work of art. How could he not stare? She'd filled out some more; finally rounded in all the right places, all of her bones covered with a layer of muscle now. She was convinced he found her ugly before, but that wasn't true. Sure she was too thin, but she would never be ugly. She was perfect. She looked over her shoulder, cat's eyes gleaming with mischief.

"Are you ogling my ass?"

"Guilty. You can't blame me though. I know what it looks like naked. My imagination won't shut up."

"Mmm, hmm. Come and kiss me. I'm too wet to move." She held up both soapy hands as proof.

Standing behind her, he took full advantage of her order, kissing her until she swayed and gripped the sink with both hands. "Better?" he murmured. "God, you taste good."

"Really? In the kitchen?"

Her man jumped like he'd been hit with a cattle prod. He jumped away from her so fast she nearly fell into the sink. Two strangers stood just inside the doorway. A young woman, close to her age maybe, crossed her arms and scowled. The scowl wasn't serious. Her eyes glittered with amusement as she shook her head in mock disapproval. She had pink hair. Well, most of it was pink. Some of it was platinum, which went with the hardware gleaming from her right ear and her face. One, two, three, four... how many studs did she have anyway? She had a hoop in one eyebrow too. An elegant angel flowed up the side of her neck. Nice tat. Odd place for it, but nice all the same. Her tight, lithe body was stuffed into skinny jeans and a black sweater that would've been classy except for the scissor slashes that gave everyone a good look at her abs and lower back. Uh...

Dec's face went through a series of fascinating expressions. Shock, horror, guilt, then finally embarrassment... he was blushing? Cute? Maybe. But not right at this second. She didn't need to be psychic to know he'd hooked up with this girl. The girl smiled cynically, but the pain in her eyes was easy to see. She was in love with him.

"Hey, Abby. I didn't hear you come in."

"Obviously. I wanted to introduce you to Josh." She looped her arm around the huge hunky man at her side. "Josh, this is my old friend Declan. He's another of Killian's brothers. You met Sean already."

To say he was cute... well, *cute* wasn't the exact word she would've used. Rugged? Interesting? His nose was crooked. He had a pale scar running from the corner of his eye to the side of his ear. His jaw needed shaving, and his blond hair needed trimming. Definitely rough around the edges. The guy's height and bulky muscle made up for the tiny imperfections of his face. He wasn't classically cute, but he was ruggedly sexy. He gave off a cocky vibe, too. Good replacement for Dec. She'd bite her tongue off before saying that out loud though. Dec was already giving her the stink eye.

Rori dried her hands and offered one to Tall and Hunky. "Do you play hockey?"

The missing front tooth confirmed it. He even had dimples. Nice ones too. He gave her hand a shake and said, "Every chance I get. I just got pulled into the Rangers' farm team." He dropped a kiss on Abby's head, adding with a huge smile, "We'll be on the road a lot this year."

Twenty minutes later, the beautiful table was a warzone. Plates, bowls, and platters were empty. There was nothing left other than a couple of olives drifting around the relish tray. It was shocking how much food they went through. There were a lot of people, but still. They'd killed a ham, a turkey, too many side dishes to count, and four bottles of wine. Mica and Killian sat beside each other at one end of the table. While conversations ebbed and flowed, they were lost in their own world. They shared an intimate look that caught Rori's eye. No one else was paying attention, but she couldn't help staring. She was fascinated.

Killian pressed his cheek against Mica's to whisper in her ear. Whatever he said made her tear up, and he tenderly thumbed away the moisture. He murmured something else with a wink, and she nodded, eyes brimming again. Completely ignoring their guests, he lifted her chin and caught her mouth in a soft, sweet kiss. Rori felt her own eyes sting in romantic sympathy.

Killian turned to face the family and said proudly, "We're having a girl."

All conversation screeched to a halt as his words sunk in and spread down the table. As quickly as it stopped, it started up again with a vengeance. Everyone spoke at once.

Abby squealed, "Awesome! When did you find out?"

Her step-mom Janet asked, "When are you due? How are you feeling?"

Several 'congratulations' were tossed out too. Mica glowed. Killian practically strutted with pride. Strangely, Dec and Sean couldn't stop laughing…

Mica noticed and froze them with a wicked glare. "Don't even think about it! She's already growing!"

Dec tiptoed out of the boys' room and carefully eased the door closed. There would be hell to pay for waking the kids up. It was way past their bedtime. He couldn't resist reading one last story and had shooed Mica out a little while ago. Poor thing was dead on her feet. She didn't hesitate when he offered. She gave him a grateful kiss and bolted. After 30 minutes, the boys finally crashed. He loved those little angels. And now he would have a goddaughter. He hoped she'd look exactly like her mother. One of these days, he wanted his own little princess.

Rori caught his eye when he came into the living room. The love in her smile warmed him from the inside out. He'd found his queen. They'd work on the princess later.

For now, he only wanted to know her, to see the world through her eyes, to bask in her love. Waxing poetic? Maybe. Nothing new for him. Hell, she'd been moving him to poetry since she tried to die in his arms. Was he in the right place at the right time? He thought so at first, but not now. There were still a few mysteries to puzzle out, a few secrets to keep, but he was wrapping his brain around it all now. No way they met by coincidence. No. Not a coincidence. Who was pulling the strings?

File that train of thought under 'to be continued.' He had one more important thing to do before Christmas day officially ended. The love of his life was curled under a quilt on the couch. Sean sprawled across the other end, boots off, feet planted on a footstool. He was sound asleep; beat down from faking happiness all day long. Mica sat on Killian's lap on the recliner. They spoke softly, eyes only on each other. Killian's palm rested protectively on her belly. The music was turned down, the fire burned low. The lights were off except for the tree. Standing in the doorway, he drank them in and burned this image into his memory. This was his family. He wouldn't trade his existence for anything. He was the luckiest soul on the planet.

Rori scooted over so he could sit her on his lap and brushed his bangs away from his eyes, soft fingers lingering on his skin. He kept thinking about cutting his hair, but she couldn't keep her hands off... why ruin a good thing?

"I have a surprise for you."

She stopped brushing. "Don't tell me you're pregnant too?" she whispered.

"Not that, wench. I didn't give you your special present."

"You bought me perfume. It's divine. I love it. You don't need to give me anything else."

"Yes, I do. I want to do something cool with you. Let's go to the penthouse for New Year's. It'll be wicked. We'll go to Times Square to see the ball drop. We'll go clubbing where ever you want. I'll even dance with you. We'll go shopping too. You can pick out a slinky dress that'll turn me on. Maybe get some lingerie that I can tear off with my teeth. Oh, and tall boots too. Whatever you want. You'll be beautiful in anything." He paused to suck in a breath. "Say yes!"

She practically bounced up and down the entire way to Manhattan. Her butt barely touched the seat. This was the best road trip ever. Of course, she had very few to compare it to... Still, Dec's plan for New Year's totally rocked. He told her to forget their problems for a day or so; live in the moment, soak up the world. They would take care of her demon stalker after the holiday. When had she given over all faith to him and his crazy friends/brothers? She couldn't pinpoint a date, but somehow they'd wormed their way into her heart. This was a chance at life after so many years of wishing it was over; now she couldn't wait for it to begin.

Dec captured her hand and lowered the volume on Concrete Blonde. "Happy, love?"

"Delirious! I feel like my life is just now starting. I can't wait to see how it turns out!" Leaning across the console, she kissed his cheek. "And it's all your fault. Did I ever thank you for saving my life? For *giving* me life?"

The wicked grin was a surprise. "Um, let me think... no, I don't think you did. You can thank me now if it makes you feel better." His eyes dropped to his lap.

Manhattan. The sun had just set, leaving a few pale shimmers of light lingering high in the sky. Almost instantly, the lights flickered on in the high-rises across the river. They were coming in on the Brooklyn Bridge. It was one of her favorites. The soaring arches caught her imagination, and she always loved the sight. It was especially stunning at night. This was the first time she'd crossed in a car though. She craned her head to see the top of the window-like structure. Was that a person up there? Crap. Not another jumper! She peered more closely, but the bridge lights winked on, chasing away the shadows. When she looked again, the silhouette was gone.

"Shit. Look at that traffic." Dec frowned at the line of taillights snaking ahead of them. From what she could see, the line was endless. Guess they'd be sitting a while. No problem. They had plenty of time.

He kept a smile on his face for Rori's sake, but the fact was he was picking up a bad vibe. Traffic on the bridge wasn't unusual. No, that was pretty common. He scanned the bridge for demons. The cars were clean, full of humans, no demons riding shotgun. Still, the crawling feeling of doom slithered over his neck. Something was up.

Azrael smiled. The Brooklyn Bridge was one of his favorite watching places. From its highest point, he arched his wings to absorb the human energy swirling around him. Millions of souls... many of them already promised to him, inhabited this city. He inhaled deeply, letting the bitter odor of those broken souls saturate his senses. So many damned, too many to count; it was a demon's paradise. Immune to the cold, he folded his wings and crossed his arms. Watching. Searching.

The traffic below slowly ground to a halt thanks to his help. The dump truck full of garbage stalled without warning. A cement truck had an unfortunate brake line rupture. Between the two of them, they managed to obstruct the entire end of the bridge. No one was moving. The resulting chaos was just what he needed.

She was with her Primani protector, her lover. The word burned his tongue. Lover? She had no right to that. She hadn't asked his permission. He owned her, body and soul. He wanted her untainted by the scent of man, of Heaven. The stink of the archangel's pet turned his stomach. It would take time and patience to purge the smell from her blood. He'd seen them naked, wrapped together by their useless *saols*, bound. Bound? That binding wouldn't save her, wouldn't keep her from him. He would sever that bond with one thrust of his cock. She'd scream, cry, beg… but in the blink of an eye, she would forget her lover. Once her soul was his, there would be no room for memories. No room for regrets. She would serve only him. See only him, until he got bored and sent her to the pit to rot for a million lifetimes.

On the bright side, she would be reunited with her mother. Just the thought of that stupid bitch pissed him off. She thought she could set conditions. Dictate terms. With him? Arrogant bitch. He'd seen right through her little games. Annalisa hadn't done well in his personal toy box. Her soul withered almost as fast as her human body bled out when he stuck a blade in her gut. He tapped the tips of his claws together and released his fangs at the memory. She thought she had 25 years. Surprise!

The Dodge Challenger was nearly directly in the center of the bridge. Stopped dead, the car wasn't going anywhere. As an added insurance, he sent a thought that ruptured the gas line. Time to move. There was hell to pay.

Landing silently beside Rori's door, he hesitated just long enough for her to notice him. The second her eyes went round with fear, he shattered the glass into a million projectiles.

Chapter 22: The Devil's in the Details

TIME STOPPED FOR NO MAN. But it sure as hell did for one woman. Every detail was crystal clear as her world moved in slow motion. The sound of smashing glass rang in her ears; glittering chunks peppered her face, clinging to skin, drawing blood. She was too shocked to scream. Before she could throw her hands up, Azrael dragged her through the busted window by her hair. Her jacket snagged on the broken glass, bunching to her armpits, baring her skin. One shoe fell off. Using her as a shield, he moved around the front of the car. Someone screamed. A car horn blared, then another. The sounds finally burst the bubble of shock. Frantically looking for Dec, she struggled to get free. If he thought she would make it easy on him, he had another thing coming. She'd claw his fucking eyes out!

Everything went red. Pellets of glass shredded Dec's face, clawed at his eyes. But the red in his vision wasn't from the blood. It was pure rage. Rage he'd never felt before. Rage that sent adrenaline coursing through him so fast he nearly exploded with the need to move, to destroy, to rip that demon's head from its body. Instantly his *saol* burst to life, filling him with strength and power. That power gleamed through the tips of his fingers as the energy coiled, ready for whatever Dec needed. The sonofabitch had his hands on Rori! Had damaged her, hurt her again. She struggled to free herself, but Azrael was twice her size, even without demonic strength. The bastard didn't even bother to hide in a human façade. He stood in full glory, wings and all. Azrael bent his head and ran his tongue across her forehead, lapping up the drops of blood.

"Mmm, sweet. Can't wait to bring her home."

Over his dead body.

Correction: Over Azrael's dead fucking body!

Starting with his forked tongue. He'd rip that thing out by the roots.

Dec sent a get-your-ass-here-now message to Sean and Killian even as he willed himself to calm down. Every instinct screamed to tackle Azrael to the ground, but he knew better. The demon wouldn't bother to fight with Rori's soul so close. He would simply vanish with her. So he stalked around the car, fists clenched, ready for anything. He moved slowly, carefully. The last thing he wanted was for Azrael to shimmer with Rori. They'd never find her; at least not before she was damaged beyond their help. Oh, hell no! That wasn't happening. Not now, not ever.

Azrael cocked his head and said silkily, "You look upset. Careful now, your halo's showing. Going to go all 'avenging' on me? That works. I could use the exercise. Bring it if you think you can."

"Let her go!"

"Or what? We both know you can't hurt me." He swung his eyes around the bridge, taking in every detail before adding, "Your friends can't help you either. A deal's a deal. Her soul is mine."

As they circled each other, people craned their heads in curiosity that ranged from a bored peek out the window, to full video mode on their cellphones. There were calls of encouragement from bloodthirsty dumbasses. Did they not see the friggin' massive black wings? Really people? That didn't set off any alarm bells? Someone screamed. Someone announced they were calling 911. Yeah, that'll help. All hell is about to break loose. You might want to duck. Or run. Or kiss your ass goodbye.

Starting now...

Against the backdrop of the center stone structure, three demons dropped from the sky. They wore matching black hooded sweatshirts that shielded their ugly faces. After landing on the hoods of parked cars, they kicked in a few windshields on their way to the ground. All carried the usual athames in their fists. Dec had no doubt they had side arms tucked in their pants too. One of them carried an AR-15 slung over a beefy shoulder. Great. There were a hundred humans still stuck on the bridge. Leave it to a demon to bring automatic weapons to a knife fight.

The air behind him thickened, and he recognized the *saols* of Sean, Killian, and Rivin without turning around. Where had Rivin come from? Didn't matter; they could use his help. If they survived, they'd get chatty over a beer later. The three Primani fell in line beside him, fanning across the lanes, eyes locked on the demons standing no more than 30 feet away. Even numbers for a fight, but the demons didn't budge. They waited on their master's leash. One stupid human got out of his car to protest his broken window. The demon closest to him whipped up the athame and gutted him without batting an eye. As the man slid to his knees, both hands trying desperately to hold his guts inside, the demon wiped the blade on the vic's leather jacket. More screaming. Probably from the guy's wife. She should shut up and run, but that was her call.

Dec didn't care. He tuned out everything but the couple in front of him. His eyes were glued to Rori, to Azrael. Concentrating, focusing his mind…

The demon nuzzled Rori's cheek and purred, "Happy birthday, baby girl. I have such a party planned for you."

Rori snapped, "It's not my birthday, asshole. I'm not going with you. Forget it!"

"What are you playing at, demon? It's not her birthday."

Azrael smiled over Rori's head. The feral smile showed off his impressive set of canines. He tugged her head back even farther to expose the delicate skin of her throat. Her pulse thudded so fast Dec could see the artery twitching. She was terrified. Putting up a good show, though. Running the backs of his claws across her throat, Azrael shrugged a wing. "Sure it is."

What the hell? "No it's not. Her birth certificate says she was born on March fourth."

He sighed long and dramatically. "Yes, I know. It's very easy to change those things. Father Joseph took care of that for me after I got rid of her mother." He shrugged again. "What can I say? Hell gets boring. It's my little games that keep me amused. The poor souls look so surprised when I come early. Trust me though. Her true birthday is today." While his eyes were locked on Dec's, he caressed her cheek, letting his hand drift across her throat, settling on her breast. "I was there when her mother pushed her out. She screamed her head off then, too. Both of them did. It was one of my finer moments."

"Well, aren't you clever? You should be proud."

He jerked Rori's head back hard enough to make her cry out. Dec flinched. Azrael laughed long and hard. The hand on her breast moved underneath to cup the soft weight in his palm. "So lovely." He snapped his gaze back to Dec's furious face. "Go ahead. Embrace that rage. You want to rip my throat out. I know it. You know it." He squeezed again, and Rori elbowed him hard in the gut. Her bravado was short lived. In response, Azrael dug his claws into her skin. She groaned like a wounded animal, eyes rolling back in her head.

"Come on, come on, you're almost there. I'm hurting your pet. Aren't you going to stop me?"

"Keep it up, motherfucker. You feel safe now, don't you? I will come at you on my terms. When you've all but forgotten me, I'll be there to rip your head off." Dec studied the demon as he bragged, keeping his image in his mind, holding it still, chipping away at the edges. He had to focus just a little longer. They always bragged. They friggin' loved the sound of their own voices. Letting him go on and on was useful for a minute. All of his Primani brothers were also watching for weakness and were poised with blades out. They'd move in a blink when it was time. Meanwhile, he carefully pushed his mind to its limits.

Think, Rori, think! Every part of her wanted to lash out and struggle against this monster. He was massively strong, massively smelly. Burnt dirt. Rotten food. Gross on every level. Curiously, she wasn't really afraid now. Pissed, yes. Scared, no. She was sick and tired of being manhandled, or demon-handled, in this case. And she was really tired of this RBD talking about her like she was some kind of freakin' prize.

He had a death grip on her hair and another hand clamped around her breast. Her body remembered his touch. Oh, yeah, she remembered it so much she wanted to puke all over his shoes. In the position she was in though, she'd only end up choking on it and ruining her jacket. So now she was pissed *and* nauseous.

Dec was doing it again. She saw the intensity in his stare and felt the ripples of power wash over her. He was homicidally pissed off, yes, but this was different. He held himself very still, face set harder than it should've been. He was focusing his energy. She didn't dare say anything that would give him away. She blinked her eyes rapidly to get his attention. He didn't see her. He was clearly letting RBD talk to stall for time. She tried to swallow a scream when those claws dug in, but she couldn't help groaning. Oh, my God, that hurt. The intensity of the pain nearly knocked her over.

And Dec nearly lost it. His hands shook until he clenched them into fists. She studied his face again. It was hard to see the strain through all the dried blood. His eyes were already bleeding...

He's bleeding inside his melon. Killian's words after the last time he'd done this. How many times could he recover? How many times would he have to push himself to the point of death just to save her ass?

Give me a chance to love you.

She wanted that chance. She wanted that chance more than anything she could imagine.

Pain throbbed behind Dec's left eye. Everything was beginning to blur. Come on, come on. This has to work. They were running out of time. *He* was running out of time. Where were they? He swept his gaze over Rori's face and froze. What was wrong with her eyes? She blinked like a crazy person before finally staring into his with such a look of longing, of love, that he felt it to his bones. What was she doing?

"Don't lose me!" She winked.

"No!"

Her body slumped in Azrael's grip.

She was gone.

The demon roared up at the sky as her soul slipped away. Completely unhinged, he threw her body to the ground, giving it a kick in the ribs for good measure. She rolled over and over before coming to rest against the wheels of a beat up Chevy Impala on the other side of the bridge. "You little bitch! Go ahead and run! I'll find you!"

As if some signal had sounded, all hell truly broke loose. Both sides exploded into action. With a shout, Sean tossed him a blade, and then it was on. The fight was bloodier than usual. Neither the demons nor the Primani were in the mood for dragging this out. It was straight up slice and dice. More demons dropped in until the bridge was swarming with them. They overturned cars; people screamed and ran for cover. Fireballs hit humans, vehicles, and the bridge itself, as the demons took the opportunity to fuck up everything they could. A pickup truck exploded, sending Rivin sailing off the side of the bridge. With arms pinwheeling, he vanished from view. Harsh laughter rang out from above. Two demons swung from the steel cables before dropping onto the bridge. Their laughter cut off abruptly, thanks to Killian. With an ugly snarl, he yanked two blades from the demons' backs before turning his attention to the asshole sneaking up behind him.

As usual, Dec and Sean fought back to back. Dec swung his blade in an arc that hit his target across the throat. The black-hooded dick gurgled in surprise, his yellow eyes going wide. In one fluid motion, Dec swung around to take the next one, while Sean finished the first guy off with a through and through to the gut. Bam! No more gurgling; just a pile of ash. Moving with rhythm and perfect synchronization, the two of them hacked and gutted their way through a Baker's Dozen without breaking a sweat.

Just like old times. Caught up in the moment, Dec flashed a grin at the next contestant and waved him forward. "Dude, I can do this all day!"

Sean barked a laugh, decapitated one of the shorter demons, and then asked, "You want to grab IHOP after this? I'm in the mood for pancakes."

He ducked a boot aimed at his head, swiped his blade out to sever the idiot's Achilles tendon. Said idiot yowled and fell to one knee. Sean took his head off in one swing. Dec tossed him a glance, "I could go for pancakes. Bring us some back. Rori's going to feel like shit when she gets back to her body. We'll be at the usual place."

Sean started to reply but was cut off by the staccato sound of a machine gun firing. He flew backwards into the railing, blood blooming from a bullet hole in his shoulder. "Sean!" He flashed to Sean's side, kicking a hooded asshole over the railing just as he was about to skewer his brother. "Sean! Get out of here."

Gritting his teeth, Sean shook his head. "Yank it out! Hurry the fuck up! Killian's about to get overrun."

He glanced over his shoulder. Killian was playing whack-a-mole with two assholes. One threw a fireball at his head, but he simply teleported out of the way. The energy hit a steel cable instead. It swung free, knocking a frantic woman completely over the side and into the freezing river below. The next demon landed behind Killian. He vanished. The next second, the demon turned to ash and joined the rest of the air pollution. Killian grinned behind him. The decision took barely a second. Killian was fine. Sean was another story. His face was white with pain, eyes dark.

"Hang on, bro. I've got this." He pressed his palm against the entry wound. Closing his eyes to concentrate, he drew the round out and sealed the hole all in one motion. "Good as new. Let's rock. Azrael's moving."

Like most of their brawls, the action could be counted in seconds, rarely in minutes. Everyone moved faster than most humans could even track with the naked eye. The fight started only minutes before and was nearly over now. No new demons had dropped in to pick up the slack. That could only mean one thing. Azrael was ready to move.

The bridge was a warzone. Burning cars puked out heavy black smoke, filling the air, making it impossible to see. Overturned cars littered the road; bridge supports hung loose, parts of the railing blown away. Worse, there were bodies everywhere. People were trapped in some of those cars; many were gunned down by the same weapon that hit Sean. The cries of wounded humans broke through his battle haze. There would be no way to contain this from the public. No way to erase this from history. Well, that was above his pay grade. He was only worried about one dark-haired woman.

Coughing in the smoke, he searched for Azrael. There! Azrael picked his way around a smashed SUV, heading towards Rori again. Before he could get close enough to grab her, Dec and Killian blocked him. Sean and Rivin materialized behind them, guarding their backs from the few demons who still wanted to fight.

He unfurled his wings and sneered, "Do you really want to do this?"

As strong as the Primani were, even together, they couldn't hold the demon back for long. His power was overwhelming. The fact that they had slowed him down at all was probably due to his wanting to play with his prey before killing them. Dec looked around feeling something like panic seizing up inside of his gut. Where were they?

"Coward!" The word rang louder than the screaming wounded and police sirens heading their way.

Primani and demons froze at the unexpected voice.

"Leave my daughter alone! Your fight is with me."

Halle-fucking-lujah!

Raphael stood beside a warrior Dec never dreamed he'd see again. He called himself Keil Stone. His real name was unpronounceable so he invented a new one. Made by Uriel, the Primani was a legend among legends. The stories claimed he fought with Genghis Khan himself back in the day. No one could either confirm or deny that. He was also known for his love of waves, women, and fighting. Taller than most of Khan's men, Keil was impressive. Women loved him; men feared him. Made when in his late 20s, he kept the powerful body and hard face he had at that time. He was big. He was pissed. And holy shit, he was Rori's father. Dec took a step back. Dripping with weapons and dressed for combat, he strode forward until he stood a few feet from Azrael.

Azrael narrowed his eyes and waved his boys back. "I thought I banished you."

The huge Primani palmed his silver blade and planted his feet. "I was thinking the same thing about you. How did you get free?"

"No matter." He shrugged, clearly not concerned. "You're years too late. Annalisa gave her soul to find you. Wanted you to know you had a kid. Scattering you in front of her was genius, if I do say so myself. The guilt of 'killing' you ate her alive. She ran straight to Father Joseph to have the stain on her soul removed."

Keil hissed, "That was you? You sonofabitch! You targeted her because of me? She was innocent!"

Azrael brought the top of his wing around his shoulder to straighten a twisted feather with his claws. He dismissed the fury that was clear in Keil's tone. Looking straight down his nose, he agreed, "Of course I did. After all, you tried to banish me. Did you think I'd forget that? I haven't survived as long as I have by letting enemies slip past."

"By the way, I don't know what you saw in her. She was the most boring lay I've ever had. No life in her at the end. She was so boring I killed her early. You could say I terminated her contract. She's been screaming in the pit ever since."

He pointed a wing tip at Rori's prone body. "Ah, now your sweet daughter Rori's been showing promise since she was just a little girl. I've been priming her up for the big day. She's got a beautiful soul. I've been drawing from it for years. She warms me from the inside out." He rubbed his hand over his crotch and smiled. "I can hardly stand the wait."

As soon as Keil showed up, Dec began shifting closer to Rori. She wasn't dead. He heard her heartbeat loud and clear. Projecting was genius. It would've been nice if she'd warned him first. He just lost a thousand years off of his life. A spike of fresh anger ran through him at the sight of her body tangled around the tire of a parked car. The car's passengers ran screaming minutes earlier. As he watched, a shimmering ribbon of water caught his eye. It flowed slowly towards her. A familiar odor filled his nose. Not water...

Rori's astral body hovered near the top of the bridge. Careful to keep hidden, she watched the drama play out below. It was crazy. She recognized Sean and Killian, of course. Another Primani showed up. With a shaved head, jeans, and black leather, he stood out from the others who wore black shirts and black camouflage pants. Dec looked relieved to see him just before they attacked. There was no way to tell exactly how long it really lasted, but the fight seemed to last only a few minutes. Short and vicious. Bodies flew all over the place. People screamed and died. It was horrifying. She'd covered her eyes for most of the whole thing.

Then *he* showed up. She felt him the instant he appeared at the back of the bridge. He and Raphael materialized out of thin air just as the fighting wound down. Her father. She knew it in her heart. Her *saol* knew it. She felt a connection to this man deep inside. She hadn't clearly understood the meaning of the word '*saol*' when Dec tried to explain. He said it was the Primani life force, the energy that kept them strong, that healed their injuries. It gave them immortality.

Immortality? Wait a minute...

Her mother was human. Her father was Primani? If he was immortal, then...did that make her...

Oh, surely not?

Raphael stepped between Azrael and Keil with an air of authority that was impossible to ignore. Despite his rage, Keil moved back to give Raphael plenty of space. The archangel had more power in his pinky than all the Primani standing there. Deference was definitely due.

Looking the demon straight in the eye, Raphael said, "This is all rather interesting from a historical perspective. But I'm sure Rori needs her rest. You should be going now, Azrael, before Uriel runs to Satan and has a little chat about you. Guarding the gates of Hell does have its perks."

Azrael snapped his wings against his back and stalked forward until he was nose to nose with Raphael. "I'm not leaving without that soul."

"I'm afraid that's not possible. I believe there was a short addendum. Annalisa had one final request. Didn't she? She insisted the father be told so he could make the decision about the child's soul if something happened to her. You agreed to make all reasonable efforts to find the 'angel' who fathered her child. But you failed to do that, didn't you? Once you put two and two together and realized you already killed the father, you thought you were home free. But he's not dead. In accordance with the original agreement, it comes to down to Rori's father. Keil, what are your thoughts?"

Keil moved closer, hand on his blade, eyes hot. "If I'm getting a vote, I'm saying go fuck yourself. The terms of that deal were dirty to begin with. You deceived Annalisa, played on her fears, her guilt, just to get back at me. You have her soul already. You're not getting Rori's. I say she stays right where she's at, and you get the fuck out of here."

Azrael's entire body swelled with the force of the anger roaring through him. He took a step towards Raphael with hate in his eyes.

Raphael curled his fingers around his sword and simply said, "Tread lightly, Azrael. This isn't a war you want to start."

Freezing in mid-step, he growled, "Not today, but war is coming. As for this soul, keep it. It's already broken. I can live with that."

He glared between Keil and Raphael, back and forth, mind racing, back and forth again, until his eyes swiveled to Rori's body. He studied it for a moment before smiling coldly. With one dip of his wing, the gasoline ignited.

Chapter 23: Resolutions

HER FATHER WAS HOT in every sense of the word. Gorgeous? Yes! Body made for ogling? Yes! Supernatural power oozing from his pores? Yes! Her mother hadn't had a chance. Rori closed her eyes to picture the scene. She could clearly see how her mom had fallen for him. What was their story though? How did they meet? Where was he for the last 25 years? She had way more questions than answers.

The sperm donor was currently buried neck deep in an intense argument with Dec. They stood on the patio, their backs to her so she couldn't see their faces. She didn't really need to see their expressions at this point. The heaving shoulders, waving hands, and crossed arms definitely didn't scream happiness and roses. She glanced at the clock on the wall. They'd been at it for an hour.

It had been less than 24 hours since the showdown with that demon who she refused to name. The name gave him an identity. It gave him power. The name made him real. As of 20 hours ago, he no longer existed in her mind. She evicted the fucker with extreme prejudice. She absolutely refused to think any more about him. It was time to move on with her life. She was still not sure what that meant. Up until now, her only driving ambition was surviving one more day. Now what?

Dec tried not to punch his old friend in the mouth. It was hard. The mad joy he felt at seeing him alive and kicking at Woodstock vanished the second he opened his trap to grill him about Rori. He ground his molars together and tightened the grip on his temper. For the past 30 minutes, the convo had gone something like this:

"I can't believe you screwed my daughter!"

"I can't believe you screwed her mother!"

"I should kick your ass!"

"Bring it!"

After going around this circle about 18 times, Sean busted out laughing, the unexpected sound breaking through the stubborn wall of testosterone.

"Why don't you two put your dicks away before someone loses an eye? Keil, buddy, it's good to have you back. You look great for a dead guy. But dude, you have no real leg to stand on here. You had no idea you had a daughter. Don't go getting all fatherly now. She's 25 years old. It's a little late, don't you think? Besides, it's not like Dec took her virginity. She knew what she was doing."

Dec took offense to that less than flattering description. "Hey! Don't make her sound like a slut! I'm only the second person she's been with."

Sean waved away his protests, mouth running on autopilot. "Whatever. The point is Rori doesn't need a father to defend her. She's survived a boatload of bullshit for all these years. She's strong enough to make up her own mind. You might want to figure out how you're going to explain how you met her mother. She's going to want all the details."

Keil grimaced, and replied, "Yeah, I know. That's a story for another day though. I don't think she's ready for this right now. It's not pretty."

Dec uncurled his fists. "Good point. Thanks, Sean."

Sean gave him the hairy eyeball and replied, "And *you* need to figure out what you want to do now. The big mystery's been solved. Rori's safe and mostly sound. What are you going to do?"

Rori watched them from the French doors. Sean caught her eye and waved. The gesture was so out of character, she paused before responding. He was up to something out there. He gave her a wink. Definitely up to something.

"You must be Rori. You have your father's eyes."

Startled, she swung around, jamming her hand against her heart to keep it from leaping out of her chest. The man appeared right behind her, so close she felt the heat wafting away from his skin. Whoa... she took an automatic step back, running smack into the door. No place to go.

She craned her neck to look into his face. He could be Raphael's twin. They shared the same aristocratic features. Square jaw, straight nose, well-defined cheekbones... but where Raphael kept his brown hair neatly trimmed, this man's hair was pulled into a long ponytail. He would be handsome if he lost the fierce scowl. There was no warmth in his eyes or the shape of his mouth. Her survival instincts twittered a warning just before he reached out to take her hand.

The shock of his touch tingled all the way to her bones. She opened her mouth to protest, but lost the ability to think. With a knowing smile, he shook her hand and said, "My blood runs through your veins, little human. What will you do with that power?" Pulling her a few inches closer, he continued in a deep, compelling voice, "Will you help the lost spirits find their rest? Or will you hide from them? Are you brave enough to use the gifts I've given you?"

"I don't understand." Gifts? What was he talking about? She'd never seen him before.

Reeling her in close enough to brush against the buttons on his jacket, he tipped her face up and captured her eyes in his. Her heart skittered so hard she couldn't breathe. Tiny spots of light blocked her vision. Surely he could feel it? See it? If he did, he didn't care.

"I'm your father's maker. You're my descendant. Because of this, I've given you the ability to help your Primani right many wrongs. Let him guide you; let him teach you. The two of you are bound for more than sensual pleasure."

Her heart was going to explode. Her breath came in shallow gasps as he sucked all of the oxygen from the room. The spots in her vision grew darker, turning to solid walls of black. His hands gripped her elbows now, holding her up, palms searing her skin. He tilted his head as he searched her eyes, looking deeply, prying through her walls, digging into her secrets. He pursed his lips to speak, hesitating a beat before smoothing them into a genuine smile that transformed his face into something glorious.

She stared, mesmerized. The black walls narrowed to a tunnel. Who was this man?

In response to her thoughts, he unfolded beautiful amber wings, chuckling as her eyes rolled back in her head.

"I see you've met Uriel." Keil's husky voice spoke somewhere just above her nose. "Can you stand?"

Shoving herself to her elbows, she blinked a couple of times to stop the spinning walls. "What happened?"

"You fainted, darlin'. Come on, I'll help you up."

"Dec! Oh, thank God!" She let him haul her to her feet before throwing her arms around his waist. Squeezing him hard enough to crack a rib, she laughed shakily into his chest. "He scared the hell out of me! Is he gone?"

He didn't answer with words, but the vibrations of silent laughter did the trick. Shit. He's right here, isn't he? She peeled her face away and swallowed hard. Yep. Still here. And standing just behind them with her father and Sean. Okay, this 'father' stuff wasn't working for her. He was too young, too... too male. He might technically be her father, but she couldn't call him that.

"Let's get something straight, Keil. I'm not calling you dad. It's way too weird for me. I'm still trying to wrap my head around the fact that you exist, I'm part Primani, and no longer have a death sentence around my neck."

"Whatever you want. Call me Keil."

Uriel came forward. Everyone rushed to move out of the way. Dec stood tall and proud next to her. His hand rested possessively on her lower back. He dipped his head respectfully.

"I must return to Hell. Before I leave, is there anything you'd like to ask of me, Rori? Anything at all?"

The gleam in his eyes suggested he already knew the answer. He just wanted to hear her ask the question. Her mind was blank. What could she possibly want from him? Snap! The light bulb went on.

"There is one thing. Is there any way you can get my mother's soul freed so she can go to Heaven? It breaks my heart to know she's suffering because of me."

Uriel actually smiled gently before nodding. "I'll see what I can do." He turned to Dec and frowned. "You've led a charmed life, Declan. Now I understand why that is. You've protected my offspring and for that I thank you. You and she are bound together by the timeless power of your *saols* and the human love that beats within your hearts. It's your remaining humanity that gives you the strength to do what you must do. Know that I am giving you my blessing. Do not disappoint me, or I will smite you."

He turned on his heel to leave, then stopped and glanced over his shoulder. "Rori, come here."

He placed both hands on the side of her head and closed his eyes. A tiny burst of golden light outlined his fingers before slipping into her veins. In the space of a heartbeat, it was done.

"There. Now you're evenly matched."

Rori stared in confusion at this angel who guarded the gates of Hell. What just happened? Dec fell to his knees, tears coursing over his cheeks, undone. "Thank you, Uriel. Thank you."

New Year's Eve. The witching hour was only minutes away. Times Square was packed with thousands of people screaming in frenzy to welcome another year. For most of these people, another year was guaranteed. No one gave it a second thought; of course the next year was coming. They didn't know any differently. But for others... well, this new year was an unexpected blessing.

Dec held his breath as Rori's fingers glided across his groin. Teasing him with her nails, she purred low in her throat when she got the reaction she wanted. With eyes closed and head flung back, he sank into the pleasure of her touch. For a full 30 seconds. Even though she touched him in all the right ways, he couldn't stop the thoughts that ran around his head like a merry-go-round. He couldn't relax.

"What is it?" She nuzzled his jaw, dropping kisses along the side. The feel of her against his chest, skin on skin, heartbeats thumping together, was almost too much. He couldn't do this anymore. He felt like a fake. He didn't want to be with her like this.

Rolling them over so she lay beneath him, he supported himself on his arms. Her look of surprise brought a smile to his face, but he quickly banished it. Now was not the time for smiling. This was serious. She pouted at his frown and traced her tongue around his lower lip. His carefully planned speech vaporized when she slid her hand between them and stroked him against her palm. Her sexy little mouth curled into a grin of victory.

Moving so fast she gasped out loud, he snagged her wrist and pinned both hands next to her head. Dipping down, he kissed her with all of the gentleness he could find within him. He wrapped his lips over hers, slowly tasting them, caressing her with his mouth, his tongue. When she was panting beneath him, he pulled back and said, "Marry me. Say yes and let me love you for eternity."

"Kiss me again, and I'm yours."

ABOUT THE AUTHOR

Hi! I'm Laurie Olerich and writing is my passion. I love to create guilty pleasures full of exciting locations, rollercoaster action, strong, quirky heroines, and steaming hot heroes who'll raise the temperature in any room you're in! Paranormal romance? Check! Urban fantasy? Check! Romantic suspense? Check! My *Primani* series combines the best of the three. When I'm not plotting, writing, or fantasizing about my next hero, I'm planning parties, traveling, and spending lazy nights with my son, my Dal pals, and my friends. I've spent many years living in New York and Germany, but have made my home in San Antonio, Texas since retiring from the United States Air Force. Thank you so much for taking a chance on a new author and picking up my story! I hope you'll fall in love with the Primani world as much as I have. If you'd like to get to know me better and keep up with my works in progress, look me up on the Internet. I'd love to hear from you!

Website: www.laurieolerich.com
Facebook: www.facebook.com/LaurieOlerichAuthor
Twitter: @LaurieOlerich
Email: laurieolerich@gmail.com

Craving more Primani? Here's a little taste of what's coming next!

"Aisling! Damn it, woman. Stop!" Alexandyr Talanov threw himself forward into a low roll that let him slide just under the knife thrown at his gut. Diving behind a wooden fence post, he allowed himself a grim smile. Finally she was getting it! Rubbing absently at a steady stream of blood soaking his shirt, he congratulated himself on his teaching skills. His newest pupil was coming along well, though a little stubborn about things, if he was being honest.

"Alexi! Come out, you big coward. I'm not going to wound you." Aisling's voice came from the other side of the fence. She was laughing at him.

Unfolding himself to his full intimidating height, he held his own knife in a defensive position and scowled down at her. "Too late. You've ruined my favorite shirt."

Aisling Andersson smothered a grin at her trainer's peevishness. Alexi was *always* scowling. It wasn't a good day unless he was angry about something. She'd known him for only a year, but it felt like lifetimes. "Oh, I think it'll wash. And you will heal." Jamming her throwing blade into its sheath, she turned away, dismissing him altogether.

Alexandyr stood with his mouth hanging open before slamming it closed. How did she do that again? She walked away from him this morning...in the middle of his lecture. She had no respect!

In two strides, he was at her side, pulling her around to face him. The shock on her face made him want to laugh, but when the shock turned to fear, he scowled instead. Paling at his nearness, she took a step back, tugging at his hand unconsciously.

Striving for patience, he ground out, "Why do you cringe? I've never hurt you." He studied her glittering blue eyes for a sign of her thoughts, her emotions, anything that would help him understand her. She made him crazy with her contradictions. He never knew which side of her he'd get to see. He'd thought they'd had a normal training session today. Her attitude was positive, and she'd shown no signs of depression. But now...

Aisling tugged her hand again, wanting nothing more than distance between them. God, didn't he know how hard it was for her? He was overwhelming her, making it hard to think, let alone come up with a rational lie for her fear. He'd never accept the truth. She'd never tell it to him. Instead of letting her go, he drew her nearer. The heat from his powerful body warmed her, and she shivered. Not with cold, not with desire, but with fear. She could never be with him. If anyone saw them, it would be the death of them both.